CLARE FRANCIS

# Keep Me Close

MACMILLAN

First published 1999 by Macmillan
an imprint of Macmillan Publishers Ltd
25 Eccleston Place, London SW1W 9NF
Basingstoke and Oxford
Associated companies throughout the world
www.macmillan.co.uk

ISBN 0 333 75270 8 (Hardback)
ISBN 0 333 78054 X (Trade Paperback)

The author and publishers would like to thank The Society of Authors
on behalf of the Estate of John Masefield for permission to
reprint the extract from 'Sea Fever' by John Masefield.

1 3 5 7 9 8 6 4 2

A CIP catalogue record for this book is available from
the British Library.

Typeset by SetSystems Ltd, Saffron Walden, Essex
Printed and bound in Great Britain by
Mackays of Chatham plc, Chatham, Kent

For Vonnie

# Chapter One

———•———

LEADEN SUMMER rain had seized the city. As the taxi inched along the humid streets, Simon felt a nervous dread. To see Catherine at last, to face the full extent of the damage, to get the whole awful business sorted out one way or the other! After the long hours at the hospital, the calls to the police, the sleepless nights, he felt as though he had been waiting for this moment for ever, though it was just – he knew it precisely – four and a half days.

The interminable journey also gave him more than enough time to brood with growing misgivings on the white roses that sat so obtrusively on the seat beside him. He had bought them hurriedly from Moyses Stevens at considerable expense, but now the arrangement seemed too formal, the roses too white, and he couldn't suppress the suspicion that they would be seen as glaringly inappropriate, more suited to a wedding or a funeral. The realisation irritated him excessively because with just a little more thought he would never have made such a ridiculous mistake.

Out of long habit, he reached for his mobile and began to make calls from the list he kept on the small white cards that fitted so neatly into his breast pocket. The list was long, it always was, yet after two calls he found himself staring blankly through the misted window at the streaming streets, the phone forgotten on his knee. A moment later he switched the thing off altogether, impatient with the cab's impossibly slow progress. At this rate there was a risk of getting to the hospital at the same time as Catherine's family, a prospect that filled him with dismay.

He called to the driver to try another route, only for the cab to enter a street that was completely blocked. As his frustration soared, the sweat sprang against his shirt, and he felt a familiar flutter high on his cheek: his certain visitor in times of stress. Removing his spectacles, he propped his elbow against the window and, finding the exact spot and angle, pressed two fingers hard against the dancing muscle until it subsided.

The cabbie cut down another side street; they began to make progress. Reaching the hospital at last, Simon resolved the problem of the flowers by thrusting them into the hands of some fellow arrivals, a shambling overweight couple bearing chocolates for some unhealthy relative. They stared at them with lumpen distrust, but he didn't waste time with explanations they wouldn't begin to understand.

The hospital was modern and showy, with expanses of steel and glass and the inevitable atrium. He followed the now familiar route along a suspended walkway past intensive care to the ward with the unpronounceable, vaguely African name. At the last set of doors he paused and, setting down his briefcase, peered critically at his outline, silhouetted in the glass. He smoothed his hair and flicked a hand over his lapels and viewed first one profile then the other, and saw a version of himself that was entirely as it should be: well-groomed, soberly dressed.

Typical of the shambolic way in which the hospital seemed to be run, there were unfamiliar faces at the nursing station for perhaps the fourth time that week, two pudding-faced girls, neither more than eighteen, both engrossed in paperwork and determined not to notice him. It was necessary to speak decisively before one of them would look up, and then in his general agitation he stumbled over Catherine's name, almost saying Langley instead of Galitza.

'Are you family?' the girl demanded curtly.

'I'm Catherine's solicitor,' Simon explained, producing his card. 'As well as a close—'

'Sorry, family only.'

'That's correct,' he agreed slowly and calmly. 'But – as I was trying to explain – I'm a close friend of the family and I have permission to see her. So long as the family haven't just arrived – have they? In which case I'll wait.'

The girl examined the card doubtfully. 'We've no instructions. I'll have to check.'

'But it was Sister Jones who called me,' Simon said with tight lips and a degree less patience. 'It was she who told me Catherine had regained consciousness. She knows I have permission to visit her.'

The girl was wavering. He tried to loosen his expression into something a little more friendly. 'You didn't say – have the family arrived yet?'

The girl went to check with the other nurse. 'No, but they're on their way over.'

'I'm aware of *that*. I was the one who contacted them, you see.'

A small exaggeration this – Simon had never attempted to contact Alice and by the time he'd got through to Duncan the old boy had already heard from the hospital – but it was enough to win the nurse over.

The nurse led the way down the corridor to Catherine's room and slipped inside. Through a chink in the curtained panel Simon could just make out the dark outline of a chair and a mass of shadowy flowers, but nothing of Catherine herself. He wasn't sure what to expect. It had been a couple of days since he'd last glimpsed her in intensive care, stretched out under bright lights amid a morass of equipment and wires. She would still be attached to tubes and machines that bleeped, he imagined, possibly to some even more disturbing apparatus which did not bear thinking about. But would she be drowsy or wide awake? Confused or coherent? When he'd made the hurried call to Duncan, the old boy had been too busy going through the motions of fatherly relief to provide any useful details.

The nurse reappeared. 'She's very drowsy. She's not up to much, but she's agreed to see you.'

The L-shaped room was dim, the blinds drawn against a day that was already overcast. Closing the door softly behind him, Simon waited in the angle of the room until his eyes had adjusted to the gloom. His nervousness came rushing back. His tongue felt thick, his shirt clammy against his back.

Soundlessly he moved forward into the pool of muted artificial light. Catherine lay flat under a thin coverlet that revealed the slightness of her body. He couldn't immediately see her eyes; her head was low, there was some sort of contraption under her chin and around her head, and wires and weights at the bedhead. Tubes were strapped to her arms, and two more emerged from beneath the coverlet and looped away through the bed frame, one to a machine on a stand that showed a green light, the other to a transparent bag half-filled with – he quickly averted his eyes.

He took a few steps towards her, the tension fluttering like a tribe of butterflies in his stomach. 'Hello, Catherine. It's Simon Jardine!'

A faint sound: gasp or sigh.

As he advanced into her field of vision her eyes swivelled down, searching for him, squinting uncertainly. Her entire head was held in a rigid cradle, he realised, a sort of surgical collar, but larger and sturdier than any he'd seen before, extending from her chin up and around the back of her head, like some bizarre Elizabethan ruff.

Her eyes narrowed again, she couldn't seem to focus on him, and, depositing his briefcase on the floor, he forced himself to move closer still, to the very edge of the bed.

'Simon?' Her voice was dry and cracked.

'Hello there.' In attempting to smile he felt his cheek give way again: a sharp shiver. 'How are you, Catherine?'

Her gaze widened, she looked at him with something like fear. 'Ohh . . . *Ohh* . . .'

For a moment he thought his heart would give out, it was beating so violently.

'Something's – happened?' she gasped with an effort. 'Something . . . Tell me . . .'

'It's all over now, Catherine. Nothing to worry about. You're in safe hands.'

She seemed to have trouble in understanding him, and he repeated the reassurances.

'But Ben? Pa?' she whispered. 'Has something—? Are they—?'

'They're fine. Really!' He produced a fiercely cheerful tone. 'Absolutely fine!'

'Fine?'

'Yes! I promise!'

She closed her eyes and gave a long ragged sigh. 'Ohh . . . I thought . . . Ohh . . .' Then, with a fresh wave of anxiety, she whispered, 'But where – are – they?'

'Oh, they'll be arriving any minute now, I'm sure. I just happened to be the nearest, that's all!' He heard himself laugh awkwardly. 'Your father's definitely on his way. He'd just popped home for a wash and brush up. I spoke to him as I left. He was just turning round to come straight back. And Alice – she'll be in after work, I expect. So you see?'

'But – *Ben*?'

'Oh, bound to be in soon! Been in twice a day, most days, sometimes even more.' *Covering for Ben again*, he thought with a burst of anger. *How often have I had to do that?*

She frowned at him. 'So why . . . are you . . . here?'

He blurted, 'Oh, I just thought I'd drop by, that's all!' *What a ridiculous thing to say*, he thought unhappily. *I'm sounding like a complete idiot.* This was his fate, it seemed: always to feel off-balance with Catherine, always to feel hopelessly awkward. 'No, it was more that' – he selected a more considered tone – 'I came to help out.'

'Help . . .?' The idea seemed to add to her general air of puzzlement.

'To look after all the tedious things that Ben and Duncan don't want to be bothered with—'

But he had lost her. Her eyes were ranging back and forth in a slow incessant searching of the walls and ceiling. Finally she murmured, 'Where is . . . this . . . again?'

He gave her the name of the hospital.

'The doctor . . . said . . . an *accident*.'

'Yes, you bumped your head. You had us worried for a while, I can tell you, but you're okay now. You're in the very *best* of hands. We've made sure of that!'

The words came faintly, like small breaths. 'My head . . .?'

'A nasty crack.'

'But it's not – it's . . .' She lost this thought, or abandoned it, and after a moment her gaze came back to him. 'A car . . .?'

'No. It was a fall, a nasty fall.'

'*Fall* . . .' She took this in slowly, with renewed bafflement.

He thought: No memory, she has no memory at all. He could hardly believe it.

He leant over her so that she could look up at him without strain. He saw that the whites of her eyes had a jaundiced tinge, from medication perhaps, or some internal damage, while the irises, which in healthier times had been such an intense blue, seemed almost bleached of colour.

There was a terrible intimacy in being so close to her, in witnessing her defencelessness; he shuddered softly, with pity and wonder, and something like longing.

He said gravely, 'It happened at home. You fell from the landing.'

'Oh . . .'

'In fact . . . during a burglary.'

Alarm and confusion passed over her face, her mouth moved loosely. 'Burglary . . .' Then, with another stab of anxiety: 'Ben wasn't . . . there? Wasn't . . . hurt?'

'Hurt? No! He got a couple of bruises, that's all. Nothing serious. They discharged him almost immediately. Four days ago now.'

'Four . . .' She frowned, though he couldn't tell if it was the thought of the lost days or the burglary that troubled her.

The odd thing was that there was no visible bruising. Nothing to show for the fall but the dulled eyes and a deep pallor. In the sepulchral light her skin looked so white and smooth and polished that she might have been an alabaster effigy. Only the area beneath her eyes revealed the slightest trace of colour, a faint smudge of violet-blue far below the surface. The effect of this terrible perfection was dreamlike, hypnotic, and he could not look away.

'You wouldn't – *lie*?'

She had startled him. 'Lie, Catherine?'

'About Ben.'

'*Ben?* Oh – absolutely not!'

'You would – say?'

'Of *course* I would say, Catherine! How long have we known each other, for heaven's sake? How long have we been friends? Good God!' The laugh came again, a jarring sound that seemed to jump unbidden from his mouth. 'No, he's perfectly okay. Promise. Tough bastard. Grappled with the burglar and got a black eye for his trouble. And then – well, two stitches. On the cheek.'

The two stitches seemed to provide the authenticity she craved and for the first time since Simon had arrived she became almost calm.

Bending still lower, Simon whispered, 'Catherine, the police have asked if they can come and talk to you.'

Her expression was almost childlike in its incomprehension and it occurred to him that she was probably dosed up to the eyeballs with sedatives.

'Police?'

'To ask if you can remember anything about the attack. But, Catherine, you don't have to see them if you don't want to. Just tell me and I'll keep them away for as long as you like!'

'Attack . . .'

'They just want to know if you can remember anything.'

'But I— No . . .'

'You don't remember anything?'

'No . . .'

He nodded sympathetically to give her more time. 'What about – oh – arriving at the flat? Nothing about that?'

A faint furrow sprang up between her eyebrows as she agonised over this.

'Or going upstairs?'

'No.' Then, as if his words had only just sunk in: '*Attack?*'

He hesitated, wondering how much he could say without planting memories in her mind. 'Well, we don't know exactly what happened of course, but it seems that the intruder attacked Ben, then – well, who knows, he may have pushed past you, something like that. Anyway, somehow or another – you fell.'

'Fell . . .'

He left it for a moment before prompting gently, 'You'd just come back from France.'

'France.' It wasn't a memory but a repetition.

'The intruder was already inside the house.'

Clearly disturbed at this, she began to breathe in snatches. '*No* – nothing – nothing—'

'It's all right,' Simon interrupted hastily. 'It really couldn't matter less. Please don't worry yourself about it. Plenty of time for all that later. *Plenty* of time! I'll tell the police not to come. I'll tell them not to bother you.'

'Yes, I . . . can't . . . can't . . .' She stared past him, the confusion chasing over her face like shadows.

'It's all right. It's all right.' He repeated the words over and over again because he couldn't think of what else to say, and because it thrilled him to be soothing her in this moment of fear and need, whispering to her like a lover in the night.

Her eyes became opaque, then closed altogether. If it hadn't been for the rapidity of her breathing and the slight crease between her eyebrows she might have been asleep.

Simon straightened up with the sense of a task completed, if only for the time being. She could recall nothing. It was a miracle, a blessing. No police, no hassle, no flashbacks, no nightmares. According to the information he had garnered from various medics concussion victims rarely recovered lost memories of events immediately surrounding a trauma.

Waiting quietly, he remembered the time he had first seen Catherine – when was it? – three years ago. No, he could be more precise than that – two years and eleven months ago – at Ascot. He had understood immediately why people should talk about her, why they should describe her as pretty, lovely, striking. Simon himself had had no hesitation in calling her beautiful, though then, as now, he would have found it hard to say exactly why. She had good eyes – extraordinary eyes – arresting, oval with a slight upwards tilt at the corners, and her hair, when it wasn't scraped back and dead-looking like this, was a rich browny-gold; yet her nose was by any standards rather long, while her mouth was a little on the wide side and very full. There was no one feature that could be described as exceptional, and yet taken together they had what his mother would have called an *effect*. From that first glimpse Simon had found it impossible not to be gripped by the sheer improbability of that brilliant face.

Later, when he'd had the chance to observe her, he'd become intrigued by her vitality, the way she moved and talked and held her head, by her low supple laughing voice and the warm conspiratorial glances she threw at those around her. She was the most vivid person Simon had ever met. He was in awe of this, and envious too, because, though he worked hard at every aspect of his life, enjoyment wasn't something that came easily to him. Watching Catherine sometimes, he was both fascinated and disturbed by the idea that such enjoyment of life could be acquired or learnt, that if he could only devote more time to the study of it he might be able to find the secret. But in his sombre and lonely heart he knew there was no secret, no trick, no easy way; it was simply that some people loved life and others had to take the promise of such things on trust.

Her hand lay on the coverlet, white and slender and smooth

as a child's. He stared at it. He pictured himself taking it, squeezing it gently, communicating reassurance and affection, perhaps even managing to leave his hand resting lightly on hers for some moments afterwards. He imagined it, almost persuaded himself to do it, but in the end it was too enormous an undertaking, and it was a relief to hold back.

The emergency staff had removed the wedding ring, he noticed. He remembered Catherine wearing it for the first time. The wedding seemed very distant now, but it was just – Simon had to think – yes, eight months ago. Remembering her then, luminous and vibrant, it seemed strange to be looking down on this diminished shadowy version of Catherine, uncharacteristically subdued, confined, devoid of everything that had made her so alive.

Who would love and value her now? he wondered emotionally. Who would warm to someone so still, so changed? Not Ben's circle of acquaintances. If Simon's understanding of her medical condition was even half right, Catherine was going to need friends rather more substantial than that.

He found himself thinking: And Ben won't be much use either. *Love is not love which alters when it alteration finds.*

A mechanical hiss broke the silence: it took him an instant to realise that it was some sort of device for redistributing air around the mattress. When he looked up again it was to find Catherine watching him through half-closed eyes.

He smiled hastily, inanely. He felt his cheek tremble. He glanced away. 'Amazing flowers.'

There were flowers along the length of the window sill, at least six vases, and several more on the floor, as well as the large arrangement next to the chair, and, propped between them on every available surface, cards, several dozen of them. A few of the arrangements were striking, with unusual mixtures of flowers, foliage and dried grasses. From fellow garden designers, presumably, or, more likely still, grateful clients. He noted fleetingly but with satisfaction that the two all-white flower arrangements looked quite out of place.

'Could you . . . move them . . . please,' Catherine murmured.

'The flowers?'

'The white . . .'

He looked at her sharply, thinking for a ludicrous moment that she had read his mind. 'Yes – rather too funereal, aren't they?' He gave a bright bark of a laugh. 'Or matrimonial! Shall I move them away?'

'Nearer.'

He felt a stab of heat in his face, as if she were making fun of him. 'Nearer?'

'I love . . . white.'

This time he managed to turn his laugh into a sharp cough. 'Of course.'

It was no easy job. The sill was so crowded that he had to move two vases temporarily to the floor before he could rearrange everything satisfactorily.

Catherine's eyes followed him back to the bedside. 'I – don't see—' For some reason she was suddenly close to tears.

'What don't you see, Catherine?'

'Why' – her voice cracked with open resentment – '*you* – came.'

His chest tightened, a sharpness burned his eyes. 'Why I came?'

Her face contorted. 'Go away,' she cried bitterly. 'I don't want you here. I want my family.'

Steadying himself, he put a hand to his glasses and settled them more precisely on his nose. 'I understand, of course . . . But someone had to liaise with the police, you see. And I thought it was the one area where I could be useful. Give Ben and your father one less thing to worry about.'

A single tear slid from Catherine's eye. 'But where – are they?' she cried pathetically. 'I want them here.'

'They'll be here any moment now.' With Catherine's rebuff still echoing painfully in his ears, Simon reached for his brief-case. 'I'm sure you'll want to rest,' he said, mustering his dignity. 'You'll want to sleep.'

The door sounded. Simon braced himself, but it was only one of the ancillary staff.

'More flowers, Catherine!' she called gaily. 'What a popular girl you are!' She brandished them in the air before plopping them on top of the television set and sweeping out of the room.

Simon took a step towards the door. 'Well . . . I'll be off then.'

'They wild?'

'Sorry?'

'The flowers.'

Simon gave them a cursory glance. 'I wouldn't know, I'm afraid.'

She lifted the fingers of one hand: a summons. Dutifully, Simon put his briefcase down again and, fetching the flowers, held them just above her where she could see them. They were arranged in a posy, a mass of tiny blue, white and pink flowers, set in a halo of leaves and miniature foliage, supported by an outer layer of cellophane.

She touched them, she seemed to lose interest, but just as Simon thought it would be safe to slip away she gave a soft cry. '*Oh*, but they – look like—' There was an envelope pinned to the cellophane; she raised a hand towards it.

He unclipped it and took out the note. 'Do you want me to read it for you?'

She blinked slowly in agreement.

He turned the note over and glanced at the signature. 'It's from someone called Terry.'

Her eyes widened, she made a harsh sound of annoyance. This reaction was so unexpected that Simon went back to the note for an address or some other clue to Terry's identity. There was none. Then, with sharpened interest, he realised precisely who it might be. If it was indeed Terry Devlin, then the man certainly had a nerve. According to Ben, this was the man who, having been shown great kindness by Catherine's family in his youth, had repaid them by acquiring the debts on their house and throwing them out.

However, it was another, largely untold story that had taken a far deeper hold on Simon's imagination. While it was generally known that Ben and Terry Devlin had worked on a deal together, the cause of their falling out had always been something of a mystery. Certainly it was not a subject that could safely be raised with Ben. But if the hints and rumours Simon had picked up were even half correct, Terry Devlin had achieved the unique distinction of having played Ben at one of his trickier games and outmanoeuvred him. Simon had always ached to know how Devlin had achieved it.

He began to read aloud. '*Dear Catherine, I am so very sorry to hear that you are in the hospital. I trust they are looking after you well. I hope these flowers from Morne will bring a little colour to your room. They were fresh picked this morning from the meadow just the other side of the bridge—*'

Catherine made a faint sound that he couldn't interpret.

'Shall I go on?'

She closed her eyes. It wasn't a request to stop.

He continued, '*The meadow is completely covered in wild flowers every May now (last year there was a lot of marsh marigold, this year ragged robin and cranesbill). I think the land there was always trying to be a flower meadow and just needed to be left alone for a while.*'

Simon felt the irritation of having been mistaken. This was obviously a gardening crony or former colleague.

Seeing that Catherine was slowly losing the battle to stay awake, he rattled rapidly through the descriptions of seeding and grazing, and slowed down only for the last bit. '*Now, you take care of yourself, Catherine. We all wish you a speedy recovery. With fond regards, your devoted friend, Terry.*'

He glanced up to find that she had drifted off. He stood and watched her for a final moment, transfixed by her helplessness. With a rush of feeling, he thought: I will care for you when the rest have drifted away, I won't abandon you. But no sooner had he allowed this thought to fill him with secret pride than it became confusing to him, and he shrank away from it.

He had been here too long. Hurriedly he deposited the letter and flowers on a chair and, scooping up his briefcase, went softly towards the door.

He was beginning to think he had escaped the family when the door swung open in his face and he was confronted by Alice, followed shortly by Duncan.

'What the hell are *you* doing here?' Alice hissed.

'Simon, old chap,' Duncan murmured, looking puzzled.

'Well?' demanded Alice.

With an arrow-like gesture of one hand, Duncan cleared a path for himself and, muttering, 'Where's my girl?', shouldered his way into the room. A moment later Simon heard him call in a broken voice, 'My dearest darling girl—'

'*Well?*' Alice's tone was uncompromising.

Simon gestured her towards the corridor. It was a perfectly polite gesture, in fact he inclined his head as he did so, which was about as polite as you could get, but Alice was not one to let manners or self-control interfere with her temper, and she stood square, blocking the doorway with her plump frame, so that Simon had no choice but to squeeze past her into the passage. He pulled tight against the wall, but she moved to block him further or possibly to provoke him because first her arm, then, as she turned, her breast, brushed against him, and he had to suppress the urge to thrust her away.

Following hard behind him, yanking at his sleeve, she hissed, 'I suppose this was *Ben's* idea!'

He didn't answer immediately, which only seemed to enrage her further.

'How dare you!' she growled. 'How *dare* you!'

'Perhaps when you're a little calmer I could explain—'

'*Explain!* You sneak in here, like you sneak in everywhere, you go and *bother* her – and you think there's anything to *explain*!'

'The alternative was the police,' he replied in measured

tones. 'I'm sure you wouldn't have wanted them to come and bother her.'

'At least *they* would have had the decency to *wait*! At least they wouldn't have barged in uninvited!'

Alice was a tall girl and several stone overweight, with a small nose and thin lips that were lost in the broad fleshy cheeks and frame of thick dark hair. Her complexion was the colour of dough and there was an unhealthy puffiness beneath her eyes. Her manner matched her temperament, sullen and irritable. Now, with her chin thrust out, her eyes glittering shrewishly, she looked positively ugly. If she had been anyone but Catherine's younger sister, Simon would have retreated without another word.

'Who gave you the *right*?' she flogged on. 'That's what I want to know! Who said you could just waltz in here?'

'It was your father, actually.'

He had caught her there, and she didn't like it one bit. Her eyes narrowed, her lips formed a jagged line.

Simon pressed home his advantage. 'He asked me if I would deal with the police – and that's exactly what I've been doing. And why I came here today, to see if it was necessary for them to bother her—'

'But you're a bloody *tax* lawyer!'

Her voice was strident, it could have commanded a hunting field. Glancing up the passage, he was aware of people looking in their direction.

With a conspicuous demonstration of restraint, he lowered his voice to a murmur. 'That's not right actually. I'm a commercial lawy—'

'But *money*! You deal in *money*!' From the way she said it money might have been one of the most noxious substances known to man.

'What I deal in are situations. This is just another situation.'

'Ha!' She wagged an exultant finger. 'Exactly! Just *another* situation you're fixing for someone else! For *Ben*, perhaps?'

This was the sort of emotionally charged, illogical argument that Simon found profoundly unpleasant. Recoiling, he lifted a splayed hand, in truce or farewell, however she cared to interpret it.

Alice chose to redirect her ire. 'What I want to know is why *Ben* isn't dealing with the police. *He* should be the one dealing with them – not *you.*'

'As I've said, your father thought—'

'Where the hell *is* Ben, anyway? God – Catherine's in this place, desperately ill, and Ben's vanished. Where's he been for the last few days, for Christ's sake?'

He put her right. 'He's been dashing in and out most of the time actually. But now – I can't tell you where he's gone.'

'Can't or *won't!*'

'Actually – can't.'

She searched his face for the lie, then, backing down, gave a grudging shrug. 'Well, he damn well *should* be here.'

'I agree.'

'When did you last speak to him?'

Simon selected his words with care. 'Not recently.'

'It's unbelievable! He doesn't even answer his mobile. Not for *me*, anyway. What about you?'

Choosing to interpret this question loosely, Simon gave a minute shake of his head. In fact, he'd managed to make contact a couple of times, but Ben had been so uncommunicative, the conversations so brief that they hardly seemed worth mentioning, particularly to Alice, who in her present mood was unlikely to believe anything so obvious as the truth.

'Just *incredible*!' Alice gave a harsh contemptuous sigh before fixing Simon with a cold eye. 'So why have *you* been dropping in the whole time, then? Oh, don't think I don't know – the staff have told me. At dawn, at *night* even. I assumed you were reporting back to Ben, but now you tell me you're not.'

'Actually I've been coming in to find out how Catherine was,' he replied solemnly.

'Oh, have you?' Her eyebrows shot up in an ironic expression of surprise. 'Really? Now why should you do that?'

When he hesitated, she declared, 'You always were a creep, Simon. Right from the beginning. Wheedling your way in, getting to know people who might be useful to you. Oh, don't think it hasn't been *obvious*—' She broke off with a dismissive gesture.

Simon felt the coldness come over him that marked his moments of deepest bewilderment and humiliation.

'Anyway,' Alice went on, 'the point is, you've been talking to the staff about Catherine!'

He said very quietly, 'Only to ask about her health.'

'That's what I mean. Getting information that wasn't any of your business. Well, whatever you've heard, whatever they've said, it's not to be passed on to anyone else. Is that absolutely clear?'

'I wouldn't dream of it.'

'No talk of her condition. No talk of – *problems*.'

'Of course not!' he retorted, letting his indignation show. 'What do you take me for? Quite apart from anything else, I'm bound by client confidentiality.'

Another raised eyebrow. 'Well, that's something, I suppose. Assuming you stick to it, of course. Assuming we have the faintest idea of who you're acting *for*.'

Simon felt a shudder of rage. It was only with the greatest effort that he managed to control his voice. 'I'm acting for Ben while he's away. And for your father. And for Catherine of course, if she needs me.'

'Well, she doesn't need you.' Alice loomed closer and he could see the faint dampness on her forehead and the darkness in her muddy-green eyes. 'And you're not to see her again without our permission. Is that quite clear?'

*My God*, he thought savagely, *she'll be asking me to kiss her arse next*. He stated stiffly, 'I will return if asked to do so. As indeed I was *today*.'

'Quite.' She gave a tight little smile, and he had no doubt that Duncan would be strictly forbidden to issue any more rash instructions.

'Well, I think I'll go and see my sister now.' She added pointedly, 'If she isn't completely exhausted, that is.'

Simon managed to hold on to his expression until he was some distance up the corridor, when he was overtaken by a shiver that caught his breath and clouded his vision. My God, what had he done to deserve that?

Ben said it was lack of sex that made Alice so spiky, though being Ben he put it rather more bluntly than that. In his more unabashed moments he also said that she resented being fat and plain in a family of attractive people. Yet Ben had been referring to Alice's normal chippiness, a carping banter that could almost pass as humour; he knew nothing of this particular and malicious delight she reserved for Simon. Alice had attacked Simon before – twice – and, then as now, he had racked his brains as to why he should provoke such hostility. He had never to his knowledge given her the slightest cause to dislike him, had never overstepped the mark in any shape or form, indeed had taken care to be polite and pleasant, going so far as to ask after her interests (she watched polo, was pro-hunting, and went skiing in Val D'Isere). No, it couldn't be anything he had said or not said.

As for *using* people . . . as for *wheedling* his way in . . . This thought stung him to the core. Was this what Alice was telling everyone? Worse, was this what they were believing? Was this what Catherine herself thought of him? The idea was especially painful because it was so unjust. He had *never* promoted himself in any inappropriate way, had never been anything but meticulous in his dealings with other people. Away from the office, he was like everyone else, he drank with his friends, went to the races with them, supported their charities, and now and again dropped in a bit of business. Everyone did it. Not only was he no worse than anyone else, he was a great deal better. The suggestion was outrageous! He had nothing to reproach himself for.

It came to him suddenly that there was something far simpler behind Alice's attack. The answer was so obvious he couldn't imagine why he hadn't thought of it before. What she really loathed was the idea of being indebted to him. She couldn't stomach the fact that he had saved her father from his own excesses, that by taking control of Duncan's tinpot wine company Simon had rescued him from financial disaster. It was nothing personal at all.

He allowed himself a last burst of indignation and relief before pushing thoughts of Alice firmly to the back of his mind. The heat had gone from him, the sweat on his shirt felt cold on his skin. He found a washroom and splashed cold water on his face before going to a quiet spot overlooking the atrium and dialling Ben's mobile. As it rang he pictured Ben squinting at the phone, reading the caller's name on the display before deciding whether to answer it.

'About to call you,' came the laconic voice. From the background babble, Simon guessed he was speaking from a large public place, a hall or concourse.

'Where are you, Ben?' Simon used a neutral tone. 'Everyone's wondering. I'm at the hospital. Catherine's come round. She's asking for you.'

'She's come round? Well, thank God for that! They said she would, didn't they? Still – a relief. And she's okay, is she? I mean, cheerful and all that.'

'She needs you here, Ben.'

'Look, I just can't make it. Not for the moment. Just can't. Cover for me, will you, Simon? It's a bit urgent.'

'What's so urgent exactly?'

'Plenty!' Ben snapped in a rare show of nerves. Then, in a more subdued voice: 'Got to be somewhere, that's all. Just getting on a plane now. Won't get back till late tonight – no, at this rate, *tomorrow*. Yes – midday, I should think. Just tell her that nothing, absolutely nothing in the world would keep me away but wild horses. Tell her exactly that, will you? Wild horses. She'll understand.'

'What about a quick word on the phone? She'd love to hear –'

'No!' he cut in. 'Look, I would, I really would, but it'd be too difficult to explain. She'd only get upset. Make herself ill or something. Better for you to tell her. Really. Much better.'

Simon said firmly, 'I need to know one thing.' He didn't add *before I agree* but that was what he meant. 'Is this anything to do with the business? Anything I should know about? Because if it is—'

'Course not! I'd bloody tell you, wouldn't I, if it was.'

Summoning all his courage, Simon took a flier. 'Nothing to do with the Polska CMC deal?'

'*No.*' He sounded incredulous. 'How could it be?'

In his thoughts Simon echoed: That's right, Ben, how could it be? 'In that case,' he said aloud, 'is it anything I can help out with?'

'No, thanks.'

'As a friend, I mean?'

'Nope. Look – got to run. They're calling the flight.'

'Can I at least tell Catherine where you've gone?'

'No,' he said in the brisk disparaging tone he always used to halt discussion. 'Just tell her I'll see her tomorrow. Okay?'

The connection went dead.

Pocketing his phone, Simon tried to remember a time when he had known Ben so rattled. Not for years, not since they had first started the business and gambled everything on the Qatar deal. On second thoughts, not even then; no, in all this time Ben had never had it this bad.

Avoiding a passing trolley, Simon crossed the corridor to the nursing station and, taking some blank paper from his brief-case, used a free end of the counter to write out Ben's message to Catherine. As he underlined *wild horses*, he became aware of a woman marching up to the desk and casting vainly about for a member of staff. Simon recognised the tall, sharp-featured blonde immediately. She was a girlfriend of Catherine's called Emma Russell, in advertising, or maybe it was PR – yes, PR for an up-market china shop – and her father was the managing director of an independent Midlands brewery.

'Hello, Emma.'

She stared at him uncertainly. 'Oh . . . hi.'

'Simon Jardine.'

Though they had met at least three times before, it was clear she hadn't placed him. He suppressed the small flutter of resentment that was apt to stir in him at such moments.

'Cheltenham Gold Cup, lunch in the marquee,' he prompted lightly.

'Oh *yes!*' she exclaimed, springing to life. 'You work for Ben. Tell me—'

'*With* him—'

'What?' Blinking briefly at the interruption, she rushed on impatiently, 'But how's Cath? Is she all right? Tell me—'

'She regained consciousness a few hours ago,' Simon reported gravely. 'She's out of intensive care.'

'Oh, thank God for that!' Emma spread a scarlet-nailed hand against her chest in an extravagant gesture of relief. 'Thank *God*. I hadn't heard anything since Monday, and what with trying to get an earlier flight and the rush – oh, thank God!' Slowing down a little, she asked, 'But what are they saying? Is she going to be all right? Will she—' She moved closer and, resting her fingers lightly on Simon's arm, fixed him with an intense rather disconcerting gaze. She had large round eyes, hazel-brown, with brilliant whites and thick lashes. Despite her height, or perhaps because of it, she tilted her head forward so that, though her gaze was level with his, she seemed to be peering up at him. 'Someone told me she'd hurt her back, that it might be serious, that' – her voice faltered – 'it might be *broken*. Is it true?'

'I don't think the doctors know anything definite about anything yet. Too soon.'

'But it's *possible*?'

'Really – no one knows.'

She removed her hand rather crossly. 'Well – what *are* they saying, then?'

'Her skull's fractured, she was badly concussed, but there are no blood clots, which are the dangerous thing apparently.'

'But are they reasonably happy with the way things are going? Do they think she's going to be okay?'

'They won't commit themselves.'

Giving up on him altogether, she narrowed her mouth and glanced away. 'Can I see her? Is it allowed?'

'Duncan's with her at the moment. And Alice. Best to ask them.'

'Oh, if they're both in there I'd better wait, hadn't I? It'd be too much to have me as well, wouldn't it?' Increasingly fidgety, she glanced around several times before grunting, 'Anywhere to smoke in this place? I've just had eight hours on a plane and a perfectly awful time in New York. The fascists there scream at you if you so much as light up in the *street*.' Another scan of the pristine white corridors and, with a sharp sigh of resignation and a pursing of her mouth, she abandoned the quest.

As if to keep her mind off nicotine, she began to speak in a rush that emphasised her high rather breathless voice. 'I only found out when I happened to call someone from New York. They told me she was on the critical list. I couldn't *believe* it. Tried to phone Ben, left dozens of messages – he never called back. I realised he must be here night and day, of course, but that only made me more frantic. Imagining the worst. So I phoned everyone I could think of. Finally got through to Jack and Amy Bellingham – you know, the restaurant people – and they told me Cath was here, in intensive care, and that she'd broken her spine and fractured her skull and the doctors weren't sure if she was going to make it. Well, you can imagine – I was just devastated. I mean, from the way they were talking it sounded so *desperate*. And when they told me she'd been *pushed* – well, for God's sake! – is it true? – did this maniac really *push* her?'

'All that anyone knows for sure is she fell.'

Emma shuddered visibly and screwed up her eyes. 'Where? How?'

Even now, four days after the event, Simon had to take a

slow breath before he could bring himself to relate it. 'She was found on the hall floor, underneath that railed landing. The banisters gave way. She fell across a large wooden chest – they think it was that which broke her back. Her head met the floor.'

Emma clasped a hand to her mouth. 'That hall – it's stone, isn't it? *God!* It's too awful to think about! Too ghastly!' She dropped her face into her hands amid curtains of hair and gave a long strangled moan. Then, lifting her head abruptly, flipping her hair back from her face, she cried, 'And this *person* – this *animal*, this piece of *scum* – he did it on purpose, did he? To get some sort of ghastly *kick*?'

'There's no way of knowing.'

'But how did he get in? Where was Ben?'

Taking care, as always, to be precise, Simon outlined what he'd been told by the police. That there were signs of a break-in, that the house had been ransacked, that Ben had been found stunned and confused, that when he'd been able to talk to the police some hours later he'd told them about finding an intruder.

Emma listened attentively with her head on one side and her arms hugged tightly round her waist. She had a slender, narrow-hipped figure, almost boyish, with a thin face that emphasised the childlike roundness of her eyes. She was dressed entirely in black, in a well-cut trouser suit rumpled from the journey. Her hair was straight and shoulder length and very blonde. Every few minutes she pushed it back from her face in what was evidently a nervous mannerism. She was probably the same age as Catherine though her angular rather pinched face made her seem older, more like thirty-two or -three.

'I always said it was a dodgy area,' she muttered. 'It's not really Notting Hill, is it? More like North Kensington. Anyway, I thought they were still meant to be in France. I didn't think they were back till this weekend.'

'Something came up.'

She declared disgustedly, 'With the bloody business, I suppose!' Then, in a voice hardly less contemptuous: 'And of course the police haven't caught this *person* yet, have they?'

Simon shook his head.

'No, *too* much to hope for. The police are *useless*! I got robbed last year *right* outside my door, and they were completely pathetic. Didn't want to know. Tried to fob me off with Victim Support. I mean, the woman was absolutely sweet and all that, but it wasn't tea I needed, it was transport – and *rapido*. I ended up missing the most fantastic party—' She broke off with a small sidelong glance at Simon and added a little defensively, 'I hope they're making a hell of a lot more effort over *this*.'

'The guy in charge seems reasonably efficient. Bright, too.'

Emma eyed Simon. 'You've met him?'

'Wilson? Very much so. Talk to him twice a day, sometimes more. I'm liaising with them, you see. On behalf of Ben and Duncan. To take a bit of the load off their shoulders.' The last comment had sounded almost boastful and he frowned at the lapse.

Emma was looking at him with new interest. '*Liaising?* I hadn't realised. In that case you'll know if they've checked—' She paused abruptly, her eyes slid away. 'No,' she said after a moment, as if taking herself in hand. 'No, perhaps . . .' Then, attempting to strike a different note, she asked casually, 'Where's Ben? Is he around?'

'He had to go away.'

'But he'll be back soon?'

'Not immediately, no.'

'You mean – *away* away?'

'Yes.'

She gave Simon a mildly resentful glance, as if Ben's unaccountable absence was in some way his fault. 'But I can get him on his mobile?'

Simon made a doubtful gesture. 'I rather think he's out of

reach. But I'm expecting him to call later. I'd be glad to pass on a message.'

Emma exhaled sharply, almost petulantly, and it occurred to him that she wasn't one to bear the trials of life with good grace. 'It'll wait,' she muttered.

Overtaken by a fresh attack of restlessness, she flicked her hair back, though now, as before, it fell forward again almost immediately. 'Do you think they'll be in there much longer, Duncan and Alice?' she said fretfully. 'Or shall I put my head round the door?'

'It might be an idea.'

But she made no move towards Catherine's room. Instead, agitating her hand, she paced off across the corridor.

A wall clock showed a quarter to five. If he got a move on Simon realised he might be able to catch DS Wilson at his desk before he knocked off for the day.

Returning to the message for Catherine, he picked up his pen again and added '*He sends tons of love*' and was immediately worried that *tons* was too breezy, even by Ben's standards, that *much* or *deepest* love would be more fitting.

He'd just decided to leave the love measured by weight when Emma came back. Leaning both forearms on the counter, she said, 'It was definitely a burglary?'

'Sorry?'

'The police – they think it was just a burglary?'

Her choice of words made him look up. 'Well – yes. Things were stolen, the house was ransacked.'

'It wasn't a stalker then?'

He stared. For an instant he thought he must have misheard her. 'A stalker? Why do you say that?'

She gave a sharp sigh, as though the whole matter had become altogether too much for her. 'That's what I wanted to talk to Ben about, you see, to ask him what he thought – whether the guy could have had anything to do with – well, *anything*. Look, it was probably nothing – Cath only mentioned it once, she didn't seem to take it seriously – but it's been on my mind, I kept thinking about it on the plane, that this *breather* might have turned out to be a complete *psycho*. You know, followed her, waited for her. I mean, it often starts with calls, doesn't it? And then they go on from there, get obsessed. But if it was just a burglary, then—'

Simon interrupted, 'Are you saying someone was stalking Catherine?'

'No – well, not then – no, it was just calls. But that's what I wanted to ask Ben – if anything else had happened, like anyone had started hanging around, or if this guy was just, you know, a sad anorak in a phone booth.' She threw up a hand. 'But, look, how do I know? It was probably nothing. It might have stopped weeks ago—'

Simon couldn't get to grips with this at all. 'Let me get this straight, someone was making nuisance calls to Catherine?'

'Yes.'

'Threatening calls?'

'Well – not quite. I think Cath said that he only ever spoke once. After that he never said a word. That's why she wasn't too fazed.'

'There was nothing else apart from the calls?'

She said touchily, 'Well . . . no.'

'He never bothered her in any other way?'

'Not that she ever—' Emma pushed a palm against her head in a gesture of stupidity. 'I'm crazy, aren't I? If this guy had shown his face, Ben would have said something, wouldn't he? If anything had happened to frighten Cath, he would have told the police.' She gave a long groan. 'I left my brain on a bar stool somewhere, didn't I? I really hadn't *thought*.'

But Simon wasn't listening, he was too busy trying to see how the police were likely to interpret this information, how it might affect the course of their investigation. 'Best to be on the safe side,' he said finally.

'What?'

'Best to tell the police. They should know everything, decide for themselves what's important.'

She shrugged, but she was relieved all the same. 'You think so? Well, in that case—' Her eye was caught by something over his shoulder. 'Oh, there's Alice!' She gave a tentative wave and prepared to move off.

Simon put the message into her hand. 'Could you read this to Catherine?'

Emma waved more strenuously to Alice and mimed greetings. 'Sure.'

'And the police may want to talk to you. Shall I call you—'

But she was already hurrying off. Just when he thought she would leave without a word she spun round and, pointing the edge of the folded message at him, sighting along it like the barrel of a gun, called, 'Got it now – you're the one into ballerina gear!'

Simon had long since taught himself to arrange his mouth into a smile whenever this subject came up. 'Ben's little joke,' he called back.

But she was already striding off and didn't hear.

Avoiding Alice's distant and frosty gaze, Simon turned away to find the pudding-faced nurse leaning over the counter, holding out a phone to him. 'A friend of Catherine's, wanting to speak to someone.'

Simon looked at the wall clock, then his watch; time was running out to see Wilson. He took the receiver hastily with a brusque, 'Yes?'

'Yes, hullo there. This is an old family friend of Catherine *Galitza*.' The soft male voice hesitated slightly over her married name. 'I wanted to know how she was.' The accent was muted but unmistakably Irish.

'I'm not at liberty to give out information over the phone.'

'I just wanted to know if she was conscious yet.'

Simon said grudgingly, 'She is.'

'*Ah*.' It was a cry of relief. 'And the operation went okay?'

'Operation?'

'Wasn't it yesterday? To stabilise the spine?'

Whoever the man was, he was astonishingly well-informed. 'Who is this?' Simon demanded.

A slight pause. 'My name is Terry.'

Simon pictured the flowers and the note, saw Catherine's reaction. 'Terry who?'

A more conspicuous hesitation. 'Devlin.'

He'd been right after all. Simon felt a brief satisfaction before his thoughts skidded off in several directions at once, all disturbing, all intriguing. How in the world had Devlin got hold of this information? Why on earth should he want it? Could he be planning to use it against the family in some way? Simon couldn't help thinking how furious Ben and Duncan would be when he told them about this call.

Now he retorted, 'The information you want is confidential.'

'I appreciate that, Doctor. I just wanted a general indication of whether she'd got through all right.'

'I'm not a doctor.'

'*What?*' There was a stunned pause. 'But the girl said— Who *am* I speaking to then?'

'This is the family solicitor.'

Another pause. 'Your name?'

'Simon Jardine.'

The silence drew out. Devlin's voice said very coldly, 'I was misinformed.'

A click and he had rung off.

With a glare at his watch, Simon strode rapidly out of the building into the last of the rain and, failing to find a cab, arrived at the police station a good twenty minutes after DS Wilson had left for the day.

# Chapter Two

TERRY DEVLIN spent the rest of the afternoon in a state of angry self-reproach. The call had been a complete misjudgement, the blunder with the lawyer nothing less than excruciating. What had he been thinking of? Why couldn't he have waited? It would only have been a matter of an hour, two at the most. The wages of impatience. Now Duncan and Alice would know he had phoned, would be appalled at his intrusion. Daring to call himself a friend of the family! Presuming to ask about Catherine's operation! Having by some despicable underhand means managed to find out about it! They would be deeply offended, and who could blame them.

Just an hour or two. Why, oh why, couldn't he have shown a little patience?

He snapped instructions into the intercom, heard the imperious note in his voice, and moderated his tone abruptly. He was leaving, he told Bridget, would she cancel the rest of the day and summon the car immediately. Please – this more reasonably. If she would be so kind – this contritely.

Bridget came in, wearing her uncompromising face. 'You have an interview with the *Sunday Independent* starting in two minutes.'

'Can't it be put off?'

'I think that would be unwise since the journalist is waiting just outside and the time and venue have already been changed twice.'

He gave in with a shake of his head. 'All right. But nothing after that.'

Bridget asked if he would like the last two meetings of the day rescheduled for the morning.

'No. Tell everyone to go ahead without me.'

This was unheard of, not Terry's style at all, and he saw Bridget hesitate and eye him cautiously, like someone who has found herself in a cage with an animal of uncertain temperament.

He sighed and raised an upturned palm in a gesture that was partly an apology, partly an expression of helplessness, and she gave a rapid nod of understanding. Terry's daughter had been seriously ill, the recuperation slow, and during the months of his wretchedness and inattention Bridget had of necessity become a master of flexibility and improvisation, as well as a holder of forts, large and small. Then, just when his daughter seemed to be recovering and Bridget and the rest of the staff had thought life was settling down again, this new and terrible anxiety had overtaken him, a crisis whose cause he couldn't begin to explain to her, nor indeed to anyone else who found themselves on the receiving end of one of his unprovoked bursts of ill temper.

'And you mentioned you had a seven-thirty appointment this evening,' she said. 'Will you still be keeping—'

'You bet!' Terry cried with such ferocity that Bridget's eyes rounded momentarily. He repeated more reasonably, 'You bet.'

She plucked up courage to ask, 'Where is the meeting, so Pat will know what time to pick you up?'

'The Shelbourne.'

He saw her eyebrows lift in unspoken surprise.

'Shall Pat pick you up from home, then, at seven ten?'

'Seven twenty.'

'You want to be late?'

'I want to be late.'

Moving on from this topic with something like relief, Bridget asked, 'Will you want to freshen up?' This was her way of saying he needed to comb his hair and make himself presentable.

Obediently, Terry went through to the adjoining bathroom and faced the glass. He saw a man who looked weary, unhealthy and overweight. Since he had given up all pretence of taking care of himself some four years ago, these were conditions he richly deserved, though this didn't prevent him from feeling disappointment at the speed and relentlessness with which his body had given up the fight. Three extra stone had fixed themselves to his midriff and surrounding areas, his knees were creaking under the strain, his eyes had grown pouches and his skin had taken on a patchy uneven tone. His hair was beginning to grey and recede and if he was being ruthlessly honest there was a bare patch on his crown which, having been the size of a fifty-pence coin, was gaining currency by the day. His doctor told him the usual things doctors were paid to say, that he should drink less and eat less and take exercise. In the meantime, he looked nearer to fifty than forty. However, it was not his age or weight that preoccupied him as he looked in the glass, but the unprecedented doubt and uncertainty he saw reflected there. Maeve's illness had pulled him up short. Catherine's accident had shaken him. It seemed that fate was trying to bring him down off his high perch, and for the first time in his life he felt he had lost confidence and direction.

'It's a feature article,' Bridget reminded him when he emerged, washed and combed. 'For the main body of the paper, to mark the opening of The Kavanagh. Being a feature, you're to expect all sorts of questions.'

'I don't want all sorts of questions.'

'Anne did warn you.'

Anne was the PR girl. He hardly remembered the briefing, but then there was no accounting for the things that passed him by these days.

'Anne will be sitting in. She'll fend off anything unsuitable.'

The journalist was a tiny girl clad in tight black trousers and skimpy top with cropped blonde hair, and so young that she might have been Maeve's age and straight out of school.

His smile appeared mechanically; he had long since learnt to hide most emotions – certainly indifference and impatience – behind a smile. Assuming the rest of his required role was more difficult, however. From the time that the business world had started to take notice of him, some fifteen years back, he had been content to take on the various guises allotted to him by the press. First it had been the boy from the bogs on the up and up, the cheeky chappie who never missed a trick; then, following a round of acquisitions, he had become the daring young entrepreneur with the Midas touch; latterly, by a mysterious process of metamorphosis, he had grown into a pillar of the business community, a champion of the New Ireland. Not that he must ever fail to mention the rockier moments in his career, nor his humble beginnings, nor his gratitude for all that life and a booming Ireland had given him. He had learnt that so far as the press was concerned no cliché was so overblown that it should be left unprinted. Local boy made good. Rags to riches. Golden touch. Sometimes he felt like a living banality.

From the start it had always been easier to give them what they wanted, a Terry Devlin who was confident, outgoing, provocative, quick to joke and quicker to laugh. Over time this simplistic and distorted version of himself had become a habit as well as a shield. But today he could summon neither the energy nor the will to step into his role, and he faced the young journalist with an empty smile fuelled by an empty heart.

The journalist went straight to the large west-facing window at the far corner of his office to gaze at the view.

'That's why I chose this site,' he said, coming up beside her. 'It's the only place you can look straight along the river for such a distance – a mile in fact. The only place you can see five bridges in a row.'

Below them, the Liffey was a pale grey beneath an insipid May sun. The water had the smooth stagnant look of a canal. From this vantage point the bridges, one behind the other, seemed to number more than five and to crowd the river.

'Wasn't it the land prices that attracted you? The fact that this was a derelict area?'

'That too, of course.'

'Two birds with one stone?'

He broadened his smile. 'And why not?'

'And you can see The Kavanagh from here, can't you?'

'Just the top storey.'

'But gratifying all the same, I imagine.'

'Nice to keep an eye. Know it's still there.'

She turned to face him. 'But you're pleased with it?'

'It's the best hotel we could build.'

'Was that your purpose, to build the finest hotel in Dublin?'

'Well, it has five stars.'

'That wasn't quite my question. I meant the hotel that would be acknowledged as the finest in the city?'

'It's intended to be the best you can get anywhere.'

She tried another tack. 'Would you describe yourself as a proud man?'

'Without wishing to split hairs, in what sense do you mean?'

'A man who is proud of his achievements.'

'Ah, in *that* sense – yes. Overall.'

'Only overall? So there are things you're not so proud of?'

'Inevitably.'

She smiled ingenuously. 'Such as?'

Scenting danger, the PR girl moved forward, ready to catch his signal.

'Well, as you will have garnered from the press cuttings I have made a few mistakes in my time.'

'Business or personal?'

He made a gesture as if to award her marks for trying. 'Business. I would only count my business mistakes to a stranger.'

'But to yourself?'

'To myself?' He made a show of considering this. 'I think I could be relied on to count all my mistakes, honestly and without favour.'

'You have regrets?'

'Everyone has regrets.'

'What are your main regrets?'

'Business or personal?' And he offered a cautionary smile to show that this was just part of the game and he had no intention of answering anything to do with his private life.

'Both.'

'In business I would say that I have most regretted misreading situations. Misjudging them.'

'Does that happen very often?'

'Not often, but occasionally.'

'With serious results?'

He shrugged. 'With less than satisfactory results.'

'Are you a forgiving person?'

The question took him off-guard and he must have let it show because she quickly rephrased it more forcefully. 'Do you forgive people who have let you down?'

'Forgive? It's usually irrelevant by the time ... I don't concern myself with holding grudges, if that's what you mean.'

'Is that because you can afford to, or because you have a forgiving nature?'

He thought about that for a moment. 'Rivalry is perfectly natural, and you could say that rivalry is based on not forgiving or forgetting that someone managed to get the better of you last time, and making darned sure that you are the one to get the upper hand at the next opportunity. Men are naturally competitive. It's one of things that makes the world go round.'

'But if someone hasn't played fair?'

'Fair has many interpretations.'

'Done the dirty on you. Tried to cheat you.'

Immediately, he thought of Ben Galitza. 'I would not forget,' he said solemnly. 'No, I would not forget.'

'Forgive?'

'I wouldn't lose sleep over it. Life's too short. One must move on.'

'Indeed? People say you don't move on. People say you never forgive.'

'I can't answer for what people say.'

'So you don't care what they say?'

'I care very much what certain people say, people I respect.'

'And in your personal life? Do you forgive and forget there?' She was fishing unashamedly, though more in hope than expectation.

'By definition, that is personal.'

She nodded philosophically. 'Would you say it's necessary to be ruthless to achieve success?'

He laughed briefly but without humour. 'It's a fine word – *ruthless*. The ruthless businessman. The ruthless operator. The ruthless bastard. Those words always go together somehow, don't they? But I wouldn't say they were mutually dependent. And certainly not something to aspire to.'

'But the description might be apposite none the less.'

'It might. But I don't think it's necessary to be ruthless. Rather, *meticulous*. Or, if I had to be described by an adjective beginning with R, *resolute*.'

'So, you never give up.'

'I'm single-minded certainly. So long as I believe the prize to be worth winning.'

'You've never remarried, Mr Devlin. No prize worth winning among the ladies of Dublin?'

He didn't attempt to answer this, nor to laugh it off. Instead he gestured her towards the conference area. 'Why don't we talk about hotels now?'

The girl had the cheek to answer, 'I thought we were.'


On the journey home, Terry kept going back over his day and found little to ease his agony of mind. At some point after they had crossed the Liffey, Pat asked him if he would like to go round by The Kavanagh, a detour they generally made once or twice a week. But Terry was in no mood for discussions with the hotel staff, nor with anyone else for that matter, and told Pat he would go straight home. So they went on past Trinity and the Castle, towards the southern suburbs, and he was aware of little else until they were turning in through the gates and Pat was confirming that he'd bring the car round again at seven twenty.

Bridget must have phoned ahead as usual because Mrs Ellis was waiting at the door, one hand restraining Conn, who was struggling to break free and jump against his chest like the crazy dog that he was.

'Well, here you are again, Mr Devlin,' said Mrs Ellis, meaning that he was home once more at a reasonable time. 'And will you be wanting dinner?'

He explained that he would be going out again at seven twenty, he wasn't sure how long for, and would find something to eat along the way. 'But for Maeve . . .?' He knew that Mrs Ellis needed no reminding, but he couldn't help asking all the same.

'She's sleeping now,' said Mrs Ellis, 'but she said to wake her at six and that she might fancy some salmon for supper, though to be on the safe side I've prepared those vegetables she likes, the kind for stir-frying.'

For someone schooled in the Irish–French cookery tradition – her own incontestable description – a stir-fry represented something of a departure not to mention a challenge, and he made a point of thanking her for taking so much trouble.

Over the last few months whenever Maeve was at home and sleeping like this he would often go upstairs and look in on her as he used to do when she was a small child. Today, however, he headed straight for his study, partly because she would be waking soon and he didn't want to disturb her prematurely, partly because Fergal's call, now thirty minutes overdue, would be coming through on his mobile at any moment and he didn't want to take it in a place where he might be overheard.

Conn, the black thief, slunk in through the study door before Terry had the chance to shut him out and limped on his three and a half good legs to his unofficial perch by the bookcase, where, in an attempt to keep a low profile, he curled up immediately and feigned sleep.

Terry sat heavily at the desk and thought: Well, what is to be salvaged then? What can be done that won't make every-thing worse?

Duncan Langley would have heard about his call by now, perhaps Alice Langley too, and would have drawn their own conclusions. There was nothing that could be done about that. But Catherine herself – he could only pray to God that the family wouldn't tell her. It was too painful to imagine how she would judge him. She would think he was prying in the most gratuitous way, or – he flinched at each new thought – having the gall to patronise her, to take some sort of perverse satisfac-tion in her tragedy, or – most unbearable of all – that he still had 'feelings' for her and in some demeaning way was trying to win her favour.

Four years ago, in a burst of madness, he'd written her a letter, a foolish outpouring born of loss and loneliness and what he'd imagined at the time to be love. The letter had embarrassed her; it had very rapidly embarrassed him. She had delivered the only reply she could have made, also in the form of a letter, which he'd promptly consigned to the bin, as he very much hoped she had done with his. His phone call today had been nothing to do with this particular aspect of the past. If Catherine thought otherwise, there was nothing he could do to put her right. And yet, and yet . . . the demon pride would not be subdued. It pierced him, and he stung.

For a moment he could see no way forward. He stared at the photographs on the desk top, cased in bulky green leather frames, and felt that everything he held dear had slipped away.

Most of the photographs were from way back: a picture of his late wife, taken a few months after their marriage; a formal shot of the wedding itself, the two of them looking so young and nervous outside the church; then a series of Maeve, as a fluffy-haired baby, as a schoolgirl in uniform with a cheeky spark in her gypsy eyes, and most recently as a student nurse, looking serene and lovely in her natural unaffected way.

These pictures stood to the left. To the right was a picture of his most successful horse, Hellinger's Dip, a sprinter with three wins to his credit; and next to this, a landscape photograph of Morne, which had been Catherine's childhood home and was now, largely by chance or so it felt, his own, though he could never bring himself to think of it in that way. The photograph dated back to the late sixties, a time when Lizzie, Catherine's mother, had herself been a young woman there, and Terry, a feckless boy of eight or nine, had passed the gates every day on his way to school or more likely to snare rabbits, and had known the place, inevitably, as 'the big house', though by Ascendancy standards it wasn't big at all, a long way short of a mansion, more a modest English vicarage. In keeping with his memories of that time this was a distant view, taken from a hill a half mile away, the house a compact oblong sheltering in its verdant demesne, a rolling upward-sloping landscape of gardens, fields and woodland, which from this high angle looked larger and more impressive than its thirty acres. He had found a print of this photograph in an attic and had it blown up, partly because it was a fine picture, but also because he was a nostalgic man and it showed in all its leafy glory a patch of ancient oak forest to the south-west of the house that had been cut for timber a few years afterwards and then abandoned to hazel and scrub.

The small snap next to this was taken many years later. It showed Catherine and Alice sitting on the terrace at Morne, with Duncan in riding clothes leaning rakishly against a wall, and Lizzie standing with a tea tray she had just picked up from the table. Catherine was just eighteen then. Typically, both she and her mother were laughing.

The tea had begun awkwardly, he remembered. It had soon become clear that the invitation had been Lizzie's alone, that

Duncan regarded it as a familiarity too far. For Duncan, Terry Devlin was still the ungrateful odd-job man who, at considerable inconvenience to the family, had stopped turning up with any regularity some four years before. Even in the days when Terry had managed to get back every month or so to do the light repairs, Duncan had failed to grasp the fact that he was busy running two pizza restaurants and fitting out three more and could no longer drop everything to fix a loose slate.

Fragments of that day had stayed with Terry. From old habit, and perhaps a sense of irony, he had walked round to the side of the house and presented himself at the back door. He had an image of Lizzie welcoming him into the kitchen with a small cry of delight, of the two of them exchanging news secretively before they could be interrupted.

The weather had been fine enough for them to sit on the terrace, which neatly avoided the awkwardness of choosing drawing room versus kitchen. He remembered Catherine appearing from the garden, a figure grown taller and fuller and astonishingly self-possessed. Humming some pop tune, she strode past him into the house with a sidelong glance, a lift of one eyebrow and a brief careless hello, the effect of which would have been splendidly sophisticated if she hadn't pulled a larky schoolgirl grimace at the last moment. Alice's arrival was a more muted affair involving a silent approach, a flop into the remotest chair, downcast eyes and a series of monosyllabic responses. When Catherine reappeared, it was to take centre stage, with the recital of a series of extravagant tales, unashamedly featuring herself and her escapades, told amid excessive laughter and much twisting of her head and arching of her neck and other postures intended to beguile. Some might have judged her rather too full of herself, and there was no doubting that she enjoyed an audience, but Terry put her exuberance down to an understandable excitement at being young and pretty and fancy-free, and the discovery that in a troubled and gloomy world vivacity set you apart.

When they had finally exhausted the subject of Catherine,

she fixed him with a challenging look. 'So, Mr Devlin,' – it had always been Terry before, and now she put a droll stress on the *Mr* – 'everyone says you're going very well, raking it in with all these restaurants. How nice to be rich!'

'Ah. It's the bank that's rich. I just keep them in profit.'

'You're *going* to be rich, then!'

He laughed. 'Well, I'm going to avoid being poor, that's for sure.'

'So, how will you spend it all? Cars? Houses? Planes?'

'I hadn't thought that far.'

She gave a cry of mock horror. 'Of course you have! Don't be so ridiculous! You've planned a Ferrari, a mansion in the country, a string of horses, enormous parties. Oh, please say you've got it all planned!'

Lizzie was eyeing her daughter tolerantly but also a little wearily.

Alice, staring fiercely into the garden, muttered in a tone of disgust, 'Oh, for God's sake.'

'I think I've got everything I want for the time being.'

'But that's hopeless!' Catherine groaned. 'I expected bigger and better things from you!'

Terry pretended to search his mind. 'I do have a new car on order.'

Catherine shot forward in her seat. 'A Porsche? No, no—' She flapped a delaying hand. 'A Merc convertible?'

'An Alfa. And not even the top model, I'm afraid.'

Alice murmured, 'He's already *got* an Alfa.'

'Have you? Have you?' Enjoying this flurry of her own making, not wanting it to end, Catherine wrinkled up her nose in disappointment. 'And you're getting *another*? Oh, how boring!'

It was then that Terry became aware of Duncan. For most of the meal Duncan had worn a distant inattentive expression, overlaid by the slightly glazed smile that was so characteristic of him. Now he was watching Terry with a glimmer of interest.

Later, while Lizzie and the girls were carrying the tea things into the house, Duncan launched into a monologue about European Community grants and interest rates and business conditions. 'Things are going pretty well already, of course, and are undoubtedly going to get better, but I've decided we'd be wise to tie up with an outfit in Britain, spread the risk, if you like.'

Failing to see the logic of this, Terry murmured non-committally, 'Aha.'

'People are getting far more confident about wine, you know. Bulk buying's going to be the big thing, no doubt about that, and we've got a real chance of cornering the market. This tie-in's going to let us negotiate the best possible terms.'

'What sort of volume are you handling, Duncan?'

'Oh . . . pretty large, pretty large.'

Terry found himself having doubts about this. In the same instant, he had a good idea of where the conversation was leading.

'You offer wine in your pizza places?' Duncan asked.

'Most certainly. We try to cover a reasonable price range. Not just plonk.'

'And who does your buying?'

He described their arrangement with a major wine importer.

'Well!' Duncan tapped the arm of his chair. 'We might be able to do something for you, you know. At least as good as they can, and probably a lot better. Why don't we talk? Never know, could be something in it for both of us.'

'Delighted.' As Terry handed him a card, he couldn't help wondering if his diplomatic skills were going to be up to the situation.

Duncan smiled magnanimously. 'Glad you're doing so well, Terry. Always nice to see a local chap getting on.' He stood up and surveyed the view. 'Well, must go and deal with the horses. Oh, yes!' He held up a forefinger, as if the matter had just come back to him. 'Terrible trouble finding anyone to repair the boiler. You wouldn't know of a good plumber by any chance? The chaps round here can't seem to handle it.'

When Terry phoned around he discovered that, in company with most other tradespeople in the area, the local plumbers were not prepared to call at Morne because of a long-standing problem with unpaid bills. In the end he sent one of his contract plumbers down from Dublin at his own expense.

It was a year later, when Lizzie had her first brush with cancer, that Duncan touched him for a personal loan.

So, he asked himself again, what is to be salvaged?

With a troubled heart, he drew out some paper, picked up his pen and began to draft a letter.

He began *Dear Cathy*, only to cross this out and replace it with *Dear Catherine*. Formality seemed more appropriate in the circumstances.

*I trust you will not feel I have overstepped the bounds of our acquaintance and what I hope, despite everything, to be our friendship, but I should tell you that I have phoned the hospital several times to ask how you were, and trust that you will not take this interest in your wellbeing amiss, but accept it as an expression of my continuing concern and affection . . .*

No, no! He'd started from entirely the wrong angle! No, this sounded terrible! Crass! He ran a line through the words and, crushing the page into a ball, threw it into the bin.

Taking another sheet, he stared at it for some time before starting again.

*Dear Catherine, I trust you continue to make progress. I hope you will not mind if I phone the nurses now and again to ask how you are (I have in fact called once or twice already). I realise that I may be overstepping the bounds of what you may regard as . . .*

With a sigh, he dropped the pen and slowly tore the page into small pieces. Never had he felt the cost of his misspent schooldays more keenly. Over the years he had taught himself to write business letters in a reasonably proficient manner, he could argue contracts and figures any day, but *this* – how to strike the right note, how to communicate one thing without letting slip another, to convey regret without guilt, concern without anger – it was beyond him.

Abandoning the letter, at least for today, he called Bridget and asked her to arrange for another posy to be made from the final flush of May flowers at Morne, put on ice and flown to London as soon as possible.

'Will there be a note?'

He hesitated. 'Not this time. Just a card, saying it's from Terry.'

'With best wishes?'

At first he said no, thinking that it sounded too impersonal, then changed his mind: detachment was more appropriate. 'Yes, best wishes.'

Before ringing off he asked for the messages. He noted there was nothing from London, no delay to the evening meeting.

On impulse, he said, 'Tell Pat seven thirty for the car, would you?'

He would be fifteen minutes late because he could not bear the idea of having to sit and wait for Ben Galitza for so much as a single second, certainly not in the hotel that was probably the most public place to meet in all Dublin, and certainly not in a hotel that wasn't one of his own and where he wouldn't be able to busy himself talking to the staff. The Shelbourne had been Galitza's choice, and while Terry was in favour of neutral ground, he would have preferred somewhere more discreet.

The call had come through to Bridget first thing that morning. Thoroughly startled, heart in mouth, he had taken it immediately – expecting what, for God's sake? News of Catherine? News of the police investigation? Fury? Accusations? Apologies? If the call hadn't taken him so completely by surprise he would have remembered that this was not Galitza's style at all, that Galitza had a breathtaking capacity for insensitivity. The voice had wrenched Terry back three years, to the joint venture on the west-coast hotel that had gathered so much speed so quickly that it seemed nothing could stop it. The voice was the same: cool, clipped, succinct. Catherine was 'recovering', Galitza had replied to Terry's enquiry, before going straight on to the matter in hand. He would like a meeting. As soon as possible. He would fly over. Terry had agreed immediately, which came as a surprise to neither of them. Whatever else, Galitza knew his man.

He hadn't said why he was coming of course; but then he hadn't needed to. Terry had never had the slightest doubt as to his purpose. The question was, how much would he have the nerve to ask for?

At ten to six Terry checked the battery and signal strength on his mobile and replaced it on the desk before him. Fergal was now almost an hour late with his report. In his general anxiety, he wondered if something had gone wrong, if Fergal had been caught or warned off. But he knew that this was to fall victim to paranoia, to overlook Fergal's experience and his infinite capacity for caution.

As if on cue a phone rang, but it wasn't the mobile, it was the house line. He answered it all the same.

'It's Dinah.' Her voice was smooth and warm as ever.

'Well now, how are you?' he asked, with as much affection as he could muster.

'Oh fine, but what about *you*?' This was her way, always to turn the subject round to him, to ask after his welfare.

'Not a great day, I have to say.'

'I'm sorry,' she said. 'And how's Maeve?'

'Oh, so-so.'

'And the food? Is she managing a bit more?'

'A little more, you know.'

'I got the phone number of that doctor everyone recommends so highly, the one in Howth. Would you like it? He's meant to be a marvel.'

'Perhaps . . . would you hang on to it? Maybe in a week or so.'

Dinah left it there. She never pushed her ideas, never tried to impose on him. In this, as in so many other ways, he could not fault her. Terry knew that if he had more sense he would persuade himself that he loved her, in so far as he understood what he meant by that nowadays; he would tell himself that she would be a good thing for him, that in her calm and accomplished way she would make him comfortable and content. Yet he retreated from the idea, some deep and stubborn part of him could not accept it, and this knowledge brought a weight of guilt. Sometimes when he stopped to think about it, it seemed to him that guilt had become the overriding emotion in his relationship with Dinah. He felt it now, corroding his thoughts.

She said, 'You'll be busy then, with Maeve.'

'Yes. I'm sorry. Perhaps next week.'

'Of course.' Her tone, as always, was light and without reproach. 'Now tell me, do you like the curtains? You must say if you don't, because if you don't I can alter them, change the trimmings or whatever.'

His mind was a blank. 'The curtains?'

She laughed softly. 'You obviously haven't been into the drawing room.'

'Give me a moment.' He picked up the portable extension and, almost tripping over Conn who dashed past him to the door, took it across the hall to the room that she called the drawing room but which he'd always been happy to call the lounge. He stared in astonishment at the mass of drapery bunched around the bay window and adjacent french windows. The curtains were huge and richly shaded in deep red and cream, with ornate curved pelmets and long tassels and great loops of fabric caught back from the windows.

'My goodness.'

'Do you like them?'

He had no idea what he liked or might be persuaded to like; no idea what was appropriate for a house such as this. In truth, he'd been quite happy with the way the room had looked before. It was only when Mrs Ellis pointed out the need for some new chair covers and a lick of paint, that he'd realised it'd been nine years since anything had been done, since two years before his wife's death. Friends had recommended Dinah for the work, and the next moment, or so it seemed, he'd found himself dining with her and signing up for a total refurbishment.

'Well, have a think about it,' she said.

'I'm sure they're fine,' he declared, though even as he said this he knew the decor was too rich and heavy for his taste and that if he had any courage at all he should tell her. Following on from this came the knowledge that he owed her other far more important truths, and that here too he was a terrible coward. He should tell her what a poor prospect he was for her, how through no fault of her own he was not husband material, but the time never seemed right, in these troubled times least of all.

'You sound rather down,' she said.

'I am a little.'

'You don't want me to come over for half an hour?'

This offer was made in a spirit of generosity, he knew, but he refused it none the less.

'Terry,' she said with uncharacteristic hesitation, 'I hate to mention it when you've so much on your mind, but the holiday, it's getting late to book. Are we still on?'

He had forgotten, or had chosen to forget, that in three weeks they were meant to be going to Royal Ascot for a couple of days, then on to the South of France for a short break. 'Oh heavens, Dinah, I don't know . . .' She made no sound, but he knew she would have been planning for it, would have bought a hat, an outfit. Steeling himself to take the sensible option, he said, 'Look, perhaps it would be safer to count me out for the summer, until things get clearer.'

She said evenly, 'Of course.' Then: 'We could always keep it to Ascot, couldn't we? Just a couple of days.'

'Best not. Too chancy—' He heard a distant ringing and realised it was his mobile, back in the study. 'Speak later!' Cutting Dinah off without chance of reply, he hurried to answer the call before the message service picked up.

'Sorry I was a bit delayed,' said Fergal in his unhurried tones.

'Nothing wrong?' asked Terry, clambering breathlessly into his chair.

'No. Fine.'

'So?'

'So – she's regained consciousness.'

It was on the tip of Terry's tongue to admit that he already knew this, but he checked himself. He didn't want to confess to having made the call.

'And she's lucid,' Fergal continued, 'which is a good indication for brain damage, by which, of course, I mean *lack* of brain damage—'

'She's talking?'

'And seeing. There's a question mark over the hearing – may be damage to one ear. But the other's fine.'

Terry shuddered with relief and anguish.

Fergal went on in his soft educated voice, 'They operated yesterday afternoon, as planned, and they're pleased with the way it went. They've also done a further round of X-rays and CT scans, so they've got as clear a picture as they're going to get for the moment—'

'What *is* the picture?'

A moment while Fergal phrased his answer. 'It's as they first thought – the spinal cord is damaged.'

'For certain?'

'For certain.'

'The operation – they couldn't fix it?'

'Spinal cord damage can't be fixed, Terry.'

Fergal never referred to him as Terry – never called him by any name at all in fact – and the unexpectedness of this only served to drive home the dread finality of his words. Terry heard an escape of breath and realised it was his own. 'Oh dear Lord,' he murmured.

'But they can't say what the effects will be, not yet—'

'Can't say or won't say?'

'Can't say. It's a bit complicated, but I can take a shot at explaining it if you like. After I got the information I went and checked it out with a doctor friend of mine. I think I've got it straight.'

Terry made an effort to clear his mind. 'Okay – go ahead.'

There was the leafing of paper as Fergal looked at his notes. 'The spine is damaged in two places, in the neck and in the thoracic region. The injury in the neck, at what they call C5/6, is a simple fracture of the vertebra – a hairline crack to you or me. It isn't likely to be a problem. The bone should mend itself over time and the scans suggest the spinal cord is undamaged. Just *suggest*, mind you, because here's where the uncertainty comes in – they won't know for sure about any effects until the body gets over the trauma and the swelling goes down and any natural healing has taken place. Then—'

'Healing? I thought you said . . .'

'I didn't say there wasn't any healing,' Fergal replied in his patient way. 'Just that damage to the spinal cord itself can't be mended.'

Terry hadn't entirely followed, but let it pass.

'Now the second injury is at the point known as T9. Here the vertebra suffered a comminuted transverse fracture. This means the bone was shattered and the spine was partially dislocated – I'm not sure that's the right word – put out of alignment, if you like. The operation fused the spine with screws and metal plates, so no further injury can occur. It's here that the scans show damage to the spinal cord, but again the doctors can't tell what the effects will be until the swelling goes down and the body has had a chance to recover generally. And that takes months, sometimes many months. There are different types of damage to the spinal cord, like to the front of it, the back of it, the side of it, and different degrees of damage, partial, complete, etcetera, and only time will tell what's what. Oh, they'll be transferring her to a spinal unit as soon as it's safe to move her, by the way. No date yet, but in two weeks, something like that.'

'But the outcome? What are they saying? What do they think?'

'That's what I mean – it's too early to say yet, they have no way of knowing.'

'Come on,' Terry protested. 'They must have their views. I mean, privately.'

'Privately?' echoed Fergal with soft irony, as if the information he'd already obtained hadn't been exclusive enough. 'The only opinion I got was sort of third-hand,' he said reluctantly, 'a junior source, if you follow me. Not to be taken as totally reliable.'

'Yes, yes – and?'

'There'll be some degree of paralysis.'

'She won't walk again?'

'They can't know, Terry – that's what I'm trying to say.'

'But it's probable?'

Fergal didn't answer and Terry took his silence to be an answer in itself.

After a moment, Fergal said, 'I'm still working on the police side of things. That might take a bit longer. Starting from scratch there, if you understand me.'

'Of course.' Terry added, 'You've done fine. Thank you. And Fergal? I want to extend the brief. Can we have a look at Ben Galitza?'

'When you say a look, are we talking surveillance or general intelligence?'

'General intelligence. For the moment anyway.'

Terry had only the vaguest idea of how Fergal obtained his information, and took care not to get any the wiser. Fergal had come from Cintel, a corporate intelligence agency Terry used from time to time. One day he had simply presented himself to Terry and asked to work for him on 'a one to one' basis because, as Fergal had put it, he wasn't really a corporate man, thereby implying that he didn't regard Terry as much of a one either. By degrees Terry had gathered that in Fergal's more misty past, before a flirtation with the priesthood, a short-lived marriage and what might have been a breakdown, he had been a lecturer in French at Trinity College, Dublin.

By any standards he had done an outstanding job this time round, and Terry said again, 'Thank you.'

'Have you had any more thoughts about the best way to play it with the police?' Fergal asked.

'I've thought.'

'You want to leave things as they are?'

'I do.'

Fergal made no comment on this, but the very fact that he'd asked was enough to send a small wedge of doubt into Terry's mind, and as soon as he'd put the phone down he sat staring out into the garden, raking over the pros and cons until he had satisfied himself once more that he had made the right decision.

Hearing a movement upstairs, he roused himself to go and see Maeve. He wondered how it would be with her this evening: whether her day would have been good or bad, whether she would eat more than a token mouthful for supper. Most of all, he wondered how he would present the day's news to her without giving himself away. He poured himself two fingers of Jameson's and, downing them in one, poured another smaller measure and polished that off as well. As he started up the stairs he made a conscious effort to relax his features so that when Maeve looked into his face she shouldn't read too many of his troubles there.

He met her coming out of her room, and went to embrace her.

'How's my darling girl?'

She came into his arms and said, 'Better today, thanks, Dadda.'

'There's my girl.'

'The iron seems to be doing some good.'

'Your mother had the anaemia too. Runs in the family.' He shook his head. 'They should have spotted it before.'

He held her at arm's length. She did look a little better. He thought he could see a touch more colour in her cheeks, though the flesh itself was still drawn against the bones, her upper arms were still little more than matchsticks under his hands. For once he tried not to dwell on the doctors' incompetence, on the terrible hours when he thought he had lost her, and keep his anger focused on more worthy targets.

'Shall we go to Morne at the weekend then?' he said in a cheerful tone. 'Get some air into our lungs, take a walk or two in the garden. What do you say, my darling?'

Her face wore the exhausted look that had become so achingly familiar to him over the last four months. Sometimes he wondered if he would ever see her eyes bright again.

'If you like,' she said.

'Oh, I think a little walking would do us both good, wouldn't it? Your father most of all!' He tapped the bulge of his belly, which was something of a joke between them. 'What does the nurse say?'

She dropped her head abruptly, and his heart sank when he realised that in his thoughtless way he had said the wrong thing. 'Not too late to go back to college,' he said coaxingly. 'They're keeping your place—'

'I won't go back, Dadda. I won't.'

'But you were made to be a nurse, darling girl. You'd be the best nurse in the world.'

'No.'

'Is it England that's the problem? We could always find you a college in Dublin, so you could live at home—'

She raised her head and her eyes were brimming. 'No.'

He managed a smile. 'If that's what you want.'

He linked her arm through his and, covering her hand where it lay on his arm, walked her downstairs.

'Is there news?' she asked.

'News?'

'Of *Catherine*.'

'Indeed! I was going to tell you the minute we got downstairs. She's regained consciousness. I just heard a moment ago—'

With a gasp Maeve stopped and turned to him, and for a moment her face came alive. 'She's going to be all right then?'

'Well, she's talking and hearing and seeing, so it's all looking good from that point of view.'

'What else?' she demanded hungrily.

'Well . . . she's off the danger list.'

'But what are they saying?'

'It's early days yet. You know – very early days. They need to wait and see.'

Instantly her mood plunged. 'What do you mean, they need to wait and see? There's something wrong, isn't there? Tell me.'

'Darling girl, they're investigating. You know better than anyone that sometimes they don't always find the problem straight away.'

'So there *is* something wrong! What is it? Tell me!'

She was taking great gulps of air and he hastened to calm her. 'Remember, darling, the fall was a terrible thing. Her body needs time to mend. Quite a while. There'll be rehabilitation, physiotherapy – all the usual things.'

Maeve shook her head and murmured, 'No, no . . .'

He persuaded her to continue down the stairs. She moved jerkily.

'I must go and see her,' she said.

'When you're better, darling girl. When you're better.'

'I can't bear it. I can't bear it. She was so kind to me, Dadda. So kind.'

Flashes of memory came to him from the long summer at Morne four years ago: a glimpse of Catherine taking Maeve off to show her something, a dress or it might have been shoes; then a picnic in the walled garden, Catherine and Maeve sitting on the grass talking companionably as though they were of an age, not eight years apart. Inevitably more painful and personal memories followed, of the weeks of his folly and the mortifying letter, but he shut these firmly from his mind.

He walked Maeve into the small sitting room, to her favourite chair facing the TV. She pressed herself into a corner of the chair and drew her legs up under her. 'She was so very good to me. So good, Dadda.'

Terry heard the crack in her voice and thought: Dear Lord, please don't let there be tears tonight.

'If they're talking of rehab and physio, there must be something seriously wrong,' Maeve cried. 'I know it. I know it!'

'Hand on heart, darling, they really don't know.'

'But she fell! She fell!'

'We have to wait and see. That's all we can do.'

'I can't bear it, Dadda.'

'You can't take all the worries of the world on your shoulders, darling girl. You must think of yourself. That's your first duty.'

But there was no soothing her during these periodic plunges into despondency and Terry wondered if he should cancel his meeting with Galitza. He asked, 'You have been taking all your pills, darling, haven't you?'

But she had turned her face away from him, her head was pressed into the back of the chair, and he knew he must attempt to cajole her out of this mood or lose her to anxiety for the rest of the evening. Sometimes he wondered if he shouldn't try to shake her out of it, literally take her by the shoulders, if it wouldn't be a kindness, but he couldn't bring himself to do such a thing, not when she had been so dreadfully ill, not when he could still remember in every terrible detail the night in the hospital when she had almost slipped away. Instead, he perched on the side of the chair and, threading an arm clumsily round her shoulders, rocked her gently, whispering softly, 'There, there, my darling girl. It'll all be fine, you wait and see.'

She murmured, 'I'm so sorry, Dadda, I'm such a nuisance to you.'

'A nuisance? That you could never be. Never!' Saying this, he remembered with a surge of emotion the only time he had felt truly frustrated by Maeve's dependence, the only time she had actually prevented him from doing anything he dearly wanted to do, and that was four days ago when he had longed with every instinct in his body to go to London and find out what had happened to Catherine and, while he was about it, to take Ben Galitza apart with his bare hands.

She was quieter now and he dared to hope that the worst might be over. He talked about the summer ahead, about the things they would do together, how he was going to take time off, a month or more, and spend it with her at Morne, how she was to invite friends, as many or as few as she wanted. When he finally ran short of words, he hummed softly to her, a poor rendering of 'Some Enchanted Evening'.

The thin summer light began to deepen imperceptibly, bringing the brilliant yellows and blues and golds that dominated the room into glaring focus. In keeping with his schizophrenic existence one inconsequential corner of Terry's mind was deciding that he really must ask Dinah to tone the colours down a bit, while another colder and more determined part was rehearsing the conversation he would have with Ben Galitza, speculating not only on how much money Ben would dare to ask for, but how much Terry would agree to give him and the heavy price that he would force him to pay.

At seven thirty he said quietly to Maeve, 'Now I have to go out for a while, just an hour or so. But you'll have to promise me you'll eat something while I'm gone. Will you? Otherwise I'll worry about you the whole time I'm away.'

She turned her face to him and fixing him with a beseeching gaze asked, 'You'll make sure Catherine's all right, won't you, Dadda?'

'Why, yes . . .' He hardly knew what to say. 'Of course I will.'

The light in her eyes faded as quickly as it had come.

Terry bent down to embrace her and felt the chill breath of uncertainty and doubt on his cheek.

Before leaving he turned the television on for her and commanded Conn to stay beside her chair. When he paused at the door to say goodbye Maeve was already staring dully at the screen.

# Chapter Three

———————

'IF YOU wouldn't mind.' Simon indicated the unlit cigarette poised between Emma Russell's fingers.

'Oh.' She looked around her with a show of exaggerated puzzlement as if a car was a perfectly natural receptacle for cigarette fumes. Then, in a tone of sudden understanding: 'Oh, it's *new*, is it?'

'No, I just don't want it smelling of cigarettes.'

She made a face and, closing her lighter with a snap, dropped the cigarette back into the packet. 'You must work *incredibly* hard to keep it this way.'

'I'm sorry?' They were crawling through the unlovely end of Earl's Court in a slow line of early-morning traffic that promised to last all the way to Notting Hill. The rain had stopped in the night but the sky was still heavy, and a dankness hung in the air. 'I'm sorry?' he said again.

'Do you ban feet?'

He glanced across at her, not quite sure of the spirit in which this remark was intended. 'I get it valeted every week.'

Her mouth twitched in a small knowing smile, as if he had just confirmed an accurate and rather unflattering picture of himself.

Irritated by this, and by the fact that he'd put himself to considerable inconvenience by offering to pick her up and drive her to the police station on what was going to be an extremely busy morning, he said, 'I get a man to look after it for me, if you really want to know. I have to. I simply don't have the time for that sort of thing. I run three companies. Three very demanding companies.'

'Aha.' She was in the midst of an enormous yawn.

'And while we're on the subject of getting things straight,' he said in the slow steady voice he used to explain things to people who weren't too quick on the uptake, 'I don't work *for* Ben – the two of us are *partners* in a company that trades with Eastern Europe. We set up the company together. As *partners*.'

'Oh . . . right.'

He wanted to add crossly: And moreover there is no ballerina gear in my flat, there is nothing faintly outrageous in my closet, only the costume my mother once wore when she danced with the Rambert, which Ben just happened to see hanging in the spare room when he invited himself to stay three years ago, when, having been kicked out by his then girlfriend at two in the morning, he was partaking of my hospitality, the shit.

He wanted to say all this and more, but he'd learnt from bitter experience that it would do him no good. If you tried to explain something like that, something that had grown into a huge joke, people weren't interested in the truth, they only wanted to roar with laughter and say how brilliant it was to be a cross-dresser, particularly such a cultured one – ah, the quips came thick and fast when people were having fun – and that he wasn't to be ashamed, not for a moment, not when it was so fantastically amusing to picture him in pink tulle. These people were shits as well, just like Ben. The secret was not to let it rankle, not to give anything away, but to rise effortlessly above it.

He did this now, saying smoothly, 'I know DS Wilson will appreciate this very much.'

'I still don't see why it can't wait,' Emma said peevishly, stifling another enormous yawn. 'I'm desperately jetlagged. My body's screaming: Three in the morning!'

Simon felt no remorse for having dragged her out. It served

her right. She had started grousing as soon as he'd called and told her the police wanted to see her, had griped about having only just got to sleep a few hours before, had demanded to know why *they* couldn't come to *her* later in the day, for Christ's sake. Simon had bitten back the impulse to say that nobody was getting much sleep at the moment – certainly not him: four hours last night? five? – and that when it came to Catherine surely nothing could be too much trouble. Instead he had explained very firmly that everything of the remotest importance to the investigation had to be followed up immediately, that DS Wilson couldn't get away from the police station to see her, and – in an effort to humour her – that her information could be immensely valuable. Emma had finally agreed, though not without a series of resentful sighs that had caused him to grit his teeth. Devoted to Catherine? She had no idea what devotion meant.

Emma's litany of complaint was bringing an unattractive shrillness to her voice. 'Well, I hope they're not expecting a statement,' she said. 'I'm not going to hang around all day.'

'They just want to hear what you have to say.'

'But that's the point – I haven't *got* anything to say, have I? Not really. Why can't they talk to Ben, for heaven's sake? He'd be able to tell them much better than me.'

'I'm sure he will, once he gets back.'

She shot him a curious look. 'Yes, why *is* he away? There's nothing wrong, is there?'

'Like I said, he had to rush off.'

She shook her head and murmured admiringly, 'Ben!'

This reaction had a dreary familiarity for Simon, who had yet to meet a woman who wasn't prepared to forgive Ben behaviour that would be judged totally unacceptable in anyone else.

They stopped at some lights.

'Why didn't she get the calls traced?' Simon asked.

'Mmm?' Emma had leant her head back against the seat and closed her eyes.

'Why didn't Catherine dial 1471? Or get an intercept put on the line.'

'Didn't take it that seriously,' Emma murmured groggily.

'She told *you*, though. She mentioned it to you.'

After a while she muttered, 'I don't think you can get an intercept on a mobile, can you?'

They were moving off again and Simon was forced to look at the road. 'The calls came on her mobile?'

'Mmm.'

'You didn't say that.'

Reopening her eyes, Emma peered blearily ahead. 'I definitely said it was her mobile.'

Letting this pass, he asked, 'How long ago did it all start?'

Emma pressed her forefingers into the corners of her eyes, the scarlet talons like tears of blood. 'November?'

'And they've been going on all this time?'

'Haven't a clue. You see? I'm really *not* the person to ask.'

'And Catherine had no idea who this guy was?'

Emma's golden hair swung around as she slowly shook her head.

'Someone who had her number at any rate.'

'Oh, that could have been anyone, couldn't it? You know how it is in her line of work.'

He didn't know, and said so.

'Well, all her *clients* would have had her number for a start, wouldn't they? *And* all her would-be clients. *And* her suppliers. *And* all the little men who lay paving stones and build arbours and plant trees, who might have got the hots for Cath over the nasturtiums, or whatever it is that turns garden people on. And then there's the TV. Once you're on TV – well, you're inviting weirdos, aren't you?'

Remembering the three or four rather serious-minded programmes on garden design that Catherine had made for a minority network, Simon failed to see how this followed. 'Weirdos?'

'Sad people. Men in anoraks. People who get fixed on

someone they see on TV. That's how I got on to the idea of a stalker. Though come to think about it, far more likely to be a wanker, isn't it? An anorak who wants a quick thrill with a soggy newspaper cutting.'

Simon winced. He could never get used to the way some women talked, the coarseness of their thinking, the ugliness of their language. 'But her number – how would he have got hold of it?'

'Oh' – she spun a hand through the air – 'a thousand ways.'

'Like?'

'Oh *God*—' She couldn't believe she was having to explain something so obvious. 'Well, he could phone the TV producers saying he wanted Cath to design this massive park for his stately home and could he have her number please, *or* he might phone the owners of one of the gardens in the programmes and say he was longing for a divine little knot garden just like theirs and what was the number of that clever little designer person, *or*—'

'I think I've got the picture,' Simon interrupted caustically, not taking kindly to being talked down to in this fashion. Staring glassily ahead, he maintained a firm silence and when he next glanced across it was to see Emma fast asleep with her head wedged against the window.

She groaned when he woke her. 'Shit. I hope this doesn't take long.'

The lobby of Notting Hill police station was built to withstand the assaults of an ungrateful public. The duty officer sat behind reinforced glass, and when Wilson appeared it was through a heavy steel pass door that swung shut behind him with a deep thud.

The sergeant was a lean wiry man of about forty with a straight back, a rapid handshake and an intense manner that suggested honesty, energy and dedication. His mouth shaped itself into a brief professional smile. 'Good of you to drop by, Miss Russell.'

'I wouldn't have called it *dropping by* exactly.'

Wilson looked mildly enquiring. 'Weren't you on your way to the hospital?'

She frowned at him. 'I wasn't on my way anywhere.'

'Good of you to come in specially, then.'

As the implications of Wilson's remark sank in, Emma threw Simon a suspicious glance.

Studiously ignoring this, Simon told Wilson he would go and wait outside in the car. 'Though I'd be glad of a brief word afterwards, if I may.'

'Sit in, if you like,' Wilson said. 'I'll find us some coffee.'

Simon said appreciatively, 'If that's all right. Thank you.'

'Dropping by!' hissed Emma sarcastically as they followed Wilson to an interview room.

Seated in front of Wilson with a coffee and a cigarette, Emma went through one of those transformations that left Simon wondering not for the first time at women's disconcerting ability to change moods at the drop of a hat. The petulant child vanished, replaced by a sympathetic and amenable woman, Catherine's dearest friend who was anxious to help in any way she could.

The story was much the same as before until Emma said, 'Sometimes he called twice a day.'

'Were these regular times?' Wilson asked.

'Oh, I don't know about that. Except . . . I think Cath said usually in the day. Yes,' she declared with greater certainty, 'the day.'

'What about weekends?'

She scooped her hair back from her forehead and tapped the ash thoughtfully off her cigarette. 'She didn't say.'

Wilson was about to ask another question when Emma interrupted with a wave of her hand, a slow dipping of splayed fingers that accelerated into a flutter as she summoned up a half-buried memory. 'Yes – there was something else that stuck in my mind – something I couldn't work out at the time. Not sure I can now, really, but anyway – she said it was someone really *sad*. No . . .' She went trawling through her memory again. 'It wasn't so much sad . . . I think she said it was a very unhappy person. Yes, a very *unhappy* person. Now in one way I thought, yeah well, it would be an unhappy person, wouldn't it? But then I got this feeling she was talking about someone in particular, that she knew for sure that this person was unhappy, if you see what I mean.'

Wilson gazed unblinkingly at Emma. 'Knew for sure? But you say Catherine didn't know who this person was?'

'That's right. I mean – not a name.'

There was a pause in which Wilson seemed to be waiting for Emma to go on. 'You're suggesting', he said eventually, 'that though she had no name for this person, she knew something about him? Something to make her think he was unhappy?'

'Yes, that's what I'm saying. Yes.'

'The caller only ever spoke once, is that right?'

'That's what she told me, yes.'

'So it was from this one conversation?'

Emma raised a shoulder and turned her mouth down in a Gallic shrug. 'I suppose so.'

'Catherine didn't tell you what he said?'

'No.'

Wilson went through the motions of asking more questions but it was obvious he wasn't expecting to learn much else and, winding things up briskly, he thanked Emma for her time.

When they reached the front hall Simon managed to catch Wilson's eye and gesture him to one side. As soon as Emma had gone ahead, Simon said, 'I was just wondering if you had any news that I could pass on to the family.'

'Nothing as yet, I'm afraid.'

'No leads?'

'Not really.'

Simon wondered if Wilson's air of efficiency was a cover for ineptitude. He was, after all, still a sergeant. 'Nothing from the labs?' Hearing himself say this Simon thought not without a certain pride that he was beginning to sound like a criminal lawyer.

'Nothing concrete,' Wilson replied carefully. 'However, there is one thing we are particularly keen to establish, and that is the identity of the man who called the ambulance.'

This was the man Simon had come to call The Good Samaritan. 'A neighbour?'

'Seems not. We've checked them all.'

'Not Ben Galitza?' Simon knew that it wasn't Ben, but he needed to play the part of the dispassionate professional.

Wilson shook his head. 'Barely conscious when the ambulance arrived. No, we're thinking along the lines of a passer-by. Saw the open door. Looked in. Spotted Catherine lying there.'

Simon had a vision of darkness and blood and silence, of a man rushing into the house and dropping onto his knees beside Catherine, staring down at her in horror, taking off his jacket and laying it over her. 'You think he might be able to help, this man?'

'Might have spotted a person leaving the scene. Could have been the very thing that made him go into the house – seeing someone running out in suspicious circumstances, leaving the door wide open.'

Simon nodded sagely. 'The call was taped, presumably?'

'Indeed.'

*Well, tell me, you bastard. Don't force me to ask.* 'Any clues there?' he enquired solemnly.

Wilson shrugged. 'Some.' For a moment it looked as though he wasn't going to elaborate, and Simon had to stifle the cry of frustration that sprang into his throat. Then Wilson was saying ruminatively, 'An educated voice – decidedly. Calm sort of type. Very businesslike. Very factual. And informed on medical matters, in the sense of having done a first-aid course, I would say. Something of that nature.'

*Educated, calm, businesslike.* This image flew around

Simon's mind, seeking shape and substance. 'The ambulance crew saw this person, presumably?'

Wilson gave a sigh. 'Indeed they did, but according to them he disappeared so smartish that they can't give a description. For which read: they didn't take a real look at him, didn't ask his name, didn't see him go.'

Wilson moved purposefully towards the main doors and Simon was forced to follow.

'No description at all, then?'

'Nothing worth having. The three of them might as well have clocked three different people.'

Wilson led the way out into the street.

Simon said, 'If this man had seen someone running away, surely he'd have reported it by now.'

'You'd think. But people don't always realise the import- ance of what they've witnessed. Believe me.'

Simon made a gesture, as if to defer to Wilson's superior knowledge. 'You'll keep me in touch? You've got my number?'

'Yes, indeed.' Wilson turned as if to hurry away, only to think better of it and strike an awkward pose of informality, hands thrust into his pockets, face lifted to the sky. 'Ah, sun.'

A few yards away, Emma was leaning against the wing of Simon's car. Seeing her heavy shoulder bag lying on the bonnet, bristling with studs and buckles, Simon tried not to think of the scratches it would make when she dragged it off.

Wilson appeared to make up his mind about something. 'Look, there is one other thing,' he said in a low confidential tone, 'but I will ask you not to mention it to the family at the present time. No point in upsetting them, if you understand me.'

Simon felt a surge of tension. 'Of course.'

Wilson thrust out his chin. 'There would appear to be a somewhat' – he searched for the word – '*bizarre* factor in all this.'

Simon thought: Dear God, what's coming now? Will I be

able to stand it? Outwardly he didn't move, didn't alter his expression of grave concern.

'I can't give you details, of course. But suffice it to say that we found some articles that give us reason to believe that the assault had overtones of – how shall I say? – a sexual or psychotic nature.'

Simon felt a rush of heat, his heart seemed to lift in his chest.

'No reason why your average burglar shouldn't be a bit of a psychopath, of course. On the side, so to speak. Or a fantasist, or any of these things they get off of the videos nowadays. But there we are, we have to take it into account.' Simon must have looked as startled as he felt because Wilson added, 'See what I mean – best not to mention it to the family.'

'When you say, *articles* . . .?'

'Well, I can't give details. You understand.'

*But I don't understand*, Simon wanted to argue. 'Of course,' he said. 'I'm just – shocked.'

Wilson was on the point of leaving. Desperate to detain him, Simon almost reached out to grab his arm. 'You're not saying she was sexually assaulted?'

'No – no evidence of that. It's just that this man appears to have been a bit – well, *sick*.'

*Sick?* He couldn't begin to think what he meant by this. His imagination roared off in a dozen different directions, all of them wild and disturbing and hopelessly mixed up. *Found some articles? Sick?* Feeling his cheek jump uncontrollably, he turned it away. 'So you'll be looking for someone with a . . . record of this sort of thing?'

'Let's just say we'll be keeping an open mind as to whether this person broke in with burglary or assault in mind.'

Simon almost laughed. 'So these calls . . .?'

'Oh, yes. Could be very significant.'

'I see.' With that, Simon was finally lost for words.

He had intended to drive straight to the hospital and leave Emma to pick up a cab there, but he was so agitated, his mind so numb, that he found himself driving her all the way back to her flat in Chelsea. At one point she asked what Wilson had told him during their huddled conversation. He fumbled for an answer, muttered something that made little sense and was unable to finish.

'You *are* in a state,' she remarked. 'What is it, for God's sake?'

He said with a break in his voice, 'They think he might have meant to harm her. Might have intended to, right from the outset.'

Emma absorbed this with a heavy sigh and a shake of her head. After a while he became aware of her watching him. She said, 'You think a lot of Cath, don't you?'

He couldn't answer, except to give an anguished nod.


'Ah, Mr Jardine. You've got me into a lot of trouble.' Sister Jones spoke in the weary tones of someone who is far too tired to get angry.

Simon looked suitably mystified, though having an idea of what was coming he felt the first stirrings of injured pride.

'The family say you're not representing them at all. They say we shouldn't have let you in to see Catherine. They say you aren't to be allowed to see her again.'

This pronouncement bore the stamp of Alice's vituperative little mind, but Simon was wounded all the same because Duncan obviously hadn't stood up for him. Even allowing for Duncan's erratic grasp on loyalty, he counted this an outright betrayal.

'They're under a lot of stress,' he said in a forgiving tone. 'I think everything will get sorted out as soon as Catherine's husband gets back.'

'But he *is* back.'

'Here?'

'Here.'

Startled, Simon looked at his watch. 'When did he arrive?'

'Oh . . . ten minutes ago?'

Simon covered his surprise with a brisk nod. Trying not to think of the work piling up at the office, he stationed himself by a window overlooking the atrium, which also offered a view of the passage leading to Catherine's room, and settled down to wait. He tried to work out where Ben could have got to last night that enabled him to fly back to London, get through the airport and into town by ten fifteen in the morning. Not Warsaw – Simon knew the timetable off by heart. Zurich? Paris? Guernsey? Not far away, that was for sure. But it must have been one hell of a panic to send him rushing all over town for three days and then off on a plane, one hell of a panic to make him leave Catherine's bedside. But listen, he wanted to say to Ben's face, what's so serious that you can't tell me about it? What's so momentous, so overwhelming that it doesn't involve me or the business in some way? Times are hard, Ben, remember? We've had a bad year, we lost the Polska CMC deal, we're seriously broke, if we're going to be in a panic about anything it should bloody well be the business. Listen, Ben – at this point he would look him dead in the eye – if you can't trust me who the hell can you trust, for God's sake? It's me, I'm your partner, remember?

There were seven messages waiting for Simon on his mobile; with the fifteen calls already listed on the white card in his breast pocket and the three meetings scheduled for the afternoon it was going to be a nightmare of a day. He needed no reminding that, yet again, he was shouldering most of the load. When it came to Duncan's wine company, this wasn't a problem. Since Simon had knocked it into shape and installed a half-decent manager it more or less ran itself. RNP was a different matter, however. RNP was a hands-on company that relied on vast amounts of time, effort and nurturing. How often had he said to Ben, *We're in the nurturing business*? Nurturing contacts, nurturing deals, nurturing the possibility of deals. In an average year, if he and Ben gave it their best shot and had a bit of luck, they managed to pull off four or five medium-sized deals. The simplest were straight sales, a shipment of grey-market Levi's from Detroit to Hungary, a cancelled order for amber from Poland to Singapore. But more often they were three-way deals, cash at both ends and a trade in the middle: a consignment of Laotian teak marooned by bankruptcy in Singapore that they traded to the Poles for a warehouse of glass, which they sold on, strictly cash on delivery, to a discount warehouse in Chicago.

They had decided right at the beginning that they weren't going to get involved in any deal so big that the whole business had to ride on it. Far too risky; they wouldn't let themselves fall into that old trap. For the first three years it hadn't been hard to stick to this policy for the simple reason that nothing very large had come their way.

Then they had got wind of the Polska CMC deal.

Simon thought briefly: I had a life before the Polska CMC deal, a life that was my own, running smoothly, going my way. The remembrance of what he had lost brought a shiver of bitterness.

Like all the best mistakes, they had been lured in effortlessly, by degrees. It had begun like any one of a dozen deals. There was a tip-off, a contact, they talked their way past the middlemen to the man in possession of the goods at Polska CMC, they got a feel for the price. A cancelled order for generators, twenty 2000-kilowatt machines originally destined for German hospitals. Dollar signs flashed huge and bright. Suspiciously huge, of course. But Ben wouldn't listen. He wanted to give it a go. *What's the harm*, he said, *we can only lose the deal.* So they had waltzed off to Warsaw with their double act, Ben the talker, the front-man, the Polish-speaking ideas man with the anglicised Polish name and the charming manner, Simon the detail man, specialist in small print and bank transfers.

Slowly but surely they had got sucked in. Slowly but surely they had neglected their other business until the other deals had melted away. Negotiations had spun out, months and months of suffocating red tape and back-slapping dinners and rousing toasts and appalling women with dubious hygiene and slobbering lips looming up in seedy Warsaw nightclubs; months and months of getting a feel for the way the wind was really blowing under the vodka-fired camaraderie, months of fine-tuning the terms and renegotiating the 'special payments'. All this while tying up the other end of the deal with the South American broker who'd found buyers across the continent and probably off it too. Getting the money in the right place at the right time was always an art form, but with this deal it was like writing a score for a hundred-piece orchestra, the web of transfers between Warsaw and Switzerland and the Caymans, banks and front companies in Panama and El Salvador and Monaco, the timing of it all, the bonds, the guarantees.

Three months ago it had been in the bag, signed, sealed, first bank transfers due any day. But as Simon should have known – did know deep down, but chose to ignore – it was precisely when something was almost in the bag that it leapt out and savaged you.

Now, as he attempted to revive the business, Simon wasn't sure whether it was his imagination or he was just suffering a general loss of heart but new deals seemed much harder to find.

He was finishing a call to Bahrain when he saw Ben emerge from Catherine's room and walk briskly down the passage towards him. He noticed Ben was wearing business clothes, a dark blue Armani suit he'd acquired a couple of months ago in Milan to add to the twenty or more suits already in his wardrobe, and a dark open-necked shirt. As he got closer Simon noticed he was unshaven and that his shirt was not as crisp as it might have been, which suggested that, against all habit and instinct, Ben had gone travelling without a change of clothes.

'Oh hi, what are you doing here?' Ben demanded vaguely, swivelling to a halt.

'I came to find out how Catherine was.'

'Oh, she's all right,' he said carelessly. 'So what's the latest?'

Simon shuddered with disbelief, he almost cried out, *How*

*can you say she's all right? How can you stand there as if nothing's happened?* Then he remembered that they were all in shock, and that Ben simply had an unusual way of showing it.

Mechanically, Simon began to summarise events at RNP while Ben stared past him into the atrium, listening with the inattentive, faintly bored expression that Simon knew so well. His face was mending quickly, Simon noticed. The bruising around the left eye was still a rather bright shade of blue-black but the swelling had gone down, and beneath its strip of transparent plaster the gash on his left cheek, sealed by the minuscule stitches, seemed to be healing neatly. In no time he would be back to normal: unmarked, unblemished, the handsome man with the winning ways. Simon found himself thinking, *All bloody wrong*, and just as quickly pushed this thought from his mind, because if you allowed yourself to get consumed by the injustices of life you could go mad.

'So Bahrain could be a goer?'

As they talked Simon tried to gauge Ben's mood. With Ben this was never easy, since it was necessary to separate the person he chose to show to the world, a Ben who might be engaging, flamboyant, boyish, provocative, lost – he kept the most mawkish of these fronts for women – from the other Ben, the 'real' Ben in so far as this could ever be pinned down, the person who might be in a quite different and more prosaic mood, frustrated, annoyed, displeased, bleak. Simon saw the real Ben more often than most, saw him in his rare unguarded moments, between meetings, between phone calls, when for the odd minute or two he dropped the pretence that every moment of life must be lived to the full, at speed and with maximum enjoyment, and revealed a side of himself that was more sombre and altogether less straightforward.

The Ben he saw now – the outer Ben – was a man bearing tragedy intensely but bravely, with restraint and a kind of gruff bewilderment. As so often, his appearance had somehow come to match his mood, and he was looking Byronic, with his bruised face and unshaven chin, his grey eyes narrowed by fatigue, his light brown hair seemingly wavier and wilder and wind-blown. Yet for all his suffering, there was a light in his eye, a glimmer of something that, if not quite confidence, was pretty close to it – resolution perhaps – and, unless Simon was very much mistaken, relief.

Was the panic over, then? Had Ben, the master escape artist, done it again? Simon wanted to laugh aloud.

Instead, seeing an opportunity, seizing it hastily, he said, 'The cash situation's getting to be a real problem, Ben.'

'Yeah?' He was staring out into the atrium again.

'We have to decide. We could go on half salary until August, we could—'

'Look – I don't think I can deal with this now.'

'Later then?'

'Not today. Not this week.' Reading Simon's expression, he protested in a tone of self-justification, 'Got to look after Cath, haven't I? From now on, that's the only thing that matters. Look after her *properly*, Simon! Whatever it takes. Come what may. The full bit. Be there for her, one hundred per cent!' He nodded emotionally, caught up by his own fervour. 'It's the whole world for her from now on! Nothing but the best.'

Simon thought: He really seems to mean it.

'I'm afraid you're going to have to fill in for me, Simon. I mean, I'll do what I can, when I can – you know that. But Singapore, Warsaw – I just won't be able to make it. And Bahrain . . .' He gestured with upturned hands.

'I can do Bahrain and Warsaw, of course,' Simon replied. 'But Singapore – I won't have time, Ben. It's going to take a week just to—'

Ben cut him short with a rapid jerk of his fingers. 'Well, just do what you can, eh? What you can.'

When Simon didn't reply Ben made one of those comradely gestures he usually kept for business contacts, a complicit touch on the arm accompanied by a rapid uplifting smile.

'What about the cash problem?' Simon asked before he could disappear. 'Shall we go for the half salary?'

'Sure, sure.'

'But will you be able to manage?'

He appeared to consider this seriously for the first time, he gave a light-hearted shrug. 'I'll have to, won't I?'

Ben had always been a big spender, living up to his income and generally well beyond it, getting stuck into his half of the profits well before the end of the year. If he had savings Simon knew that they couldn't be large. The house had been bought with Catherine's only inheritance and a large mortgage.

He said, 'If it's a problem, I could always look into the chances of getting the Bahrain money up front.'

'Christ, no. We'd get stinking terms! No, no – let's cross bridges when we damn well come to them.'

A cash crisis was hardly a bridge to leave to the last minute, but Simon knew better than to push the issue when Ben was in one of his more impatient moods.

'So, is that it, then?' Ben asked briskly.

'You got my message about the police all right? To say I was taking Emma Russell to see them this morning?'

He pulled an elaborate face. 'What?'

'I left a message at about eight—'

'Why the hell did you take *Emma* to the police?'

'Well, she told me about the nuisance calls and I thought she should go and tell Wilson—'

'What nuisance calls?'

'The calls that Catherine had been getting on her mobile.'

Ben screwed up his handsome face still further into an exaggerated expression of incredulity. 'For God's sake, what are you talking about?'

'I thought you knew. I thought you'd just forgotten.'

'I've never heard of any calls! Never! This is rubbish!' He was angry.

'Well, according to Emma, Catherine had been getting calls for some time, since about November. Sometimes as often as twice a day.'

'Look, you don't know what you're talking about,' Ben

retorted in a shoot-the-messenger tone. 'Emma must have gone and got her wires completely crossed.'

'She seemed fairly certain.'

'For heaven's sake, Cath would have told me about something like that. If it was in the slightest bit *serious*, I mean.' He glared at Simon. 'And you went and took Emma to the police with it! Jesus, Simon, you might have waited, you might have talked to me first. Really! For God's sake!'

'You weren't around. I thought it was the right thing to do. And the police do seem to think it could be important. They're certainly taking it seriously.'

'That's all we need! Emma making a drama out of a crisis. Jesus! I'll have to go and sort it out with the police, I suppose. Tell them they've been sold a load of cobblers.' He gave a heavy sigh of forbearance. 'Oh, and speaking of dramas' – he jabbed a finger at Simon – 'Alice tells me you barged in on Cath when she was barely conscious. For Christ's sake, what's wrong with you? Have you gone mad?'

Simon took a deep breath. 'I didn't barge in on her, as you put it. I simply had a very quiet word to establish if she had any memory of the attack, so that I could keep the police away. I thought that was the idea – to make sure she wasn't hassled by them. Now if I've done the wrong thing, then excuse me!' He put a hand to his chest, his voice shook with aggrievement. 'But if I may remind you there's been no one else around to organise anything, to deal with the police and sort everything out. You were very glad of my help at the beginning, if you remember. Getting the locks changed and tidying up and everything else you couldn't deal with. And that was quite apart from the *business*. Now, don't get me wrong – I was *glad* to help, more than glad. I'd do anything, anything at all, you know that. But when you *disappeared*' – he emphasised the word mercilessly – 'and Duncan asked me to deal with the police, what was I meant to do – refuse? And after all that, what do I get but a bollocking from Alice!'

'All right, all right, keep your hair on. It's just Alice being Alice, you know how she is.'

'Incredibly, unbelievably rude.'

'Needs a good screw, as usual.' Ben threw out such remarks all the time, the more outrageous the better. They were made largely for effect, but also because for him there was more than a grain of truth in such primitive beliefs.

'You don't understand,' Simon cried, 'it's *me* she's got it in for. You should have seen her. It was hideous.'

'Perhaps it's you she wants to shag.' This thought caused him such amusement that he laughed loudly and suddenly.

*'Oh, for God's sake!'*

Simon's explosion of fury was so violent that it startled both of them. Ben thrust out a quieting hand. 'Look, calm down, will you? Calm down. It was only Alice. She's a pain, everyone knows that.' Then, dropping his head and looking at the floor, he muttered grudgingly, 'Listen, I do appreciate everything you've done. Really. I'm very grateful.'

Simon thought: And well may you look guilty, you shit. You should be bloody ashamed of yourself.

Ben looked at his watch. 'Hell – I'm late. Are we done? Anything else?'

'One thing,' Simon said. 'There was a call yesterday from Terry Devlin.'

'Oh yeah?'

'He seemed to know an awful lot about Catherine – about her condition, I mean.'

Ben was checking the time on the wall clock over the nursing station.

'Medical information,' Simon persisted. 'Stuff he could only have got from someone here.'

'Aha.' He was determined not to pay attention.

'*Ben*, are you listening? Someone's been talking out of turn, passing on confidential information.'

Ben was combing his fingers through his hair and pulling

his shirt collar into shape. 'Well, it wasn't any of *us*, was it?' He was looking around for some shiny surface in which to check his reflection.

'Well, if it was any of the staff we should make a strong complaint.'

'I'll look into it.' It was the tone Ben used to humour people when he wanted them off his back.

'Aren't you bothered? I mean, it's none of his damned business.'

'Mmm?'

'But why would he want it—'

Ben gave the sudden explosive sigh of someone who is being sorely tried. 'Simon – for God's sake, because he's a control freak. Because he's got this thing about the family. Because he can't let go.'

When Simon still didn't get it Ben took a long-suffering breath and spelled it out as if for an idiot. 'Because he's soft – in – the – head.' He raised his eyebrows, he lifted a palm in the pose of someone awaiting a sign of comprehension. 'About – *Cath*.'

'You mean . . .'

'He had a thing for Cath's ma, Lizzie. Now he's transferred it to Cath. Call it continuity.'

'Oh.'

'Sort of sick really.'

'But I thought he pulled a fast one over the Langleys' house in Ireland.'

'He did. But then, that's always been his way of showing affection – to shaft his friends. Though it has to be said that Duncan was easy meat. Bit off more than he could chew . . .'

In the flow of people along the corridors Simon became aware of a familiar figure heading towards them and signalled a warning to Ben.

'. . . Out of his league on every front, silly old fool. Always been clueless when it comes to—' Catching the signal, Ben turned and, without a break in his flow, said easily to Duncan,

'Hey ho, Dunc. We were just sorting a few things out. *So* . . . I'm off to Fortnum's now to get some goodies for Cath. Cheer her up. Bit of champagne and caviar.'

'Good idea,' said Duncan, taking it literally. 'Can't do any harm, can it? Just a spoonful.'

Clapping Duncan on the arm, Ben gave a delighted chuckle, and for an instant he was the old Ben, the hard-living, hard-playing rogue with the appetite for life. 'No harm at all!'

As Duncan watched his son-in-law stride off, his lip trembled, he seemed to control his feelings with difficulty. 'What a thing for the poor chap. Married less than a year! Just setting out on the road of life. What a start! And being so bloody *good* about it. Determined to do his best for Cathy, you know. Going to pull out all the stops. Makes one feel very *moved*, you know. Very proud.' His voice reverberated with such honeyed, almost theatrical emotion that Simon couldn't help thinking that on some typically ill-judged level Duncan was rather enjoying the drama surrounding his daughter.

'How is Catherine?'

'Mmm?' Duncan turned and looked at Simon with faint surprise as if registering his presence for the first time. 'Oh, coming along. Coming along. The doctors are doing a marvellous job. Under the best chap in London, you know, the very best. I made sure of that.'

Selective amnesia was a peculiar talent of Duncan's and his memory was never more uneven, it seemed, than when Simon had done him a favour. Not only had Simon been the person to suggest they should check out the consultant, but at Duncan's request he had also been the one to make the necessary enquiries.

'The operation yesterday – was it a success?'

'Oh, absolutely!' Duncan said expansively. 'Went very smoothly. Of course, it'll be quite a while before she's back on her feet. You know – lots of physiotherapy, lots of rest.'

Back on her feet. Could it be true? Everything Simon had heard told him it was unlikely, yet this didn't stop a small bubble of hope from rising irrepressibly to the surface of his mind. 'So . . . is that what they're saying, that she's going to be all right?'

'Oh – in time! In time! You know.'

Simon's hopes subsided. He should have remembered that making the right noises was part of Duncan's stock in trade, like his easy charm and air of patrician authority. For this reason it was never easy to get a fix on Duncan, never easy to tell what, if any, of his utterances were true.

'And how about her memory, Duncan?' he asked solicitously. 'Has it come back at all?'

'Memory?'

'The attack – does she remember anything?'

'Good God, haven't asked her!'

'It's just that I told the police that she couldn't remember anything, and it's on that basis that they're staying away.'

Duncan looked blank.

'You did ask me to deal with the police, if you remember.'

'Did I? Well, there we are. But now that things are quieter . . .'

'You did ask me to see the police, Duncan. Very definitely. And I'd be grateful if you could tell Alice, so that she doesn't go around saying that I—'

They were interrupted by an apologetic Sister Jones, pausing in a rapid flight up the corridor to confirm some arrangement with Duncan. Instantly Duncan produced his ready smile, his twinkling gaze, his attentive manner. With his fine even features, his high forehead and greying hair combed back to reveal a widow's peak, his lean stooped figure clad in a well-cut summer suit and clubbish tie, he had the distinguished air of the international boardroom, the embassy or the judge's chambers. By background, you would guess county and a well-trodden path through public school and Oxbridge. The truth, Simon knew, was somewhat closer to the Eastbourne suburbs, an independent day school and a short stint at some non-accredited college in America. From his father Duncan had inherited a love of horseflesh, though like his father it was invariably the laggardly and lame that attracted his money, and barely a month went by that Duncan didn't fret about his salary, his shares and the scandalous cost of living.

As Sister Jones hurried away, Duncan assumed an industrious expression. 'Before you go, Jardine – about Ben. I'm worried . . . He needs to have some of the load taken off his shoulders, you know.'

'When you say *load*, Duncan?' It always got Simon's back up when Duncan called him by his last name, like some sort of hired hand.

'His workload,' Duncan declared as if this should have been self-evident. 'The thing is, while Ben's got so much on his plate – taking care of Catherine, dealing with the doctors – he won't have the time to run the business as he'd like. Simply not possible.' He spoke in the sonorous tone he used for board meetings, the inflated voice of authority and experience. 'And if I may say so, he shouldn't have to dash around the place like he did yesterday.' He shook his head reproachfully. 'Something *you* could have done, surely, Jardine. Not too much to ask, to step in and do the smaller trips.'

'He wasn't actually on RNP business yesterday, Duncan.'

Duncan frowned, as though Simon were making a rather shoddy attempt to deflect the argument. 'Difficult for you to deal with the core business on your own, of course – I do understand that. But I was thinking that if you liaised with Ben on a day-to-day basis, took instructions on the main decisions, then you might be able to keep things ticking over until Ben can get his eye on the ball again. I know it's a hell of a gap to fill—'

Simon said stiffly, 'I'm filling most of the gaps already, Duncan.'

'But you don't speak Polish.'

'I speak enough.'

'But you don't speak it *fluently*,' he argued triumphantly. 'And then there are all Ben's *contacts*. No, no—' He shook his

head decisively. 'You couldn't be expected . . . not on your own
. . . The thing is, what I wanted to say was that if things
threaten to go belly up in any way, I know this fellow who
might be able to step in. Excellent chap. Bit of a linguist.
Excellent contacts—'

Simon snapped, 'I think I can handle things on my own,
Duncan.'

'Oh? Well, if you're sure,' he said doubtfully.

'Just like I handled *your* little crisis.'

Duncan didn't like to be reminded that his business had
been in need of rescue. 'Hardly did it on your own, old chap,'
he corrected him pedantically. 'A team effort. That's all I was
suggesting—' Reading Simon's expression, he broke off with a
look of mild injury. 'Never doubted you would do your best,
er – Simon. It was just a suggestion, that's all. Just trying to
help. Just trying to do the right thing by Ben.'

It was typical of Duncan to back off suddenly, to justify
himself with an air of baffled innocence, but it didn't wash with
Simon who had no time for insincerity of this or any other
kind.

'So – Alice,' Simon said resolutely. 'You'll tell her I was
acting on your instructions?'

'The thing is, I know you meant well, Simon – no doubt
about that – but it was a bit much, you know. Going in and
bothering Catherine like that.'

'I didn't *bother* her.'

'She was upset.'

'She was upset because of what has happened to her,
Duncan. Not because of *me*.'

'You didn't have to tell her. It was up to us, her family.'

'I'm sorry, she asked me what happened and I told her.
Very gently. Incredibly gently. What was I going to do – pretend
she'd been in a car accident?' Simon was unable to prevent his
voice from breaking slightly as he added, 'I think the world of
Catherine. I would never do anything to harm her.'

'Oh well, there we are, there we are,' Duncan muttered,

with a glance around the hall. 'But, look, Simon, the thing is, Ben and I will be able to handle everything from now on. So, er – you know.'

'I don't think I do know.'

'No longer necessary for you to deal with the police. And, er, while we appreciate your concern – your support – well, we're fine here too.' He angled his elegant head, waiting for a sign from Simon that he had understood. Forced by Simon's silence to elaborate, he said, 'No visitors except family, you see.'

'I see,' Simon said tightly. 'When she's a little better then?'

Duncan made the sort of gesture that could have meant anything, but which Simon recognised from long experience to be a rejection. From equally long experience, Simon carried off his departure with a composure and style that even Duncan with his fastidious eye for the social niceties couldn't have faulted. It wasn't until Simon reached the street that he allowed his humiliation and anger full rein. After all he'd done! After all the work he'd put in! Duncan and Alice had the nerve to treat him this way, like some paid hand! Had the nerve, he thought with a steadier passion, to think they could manage without him. Well, he thought grimly, time would teach them otherwise.

He continued to quiver with repressed indignation as he drove home to Chelsea to drop the car off. It was only in the cab on his way to the office in Marylebone that his deeper disquiet about Wilson's words worked its way to the surface once more, and he again brooded unhappily on the 'overtones', the 'articles' that had been found next to Catherine. He racked his imagination as to what this something could be, his mind flitted across horrors and obscenities culled from films and books, and each image distressed and frightened him more than the last. He thought with a swell of emotion: I must stay close to her, I must protect her. And the thought of the months of guardianship ahead filled him with quiet joy.

Reaching the office, he got through his own work and much

of Ben's as well, and some of the secretary's too because she was off sick. He worked quickly and conscientiously because it was not in his nature to do anything sloppily, but at some point in that long day a thought came to him and kept returning until it took on the solidity of a decision. He would give Ben and the business three months before leaving; he would not abandon either until they were functioning properly again. *He* at least understood the meaning of loyalty. He searched his compendious memory for the apt quotation and located it with satisfaction. *I'll prove more true than those that have more cunning to be strange.*

It was nine when he finally locked up. He took a cab to a fashionable media bar in Soho and drank two Manhattans before going on to a club he knew well, where the pleasures were certain and the price well within his budget.

# Chapter Four

In the afternoons Catherine slept fitfully; a way of passing time or of postponing it. The interventions and routines of medical rounds were over, the physiotherapist gone, the family not expected nor encouraged until after five. She lay, eyes closed, absorbing the sounds of the city: the swish of tyres in the monsoon wet, the suppressed throb of the hot dry days, the rumbling of a stationary bus in the build-up to the rush hour. With these sounds came dreamy half-realised images of umbrellas and scorching sunshine and pallid faces on the number 19 of her student days. A life passing her by.

Her sense of detachment was reinforced by listening at a remove, with one ear only, for while her right ear had become attuned to the world beyond the window, the other explored an obscure inner world, a new-found universe in which reverberations and echoes moved secretively through layers of silence. The bones of her left ear had been damaged in the fall. Oddly, or perhaps not oddly at all, she concentrated her resentment and irritation on this one deadened ear, which of all her injuries seemed openly offensive.

Sleep, when it came, was uneasy, filled less with nightmares than a deep extended anxiety. Sometimes when she was disturbed by one of the staff she woke to find another more particular image imprinted on her mind, of an amorphous shadow blotting out the light, of seeing herself running, running, though never quite fast enough, so that she felt the heat of his hand inches from her shoulder. This scene repeated

endlessly with different variations, darkness, light, doors, corridors. An anxiety dream. Or a reality dream.

'Catherine?'

She woke with a beat of alarm.

'Sorry to disturb you.' It was one of the black nurses, a
woman with a rich mellifluous voice.

It was a moment before Catherine regained her bearings.
Late afternoon. Hot and airless. Her last day before being
moved.

'There's two police,' the nurse said. 'They want to know if
they can talk to you. One is named Wilson. He says you know
him.'

'Yes,' she said. 'I'll see them.' *And get the whole business
over and done with.*

She asked the nurse to bring her a face-wipe, comb and
mirror and to give her a few minutes before letting them in.
Since losing most rights over her body, tidiness had become
excessively important to her.

She did not realise that Wilson had entered the room until
she felt the gaze of his button eyes. Behind him came the broad
smiling face of Denise Cox. When Wilson made for Catherine's
deaf side it was Denise who called him back with a diplomatic
'Boss?' and signalled him round to the other side of the bed.

'Right,' said Wilson, backtracking.

Denise was the victim liaison officer, a big-boned big-busted
woman of about Catherine's age with cropped bleached hair,
startlingly blue eyes and a soft confiding voice.

'So,' Denise said, 'off on your travels tomorrow.'

'Out of jail,' Catherine said. 'Into prison.'

Denise chuckled. 'They say prison's an improvement. Still
running a florist's shop, I see.'

The flowers had kept coming, many from names she didn't
recognise, people she and Ben must have met at the races or
weekends away, others from distant friends of the family, or,
on Ben's side, émigrés and ancient Polish countesses. 'Don't
know half of them,' she said. 'Don't know how they heard.'

'Catherine, it was in the newspaper.'

This startled her. 'Why?'

'You've appeared on television. It made a story.'

'I don't want to be a *story*. Why was it a story?'

Denise used her reassuring voice. 'It was just a small piece. Nothing since.'

Wilson moved forward. 'We have no particular developments to report on your case as yet. But we still have several avenues to pursue. Three detectives are on the case this week.'

Catherine said, 'You're putting in a lot of work.'

'And will continue to do so,' he replied, adding one of his rather forced smiles.

He had no idea of how little she expected from him. She had no wish to know anything about her attacker, no wish to discover any details of his doubtless miserable life. While he remained an abstraction he remained safely in the past, like an encounter with lightning or a tornado, something which, though catastrophic at the time, would never touch her again.

'There's one thing we're having difficulty with,' Wilson said in his rather high voice, 'and that's the list of stolen property. Is your husband away? Abroad perhaps?'

'No.'

'Oh?' He looked a little puzzled. 'I see . . . He promised us a comprehensive list of missing items some time ago, but we can't seem to make contact. We've left numerous messages.'

Automatically coming to Ben's defence, Catherine said, 'He's always very busy. He works very hard.'

'But he's in London? He's been in to see you.'

'Oh yes.'

Wilson's mouth twitched. 'Could you ask him to get in touch? It would be most helpful.' Lifting his head, drawing himself up as if to indicate the start of the real business, he said, 'WPC Cox informs me that you have something to tell us.'

'I have very little to tell you,' Catherine informed him. 'I hope she explained.'

At Wilson's shoulder Denise nodded in confirmation.

Wilson made a concessionary gesture. 'You've remembered something at any rate.'

Catherine persisted, 'Nothing useful, really.'

'All the same, we'll take it down as a statement and ask you to sign it, if that's all right.' He half turned to Denise, as if to remind himself of the right procedure for hospital cases. 'Yes – so long as you're up to it. You will stop me if it's too much?'

Catherine told herself, *Soon it will be over and done with*.

Denise produced a pad and sat down near the foot of the bed, so that all Catherine could see of her was the crown of brilliant yellow hair.

Wilson remained standing, hands in pockets, affecting an unhurried air that was belied by the restlessness in his eyes. 'If we could just get the matter of these calls out of the way. For the record. You say they were wrong numbers, not nuisance calls as such?'

'That's right. I'm sorry you were told otherwise.'

'How could you be sure they were wrong numbers?'

'A man asked for someone I'd never heard of.'

'He asked for the same person every time?'

'The other times he just rang off when he realised he was still getting the wrong number.'

'So in fact – forgive me – but you had no way of knowing it *was* the same caller?'

She explained slowly, 'But I do, I did. The other calls came regularly after that first call. And once I got the last call details.'

'Last call details?'

'The number. Off the 'last call' thingummy . . . function. It was the same number both times, not one I knew.'

'Did you make a note of the number?'

'No.'

'It wouldn't be stored on your mobile?'

'No. It only keeps the last – I think – ten calls.'

Wilson accepted this with no sign of disappointment. 'Do

you remember if it was a London or country number? Or a mobile?'

'Really, it's so long ago. But . . . London, I think.'

'And how many calls did you get in all?'

She didn't try to suppress the flutter of exasperation in her voice. 'Oh – five? Six?'

'And all on your mobile?'

'Yes.'

'Spread over what length of time?'

'Look, I really can't remember.'

'But somewhere around Christmas?'

'I suppose so, yes.'

Wilson appeared to absorb this slowly. 'I'm not clear, then, why you told Emma Russell that you'd been having nuisance calls since November.'

'Emma was there when I got one of these calls. She got the wrong end of the stick. That's all.'

'She sounded very sure.'

'She always does.'

'Ah.'

And still Wilson seemed reluctant to let it go. Did he actively disbelieve her? Or did he think she'd forgotten to mention something whose significance only he could recognise?

'The television series you did, Catherine – it came out last autumn, didn't it? Did you get any calls as a result?'

'From possible clients, yes.'

'Is there a list?'

'It'll be on my desk at home somewhere.'

'Could someone find it for us, do you think?'

'I'll ask Ben. But, really, they were just ordinary people – people with gardens.'

'That may well be so, but we need to check all the same.' He moved on at last. 'Now the evening of the burglary . . . Why don't you take it at your own pace. In your own time.'

It was hard to get started. She looked up at the ceiling and tried to fix on the fragments of memory that had been coming back to her mysteriously and haphazardly, like snapshots arranged out of order.

'I remember the journey home from France,' she said. 'I remember the airport, and picking up the car and arriving at the house. I remember finding we had been burgled and hearing the sounds of a fight and running upstairs. Then this . . . shape rushed at me out of the darkness. I'm afraid that's all, from that time anyway. Later . . . I remember someone being there. I remember someone saying that help was on its way.' Catherine pulled a face. 'There you are. I warned you that it wasn't very much.'

Wilson nodded again, sombrely. 'Could I ask about the trip to France?' he asked in his rather nasal voice. 'This was a holiday?'

'A short break, yes.'

'You were away how long?'

'Three . . . four days.'

'You were planning to stay longer though?'

'Yes . . . Ben had to come back a couple of days early, and in the end I decided to come back with him.'

'Who knew about your plans?'

'What?' She had to think about this. 'My father . . .' She corrected herself uncertainly, 'No . . . I don't think I told him in fact. I don't think I told anyone. Not that I remember anyway.'

'The people you were staying with in France,' he prompted.

'Oh yes – them.'

'And your husband, he was coming back for a meeting, I believe?'

'He was going to America for a meeting the next day.'

'Ah, so his business associates in America would have known. Anyone in England?'

She sighed. 'You would have to ask him.'

Wilson made a show of absorbing this suggestion, and Catherine wondered if he was rather slow or rather pedantic or both.

'Could I ask about when you got to the house?' he said. 'It was your husband who unlocked the door, was it?'

'Yes.'

'And went in first?'

'Oh yes. I was still in the car, I was going to park it. I only waited till I was sure he was in the house.'

'And he got in all right?'

'Eventually.' This picture was strangely clear. 'He had a bit of trouble. That's why I waited. The key . . . it took him several tries. He even looked to see if he was using the right key. He had to sort of swing on the lock before he could get in. Then he turned and waved to show he was in.'

'And how long was it before you parked and got back to the house?'

'Oh – five minutes? There were no parking places. I had to go into the next street.'

'When you got back?'

'I knew something was wrong immediately. The house was dark. And I heard a strange sound. I called out.'

'What did you hear?'

'A shout,' she answered with reasonable confidence. 'Ben . . . shouting.'

'Do you remember what he was saying?'

'Saying?' Such detail was beyond her. 'No . . . I can't remember. No . . .'

'You say the house was dark. Were there no lights at all?'

Reluctantly, she dug deeper into her memory. 'There was one on, I think. Maybe two. But across the hall.'

'In other rooms?'

She closed her eyes for a moment, better to see the night. 'Yes.'

'Can you remember which?'

'The sitting room, I think. And the kitchen. Or it may have been . . . No, the kitchen. Down the passage. Yes, I remember that.'

'No light in the hall?'

She thought about this. 'No.'

'You didn't try to turn the hall light on?'

She was slow to speak because her answer was going to sound odd, even to herself. 'I don't think I did, no.'

'The kitchen and sitting-room lights,' Wilson continued, 'they hadn't been left on while you were away?'

Again she couldn't think why he should want such detail; again she answered obediently. 'The sitting room has a light on a time switch. A small lamp. I think it may just have been that one light, yes. But the kitchen – we never leave a light on in there, never.'

Wilson shifted his weight and attempted an expression of encouragement. 'Please – do go on again. From the moment you heard the sound and realised something was wrong.'

A pause while she searched through her memory so that she could be sure to stick to the steadier images, to what was reasonably certain, and stay clear of the less reliable visions that flickered uncertainly at the edges of her memory, like unfocused photographs. 'Yes . . .' she resumed with an effort. 'I heard Ben shouting upstairs. I called, but he only shouted again, so I ran upstairs.'

'And you don't remember what he was shouting?'

'No.' But this was Wilson's trick, of course, to make her slow the action that was spooling through her head, to wind the film back and replay it if she could. Following his unspoken command, she took herself back to the door of the house once again, she stood at the foot of the stairs. After a long while she murmured, 'He said something like "Get out, you bastard" or "What the hell are you doing, you bastard?" Something along those lines.'

As Ben's voice came back to her, she heard the rage in it, the roar of aggression; behind this, like an echo, she heard herself screaming at him, she felt the fear stir in her stomach like a reflex.

After a time Wilson prompted, 'Did you hear another voice at this stage?'

'Another? I don't think so.' Wanting to be clear, she added, 'What I mean is, I only remember Ben's voice. At that time. Yes . . .' She held up the remnant of memory as if to a strong light. 'Yes,' she confirmed. 'Only his.' But even as she said this another sound resonated faintly on the periphery of her mind, a sound that seemed to strike a lower and colder note. Another voice? Or Ben speaking in a different tone? Or was her imagination simply building on Wilson's suggestion? She excavated the moment more deeply and it seemed to her that the sound resonated again.

'Perhaps you should ask him that yourself,' she suggested again.

'Yes, but it always helps to have a story from two different witnesses,' Wilson explained in a speech he had obviously made dozens of times before. 'It's amazing what comes out. Things that the other person didn't notice. Or simply forgot.' He gave a brief professional smile. 'You're doing fine, Catherine. How're you feeling? Up to going on?'

Taking her silence as tacit agreement, he took her forward. 'So – you went upstairs?'

She returned to the scene with reluctance. 'It was dark up there. On the landing. I stopped. I reached across to the light switch and then . . . I wasn't sure if it was the best thing to do, to put the light on. Half of me . . .' She found herself on the brink of saying *wanted to hide*, and realised that it was true, that her sense of danger had been very strong. 'I wasn't sure what to do. I remember shouting Ben's name. Over and over again. I thought he might be hurt, I thought – well, I thought terrible things were happening.'

'There was noise?'

'Oh yes. Incredible noise. Crashing. Breaking. It sounded as though the place was being wrecked,' she whispered.

'But no voices?'

'No,' she decided, and immediately paused to examine the possibility again. 'No – only my own. I think I was yelling.'

'And where was this noise coming from?'

'The spare room. Which is our study.'

'And you couldn't see anything?'

'No. No, I couldn't see anything until . . .' Her breath locked high in her chest.

From the end of the bed Denise's head popped up, her eyebrows raised in silent enquiry.

'Take your time,' Wilson said quietly.

The rushing shadow had jumped into dark focus and, with it, the fear. Catherine took two long pulls of air. 'It all happened very quickly. I don't remember much. Just . . . this figure coming from nowhere. Suddenly. *Suddenly*. Rushing at me. And—' Another recollection came to her so unexpectedly that her first instinct was to distrust it, yet almost immediately it took on the shape and rigidity of memory. 'I forgot,' she added dutifully, 'there was this silence. Just before he came for me. This . . . long silence.'

Why had she stopped shouting? Why hadn't she called Ben's name one more time? If the thief had realised she was there, he might not have reacted so violently. Might not have attacked her. But even as she agonised over this she remembered the grip of that dreadful intense silence and knew that she had been incapable of breaking it.

'That's all I remember,' she said, though that wasn't quite true. In some fraction of time before the shadowy figure struck her she remembered a shrill unfamiliar sound, which was the sound of her own scream.

Wilson nodded slowly. 'You can't describe this man in any way?'

'No. It was so dark. He was just a – shape. Rushing. Very quickly.'

'Was he carrying anything? Holding anything? A weapon?'

She thought about this for some time. 'I . . . just don't know.'

Wilson turned away to say something to Denise, which she didn't hear. When he swung back his eyes fixed thoughtfully on Catherine's again. 'And later? After the accident?'

'Later,' she murmured. 'Well, I don't remember much, of course. A couple of small things, that's all.' She measured each word, to be sure of getting it right, but also to give substance to the little she did have to say. 'I remember being on the floor. It was like . . . coming round from an anaesthetic. I felt sick, totally disorientated. I knew . . . it was bad. I thought . . .' What she had thought was that she was going to die. Dimly, through the shock and injury, she had thought: So this is how it feels to die. 'The things I remember – they're pretty hazy.'

The door sounded and someone came into the room. Wilson turned sharply, there was a muttered exchange and whoever it was left again.

Wilson bent forward over the bed. 'You were saying?'

'Just two things. I'm not sure which came first.'

'That's all right.'

'In one there were blinding lights. Well . . . lights anyway. Perhaps they just seemed bright. I knew I was on the floor. And I knew there was someone there. Beside me. Kneeling or . . . I can't tell you who . . . or anything about them . . . I only know this person was there. It could have been an ambulance man, couldn't it?' she asked, wanting the reassurance of the obvious. 'Or whoever called the ambulance?'

Wilson nodded vaguely. 'Anything else you remember from this time?'

He already knew the answer, of course; Denise would have relayed it to him three days ago, when Catherine had told her.

'I remember something close to my face.'

'What sort of thing?'

'Something . . . softish. Fabric.'

'Now when you say close to your face – I'd like to be clear – do you mean it was being held over your face?'

'Not over, no,' she replied firmly. 'No, I was on my left side . . . well, my head was over to the left anyway. And this soft stuff was just . . . I don't know, against my face. Not pressed into it, just . . . against my face.'

'Touching your nose?'

'Well . . . yes.'

'And mouth?'

She knew where this was leading and she wanted to put him straight. 'Touching my mouth, but not pushed against it.'

'So there was no pressure as such?'

'You mean,' she said, 'was this person trying to suffocate me?'

Wilson's button eyes did not waver. 'I just want to be clear.'

Catherine exhaled slowly. 'There was no pressure.'

'Anything else you recall?'

With a final effort of memory, she stared at the blank screen of the ceiling and summoned the kneeling figure once again. This time, however, the effect was to blur the existing picture. How had she known this person was there? How had she known he was kneeling? Had this person spoken, or was it just the later one? Had there been two people at all, or had she doubled up one in a trick of memory? Before everything became irretrievably confused, she said, 'That's all I can tell you.'

'And the second occasion?'

'I think it was later, though I can't be sure. There was a voice. A man's voice. Calling my name.'

Denise's head tilted upwards. Wilson waited, motionless.

'I was still on the floor. In the same place – well, I assume so anyway. He said my name and something like, "They're on their way."'

'When you say he called you by your name . . .?'

'Catherine.'

'You're sure?'

'Yes.'

'And he said "They're on their way"?'

'Something like that. And "You're going to be all right." He said that several times.'

Another phrase came to her, something like *rest easy* or *lie easy*. But she might have lifted that from a film.

'Did you recognise the voice?'

'I don't think so.'

'Do you think you'd recognise this voice if you heard it again?'

She thought about this for a long time. 'I can't say,' she answered finally.

'Anything else you remember?'

'No, I . . . No.'

Wilson turned away and, bending down out of sight, said something to Denise in a low voice. Catherine heard a rustling and he straightened up again. 'Would you look at these items, Catherine, and tell me if you recognise them?'

'What are they?'

'If you could just tell me if you've seen them before. This is the first.'

He held up a transparent plastic bag bearing a white rectangular label marked with some sort of code number. Inside was a small amount of lacy fabric that had once been white but was now stained and grubby. She reached up a hand to bring the bag closer.

'What are they – panties?'

'Yes.'

She felt a descent into cold. She whispered, 'Are you saying . . . they're *mine*?' Her mind raced on, making connections that filled her with foreboding.

Denise shot to her feet. Catherine stared at her helplessly. 'No, no,' Denise said. 'No, you were fully dressed when you were found.'

'Ah!'

'I swear,' Denise reassured her again. 'It wasn't like that.'

Catherine gave a short nervous laugh. 'For a moment there I thought I'd suffered a fate worse than death.' And then she laughed again, even more strangely, because the real joke was that, given the choice between sexual and neurological violation, she would have taken rape any day.

'Can I have a better look?' she asked.

Wilson had clearly allowed for this possibility because he produced plastic gloves and slipped them on before lifting the panties out of the plastic by one corner and holding them up.

The panties were not soiled with dirt, she saw now, but with what looked like dried blood, lots of it, covering almost every part of the fabric.

Wilson said, 'Take as long as you like.'

The panties were bikini style made from ersatz satin with lace trim at the leg, the sort that were sold everywhere. 'I don't think they're mine,' she said eventually. 'But I can't be sure.'

'You have some like these?'

'Sort of . . . but I think the lace was different. I can't be sure. Sorry.'

Wilson pushed out his lower lip in disappointment or resignation.

Catherine had to ask, 'The blood – is it mine?'

Wilson hesitated as he put the panties carefully back in the bag and re-sealed it. 'I'd rather not answer that just at the moment, if you don't mind.'

He reached down again towards his feet and produced another transparent bag. Inside was a length of skimpy diaphanous fabric, probably silk, in aqua green, also stained with blood, but not so extensively, just a series of blotches.

'No,' she said without hesitation. 'I've never seen it before.'

'You're absolutely certain?'

'It's a scarf, isn't it?' When Wilson nodded, she confirmed, 'No, definitely not mine.'

Wilson seemed neither surprised nor disappointed.

'Where did you find them, these things?'

He took his time before saying, 'At the scene. Thank you,' he added quickly, as if to curtail any further questions. 'You've been very helpful.'

'I don't think so,' she said. 'I don't think I've helped at all.'

*

She had come to look forward to the evenings. The family usually left by eight, and by nine the corridors were falling quiet as the last visitors to the surrounding wards drifted away. After Sister's rounds the night staff would come to check her mattress and lines and collar, and if they weren't too busy would chat for a while. When she was low she liked to talk to the Filipinos because they were practical and without sentiment, they did not share the universal reverence for the brave front; they believed in God striking you down and yours not to reason why and shifting for yourself by all the means at your disposal. When she was in a lighter mood she'd hope for an Irish nurse and some talk of men and parties and pubs. They could be offhand, even abrupt, these women from Limerick and Donegal, with their cutting tongues and acid wit, but she liked that too, because they expected nothing in return.

By ten there was silence over the floor apart from the click of an occasional door and the murmur of the traffic beyond the window. Then, with Walkman and headphones on, adjusted for mono listening, eyes closed, she would put on some baroque music and take a walk on strong striding legs into a garden. Sometimes it would be a garden from the past, one she'd seen through to completion, but more often than not she would walk her way through her current commission, a traditional country-house garden in Gloucestershire.

Her journey to the garden could be unpredictable. Sometimes it was like trying to cling to a fast escaping dream in the moment after you wake up; she scarcely made it to the gate before she found herself slipping back into reality and having to begin the journey all over again. Sometimes she never made it at all, and then the night seemed long.

Tonight, however, aided and abetted by two long swigs of brandy – extremely medicinal – and some Scarlatti cantatas the journey was a doddle, just a quick flight, and she went straight to the large walled garden at one side of the Gloucestershire house. This was the part of the garden she saw most clearly.

Once the derelict fruit cages and cold frames were removed, it would make a perfect ornamental garden, half vegetable, half flower garden; with secluded arbours and long vistas that drew you forward to the next turning, the next composition. There would be geometric beds containing decorative vegetables, purple- and silver-leaved, such as chard and artichoke, interspersed with red-leaved and exotic salads. In the centre there would be a fountain encircled by festooned plum trees, and against the walls espaliers of apple and pear and peach, while around the perimeter the wide flower and shrub borders would be themed by colour. Naturally there would be a white border – she was famous for her white borders – also a blue one, a pinky-mauve one, and what she called a 'Spanish' border, containing the passionate crimsons and inky-blues that went so well together: blood and death in the arena. She would bring in plenty of autumn and winter interest too, with winter honeysuckle and viburnums and early camellias.

The garden would be divided into seven areas, each with its own geometry. In the salad area there would be squares formed by the wider paths and edged in box. Within the squares, however, she had yet to decide between running the paths diagonally to make triangular beds, or at right angles to make smaller squares, or in two concentric circles intersecting a cross, in the style of a Celtic labyrinth.

In the real world someone touched her arm.

She opened her eyes with a start to see Ben. She pulled off the earphones. 'You gave me a shock.'

'A shock?' he cooed with sham sympathy. 'Thought you were awake, Moggy. They said you were.'

Catherine didn't have to catch the wine on his breathy kiss to realise that he was on his way back from dinner: his voice rang with affability, his eyes were heavy-lidded, his smile was addressed to the world at large.

'How's my girl, then? How's my Moggy?'

For the first week Catherine had not known how to answer this question, but now she said, 'Fine.'

'What, here on your lonesome?' Ben looked around with a show of surprise. 'I thought Alice was going to be here. Where's Alice?'

'She went ages ago. She had a date.'

'Not a *date* date?' He gave a mock leer.

'She didn't say.'

He hovered indecisively, as though in the absence of other people he might only stay a minute. She knew he found it easier when the family were there, or Emma, who was the only friend Catherine allowed to visit her, because then the burden of conversation was shared, the tone light-hearted. Whenever they were alone, his manner became rather forced, his talk wild and rambling, and then she had to remind herself how hard it must be for him, for all the family: the strain of seeing her stretched out like a piece of medical meat; the fear of mentioning the p-for-paralysis word; the need to put on a cheerful front.

'Good dinner?' she asked.

'Oh, you know, the usual blow out. That's what they always want.'

It had been a business do, Catherine remembered. Some Poles in London for a couple of days.

'A surprise for you!' Lifting his briefcase onto the bed, he pulled out a small package and brandished it aloft, like a conjurer producing his best trick.

Another present. She said, 'I wish you wouldn't.'

'What do you mean, *wish I wouldn't*?' The lightness of his voice didn't conceal the note of rebuke. 'Open it!' He thrust it into her hands.

The wrapping was well sealed and it took her a moment to find a way in. Pulling the paper off at last, she held up a miniature television designed to fit into the palm of one hand. She couldn't imagine when she would use it. 'Thanks.'

Her tone must have sounded less than enthusiastic because he made an expression of offence that was half-serious. '*Thanks*? But you haven't even looked at it yet. Turn it on – see what a great picture it's got.' When she failed to find the switch he plucked it from her grasp and fiddled with the controls. 'See?' He held it close above her face.

'It's amazing.'

Like a boy with a new toy, he showed her every channel and button, looking to her expectantly for suitable expressions of wonderment and appreciation. She realised he'd had more than just a glass or two of wine when he swayed gently and put out a hand to steady himself, though he managed to fuse it into one seamless movement that to anyone else would have appeared deliberate.

Putting the television to one side at last, he declared, 'It's for when everyone's driving you nuts!'

'All the time, you mean?'

He liked it when she showed the right spirit. 'All the time,' he echoed with a warm chuckle of approval. 'Absolutely!'

She felt a burst of love for him, for his quirky smile, his mischievous eyes, for the marvellous familiarity of him, and the novelty too, because however hard she tried her memory could never quite do him justice. Close behind this came a plunge of anxiety, which brought her up with a hard jolt. Would they ever survive this? Could any marriage survive this?

She asked, 'How's work?'

A lazy shrug. 'Got a lot of catching up to do. Sort out some nonsenses.'

'Nothing serious?'

'No, no.'

'Simon can't do it for you?'

'Ha! I wish!' Still in expansive mood, he asked, 'So, my darling Moggy, how are things?' Neither of them could remember how or why he had come to call her Moggy – they weren't cat lovers – but somehow the name had stuck.

She didn't attempt to list the various indignities of her day, nor describe the auditory tests that had showed almost no hearing in her damaged ear; like her moments of panic, anxiety and dread, these were things she had learnt not to talk about. 'Emma packed for me.'

Faint puzzlement flickered over his face and she knew that for a moment he'd forgotten she was being moved to the spinal unit the next day. 'Oh, right,' he said airily. This was Ben's way, to ignore the more unsettling things in life and concentrate on the positive. It was one of the things that had drawn Catherine to him, this belief that life could be lived in a permanent state of confidence and enthusiasm.

'There's an awful lot of champagne left over,' she mentioned. 'Could you take it home?'

'What, haven't we drunk it all? Hell! We'll soon put that right when you get to the new place! Lots of people coming to see you, Cath. They're all queuing up.'

'I don't want to see anyone. Please, Ben, tell them to stay away. Will you? *Please.*'

'Might cheer you up, you know.'

The thought of small talk appalled her, but what appalled her most of all was the thought of their curiosity and pity. 'No. Absolutely not. I would really hate it.'

'But they love you, darling heart. They want to come and dish out all the gossip. Give you the latest.' Catching her expression, he shook his head reprovingly and his voice took on a mildly exasperated edge. 'Mad to cut yourself off, Moggy. Got to have a bit of light relief sometimes, you know!'

When she didn't reply his eyes drooped, he gave a slight shrug and, reaching for a chair, pulled it up to the bed.

'Can't see you down there,' she reminded him as he sank down onto it with a sigh.

'No?' he murmured lazily. He stood up again and, having shifted indecisively once or twice, perched on the edge of the bed, which had long been established as the only place where she could see anyone properly.

'Now, what have I got to tell you?' he said abruptly, coming alive to the need for news. 'Yes! Got a call from Sam Blake. You know – Sam and Livvy? Want us to go and stay with them in Barbados next Christmas. Bit of a wild child in his City days, of course, old Sam. Sailed close to the wind, so they say, but one hell of an operator, no doubt about that. Running an investment company now. On his way to a second bloody fortune, jammy bastard! But a fantastic place they've got in Barbados, apparently. *Her* family has pots of moolah, of course—'

Catherine found herself listening but not listening. This was the trick, she had learnt: to disconnect herself from such moments, from such conversations, from Ben's life, from her own too, though quite what her life involved now she couldn't have said. The only world she could focus on was small and contained: this room, this bed, this body, and the unit they were transferring her to in the morning. If she listened too closely to what Ben was saying it was like touching some terrible heat, the pain made her pull away.

Finally, when the word 'Barbados' filtered through yet again, she could bear it no longer and interrupted him in a voice that was too loud and too sharp. 'I forgot,' she said, 'the police were here.'

'Oh.' His smile had a glassy veneer. 'Wilson?'

'And the WPC.'

'The blonde job with the big boobs?'

'Well, it was the same one as before, anyway.' She heard the note of criticism in her voice and thought: This is no way to go, I'm sounding difficult. 'Yes, the blonde job. They said they'd been trying to get in touch with you.'

He rolled his eyes. 'For God's sake, I called them! Yesterday? Monday? They're never there. Hopeless! What did they want, anyway? Let me guess,' he jeered languidly, 'to tell us they've found *nothing*.'

'More or less.'

'I knew it. And they came and bothered you just to tell you that? Sorry, darling, I should have got hold of them, shouldn't I? Should have told them to get lost. Forgive me?' He rolled towards her with an endearing boyish smile. 'Poor Moggy. Poor darling.' His voice had a bleary sentimental note. He squeezed her hand, then after a moment's hesitation reached out a second time and, still not entirely at ease with the role of bedside companion, laid his hand rather awkwardly in hers. He asked, 'What did they say? They've given up on the stupid phantom caller, I hope.'

'Yes. There's no way of tracing the calls.'

'Of course there isn't! And it wasn't anybody who had anything to do with anything – you said so yourself.'

'That's right,' she murmured.

'That's exactly what I told Simon! He should never have made such a big thing about it with the police. Never have encouraged Emma to make all those ridiculous statements!' With a final press of her hand he withdrew his own and in the process of settling himself more comfortably on the edge of the bed turned away slightly so that his face was partly in shadow.

She said, 'Wilson wanted a statement.'

'But I've given him a statement.'

'No, from me.'

He turned down his mouth in an expression of mystification. 'But why? To say what?'

'Just what I remember.'

'But, darling, you don't remember anything.'

'I remember going into the house.'

He shook his head firmly. 'No, no, you said you didn't—'

'But I do now. I remember now.'

His eyes narrowed almost to the point of invisibility, she sensed a sudden alertness in him. 'Since when?'

'Oh, I don't know. Things have been coming back to me in bits and pieces.'

'But are you sure?' he asked easily. 'It couldn't be' – he rotated a finger next to his temple, signalling brain problems – 'you've got a bit mixed up?'

'No, I remember moving into the driving seat to go and park, I remember you taking the cases up to the door.'

'You didn't say anything.' It was an accusation.

'It didn't seem terribly important.'

'Didn't seem important!' he jeered, flashing cold shark eyes at her.

She realised her mistake. It was like pressing a button, this route to Ben's insecurities. He couldn't bear the thought of being excluded in any way, of having even the smallest item of information kept from him. His mother had walked out when he was twelve and no one had given him a word of explanation, not then, and not later, certainly not his mother herself, who'd gone to America and barely been in contact since. He'd been brought up by a profligate and largely absent father who, among his other notable acts, had twice forgotten to pick Ben up from school at the end of term, and had once left him to find his own way back from France after taking up an invitation to go and stay with a minor *principessa* on Lake Como. Not surprisingly, Ben hated to feel he wasn't being told the full facts, or, worse still, that decisions were being made behind his back.

'Sorry,' Catherine said. 'I didn't realise I'd remembered anything very significant until the police asked me.'

Ben forced enthusiasm into a voice that was still cool with injury. 'So! Memory all coming back! That brain of yours! All there! All working! That's great!' Then, thinking this through, he leant towards her with an unfocused look of concern. 'Haven't remembered anything *upsetting* though, have you, my darling?'

'No.'

'Nothing about that *man*?'

'No,' she lied again.

He straightened up. 'Good! Can't have you upsetting yourself!'

This was the official family line, she had realised some days ago. Everything must be done to make sure she did not get upset, though this strategy rather awkwardly ruled out discussion of the immediate past and indefinite future.

She said reminiscently, 'But tell me – I can't quite remember

– when you were at the door, trying to get in, you called something back to me. Something about the lock. Something . . .' She gave up. 'What was it?'

He was cautious suddenly, or slow, or distracted. 'What? Oh, I said the lock felt strange. Stiff.'

'Ah,' she breathed. It came back to her now. 'Yes . . . And the lights – I'm not going mad, am I? You didn't put any on, except for a couple at the back of the house.'

Ben drew his head back with a frown. 'No, darling, where on earth did you get that from? No, I put the hall light on, then when I realised the alarm wasn't set I went off on a hunt – saw the mess in the living room – did a complete round. No, I turned on every light in the place! Of course I did!' He shook his head firmly. 'But, Moggy darling, why go into all this now? What's the point?'

'I want to get a picture, I want to get it clear in my head, so that I can forget about it. That's all.'

He shrugged as though he was being persuaded against his better judgement.

She continued, 'What about when you went upstairs? Did you leave the hall light on?'

'Of course! And I put the landing light on, and then – well, I would have put the study light on, but the bastard was waiting for me, wasn't he?'

'I thought it was dark when I came in.'

He scoffed, 'No, darling. Now I know you've got it all mixed up!'

'Oh . . . well, then.'

'For God's sake, the lights were definitely on!' he insisted as if she had argued against him. 'Is that what you told the police, that the place was dark?'

'I said I thought the only lights were in the kitchen and the sitting room. But I must have got it wrong.'

'Totally!' He shook his head firmly. 'That's going to be great, isn't it? You saying it was dark, and me saying it was lit up like a Christmas tree. Ha!' He was annoyed certainly, but also rather amused, as if the idea of being an unreliable witness rather appealed to him.

'Sorry.'

He brushed it aside with a lift of one hand.

'One last thing.'

His attention was fading fast.

'Upstairs – when I got upstairs – someone was shouting. Yelling. It was you, wasn't it?'

'I should think so,' he said without hesitation. 'Well, I was bloody furious, wasn't I?' His eyes gleamed briefly.

'Did the man speak?'

'Mmm?' He had heard all right, but either he was thinking about it or he didn't know the answer. 'What a question, Moggy.'

He would have left it there if she hadn't pressed him. 'Did he say anything?'

Realising some effort of concentration was expected of him, Ben screwed up his eyes, he pushed out his lip, he exhaled slowly before shaking his head. 'Can't remember now. All lost in the mists.'

She was silent.

'Is that it?' He looked tired, or possibly the worse for alcohol.

'I think so.'

'Got your *picture*?'

'What?'

'You wanted a picture, you said. To get it clear in your head.'

'Yes, got my picture.'

'Good!' He lumbered to his feet. 'So, what time would you like me here in the morning?'

'Ten, if you wouldn't mind. I'm rather nervous.'

'Nervous? Why *nervous*, Moggy?'

'The thought of being moved.' She was aware that in showing this loss of nerve she was failing to show the kind of doughty spirit expected of her.

'Hey!' He pressed his palm tenderly to the side of her face. 'Not to worry. There's my girl!'

He bent down to kiss her and rest his cheek against hers, and she closed her eyes, better to draw in the warmth of him, the scent of him, the texture of his skin. She felt a rush of memory, an amalgam of the hundreds of nights they had spent together. In a surge of feeling, she put a hand around his head to bring his face still closer to hers, but just as her fingers tightened against the thick silky hair he pulled away.

'I miss you,' she whispered. Saying this was like breaching a dam, just a trickle for the moment but one sudden move and there'd be a torrent. The urge to give way to it was very strong. Her throat swelled, she felt all the pressure of her grief and self-pity. Yet something warned her against expressions of anguish. Partly, she had an irrational fear of voicing her terrors, as if this alone could give them the dread solidity of fact. More practically, she feared Ben's revulsion and dismay. Having no use for displays of emotion himself, he looked on them with mistrust and embarrassment.

In the end she said simply, 'Miss you so much.'

'Miss you too,' Ben said breezily. Then, clearly feeling that something else was expected of him, he added in a suggestive growl, 'Won't be long now!'

She managed to maintain her expression until he had gone, and then she began to weep, slowly at first, a trickle of hot silent tears that slipped coolly into her ears and hair. When these failed to take the edge off things, she cried with a sense of anger. Finally she remembered the brandy bottle. Reaching for it, she managed to knock it to the floor and had to call the nurse.

The bell was answered by an Irish girl named Kathleen: 'But you can call me Kate'.

'There's a bottle of brandy on the floor.'

She laughed. 'A nightcap, is it?'

'Have one yourself.'

'Trying to get me fired!' She found the bottle and, pushing

a straw into the neck, held it to Catherine's mouth. If she noticed Catherine's undried tears she didn't mention them. When one sip stretched to four she exclaimed in mock disapproval, 'Steady on!'

'I'm leaving tomorrow.'

'So you are.'

'I'm frightened.'

'No need, I'm sure. They'll look after you better there. They'll be able to give you a lot more time than we can.' Capping the brandy bottle she put it back in the locker. 'Anything else I can do for you?'

'Give me another drink?'

'You're a devil! As bad as a Paddy.'

Catherine didn't want to be left alone quite yet. 'There're some letters on the locker,' she said. 'Would you read them to me?'

'Only one I can see.' She moved chocolates and tissues and paraphernalia. 'No, only one.'

'Well, that one, then.'

She saw Kate baulk at the length of it, five pages or so, but, perching on the edge of the bed, she began to read without complaint.

'*Dear Catherine, I hope you're continuing to make progress and that the flowers arrived safely. The roses were the last from the climbers on the west wall, which have blossomed so profusely though alas so briefly. I do not of course know their name – my ignorance would be laughable if it were not so shameful. However, I'm taking myself in hand, so far as common names go at least – I think it would be unrealistic to aspire to Latin at my age when I've still trouble enough with the spelling of the English language. A Mrs Kent is coming to tell me what's what. She is said to be an expert on gardens hereabouts (she's done quite a few gardens in Wicklow)—*'

'Wicklow!'

'Careful – my mam was a Wicklow girl.'

'Wicklow's got poncy gardens.'

'Poncy?' Kate laughed. '*Poncy*. Now there's a word!' Still laughing, she went back to the letter. 'Where are we? Ah yes, Mrs Kent . . . *I'm hoping she can tell me what's here and what Mick should or shouldn't be doing to keep everything in fine shape. I have a suspicion that Mick has done damage again – the shrubs down by the stream are looking hacked about and forlorn. But of course it's hard for me to say anything from a position of horticultural iliteracy.*' Kate looked up with a quick smile. 'He's misspelt illiteracy. *Now is the time to come clean and admit that the rhododendrons met with an unfortunate accident last year. Someone said that they were a menace and strangling the trees, so I told Mick to deal with them. The result, I'm afraid to say, was nothing short of slaughter. Mick got a bulldozer, although it may have been a JCB – I found it too painful to ask which particular weapon of mass destruction he had been let loose on. Not only did he uproot the rhododendrons around the trees to the north of the house (the ones I meant him to deal with) but also managed to lay waste to those on either side of the drive. I have not yet recovered from the shock of seeing the devastation, my stomach is still somewhere out by the gates, where it dropped through the bottom of my boots, but it taught me that Mick was not be trusted with shrubs and, apart from those down by the stream, I have curbed his worst impulses to slash at vegetation with a blunt instrument.*'

'For heaven's sake. Why does he write? Why does he bother?'

'What's that?'

'I wish I knew what he was after.'

'Why would he be after anything?'

'He has to be.'

'Are we stopping or are we going on?' She examined Catherine's face. 'Shall I just whisk through the rest? *So when Mrs Kent comes I will ask her what she recommends for the drive, whether to replant rhodies or to try some other shrubs. Aware of my responsibilities to Morne, I am determined to go cautiously and to obtain advice from every possible quarter. Of course I would dispense with all such opinions if I thought there was a chance of you coming and advising us on how to restore the gardens to their proper glory. I know that you must be thinking only of recovery at present, but once you see your way clear you would only have to give the smallest indication that you might consider it and I would keep all other ideas on hold. There is nothing more precious to me than the thought of restoring Morne to its former glory, as your mamma would have wished it to be, for as you know I hold her memory most dear.'*

'Really!'

'The idea doesn't appeal?'

'What idea?'

'The garden.'

'I'd rather die.'

'Sounds a nice job.'

'That's my home he's talking about. He stole it after my mother died. Got hold of the mortgage. Forced my father out. Everything's a deal. Everything's an opportunity to make a killing.' She remembered the expression her father used. 'He'd as soon sell his grandmother.'

'Ah,' Kate said heavily. 'I see. It couldn't be that he's got a conscience about it? Trying to make amends.'

'I doubt it.'

'A guilty conscience can strike us all,' Kate offered solemnly before returning once again to the letter. *'I am safer with trees – or should I say that trees are safer with me? I have been doing serious homework in the last couple of years and have discovered what you will know already, that there are some remarkable trees at Morne – the Irish yews around the hollow, surely older than the house itself, the oak on the south lawn, which Old Patrick from the village estimates to be 300 years old (do you think this is possible?), and the beeches, which seem to reach beyond the sky, but which I am told may go any day in a storm because they have shallow roots. It is a terrible*

*thought, that they may go, so I have had some new beeches*
*planted, ones of good size, already some twenty feet high, so*
*that there will be some equally majestic trees in fifty years or*
*so.'*

'That's enough, thanks.'

'There's only a few more lines. Just' – she scanned the page
'news of Maeve, who's been unwell but is now recovering—'

'Chuck it in the bin.'

'Why don't I just put it on the side here?'

'I want it in the bin. If I could move from this bloody bed I
would put it in the bin.'

'The bin it is, then.'

Despite the brandy, it took Catherine a long time to get to
sleep, and then it was to dream all night, or so it seemed. She
revisited the scenes she had described to Wilson, re-enacting
them time and again, but with variations and additions that
might or might not have been borrowed from other times and
other dreams. In the morning two images remained intact. In
one, which was recognisably a nightmare, she was in a dark
place, making her way towards a series of rooms with half-
open doors that radiated brilliant light. The floor was littered
with what she took to be debris, but which turned out to be the
heavy glutinous leaves of some vigorous plant whose tendrils
wrapped themselves tighter and tighter around her legs, pulling
her slowly to the floor. When she was completely immobilised
something soft brushed against her face and clung to her nose
and mouth and eyes, threatening to rob her of air. She would
have fought the soft thing off but she couldn't move her arms.
Someone who was Alice and then not Alice was somewhere
close by, weeping and wailing softly.

In the other scene she replayed her arrival from France. She
ran upstairs as before but, instead of stopping on the landing
as she had described to Wilson, she ran on into the room where
Ben and the man were fighting and found herself caught up in
the struggle, though mysteriously unaffected by it. It was dark,
but this didn't prevent her from seeing a weapon in the man's

hand, a long baton that she identified as a baseball bat. In the instant she saw it, she realised that the man had finished with Ben, or perhaps Ben wasn't there any more, and was coming for her so fast that she didn't have time to raise her arms and ward off the blows. In the next instant she was back on the landing and the man was looming over her. As she cowered before him she saw the bat raised above his head, ready to strike.

In the morning the image of the baseball bat stayed with her and she decided to ask Ben if he thought the man might have used it in the attack. While she was about it she would also tell Ben what for some reason she'd failed to tell him the night before, about the blood-stained panties and scarf the police had asked her to identify.

In the event she mentioned neither. Ben arrived late, just behind the ambulance men, and by the time they had the chance to talk she'd realised that the baseball bat was probably a trick of her mind. Ben had always kept a baseball bat under the bed in case of intruders and, by association, her subconscious had in all likelihood transposed it into the dream.

She decided against mention of the blood-stained clothing for a very different reason, because despite police reassurances to the contrary Ben might believe she had been sexually assaulted, and that was one burden he didn't need.

# Chapter Five

TERRY WAITED impatiently while Fergal arranged his long limbs untidily in the chair opposite, arms at every angle, legs skewed out to one side, like an abandoned marionette. Settled at last, he began to speak in a soft unhurried voice. 'I am giving you the dry bones of the situation as *they* see it. You follow me? No interpretation, no perspective. This is the official version, pure and simple.'

Terry could only nod.

'In essence, they have no suspects and no prospect of any suspects.'

'They're still thinking in terms of a straight burglary?'

Fergal hesitated, which wasn't like him at all. 'I'll come to that in a moment, if I may. It would be simpler if we could leave the questions till the end.'

Suitably corrected, Terry slid his elbows onto the desk and propped his chin on clenched fists. Thereafter he did not shift his gaze, did not move, as if to will Fergal forward by the intensity of his attention.

'The forensic people have found nothing obvious in the house,' Fergal began again, his accent belonging more than ever to some uncharted point midway across the Irish Sea. 'No known fingerprints, nothing of that nature. Signs of forced entry on the front door, but a neat professional job, a drill on the mortice, a pick on the latch. As for the alarm . . . Here, I have to say, my contact was short on information.' From his time-worn expression of forbearance he might have been a lecturer again, in receipt of a sloppy essay. 'He could not say if the alarm was linked to a security company, so we do not know if an automatic alarm call was sent, nor for that matter if one was received. All he could tell me was that the neighbours do not remember hearing an alarm bell ringing. Not of course that this means a great deal. False alarms are two a penny in that part of London.'

Terry remembered that Fergal had lived in London during his Cintel years, and perhaps at other less accountable times.

'However, if the exterior bell did indeed sound, it would have switched itself off after fifteen minutes. That is the law – no more than fifteen minutes. The ambulance people did not report hearing an alarm ringing when they arrived, nor was an alarm audible on the call to the emergency services, which suggests that if the alarm was triggered it occurred more than fifteen minutes before Catherine was . . . *discovered*. It's equally possible, of course, that the alarm was never set.'

By an effort of will, Terry remained silent. He tried to see this information through a police investigator's eyes, tried to find a pattern that would steer a thinking mind in the right direction.

Fergal twisted around in his seat. Any movement for Fergal was a performance: limbs drawn in, tall frame realigned, arms and legs uncoiled haphazardly. He turned his eyes to the thin Dublin sun, revealing the punishment of fifty-five troubled years, a poor diet and sixty a day, only recently abandoned. His sad intelligent face was long and thin, with a nose to match and a flop of lank greying hair. His skin was criss-crossed with deep lines, his eyelids heavy and drooping at the corners, while his forehead was set into a perpetual frown, as if to warn strangers away.

When he began to speak again, there was a rare tension about him which filled Terry with foreboding.

'The place was ransacked. *Their* word. I'm trying to obtain details. To find out whether every room had been searched, every cupboard, whether papers were rifled, or clothing, or everything. At any rate, things were stolen, though they don't yet have a complete list of what is missing. It seems that Ben Galitza has been somewhat difficult to pin down on that score. However, so far as they can tell it was mainly light stuff. Jewellery, ornaments, some silver. There was a small strong-box containing a few hundred pounds in cash, which was forced open.

'Just cash?'

'That is what has been reported to the police.'

'Yes, yes,' Terry gasped apologetically.

'They're not sure what sort of weapon was used to attack Ben Galitza. Some sort of cosh, they think. They haven't found anything resembling a weapon, at any rate not in the house, not in the surrounding gardens.' Fergal's voice took on an abstracted tone. 'They are no nearer to discovering who made the ambulance call either. The ambulance crew didn't get a proper look at the man and he wasn't seen leaving.'

'Presumably, though, they would recognise him again if they saw him.'

'I have no information on that.'

Terry drew in a sharp breath. 'All right, but was anyone else seen leaving?'

'No reports of anyone, no.'

'Go on.'

Fergal fixed his sombre gaze on a point just below Terry's line of sight, and Terry knew that the bad news, whatever it might be, was very close.

'So, we have a burglary, we have a professional break-in. However, the police have reason to think that there was more to it than that. They think the intruder might have selected the Galitzas' home purposely, that he might have wanted to . . . get close to Catherine.' Fergal's eyes met Terry's alarmed gaze and continued stolidly, 'There had been calls for some months, silent calls to her mobile telephone, which cannot be traced. Also' – the hesitation again – 'certain *items* were discovered with Catherine. Close to Catherine.' He proceeded yet more slowly, weighing each word. 'There was a pair of panties . . . found under her head—'

'Her *own*, you mean?'

'Possibly. But not the ones she was wearing at the time. Her clothing was intact. No, the police are thinking that these panties might have been acquired from upstairs. Part of the burglar's haul, if you like.'

Terry repeated incredulously, 'His *haul* . . .?'

'We have an unbalanced person here,' Fergal informed him sternly. 'Someone who has broken in with the intention of thieving – no doubt about that – but also of getting some vicarious thrill from being near Catherine, from acquiring her underclothing. Are you with me now?'

It was several seconds before Terry managed a feeble nod.

'It was one of the ambulance crew who noticed these panties under her head. He pushed them aside when he fitted the collar to her neck and the police picked them up later. If you can imagine her lying on the hall floor with her head over to one side, to the left, then the panties were found between her ear and the floor. The thought is that these panties were placed against her ear to staunch the bleeding.' He held up an index finger as if to admonish himself. 'I should have mentioned that she was bleeding from her ear when they found her. I didn't mention that, did I? No . . . Well, she was bleeding quite profusely. Subsequently, tests have established that this blood on the panties was indeed Catherine's.'

'So it could simply have been someone trying to stop the bleeding?' Terry argued hopefully. 'Nothing sinister at all?'

'It *could* have been, yes.' But his tone suggested a very different tale and Terry prepared himself for whatever was still to come.

Fergal's expression darkened. 'Later on, when she arrived at the hospital, a scarf was found. A lady's silk scarf.' He looked down, his voice grew flat and urgent. 'It was found bundled up inside her skirt. Between her legs. This scarf had more blood on it.'

Terry stared at Fergal, groping for understanding. 'You mean she was *attacked*?'

'There was no evidence of that, no. There was no obvious source for the blood, you see . . . in that place. Besides which – most significantly – the blood was not Catherine's.'

Again Terry was floundering. 'Not Catherine's?' he repeated stupidly. 'But . . . You mean . . .' Fear lurched in his stomach.

'The blood was old. It belonged to a woman. They are thinking that it might have come from another victim of this attacker.'

It was all too much for Terry. Shuddering, he pushed himself back in his chair and pressed his hands over his face. 'Jesus, Jesus.' Among the conflicting thoughts that collided and jostled in his mind, one terrifying notion came roaring to the fore. Dropping his hands, he began urgently, 'Have they considered the possibility that—'

'No, we are not having random thoughts on this. This is the police, remember? They only know what they know. For the moment it has occurred to them to check the scarf, to find out if it belongs to Catherine. It does not. And if they have not already done so, they will check the DNA on the scarf against the national DNA data bank. They will check known offenders, discover who might have been in the area without an alibi. Then . . .' He lifted his shoulders, he spread his hands.

'But where will it lead, Fergal? That's the thing. Where will it end?'

He blew out his cheeks. 'At a guess? I would say that it will go nowhere. That in a month or so when they have failed to find a suspect they will wind the investigation down.'

Terry asked unhappily, 'And what will we do when that happens?'

Fergal's steady gaze contained a warning. 'We will do nothing.'

Terry wrestled with this idea, and finally submitted with a long sigh. 'If we must.'

With a last cautionary frown, Fergal pulled a small notebook from his breast pocket and flicked through it. 'So . . . the rest. Nothing more on Ben Galitza. He's generally regarded as a bit of an operator, but good for his debts. A big spender, but not thought to have any serious money worries. Seen as on the up and up, destined for bigger and better things, though likely to sail close to the wind with the regulations, tax laws, etcetera. Some people regard him as a one-man band – seem to be unaware of the partnership with Simon Jardine. Others say it's the link with Jardine that's the key to Galitza's success, Jardine being the money man, the steadying influence.' He looked up. 'That's about it. Unless you want a deeper look.'

Again Terry was uncertain. 'What about surveillance?'

'That all depends on what you are expecting – or hoping – to find.'

'I don't really know.'

'I think that rather answers your question then. Surveillance is very expensive and if you're not sure what you're after, then you could be talking weeks and weeks.'

Terry was already nodding rapidly. 'You're right. Forget it.'

Fergal produced a sheet of paper and slid it across the desk. 'The address of the spinal unit. I don't yet have the room number.' He looked at his watch, keen to get away. He had an invalid mother in a nursing home somewhere near Malahide whom he came back to visit once a fortnight.

Terry indicated one last question. 'I'm using Cintel for a job in Warsaw. Their man there is called Malinowski – do you know him? Is he all right?'

If Fergal was curious about Terry's interest in Poland he gave no sign. 'In my day Malinowski was a freelance,' he said. 'Mixed Cintel work with journalism. But solid, I'd say. Yes, solid.'

After he had gone, Terry went and stood at the window that overlooked the Liffey, his habitual retreat in times of crisis or distraction. The sky was dark with unshed rain, the water had taken on a benign silvery sheen, and on O'Connell Bridge two garishly painted tourist coaches were caught in the traffic. His eye strayed to the south bank and the top storey of The Kavanagh. Built from the shell of a former bank headquarters – appropriately the bank he himself used – the project had consumed his life for over two years. He had been obsessed by the determination to get it finished on schedule. In the event it had opened only two weeks late, which was no mean achievement in boom-time Dublin. But already the struggle seemed remote, the obsession curious and the duty he now owed the place oppressive, like a marriage after the passion has died.

Restlessly he went back to his desk and scooped up the Cintel report. He went through it once again, but found nothing he hadn't gleaned at the first two readings. Ben Galitza had been involved in protracted negotiations to buy some generators but the deal had collapsed for no apparent reason. One of the leading Warsaw-based speculators claimed to have been cheated over the lost deal but, coincidentally or not, he was locked in a power struggle with a rival for control of two vodka distilleries. Was this struggle connected? Who had ownership of the generators, or actively controlled them? Were they still for sale, or had they gone to another buyer?

Terry drafted a fax to Malinowski. He began with three questions: *Where are the generators? If they've been sold, who bought them? If not sold, why were they withdrawn from sale?* He knew there was something else he should ask but uncharacteristically it took him some minutes before he pinned it down and added a fourth question. *Has Galitza got involved in some other deal?* And still he wasn't ready to hand it to Bridget for transmission. There was something more, something obvious, which hovered stubbornly out of reach. He nursed several ideas and rejected them before it finally came to him. He grunted with satisfaction. He extended the last question to: *Has Galitza got involved in some other totally separate deal? Or has he done a secret back-door deal for the generators?*

For lunch he stayed at his desk and had a chicken salad with oil-free dressing and a glass of mineral water: part of a new regime to smarten up his waistline and his life. To the same end, he phoned Dinah and apologised for not having been in touch. She was sweet and understanding as ever; from her tone he might have dropped out of her life for two days rather than two weeks. He felt humbled by her seemingly endless capacity for forgiveness, and perhaps rather daunted by it too, though he quickly rejected this thought as negative and unworthy. No, he was lucky to have her, and it was high time he realised it. She would be good for him, he was mad not to grab her while he still had the chance. Feeling a little happier at this thought, he invited her down to Morne for Saturday evening with the understanding that she would stay on until Sunday night.

In the afternoon he chaired two meetings whose proceedings he first hurried along mercilessly then virtually ignored, so that no one was certain that the decisions he'd forced through with such despatch would survive the week.

It was a Thursday and, though Terry had decided to take a long weekend starting at four, he was still in his office at ten past, journeying back and forth through Fergal's report in his mind, one minute tormented by the possibility that he had missed something, the next racked by the possibility that he had not.

Finally he snatched up the phone and called Bridget in. 'Three years ago when I had dealings with Ben Galitza he had a girlfriend called Rebecca Child,' he told her. 'We all went to the Curragh together.'

'I remember. It was the Derby,' Bridget confirmed.

'I need to speak to her. Can we find her number?'

'Do we have an address?'

'London, I would think.'

Bridget pursed her mouth. She liked a challenge but only when she thought she could pull it off.

Terry said, 'I think she married.'

Bridget lifted one eyebrow. 'Well, that narrows the field.'

'There might be something in a British newspaper. If I remember, she married into a prominent Jewish family.'


Terry took the slow road to Morne because the main road would be busy and he liked the idea of driving Maeve in a leisurely fashion, with the radio on and Conn's broad head blocking the rear-view mirror, just like a regular family. The rain that had been threatening all day finally came on at six but obligingly fell all at once, so that by the time they were entering the Slaney valley the clouds were evaporating fast and shafts of golden light were brushing the slopes of the Wicklow Mountains.

Maeve sat quietly for most of the journey, only stirring to change the radio station or take her homeopathic hay fever remedy and blow her nose, but as they approached Morne he noticed that her hands were clenched against her legs and she seemed to be holding her breath. 'Dadda?' she whispered as he glanced across at her. 'Have you thought about . . .'

But her soft words were lost under the music. Hastily he reached forward to turn the radio off. 'Say again, my darling.'

She hesitated, as though she had suddenly thought better of the idea, and he laid an encouraging hand over hers. 'Have I thought . . .?' he prompted.

She took a deep breath. 'Have you thought about . . . who might have done this thing to Catherine?'

Now what in heaven is all this about? he wondered. What on this earth is going through her head? Deliberately choosing to take the question at face value, he said, 'It'll be a habitual thief. Young, probably on drugs, undoubtedly from a deprived background. In fact, your average criminal.'

'You don't think . . . it was someone who was trying to harm her?'

'What? You mean, *intentionally*?' He swept this idea aside with a sharp exclamation. 'No, I don't! No! Goodness! Why would anyone want to do that?'

'Or Ben?'

'What do you mean *Ben*?'

'Setting out to harm Ben but ending up hurting Catherine instead.'

'No, my darling! There's nothing to give an inkling of a thing like that. Goodness!' His laughter sounded unnatural. 'No, it was this fella barging his way out, that's all! In a panic at being discovered. A thief who found someone in his way!'

Maeve was frowning.

'No,' he hastened to reassure her again, 'it was a truly terrible thing to happen, of course it was! But it was an accident, my darling girl. Just an accident. Now, don't go thinking anything else. Don't go worrying yourself.'

She looked down at her lap, she flexed her hands. He sensed some deep reservation.

'There's no doubt about it, my darling. Cross my heart.'

Her eyes came up to his face.

He declared again, with a false laugh, 'Cross my heart!'

He was aware of her watching him for some time before she nodded, just the once, very slowly.

He cried brightly, 'Now, look – we're almost here!' They were entering the lane that twisted up through pastureland and tall hedgerows towards the groves of oak and beech that concealed Morne from the east. 'Just look at this summer! Just look at the trees! Have you ever seen them so heavy and so green!' He laughed with a joy that was only a little forced. 'I do so love this place! I do so love it here!'

'I loved Creagh,' Meave said in the voice of a child. 'Why didn't we stay at Creagh? Mamma had made it so fine.'

He kept a judicious silence. Creagh was the small house in an unprepossessing Dublin suburb that he and his late wife had bought in the first years of his success and subsequently built on to a couple of times with less than satisfactory results, before giving up on the place and moving to Foxrock. If Maeve felt a sense of loss he felt sure it was not for the house itself but for her mamma, who had died of a thrombosis when Maeve was thirteen, and for the difficult motherless years of her adolescence.

'Creagh was a good house,' he said at last. 'It did us well, no doubt about that. But you just wait until Morne's finished. Wait until the garden's planted and the decorating's done. It will be the finest place you ever saw.'

'Oh, Dadda,' she said with a weary shake of her head, 'but you'll never finish it, will you?'

This accusation took him aback. 'Good heavens, of course I will!'

'You've hardly started as it is.'

'The roof is insulated. And the windows all repaired.'

Maeve continued to shake her head. 'You'll never finish.'

He was still smarting at this curious and unwarranted remark when they turned in through the latticed iron gates of Morne.

With the demise of the rhododendrons the narrow winding drive had lost much of its capacity to tantalise and enthral; the house was now clearly visible over the inglorious tangle of roots and stumps. Yet, for Terry, it remained a stirring sight. Architecturally the house was nothing exceptional, indeed many would judge it excessively plain compared to the other landed houses in the neighbourhood. It was a two-storey oblong, two windows either side of the front door and five above, with a grey pebble-dash exterior and grey slate roof, and at the back, a small wing, two-up two-down, while across a cobbled court-yard were a number of dark outhouses and stabling for four horses. For Terry, the excessive simplicity of the frontage was redeemed by the long sash windows that reached almost to the ground, and the pillared portico that guarded the glass-panelled door, and the flowering creepers that adorned the grey façade, the whole given life and grandeur by the frame of splendid trees, yew and cedar to the left, oak and beech to the right. The house had four bedrooms, including one in the wing, and two ancient bathrooms with large-bore plumbing that rattled and sang, and a kitchen that had been poorly modernised in the sixties. It was a modest house for a rich man, but grand enough for him.

Would he ever finish doing it up? Did he want to? Had Maeve touched on some unexpected truth? Standing in front of the house, he surveyed the unkempt garden, the nettles footing the courtyard wall, the brambles fanning out from behind the outhouses, the weeds peeping through the gravel on the drive, and tried to picture the place as it would be once he'd got to grips with it, and though he couldn't quite visualise the flowers and shrubs that might come to be planted, he had no trouble in seeing the garden as an ordered place with neat beds and clipped hedges and smooth grass. It would happen in good time, once there was a plan.

'We'll see!' he said to the garden in general. 'We'll see what Mrs Kent says!'

Inside, the house had a musty unused smell, and he was the first to admit that the paintwork was shabby, the walls peeling in odd corners, and one of the kitchen units was losing its door. But he'd held back on repainting, just as he'd held back on the curtains and carpets, until he'd decided how to tackle the house as a whole. This was reasonable surely? This didn't imply a lack of will? The Langleys had left nothing behind, not a curtain, not a scrap of carpet, not a working light bulb. Having to start from scratch in this way it would have been easy to employ someone like Dinah, to give the place a 'look', but while he wasn't bothered by the tarting and titivating being visited on the Dublin house in the name of interior design, he baulked at the thought of imposing such ideas here, where such luxury and artificiality would be an affront. He wanted everything in the house to look natural and – the word came to him – timeless, and when he saw a way to achieve this, it would be done. If that was a sorry motive, he was guilty as charged.

So for the moment rugs covered odd sections of the floorboards, while the windows relied on shutters or cheap curtains. For furniture he'd bought a few antiques through a dealer employed on one of his hotels, he'd picked up an old pine table and chairs for the dining room from a shop in Cheltenham, and had chosen two new sofas and easy chairs to stand in the long living room which ran the depth of the house. The sofas and chairs weren't right, he knew that. For one thing, they looked too modern; for another, they all matched, something you never saw in old houses. But, as with everything else, he wasn't in a mind to do anything about them quite yet.

He might have been slow with the decorations, but he was quick to maintain the fabric, and while Maeve went to the kitchen to unpack the food he made a round of the place, inspecting stone, brick, pointing, slates, gutters, paths; anything that might be in need of the odd spot of repair.

This was an old routine; it had been his job as a kid, to fix everything at Morne. It had started when he was thirteen and Lizzie, alone for much of the time with one baby and another on the way, had needed someone to clear the snow. He'd resisted going, he'd found every excuse – these were Anglos after all, and Mr Langley the worst sort – but he'd needed the money and it was only the once, he'd told himself, on account of the snow. Ten years later he was still turning up almost every Saturday, even after he'd established his own building company, and started the first of his pizza restaurants.

It had been Lizzie he'd kept coming back for, of course. Her talk, her reading, her encouragement, her joy in friendship, which, he understood much later, was underscored by the strains of her marriage. It was she who'd bribed Terry to go to school, who'd cajoled him to do his homework, who'd declared him capable of conquering the world, and at some level he must have believed her because here he was, somewhere near the top of the muck heap. Why had she chosen to have faith in him? Why had she bothered? She used to say it was the challenge, but really it was the goodness of her quiet and unassuming heart.

Nowadays the study was the one room at Morne where he felt a little less like a visitor. It was a small west-facing room in the back extension, looking on to the terrace and lawn, with the avenue of yews beyond, and pasture and woodland in the distance.

Two years ago when he'd first acquired the house, he'd installed a desk, a chair and a couple of side tables in here with the idea of making it his workroom, a study in the strict sense of the word. Then, finding that he was spending much of his time here, he'd had the chimney reopened and added armchairs on either side of the fireplace. In no time a television and books had followed and, though the room was cramped and the desk squeezed into one corner, it was at least a cosy space that he could call his own.

Now he opened a window to let in the evening air and poured himself a stiff Jameson's while he picked up the messages that Bridget had left on his answering service. Her voice hummed with satisfaction when she announced that she had found a phone number for Rebecca Child, whose married name was Wiseman.

Terry settled himself at his desk and took several more sips of whiskey before dialling the number in London.

It rang for some time before an answering machine picked up with an announcement delivered by a cool female voice that he did not immediately recognise as Rebecca's. He was just about to put the phone down with the idea of calling later when the tape was interrupted by a sharp 'Hello?'

'Is this Rebecca Wiseman?'

'It is.'

'This is Terry Devlin.'

'Well, well!' she laughed. 'Hello, Mr Terry Devlin. Where are you – Ireland?'

'I am.'

'*Pity!* Otherwise I'd say let's meet for a drink!' The merriment in her voice, the slight blur to her words, made him suspect that she had started the party without him. 'Now how are you, Terry?'

'I'm not complaining. And how are you, Rebecca?'

'Ahh.' The sound drew out into a lingering lament. 'Married on the rebound, repenting in the lawyer's office. I'm getting a divorce.'

He tried to think how long it had been since she married. Two years? 'I'm really sorry to hear that.'

'I told myself I was doing the sensible thing, Terry, getting married. I told myself we had everything in common. Background, religion, interests. There was only one problem.'

'You didn't love him?'

'No passion either. And at the end of the day, there's got to be love or passion. If you don't fancy someone, you can't pretend. At least I can't.'

'No sticking it out?'

'I wish. But we can't all be good Catholics, Terry, not like you lot. For me, it's a case of one life, one chance. I want another shot at it. All or nothing.'

'Well . . . I wish you the best of luck.'

'Not free yourself?' There was a raunchy note to her voice.

He laughed. 'More trouble than I'm worth.'

'It was Ben,' she said in a voice suddenly drained of humour. 'If he hadn't dumped me quite so massively . . . I wanted to show him, you know? I wanted him to realise I could find someone else, snap of the fingers, no problem at all. Oh—' She pulled up short. 'You've heard about his wife?'

'I've heard.'

'Terrible.'

'Yes.'

'I only met her the once, you know.'

'Yes.'

He needed no reminding of that day; it was emblazoned on his memory perhaps even more vividly than on Rebecca's. It was the day of the Irish Derby, the day that Ben had met

Catherine for the first time, and Rebecca had lost him. And, God save his soul, it had been Terry who'd introduced them.

'In fact it was Ben I was calling about,' Terry admitted.

'Ben? Oh for God's sake, Terry – I haven't seen him since we bust up.'

'Ah. I thought maybe . . . You're not in touch with anyone who knows him?'

'Hardly,' she scoffed. 'I made our friends choose when we split up – him or me. There was no fence-sitting, not the way I felt about things. No, if I hear about Ben at all nowadays – which I try not to – it's third-hand.'

'Ah. In that case . . .'

'Why're you asking, Terry? Come clean!'

'I just wondered how things were with Ben, that's all. What he was up to.'

'What – work? Money?'

'An overall picture – anything, everything. Money. Work. Life.'

'Life . . .? *Oh.*' It was a knowing sound. 'You mean, is he playing away?'

'I suppose that too, yes.'

'Shit, Terry, you're asking me what men like Ben get up to when their wives are unwell? Like I'm an expert or something?' She guffawed at the thought. 'But you still haven't told me – why the interest? He hasn't gone and got himself on the wrong side of you again, has he?'

'Something like that.'

'Well, *well*! You'd think he'd have learnt the first time round. You'd think he'd know it was mad to tangle with *you*, Terry! But then he was never too bright about that sort of thing, was he? Look, I wish I could help . . .' He could almost picture her lifting her shoulders in one of her more expansive gestures.

'Well . . . if you hear anything.'

'*If I hear!* You're a funny one. But I'll say yes to dinner when you're next in London.'

'I'll call you.'

'Promise?'

'It's a certainty, Rebecca.'

Ringing off, he poured himself another whiskey and saw again the day three years ago when he'd invited Ben and Rebecca to the Derby. Strange the details that had stayed in his mind: the stillness of the air, the sunshine falling on the women's hats, the pretty blue dress Maeve had been wearing. He remembered thinking what a fine couple Ben and Rebecca made, how well suited they seemed, how much he liked her. Over lunch, mellow with champagne, he remembered feeling something close to contentment, with his business going well, and Maeve by his side, a picture at seventeen and not a care in the world.

After the second race the four of them had decided to wander down to the paddock. Had it been his idea? It hardly mattered now. There was quite a crowd below the stand, Terry took the lead as they eased their way through the mob. He paused to greet one or two people, turned to wave to someone in the distance and swung back to find Duncan and Catherine standing in his path. It was the first time he'd seen Catherine since the episode with the letter more than a year before. Time had done nothing to protect him from the lurch of mortification he felt at the sight of her. Somehow he managed a smile, a greeting; he bent to kiss her cheek. By some miracle of social programming he remembered to introduce everyone, and without muffing their names either. Ben and Catherine shook hands, said all the mundane things that people say when they are meeting for the first time on a beautiful day at the races. For Terry, the awkwardness seemed to have passed. The two parties moved on, the day sparkled, Terry felt a little easier in his mind. There was nothing to suggest that anything momentous had happened, nothing to suggest that Ben and Catherine's meeting was in any way significant, yet in those few minutes the world had shifted for all of them: by such insignificant events is one's whole future determined. Terry often wondered what direction their lives would have taken if he hadn't invited Ben and Rebecca to the Curragh that day, if instead of going to the paddock the four of them had chosen to visit one of the many boxes to which he had an invitation. But thoughts of that sort were a whip for one's own back, and there was no sense in meting out more punishment.

It was the next evening near midnight, when the whiskey was roaring and chasing through his veins, that Terry began a new letter. *Morne*, he wrote carefully at the top, and *Friday* because he couldn't remember the date. *Dear Catherine, I hope you will not mind me dropping you a line in your new place, but I thought I should report on the visit of the celebrated Mrs Kent. First, may I say that I hope your new place is to your liking and that the staff are looking after you well. If the food is half good and the other inhabitants do not speak unless spoken to I always think one is in with a chance . . .*

*So, Morne received a visit from the illustrious Mrs Kent . . . I have to say that things did not get off to the best of starts when Conn took exception to her. Under normal circumstances Conn is not a partial dog – he would as soon lick an intruder's face as bite him – but for some reason he took against Mrs Kent. Perhaps it was her voice – commanding, I think, would be a fair description – perhaps she had the scent of a Rottweiler on her – we will never know – but he bared every one of his rickety teeth and shivered and shook and generally carried on alarmingly until I hauled him back into the house and locked him up.*

*This counted against me with Mrs K, along, so it appeared, with much else. She is a forceful personage, not so very old in years (forty?) but mature in manner, who carries her knowledge like an encyclopaedia. I went to the bottom of the class because I knew no plant names, had not rooted out the Russian vine that is growing through one of the yews, and had failed to realise that half the fruit trees had canker – or would it be fungus? As for the shrubs that bore the marks of Mick's blunt machete, she said that it didn't terribly matter since they should never have been planted there in the first place (the soil?). She said it was a pity the garden had fallen into such neglect, since some of the best things would be difficult to save. Like what? I asked. Like the avenue and the lavender garden and the rose arches, she said. It was then I began to wonder if we were going to see eye to eye, Mrs K and I. I love the lavender garden, you see. And the avenue, for that matter. And even the rose arches, though I'll admit that they're a little thin and scrawny. Be that as it may, after much tutting and sucking in of breath and looking at the angle of the sun (another black mark – I could not fix on south, let alone east or west), she decided she might, on reflection, advise on a grand plan. She began to describe a few possibilities, but I couldn't take them in – I think I was still smarting from the accusation of neglect (your mamma loved the place a bit wild, didn't she? and I'm sure she was right). However, I've said yes to an outline plan and a few drawings, and we'll see where we go from there.*

He read this through in despair. What would she make of this nonsense? He thought of tearing it up and starting again, but after pouring himself another whiskey he fell asleep in the armchair, to be awoken several hours later, cold and stiff-necked, by the sound of his own snoring. The next morning he signed the letter without reading it through, and posted it in the village before he had the chance to think better of it.

# Chapter Six

———•———

THE MATCH flared in the darkness, illuminating Julie Basing's plump face. Holding the hand-rolled smoke like a peashooter, she lit it with a short puff quickly followed by a second lingering drag. 'Hey,' she murmured contentedly, 'truly vicious.' She held it out to Catherine.

Catherine hesitated before taking it. This hesitation was as much a part of the nightly ritual as her acceptance. Inhaling, she felt her head swim almost immediately. 'Help.'

'Dunno what you been missin' till you get good stuff.'

Catherine passed it back. 'A bit strong for me.'

They sat side by side in a corner of the unit garden, on the farthest loop of the farthest path. From behind them, the lights of the wing cast a feeble glimmer. The night was warm and still. Above the horizon, the sky was tinted a hazy orange from the town, but high over their heads one or two stars were showing through, faint pinpricks in the velvety dome. Catherine watched the steady unblinking dot of a satellite moving mesmerically across the sky towards the mass of nearby trees, which stood like giant sentries, tall and silent and heavy, bowed down by the last heat of the long summer. Even before the first trees began to turn, it seemed to her that she could smell mouldering leaves and woodsmoke.

'I used to love autumn,' she said.

'Nah,' scoffed Julie, 'summer, Spain and sangria for me.'

'In autumn you can plan for the next season. Move plants that aren't thriving. Make good your mistakes.'

'No sortin' my mistakes,' laughed Julie, who at twenty-five

had two children by different fathers and no man to support her. 'You know, this stuff is *truly* great. Why don' I roll you a couple of joints for tomorrow?'

For an instant Catherine was tempted.

'Or you gonna stay ratted all weekend?'

Catherine gave an ironic laugh. 'Why not?'

'Shove some vodka in an Evian bottle, then you can take nips mornin' and afternoon.'

'There'll be champagne, I expect.'

Julie was unimpressed. '*And?*'

'My sister's doing the food so . . . smoked salmon, I should think.' At the thought of the party Catherine felt a fresh stab of apprehension and, against routine and instinct, accepted a second smoke. She took a deep pull, savouring the workings of the drug, the languor, the sense of lightness, most of all the blunting of anxiety, which was like a small but perfect miracle.

Julie leant across and tapped her arm. 'Hey, it'll be okay.'

'I told Ben I didn't want a party.' Catherine saw again his closed expression, the distracted smile, the narrow unresponsive eyes.

'Look at it this way, it's your birthday, and they're just tryin' to make you happy.'

'They'll fuss, I know they will. I'm dreading it.'

'I did, didn' I, first time back.'

'But you knew what to expect.'

'You're kiddin'. Me nan ran about like a strangled chicken, pushin' food at me. Me dad, he kept talkin' to me brother about the Cup, 'cos then he didn' have to look at me an' the big bad wheelchair. And me mum, she just went and cried her eyes out in the kitchen.' Julie had been riding pillion on her boyfriend's motorbike when they'd collided with a lorry and she'd been thrown thirty foot onto a low wall.

Catherine said, 'At least they didn't give you a party.'

'Yeah, well – they're all gonna say the wrong thing. Right? They're gonna treat you like a child. Right? They're gonna say' – she put on a Knightsbridge accent – '*We think you're so*

*marvellous! We think you're so brave!* They can' help it. They
dunno no better. Just sink another dose o' champagne, get
wasted, have a laugh.'

Julie's creed was simple. You made the most of everything
life had to offer and ignored the rest. While this approach left
out too much, it perfectly suited her own stubborn nature and
the philosophy of the spinal unit, which was pragmatic and
upbeat. As if in echo of this, a distant shout of laughter floated
across the garden on the torpid air, followed by a ripple of
good-natured jeers.

On her arrival, Catherine had been quietly appalled by the
quasi-military camaraderie, the blind devotion to sports and
team games, the institutional humour. For some weeks she had
resisted the pressure to join in everything from quiz nights to
group discussions and counselling sessions, where, against all
instinct, you were expected to offer up your most private and
painful thoughts to strangers. Yet before long she too had
succumbed, as all but the most stubborn must succumb,
because in the end it was a relief to fight on only one front at a
time, to be carried along by the routine, the sense of shared
experience, the knowledge that, for what was probably the last
time in your life, no explanations were due. She had responded
to the atmosphere of, if not mutual support, then mutual
resistance, a unifying scorn for the preconceptions and mawkish
sympathies of the outside world, and learnt to joke loudly and
laugh falsely at a great many things that by most standards
were not very funny.

Her family had greeted this flippant mood with transparent
relief and renewed attempts to get her back into the swing, as
they liked to call it. The birthday party was one of their more
obvious tactics. They seemed to believe that social contact, no
matter how superficial, was like good medicine, hard to take at
first, but immensely beneficial in the long run.

'Ben comin' to get you?' Julie asked. 'He could chat up that
boot-faced bint across the corridor again, then we might get a
few more laughs.'

'He's coming at nine.'

'Been away again, has he?'

'Just very busy.'

'He works like crazy, don' he? Least you got that. A bloke who brings home the bread.'

Catherine murmured, 'I'm not so sure.' She said it softly but not so softly that Julie couldn't hear.

The pale disc of Julie's face turned and peered at her in the darkness. 'Not sure, how?'

It was a while before Catherine answered. 'I'm not sure if I've got the bloke, and I'm not sure if we've got any money.'

Julie drew in a long thoughtful breath. 'Ooops. You think he's playin' away?'

Catherine chose her words carefully, and each still felt like a small betrayal. 'I think there are things we need to talk about that we don't talk about.'

'Yeah, well, men never talk, do they, not unless they've got a gun to their heads.' She glanced around again and said in a tone of friendliness, 'Wanna talk about it now?'

'Not much to say really,' she lied.

'Talked to the shrink?'

'He says that Ben's showing the classic symptoms of survivor guilt. Or rather, double survivor guilt, because he didn't manage to protect me, and because it was me and not him who was severely injured. Something like that.'

'What's that got to do with playin' around, for Chris'sake?' Julie declared in a combative tone.

'Ah, well – how did he put it?' Catherine went through the motions of recalling the psychiatrist's argument, though she remembered it perfectly well. 'Dr Fellowes said that when a man's failed in his most basic role as protector it leaves him feeling unworthy and emasculated. And that if he feels bad enough he may go and do things that are out of character.'

'Oh, p-l-ease!' Julie gave a hearty groan. 'So they feel guilty, these men, so it's okay for them to go and fool around. I tell you, if it was a woman they'd say she was a load of rubbish.

Shit, Cath – what I mean is that men get all the breaks. *That's* what I mean. So . . . ol' Shrinko – what's he suggest, then? Therapy?'

'He says I should make it clear to Ben that I don't hold him responsible in any way. That I still respect and esteem him.'

'Yeah, well – so? That's what men want all the time, innit? Respect and no bother.'

Sometimes in her bleaker moments Catherine remembered how Ben seemed to avoid contact with her new body. Occasionally, when she really wanted to torture herself, she thought he was actively repulsed by it. But then, as the group discussions had taught her, there was no state of paranoia from which the newly disabled were immune.

'That Shrinko,' Julie muttered, 'he's a case, if you ask me.'

Catherine said, 'He doesn't rate my own guilt much.'

'What's wrong with it, then? Not good enough, or what?'

Catherine began slowly, trying to make sense of it all over again. 'Ben and I had a terrible row in France. Our first really serious row. I felt it was hanging over us – I *still* feel it's hanging over us. I keep thinking that if it hadn't been for the stupid row the accident would never have happened.'

'What?' Julie gave an exaggerated sigh of disbelief. 'Now, *how* in God's heaven do you work *that* one out?'

'I was going to stay on in France while Ben went to America, but at the last minute I came back with him. Because of the row. You know – trying to make amends, hating the thought of parting badly. But all I managed to do was stir it up again. We had another tiff on the way in from the airport. So stupid – about something so unbelievably trivial—'

'Like what?'

'Oh, about whether these friends we'd been staying with had taken offence at this nickname Ben had given their child.'

'What name d'he call it?'

'Raucous.'

'And was it?'

'Well, yes, it was, but then all small children make a racket, don't they? The point was, it became an issue. So ridiculous! It just made everything worse again. And I just can't get it out of my head that if we hadn't been arguing then Ben would never have stormed up and tried to fight it out with the intruder. He would have called the police or got a neighbour or . . . well, *something* else.'

'Wan' my opinion? Sounds like a load of complete bollocks to me. Men fight. It's in the blood. Can' help it. Every bloke I've ever known has been a fighter, and I'm not just talking push and shove either. It's in their terosterone, or whatever you call it.' She took a second equally unsuccessful stab at it. 'Trerosterone? Anyway – second bloody nature.'

'But he was angry. He was tense. He wasn't thinking straight. If he'd been thinking straight . . .'

'So this makes it *your* fault? Give us a break, Cath! You did *nothin'* that no woman ain' done through history – you had a barny with your old man. What was the big row about the first time, anyway? What was the big tangle about in France?'

Music came on somewhere, a tinny jangle that pulsated across the darkened garden. 'Oh,' she sighed, 'money.'

'Well, that wouldn' be a first either, would it? Men spend, women mend.'

'It was awful. I've never seen him so angry.'

'They never like bein' told they're not safe with money, do they? Can' take it. Never have, never will.' Julie performed her nightly ritual, pinching off the burnt end of the joint and stashing the tiny stub in her tobacco tin. Then, matter-of-factly: 'So now you think you're broke? Broke, like no Caribbean this year? Or broke, like no rent money?'

An aircraft flew so high above that it might have been at the same altitude as the satellite, on the very edges of space. Catherine looked up and thought of the intense phone conversations that took Ben out into the garden for up to half an hour on end when he came to visit, the way he prowled up and down and gesticulated as he talked, and the tension in his face when he returned. She could think of nothing that could put that sort of fear into him but money. 'I don't know. Could be no rent money.'

'You can earn, then,' said Julie sweepingly. 'Go an' do yer gardens.'

'No money in gardens. No real money.'

'Skip away to Ireland, then. That Terry keeps askin' you to do his garden, don' he? An' he's hyper-rich. Sting him for a deadly sum, why don' you? What've you gotta lose?'

This was a subject they had covered several times before. Julie, who was far more sentimental than she liked to pretend, had fallen for the dubious charms of Terry's weekly epistles to the glories of dogs, gardens and rural life, which she stole as soon as Catherine had discarded them.

'I've told you,' Catherine repeated, 'I'll never go to Morne while Terry Devlin's there.'

'But his letters – he's tryin' to be friendly.'

'Ah, but why? That's what you always have to ask – why.'

'Goodness of his heart? Tryin' to make amends for what he did to yer dad?'

'I think not.' She spoke in a tone of great certainty, but in truth she still couldn't make up her mind about the letters, which arrived with unerring regularity every Tuesday and which she had come to read with rather more enjoyment than she liked to admit. Was Terry really trying to say sorry? Or was he completing the reversal of fortunes by taking a paternalistic and patronising interest in her welfare?

'Well, he can' be *all* bad, not if he's stinkin' rich,' Julie declared with her own unanswerable logic. 'Play him at his own game, I say. Take the job. Get him to lay on the private plane, the cars, the whole bit. Make it champagne all the way. Take the money and—' Julie broke off abruptly and turned her head to some distant sound that Catherine had missed. 'Someone callin' for you, Cath.' Swivelling her chair, she added waspishly, 'Well, well, if it isn't your secret admirer.'

Catherine turned herself around and saw a man silhouetted against the french windows. Even before he began to walk towards them she recognised Simon's lean upright figure and stifled a guilty sense of dismay.

Julie said in a low voice, 'Mr Dark Horse.'

'What?'

'Hidden depths. But murky, I'd say.'

'He's been a good friend,' Catherine hissed reprovingly before calling out, 'Hello, Simon.'

'I'm off then,' sang Julie and pushed herself rapidly away.

As Simon stooped to kiss Catherine on the cheek she caught the scent of his aftershave, which still managed to take her by surprise because it was so spicy.

'How are you, Catherine?'

As always he had brought flowers; as always they were white, exotic and almost certainly expensive.

'Thank you,' she said. 'How lovely.'

'And . . . this.' He thrust a slim volume into her hand and said in a breathless excited tone, 'I managed to find a copy!'

She couldn't think what it was, and in the dark it was impossible to read the title. 'Thank you.'

'It's a new edition. They've taken out some of the minor works and added a few more in the name of revisionism. But it's still got the best ones.'

She realised it was a book of poetry he'd talked about, and she in an unthinking moment had said she'd love to read it. 'That's very kind.'

'I hope you don't mind me turning up out of the blue, without letting you know,' he said in his soft deferential voice.

'Not at all.'

It was almost nine and a Friday. Unless he was abroad Simon usually came on Sundays first thing in the morning and on Wednesdays in the evening. Before leaving he would punctiliously arrange the day and time for his next visit.

'So . . .' Catherine stalled immediately. For no reason she could ever identify conversation with Simon did not flow easily. 'Why this unexpected surprise?'

'Have you spoken to Ben today?' he asked.

'No. But then he's picking me up at nine tomorrow. I'm going home for the weekend.'

'Of course. I forgot.'

Simon was not someone to forget anything, however small, and this, along with his unexpected appearance, made her ask, 'Nothing wrong?'

'No, no. I was just passing.' The attempt at casualness didn't come off. 'And . . . well, I've got a bit of news.'

'Good news, I hope.'

'Shall we go inside?'

'Simon! You're making me nervous.'

'Nothing bad, really. It'd be nice to sit somewhere, that's all. Shall I . . .?' He was offering to push her along the path.

They went to a corner of the smoking room, an airless box of a room in the style of an airport lounge with rows of chairs along the walls and bright overhead lights and coffee tables patterned with rings and cigarette burns. The place was empty except for a couple of girls puffing greedily under an anti-smoking poster.

Simon moved a chair round, positioning it at a precise angle to her wheelchair before sitting on the edge and leaning forward with his elbows on his knees. As always he was smartly dressed, wearing a light grey Italian suit with a deep blue shirt and silk tie. His dark hair was sleek and newly combed, his small rimless spectacles flawlessly polished, his tapered hands exceptionally white and soft-looking. She had long since guessed that he spent time grooming himself in the Gents before coming in search of her.

'Well?' she prompted lightly.

'First, how are you?' he asked, his eyes fixed hungrily on her face. 'How's the physio going?'

'Oh, I've finally understood how one can be driven to kill. The physios are deaf to shouts of pain.'

He examined her face carefully to gauge her mood before deciding to smile. 'But . . . progress?'

'It's better than sitting on my bum all day.'

Catherine had been lucky, her spinal cord was only partially severed. On a good day, which meant a day when the physios managed to goad her sufficiently, Catherine could manage one or two uncertain steps on callipers and crutches, rolling along like a caricature of a peg-legged sailor. The physios had promised that with 'just' a few more weeks' work she'd be able to manoeuvre herself quite a distance, still with callipers and crutches of course, and on surfaces that were hard and level. For uneven surfaces however, pavements, shops, the outside world in general, wheels would have to remain what they termed the 'chosen' form of transport, at least for the moment. Either from ignorance or tact, no one had suggested how she was going to get around gardens yet.

'And the new callipers?' Simon asked conscientiously. As always he forgot nothing.

He listened to her report with a loyal smile, and she remembered how strained his smile had been when he'd started visiting her almost three months ago, how his cheek used to flutter so violently that he would turn away to hide it, and how very wearing she had found him in those days, with his overwhelming attentiveness, his intense desire to please. At some point, thank heaven, he must have puzzled over the tension he seemed to engender in her and finally understood that he must pull back a little, he must have realised that even the best-intentioned concern must have its limits, because as the weeks had passed he'd moderated his attention, or at least concealed it. He'd learnt to laugh with something like spontaneity, to give the appearance of being at ease, he'd learnt not to scrutinise her every move, though nothing, it seemed, could ever quite dislodge the watchfulness from his dark steady eyes. It was as though he felt the need to remain constantly alert to the dangers of misunderstanding or misjudgement.

At first she could only get him to talk about his social life, the films and plays he'd seen, the charity dos he'd attended. He took peculiar pride in these activities, he talked about the famous names he'd met, as though this proved his credentials as a gregarious member of a racy crowd, which only made her suspect that he was rather lonely, an impression borne out by his mention of numerous girlfriends, but no one in particular.

Having exhausted his social life the conversation would often flag, and once, when the silence had stretched out longer than normal and Catherine was feeling unusually irritable, she'd turned to the subject she had been warned to avoid. She asked him about his background.

The effect had been unexpected. It was as though he'd been waiting for her question, had even prepared for it. With a slow nod and a glimmer of anticipation, he'd proceeded with solemnity to tell her that his paternal grandparents had been German Jewish immigrants, who'd settled in Manchester before the war. Simon's father had been the youngest of their six children. Simon had lost contact with him years ago, but believed he was running a business up north somewhere. Simon's mother was living with a sister who ran a clothes shop in Chigwell. His mother had grown up in Ilford in Essex, the daughter of a trade union official. She had gone to the Royal Ballet School on a scholarship and become a star of the Ballet Rambert – a fact Simon recounted with immense pride – until she gave up the touring life to have Simon, her only child. She and Simon's father had split up when Simon was four – acrimoniously, Catherine gathered – and Simon had lived with his mother in a small flat in Islington – 'not the smart end' – until he won a place at the City of London School, when they had moved out to a flat in Manor Park. Reading between the lines, Catherine guessed that the move to Manor Park had been forced on them by lack of money, and that for Simon's mother life as a jobbing dance teacher had been an unwelcome comedown.

In a further show of confidence, unprompted but not, she felt, unrehearsed, Simon had told her with a kind of offhand bravado that did not sit easily on him that he'd been unhappy at school, unhappy at university and only started to enjoy life when he'd qualified and begun to make money. 'I realised money was the way out,' he'd declared. '*The greatest of evils and the worst of crimes is poverty.*' He'd laughed, though she'd sensed that for him it wasn't much of a joke.

Over the weeks, Simon continued to volunteer more particles of his history like precious gifts, given willingly but also with some anxiety as to how they would be received and safeguarded. She couldn't imagine why he was so sensitive about his past. It couldn't be his origins, not in an era when it was entirely fashionable to have poor immigrant grandparents, nor his schooling, which had taken him to Cambridge and a law degree. His parents, then? If so, Catherine guessed it was his mother, whose life story seemed to have stopped some ten years ago when she'd gone to live with the sister in Chigwell. Though Simon clearly loved and admired his mother, he never talked about her in the present tense, nor explained how she passed her time, except to say 'quietly'. Catherine imagined Alzheimer's or mental illness.

This, then, was the uncertain basis of their unlikely relationship: medical updates, social reports and occasional confidences. She would have hesitated to call it a friendship, she wasn't even sure why she'd let the visits drift on week after week. Possibly because he made few demands on her, possibly because for all his awkwardness she felt oddly comfortable with him. If she'd stopped to wonder why he should want to come and see her quite so often, she would have put it down to his nature, which would always search out some cause to which he could offer his rather dutiful brand of devotion.

Only once had he unnerved her. 'Do you believe in fate?' he'd asked one evening. 'I don't mean in the Buddhist sense. Rather the coincidental sense. The belief that coincidence signals and determines our destinies.'

'That depends on the kind of coincidence. Nice ones, yes. Nasty ones, it's all a horrible plot.'

'I mean certain . . . *bonds*. Certain connections. You don't think they're significant? That they indicate a predisposition for two people to meet?' He was strangely agitated, his voice breathy and rushed, his mouth jerking slightly as he talked.

'It all seems like chance to me, how people meet.'

'But take *us*! You don't realise, there's no way you could know – there's a bond between *us*!'

'There is?'

'I've never told you before!' He almost lost his nerve then. He said with a false laugh, 'You're going to think it's stupid.'

'Try me.'

As so often before, she felt that it took an enormous effort of faith for him to voice his more private thoughts. 'My family,' he said at last with a gasp. 'When they came over from Germany – well, their name was Gartenbauer!' He watched eagerly for her reaction.

Catherine got half way there. 'Garden. Garden-*something*.'

'Garden builder!'

'Oh.' Now she was beginning to see. 'You mean – like me.'

He nodded happily, with a wide almost ecstatic grin. 'Both of us – garden builders!'

'But you became Jardine?' she asked, more to move the conversation along than from any real curiosity.

'Oh, my grandfather was all for anglicising the name to Garden, but my grandmother thought something French-sounding would be more distinguished.'

'Coming from Germany, was your grandfather interned during the war?'

She had startled him completely. 'Yes,' he whispered, and again the strange ecstasy came over his face. 'Yes ... You knew.'

'I guessed.'

'That's what I mean – you're intuitive.'

'I wish,' she said, making light of it. 'Most of the time my intuition is precisely nil.'

'But there's intuition between *us*, isn't there? That's what I mean – a bond. Garden builders!'

She smiled and looked away.

'I can't talk to anyone like I talk to you, Catherine.' When she looked back, his eyes were hard and bright and needy.

'What about girlfriends? Isn't there someone special?'

A defensiveness came over his face. 'No one special, no.'

'One day, though.'

'I don't know. I think my standards are too high.'

'Ah, women don't suit pedestals. Too easy to topple off. I come off mine almost instantly. With Ben I think it was the third time we met when he found me picking some rough bits off my feet.'

With that, the strange intense moment had passed.

Watching him now, though, she saw the same tension in him, like a charge of electricity.

'So, what's this news?' she asked.

He sat upright and fixed her with his dark damp eyes. 'I wouldn't bother you with this, not tonight, but I wanted you to hear it from me before you heard it from – anyone else. I couldn't bear it if you thought the wrong thing, Catherine. I really couldn't bear it.'

It was the hint of supplication in his voice that always jarred slightly, the invitation to be liked. She smiled quickly to reassure him.

'You see, I wouldn't want you to hear anything that wasn't entirely . . . *accurate*.'

She urged him forward again with a nod.

'The thing is . . . with enormous regret . . . I've made the decision to leave RNP. The fact is that Ben and I have ceased to pull in the same direction. In fact, it's been wrong for a long time. It's got to the stage where we'd be better off on our own. I'm deeply sorry, Catherine. Believe me.'

He had spoken in the hushed tones of someone imparting momentous news, and Catherine found herself replying with equal gravity. 'I'm sure Ben will be very sorry to lose you.'

The dark eyes did not leave hers. 'Obviously, if there had been any way of avoiding it, I would have moved heaven and earth. You know that. *Heaven and earth*, Catherine.'

'These things happen.'

'It wasn't lack of trying.'

'No, I understand.'

'Really?' His anxious gaze searched her face, looking for confirmation or reassurance. 'And I'd like you to know that it was no split-second decision. It's been obvious to me for a long time that it couldn't be made to work. But of course I wasn't going to do anything while Ben couldn't get away, while he was needed here with *you*.' His voice trembled slightly, his expression softened, as though the very mention of her was enough to move him. 'But now that he's back at work, now he's travelling again, I feel that I have no choice, I can't leave it any longer.'

'It's good of you to have waited. I'm sure Ben's very grateful.'

'Good of me?' He recoiled fastidiously at the suggestion. 'It wasn't a question of good. It was the *right* thing to do, Catherine, from every point of view. The *right* thing.'

She thought what a strange unfathomable person he was, so racked by the proprieties of life. There were moments when she felt in awe of his old-fashioned rectitude.

'But now,' he stated with a break in his voice, 'the time has finally come. I do hope you understand, Catherine. Believe me, if there'd been any other way . . .'

'You must do what you must do, Simon.'

He gave his odd breathy laugh, which seemed to jump out of his throat at the most incongruous moments. 'I have to say Ben's pretty angry about it.'

'He probably needs time to get used to the idea.'

'I'd like to think so, Catherine, I really would, but he's saying that I'm in breach of our agreement, that I'm not leaving him enough time to find someone else. But that's absolutely not true. I'm following the terms of our agreement to the letter. I want you to know that, Catherine. You have my word.' He examined her face again, searching for whatever it was he feared to find there. 'He's also accused me of leaving him in the lurch. He says I couldn't have chosen a worse time.'

'There's a lot on?'

'Nothing unusual. No, what he's complaining about is money. Saying we've got no money. But it's simply not true!' he argued vehemently. 'Completely the opposite! Catherine – I've been working flat out for the last four months to get us out of the woods, and now we're there. We're actually there. He's talking nonsense.'

'When you say *there* . . .?'

'Oh, the extra loans have been paid off, the extra overdrafts we took out in March. And we've enough left over to make up our back pay.'

Catherine prompted cautiously, 'But there was a bad patch?'

'Yes, but way back in the winter. *Now* . . . well, we haven't made a packet this financial year, but we haven't done badly either. I don't know what he's on about, Catherine, I really don't.'

'I see,' she said, though all that she saw was that Ben's worries must lie outside the business.

'What caused the glitch in the winter?' she asked after a while. 'Ben never really explained it to me.'

'Ah.' Simon exhaled heavily. 'It was the deal with Polska CMC. Twenty generators. A million quid each. We spent months setting it up and then it just . . . evaporated.' His voice rose at the memory. 'We never knew why. I tried to find out what had happened, I did everything I could to resurrect it, but it'd gone stone cold.' He gave a slow shrug, a lift of the shoulders, an upturn of both hands. 'We put everything into it. The set-up costs were huge, we lost a packet. It's taken all this time to claw our way back. Finally got there with the Bahrain contract. I tell you, Catherine, I've been eating, sleeping, *breathing* the goddam Bahrain contract. But now, at long last, we're there. By the skin of our teeth, I have to say. But we've made it.' He added in renewed indignation, 'And now Ben's saying I'm leaving at a bad time.'

There was nothing she could say to this.

'It's really not fair, Catherine.'

Was he really expecting her to take his side against Ben's? She said non-committally, 'I'll be sorry if you and Ben part on bad terms.'

He leant forward again, his moist eyes glowing with a passionate light. He reached out to touch her hand and she noticed that his own was rigid and trembling slightly. 'I couldn't bear it if you thought I was abandoning Ben at a bad time.'

It was at moments like this that Catherine remembered why she could find Simon rather trying. She gave a minute shrug.

'I rate loyalty above everything, Catherine. If you abandon your friends – well, it's all meaningless, isn't it?'

She nodded in the hope that he would drop the matter, but Simon was not someone to leave a subject before he had made his point.

He said, 'You do understand that I've tried to do everything possible to avoid this?'

She replied with heavy emphasis, 'I do understand, Simon.'

'Really?'

She held up both hands. 'Really!'

'It was just that—'

She shook with sudden anger. 'You don't have to go on! Please don't go on!'

He pulled back sharply as if she had struck him and looked quickly down at the floor, but not before she had seen the dart of injury in his face.

She sighed inwardly. This was the way with Simon, to push too far and then be astonished by the reaction. She muttered, 'I'm tired. It's been a long day.'

His face tightened with remorse. 'Of course. I wasn't thinking. Of course. How stupid. It's late. I should never have . . .'

They both took a moment to recover.

Catherine said, 'I'm sorry. I'm glad you came to tell me. You've been such a good friend . . .'

'No, my fault. My fault entirely.' He offered a soft unhappy smile.

Letting the last of her anger go, she touched his arm briefly and declared brightly, 'Well, then – pastures new for you and Ben!'

He said, 'There's one other bit of news.'

When he hesitated, when his cheek fluttered and jerked, she thought he was still smarting from her rebuke. Nothing in his manner prepared her for what he was about to say.

'The police are questioning someone.'

She stared at him.

'Since yesterday. That's why I asked if Ben had called. I thought he might have told you.'

And still she couldn't speak.

'But, Catherine, he's not the guy. He's just someone who's got caught with some of your property. They'll do him for receiving.'

'Receiving?' she echoed stupidly, as if she were unfamiliar with the term.

'He had a piece of your jewellery on him.'

Catherine had never thought that any of the stolen property would turn up, had never allowed herself to imagine seeing it again. 'What sort of jewellery?'

'A brooch, I think.'

She had only ever owned one brooch, a sunburst in malachite and amber given to her by her mother. She had kept it in her jewellery box in a chest of drawers in the bedroom.

'Who is he, this man?'

'Oh . . .' Simon made a dismissive gesture. 'The police gave minimal details. Mediterranean appearance, aged twenty-eight, I think.'

'And . . . is he known for this sort of thing?'

'They didn't say. But, Catherine,' Simon insisted in his most solicitous tone, 'I really wouldn't worry about it.'

But I do, she thought. This man had handled her mother's brooch, this man had touched her life and brought the burglary back into focus.

Simon leant forward and rested a hand on her forearm,

then after the tiniest hesitation and a quick upward glance, shifted it onto her hand. The coolness of his touch belied the faint dampness on his forehead. 'I'll keep a watch on everything, Catherine. I'll make sure there's nothing for you to worry about. Really – you mustn't give this man another thought.'

She did, though. She thought about him for the rest of the evening and between disturbing dreams and when she woke early the next morning to face her twenty-ninth birthday.

# Chapter Seven

———•———

'NEARLY THERE,' Emma cried rousingly. She was perched in the back of the car, sitting forward with her elbows resting on the two front seats, her head at Catherine's shoulder, a cigarette brandished aloft, within an inch of Ben's head.

Ben drove silently, with concentration. Catherine stared steadfastly ahead. They were passing along Holland Park Avenue, through air hazy with dust and fumes and heat that had gone on too long. On Campden Hill a chestnut drooped in the moistureless air, its outer leaves shrivelled like brown paper, in declaration of an early autumn.

For no apparent reason Emma squeezed Catherine's shoulder.

'We did tell you Jamie and Sue were coming, didn't we, darling? We couldn't leave them out – they just insisted on coming. Wanted to pop in for a quick drink, but in the end – well, we felt we couldn't *not* invite them to lunch. Could we, Ben? But we're still only ten. Oh – maybe it's twelve. Is it twelve?' This addressed to Ben. 'Anyway, darling, it's still nice and small, like you wanted.' Making a futile attempt to blow smoke backwards over her shoulder, she cried, 'But you must tell us exactly what *you* want to do, Cath. Just tell us! We'll kick them all out at two thirty sharp if you need to lie down and rest. Quickest lunch in history. Honestly, darling – the *lot*! You must just tell us.'

They turned into Ladbroke Grove and, cresting Notting Hill, sped down the other side before turning east and crossing the fruit-and-vegetable end of the Portobello Road, which was thronged with stalls and shoppers and bands of shuffling tourists.

'God. Bloody Saturday,' Ben sighed. 'Bloody parking.'

'I found a space in All Saints Road last week,' Emma responded. 'The far end.'

And still Catherine looked ahead. Last Saturday Ben had not come to see her, neither had Emma. Ben, she remembered, had been tied up with a meeting.

'I can go and park the car, if you like,' Emma volunteered.

'Sure,' Ben murmured.

Nearing Westbourne Park, they made the last turn into the street of small stuccoed villas. Catherine registered the bunch of brilliantly coloured balloons attached to someone's front door and dimly attributed them to some kids' party. It was only when they got closer and she picked out the house that she said in cold anger, 'Could you remove them, please?'

Ben slowed the car and double-parked outside. There was a pause in which no one moved.

Catherine stated quietly, 'I'll wait here until the balloons have gone.'

Emma scrambled for her door. 'I'll do it.' She ran up the short path and began to pick at the ties holding the balloons to the door knocker.

Ben offered a rueful expression. '*Not* my idea.' He looked her full in the face, and in the harsh sunlight she noticed that his eyes had grown a web of small lines at the corners, an unhealthy puffiness beneath, and whites that were red from lack of sleep or strain, or both.

She said, 'You look so tired. Have you been overdoing it?'

He gave a short smile and ran his fingers lightly over her hand. 'No more than usual, Moggy. Just a bit hectic, that's all.'

'The business?'

He made a soothing gesture, a slow weave of his hand from side to side, to suggest that he didn't want to bother her with such things.

'You must tell me.'

'Oh, just a small glitch.'

'Is it Simon leaving the partnership? He told me last night.'

'God, no!' he exclaimed derisively. 'No – that's a blessing! He's been a complete pain. A real old woman. No – it's not Simon!'

'Then . . .? Tell me.'

He seemed to come to a decision. Taking her hand, he lifted it solemnly to his mouth and kissed it. 'Nothing I can't manage if you're there to help me through, Moggy. Nothing we can't battle together.'

'But what is it? A deal? A contract?'

He flinched slightly and offered a brave tortured smile. 'Sort of.'

It was a show of defencelessness so uncharacteristic of him that it filled her with alarm. In the same instant it came to her that this had been the reason for the barrier between them. There was no estrangement, it had all been in her head, it was just this bad deal, they were going to be all right. At this realisation something overturned inside her, she felt a wrench of love and longing. 'What is it, darling? You know I'll do anything to help.'

He gave his same forlorn smile. 'Later. We'll talk about it later. As soon as we get a quiet moment.'

'Whatever it is, I wish you'd told me before. Why didn't you tell me?'

He grimaced and gestured impossibility. 'Couldn't, could I?'

'But if you can't tell *me* . . .'

'Didn't want to worry you, Moggy.'

She shook her head gently. 'Oh, Ben. Far better to *know* . . .'

He would have climbed out then if she hadn't reached across and touched his arm. 'We'll get rid of everyone as soon as we can, won't we, darling? Be on our own? So we can talk. I feel we never have the chance to talk.'

Reaching for the door again, he said, 'Sure.'

Like a child, she called after him, 'Promise?'

'Promise.'

While he retrieved the wheelchair from the back, Catherine watched Emma remove the last of the balloons from the door and take them inside. She had loved this house from the moment she and Ben had first seen it. It was narrow and red and gothic, a garish interloper in a sedate low-built terrace of stucco and grey brick. Built in 1896 for the pastor of the Methodist chapel that had once stood in the adjacent street, the house wasn't much bigger than its humble two-up two-down neighbours, yet it dominated the street by the stridency of its red brick, the height of its leaded windows and the precipitous barge-boarded gable end that rose above the smooth line of slate roofs like the prow of a ship. Seeing it again after all these months, a number of images spooled through Catherine's mind: of the rain-soaked day she and Ben had moved in; of the weekend she had planted the tubs with early geraniums, now parched and bent; of a day just before the wedding when she had stood opposite the house and thought: *This is where I will live as a wife – a wife!*

Darker images crowded in from another time, only to vanish as Ben wrenched the door open and reached in to lift her out. He had set up the wheelchair as close as possible to the door, in the gap between two parked cars. Since the road was heavily cambered, the gap between the parked cars not all it might be and this was a piece of choreography they had never tried before, she arrived in the wheelchair at an odd angle with one hip in the air and without her cushion, and with the brake off so that the chair began to roll backwards towards the gutter. In the process of lunging out to grab the chair, Ben lost his balance and, teetering precariously on one foot, almost fell across her, only saving himself by twisting his body round in an awkward jerky motion and throwing his other foot to the ground. For an uncertain moment he hung all his weight on the chair arm. The chair rocked, jolted back, trembled, and was finally still. Ben, pinioned against a Jeep, pushed himself upright, panting hard.

Catherine had long since forced herself to find irony in such situations. She gave a raucous bray of laughter. 'Fuckin' Ada!' she yelped in mimicry of Julie. 'Almost a gonner!'

Ben glared at her in shock and what might have been rage, his skin white, his lips drawn back against his teeth.

'Hey, it's okay,' she said placatingly. 'It's okay.' This was what she always failed to take into account – how even the smallest humiliation cut him to the quick.

Still breathing furiously, Ben squeezed rapidly between the chair and the Jeep and hauled her backwards onto the pavement. As he spun the wheelchair round to face the house Catherine murmured again, 'It's okay,' and reached over her shoulder to touch his hand, but either he'd removed it from the handle or she didn't reach far enough because she couldn't seem to make contact.

A cry and Alice hurried from the house. 'Sorry – on the phone!' She stooped to give Catherine a small hug, a show of affection that by Alice's standards was decidedly effusive. 'Happy birthday!' she cried.

'You look fantastic,' Catherine said.

A small smile of satisfaction twitched at Alice's mouth, she bowed her head in acknowledgement. 'Why, thank you.'

Until now Catherine hadn't appreciated quite how much weight Alice had lost. She was dressed in clothes she wouldn't have dreamt of wearing a few months ago, a skimpy top and tight trousers that emphasised the shape and curves of her new figure. She must have lost two stone, maybe more. Her hair was different too, newly cut and subtly highlighted with hints of amber. Her make-up, rather haphazard in the past, was dramatic and flawlessly applied, as though she'd been taking lessons from a professional. Overall, the effect was of transformation.

Catherine said, 'You're still eating now and again, I hope.'

'In restaurants,' Alice replied archly. 'Still got half a stone to go, though.'

'Don't overdo it.'

'No danger of that,' she declared drily. 'Never too thin, never too rich.'

'You're having a good time, then?'

Out of old instinct Alice bristled slightly – she had always resented family enquiries into her social life – before submitting with an expression of magnanimity. 'Mmm,' she smiled. 'A *great* time, actually.'

As Alice caught some signal from Ben and stepped back to let the wheelchair pass, Catherine thought: She's feeling good about herself. She's probably got a man. She's going to be happy after all.

Ahead, Emma was standing on the threshold, one hand resting on the open door, a broad smile on her face, and now Catherine was overtaken by a more disturbing thought, that Emma was welcoming her into her own home.

Inside, there were rapid discussions about cars, parking and luggage. People hurried about and dispersed, and for a moment Catherine was left alone in the hall.

Flowers stood on the side table, and, propped against the vase, a batch of brightly coloured envelopes, addressed to her. On the wall beyond, a new picture had appeared, a pen-and-ink drawing of a mediaeval street that might have been Prague or Warsaw. In the far corner the work to widen the loo door was evident in the bare patched-in plasterwork and primed but unpainted woodwork. The sixteenth-century blanket chest from Morne that used to stand tucked into the bend of the stairs had been shifted around at right angles until it stuck out beyond the newel post into the hall. It didn't fit in that position, it looked all wrong, but she supposed it had been put there to spare her feelings. According to whoever worked these things out, it was the front edge of the chest that had broken her back, although, in one of the more interesting ironies, it had also in all probability saved her life by breaking her fall and preventing her skull from meeting the stone floor at full force.

Finally she looked up the stairs, which rose with two turns

to the short stretch of railed landing at the top. There was no sign of her fall. The weak rail had been replaced, the splintered banisters repaired. Directly below, the stone was smooth and unblemished. A little closer, however, she noticed a faint mark on one of the flags, a large irregular splodge the colour of tea. Blood? Or an old mark she hadn't noticed before? A memory tugged at her, she looked back towards the still-open door, and, in a faded image like sepia, she saw herself lying here at this spot, her cheek pressed against the flagstone, looking along the distance of the grey surface, out through the door towards the street.

'Champagne? Coffee?' Alice asked brightly, bending forward with her hands propped on her knees. 'Loo? Wash and brush up?'

Catherine usually asked people not to bend over her in the same way they bent over prams and pushchairs because, subconsciously or otherwise, they were apt to speak to her in the same over-precise over-loud tones they used for small children.

'Or guided tour?' Alice continued, like an energetic scout mistress.

'Guided tour?'

'Your new bedroom.'

'I think I can manage that myself, thank you.'

Catherine must have spoken more sharply than she meant to because Alice stiffened and shot upright. 'Of course. I'll leave you to it.'

Catherine hesitated at the door of what in the house's clerical days would have been the front parlour, but which from the first day of their occupancy she and Ben had agreed could only be a dining room. North-facing, noisy and dusty from the street, starved of sun except for a few fragile rays that slanted in on midsummer evenings, it had become a room for late dinners and candlelight, with its dark polished floorboards, rich terracotta walls, large splashy paintings and matt black woodwork and fireplace.

There had been alterations since her accident, but Ben's description had been sketchy and as she wheeled herself in she still wasn't sure what to expect.

The table and chairs had gone into storage. In their place was a bed, a bedside table with phone, and a television on a trolley. The black woodwork had been painted white – hastily by the look of the finish – the floorboards had been covered by a fitted carpet in deep parchment – laid recently from the amount of fluff – while the windows had been hung with muslin day curtains. But it was the bed that drew Catherine's unhappy gaze. It was what the English have the nerve to call a small double, but which by any reasonable standards cannot hold two people in harmony unless they sleep facing the same direction and turn in unison. Catherine told herself that this bed had been chosen because its head fitted neatly against the only available wall space while leaving room for the bedside table on one side and wheelchair access on the other. She told herself that nothing bigger would have been practical, since the window took up much of the second wall, the fireplace the next, the double doors to the sitting room the fourth. Yet even as she tried to persuade herself of this, she saw again the white melamine bedside table, the ugly utilitarian trolley, and, what she hadn't noticed before, tucked away behind the television, a cantilevered table on castors for taking meals in bed, and it came to her in a burst of humiliation that the place had been fitted out for an invalid.

Her mood did not improve when she realised that the rich terracotta walls that had seemed so atmospheric for suppers with wine and candlelight were going to look saturnine and claustrophobic in the cold light of morning, and – if worse were needed – Alice's voice suddenly rang through from the sitting room, each word audible, and she realised that the double doors were going to provide almost no barrier to sound.

In the hall Ben was calling her name. Sweeping in, he cried, 'There you are! Well, what do you think?' Stationing himself in front of the fireplace he surveyed the room as an estate agent might inspect a property that with just a little more attention might yet come up to scratch. 'Not too bad, is it? What do you think about the walls? Could do with a different colour perhaps.' He cast her a hasty smile, which to Catherine in her new mood seemed evasive. 'What do you think? Cream? White? Or maybe some sort of wallpaper? God, I'm hopeless on these things,' he added with the perverse masculine pride that men take in their deficiencies at renovations. 'What do you think, Moggy?'

In the instant before she answered, it occurred to her that she could do this gently, with tact, she could put it in such a way that he would come to understand her slowly and with less chance of taking offence; it occurred to her that only moments ago everything had been mending between them and this might set them back; but it was too late, her anger was too fierce, it carried her forward in a red-hot sea and she said bitterly, 'I hate it!'

'Well, that's what I'm saying – it can be changed—'

'No,' she cut in sharply, 'the *room*. I hate the entire room! Everything about it. Everything! I don't want to stay here – I don't want to be in here at all! I want to sleep upstairs.'

Ben's eyes darkened, his mouth curved downwards. 'But Moggy . . .' He gestured helplessness. 'How?'

'You could carry me!'

'You mean, just for tonight?' The lightness in his voice betrayed a premature relief.

'No, I mean, always,' she snapped, trembling.

He took a long laboured breath.

'Why not?' she cried, hating the petulance in her voice.

'Well, I could carry you up *sometimes*, of course I could.' Appearing to realise how grudging this must sound, he repeated with more enthusiasm, 'Of *course* I could! But what if I wasn't here? You'd be stuck.'

'What about a stairlift? I don't see why there can't be a stairlift!'

'I told you, Moggy,' he explained in a tone of great patience, 'it'd be a complicated business. All the bends, the landings . . . And if we decide to move – well!' He threw up a hand as if the argument were self-evident.

Her heart gave a tight thump. 'But we're not moving. We decided.' She heard her voice rise. 'I thought we'd decided. Hadn't we?' When he still didn't answer, she demanded unsteadily, 'Hadn't we, Ben?'

He muttered testily, 'Sure.'

'Well, then.' She forced a note of reason into her voice. 'You do see, darling, don't you, it'll be hopeless if I can't get upstairs.'

'Stairlifts are expensive, Cath.'

'Well, how expensive?'

'A lot.'

'But how much exactly?'

He dropped his gaze and his jaw tightened.

As the silence drew out, her throat seized, her eyes burnt hotly. 'You said you were getting a quote.'

He didn't like being caught out. His gaze sharpened, his lips compressed. 'There was no point. It was going to be something like six or seven thousand, and the fact is, Cath' – he tipped her an unhappy glance – 'I can't manage that sort of money right now.'

She stared at him. 'You mean . . . that's the reason?'

'Yup.'

'Money?' she asked stupidly, as if he hadn't made the situation perfectly clear.

'If I'd had anything to spare, Moggy, *anything* . . .' He gestured the whole world.

'But I thought . . . Simon said you'd managed to claw back the money, to pay off the overdrafts. He said you were back to where you were before this thing in Poland—'

Ben's anger was very sudden. He held up a splayed hand that trembled visibly, he said in a furious voice, 'This is nothing to do with Simon! How dare he try and interfere! Christ!'

'He didn't. I mean, he just told me that RNP was back on its feet. That's all. Nothing else.'

'He knows nothing about anything!' Ben cut a swathe through the air. 'Nothing!'

She slumped a little in her seat. 'Okay, okay . . .'

For a moment he stood still, locked into his anger. She called his name. When he didn't reply she called a second time and held out a conciliatory hand.

He turned at last and, seeing her hand, came and crouched beside the wheelchair. Wrapping his hand around hers, he smiled with a touch of the old tenderness. 'The thing is, Moggy . . .' He sighed as if he hardly knew how to go on. 'I would have preferred to talk about all this later when we've got more time but since it's come up . . . You don't mind?'

'Don't mind?'

'Talking about this now?'

'No, no,' she said eagerly.

'The thing is,' he said, 'I'm not just a bit short.'

'You mean . . .?'

He hated having to spell it out. He said sharply, 'I'm broke!'

She felt a pull of dread. 'When you say broke . . .?'

'Spectacularly. Incredibly. Completely.'

She gripped his hand more tightly. 'Tell me. How much?'

He gave an odd snort and muttered under his breath something that could have been, 'Bled dry.'

Her bad ear seemed to ring with the effort of trying to hear him. 'Did you say bled dry?'

He held up a hand as if to withdraw the remark, then, rising from his haunches, swung round and sat down on the bed, his elbows on his knees, his hands clasped tightly in front of him. Behind the faint smile that was his mask against all eventualities, his face was pitted with anxiety.

'Got into this agreement,' he said at last. 'Can't get out of it. Got to pay. No choice.' He shook his head slowly from side to side as if he still couldn't believe he had got himself into such a mess.

'How much do you owe?'

'Ah, there we are. It's a nice round two hundred thousand.' He gave a broken laugh. 'No half measures, Moggy!'

There was a long silence broken only by the sound of Emma calling to Alice in the next room, asking about a bowl for the olives.

Catherine was very still, as if this might help her to absorb what he was saying. She must have been holding her breath because she had to exhale suddenly and take a gulp of air. 'God.' And still she couldn't take it in. 'God,' she gasped again. Eventually she managed to say, 'It can't be put off, this debt?'

'No.'

'It can't be – renegotiated?'

He gave a small shake of his head, and there was a glint of brilliance in his eyes.

'But the overdraft – the one you paid off after the Poland thing – can't you go back and rearrange it? Can't you—'

His fury reared up as rapidly as before. The blood rushed into his face, he shook slightly. 'I told you – Simon doesn't know what the hell he's talking about. Overdrafts! For God's sake! Stupid bloody idiot!'

'Can't it – I don't know – be paid in instalments?' She hadn't spoken particularly loudly but Ben flicked his eyes towards the double doors and shot her a furious warning. Catherine closed her eyes for a moment. 'What about instalments?' she repeated in a whisper.

Still in the grip of his indignation, he said tightly, 'No.'

The front door banged, a phone started ringing, voices sounded dimly in the hall. Catherine thought she recognised her father's laugh.

She said, 'But surely they'd agree to—'

'*No!*' he insisted with a small shudder. Then, almost by way of apology, he said bleakly, 'It's already in instalments, you see.'

She felt the blankness come over her that was her protection against bad news. 'You mean . . . there's more to pay?'

'Been paid.'

She went on asking questions mechanically, unemotionally, like an investigator who must collect the facts. 'There've been other instalments?'

He made another attempt at black humour. 'Ah – just a few! Three, actually.'

'Three,' she echoed dully. 'And this one . . .?'

'Is the last.'

'The earlier payments, were they . . .?' Seeing the answer in his face, she turned it into a statement. 'They were for the same amount.'

He held her gaze: it wasn't a denial.

Out in the street a child gave a sudden wail and a father's voice called out wearily.

Some part of her was in free fall, she had to hold herself steady. 'The money so far, how did you raise it? Where did it come from?'

'Oh, here and there.'

'Here and—!' She pulled herself up short. 'Tell me – where?'

'I don't know. Cash. Loans. Overdrafts. Anything I could get my hands on.'

Her calmness finally deserted her. 'But so *much*, Ben! Six hundred thousand! How was it possible to borrow so *much*?'

'Never mind *how* I borrowed it,' he said ominously. 'The point is, I did it. I've managed to pay off three quarters of the bloody debt. Something to be congratulated on, I would have thought!'

There was a pause like darkness.

'But it'll have to be repaid, won't it? How will we ever repay it, Ben? So *much*.'

'Oh, it'll only take a couple of years, maybe less,' he said dismissively. 'I've turned over far more than that before now. I can do it again.'

She was finally reduced to a bewildered silence. He'd never mentioned this sort of money before. He'd always told her that cash was tight.

'In the meantime, I've got to find this last bloody payment,' he said. 'And that's the problem, you see. Run out of people to lend it to me.' He gave a grim chuckle. 'Not much to be said at the end of the day, is there, Moggy? I've really fucked up this time.'

Knowing how proud he was, realising how much this admission must have cost him, she avoided anything that might be taken as a reproach and said carefully, 'There must be something. What about going bankrupt? All sorts of people go bankrupt. In fact, rich people seem to do it all the time.'

'Not an option.'

'But it's not such a dreadful thing nowadays,' she argued lightly. 'It's almost—'

'Just can't.'

She left this alone for the moment. 'All right. So what happens if you don't pay? They can only sue you, surely. And in the time it takes to get to court we might have found some money—'

'No.'

'I don't see why you can't stall them. There must be a way.'

He reverted to a flippant tone. 'Ah, well, you see they're threatening to *tell*. Have me locked up.'

'Locked up? How do you mean locked up?' She laughed nervously.

He threw her an irritated glance, as if she were being exceptionally dense.

There was a rap on the door. Even as her father called her name, she cried, 'Later!' in a fierce voice. She heard his steps shuffle a little before moving away.

She turned back to Ben. 'You mean that they could get you into trouble?'

'They think so.'

'Who *are* these people? How can they threaten you like this?'

He gave a defiant shrug. 'Just people who have come across

something that – how shall I put it? – could be misinterpreted. They reckon I owe them some money and now they want it back. And if I don't give it to them, they'll drop me into what you might describe as deep shit.' He spread both hands, he tilted his head to one side: the storyteller reaching the end of his tale.

She stared at him blankly.

'For God's sake, don't get all disapproving on me, Moggy. I didn't do anything very terrible. Really! Lots of people have done the same. It's just that – well, technically speaking, it wasn't quite . . .' He sucked in his breath.

'Legal?'

He rolled his eyes a little roguishly, like a schoolboy who has been caught out in a misdemeanour but, given half a chance, would commit the same offence all over again.

'What you're saying is that these people are *blackmailing* you?'

He turned this idea over in his mind and agreed without rancour, 'If you like.'

'But who are they, for God's sake? What sort of people?'

'Oh . . .' He brushed this aside. 'Doesn't matter.'

'Doesn't matter?' she whispered incredulously.

In one of his rapid switches of mood, he shot her a look of sudden resentment. 'It's complicated!' he snapped. Scrambling to his feet, he paced restlessly off across the room.

She bit back her thoughts with difficulty. 'So what's to be done?' she said.

He came and stood before her, his arms hanging limply at his sides, back in the role of the lost boy. He made a show of hunting through the possibilities, but she knew what was coming, she knew there was only one option.

In the end it was easier to say it for him. 'The house,' she murmured.

His gaze, the small regretful outward turn of his hands, gave her his answer.

A knock at the door again. Alice's voice said, 'Catherine? Ben? The police are here to see you.'

Ben's head jerked up. He muttered, 'Christ.' Meeting Catherine's eyes, he gave a nervy laugh. 'Thought we'd seen the last of them.'

# Chapter Eight

———•———

'I HAVE to notify you,' Denise began formally, 'that last night we charged a man in relation to your case. The charges are aggravated burglary and grievous bodily harm.'

There was a moment of complete stillness. At some level, far removed from this news, Catherine took in the changes to the living room, the way the sofas had been pressed back against the walls, the arrival of a table lamp she'd never seen before and didn't like, with a tall entwined-metal base and a Japanese crushed-paper shade.

Ben, perched on a chair arm beside her, broke the silence with a sharp explosive hiss, a sound of disgust or dismay. 'Christ!' he muttered weakly.

Catherine was simply lost. 'I thought it was just my brooch. You'd found someone with the brooch.'

Denise's reply was deflected by Ben's insistent: 'Who is this guy?'

'His name is Jan Pavlik, commonly known as Johnny Pavlik.'

'*Pavlik?*' Seemingly unaware that this had sounded like a trumpet of recognition, it was a moment before Ben answered Catherine's searching gaze with a brusque indignant shrug. 'Strange sort of name,' he argued irritably.

Denise said, 'He came from the Czech Republic originally.'

'Don't tell me,' Ben scoffed, 'an illegal immigrant down on his luck.'

'He's an illegal immigrant, yes.'

'Ha!' Ben exclaimed, half surprised at the accuracy of his

own prediction. 'How did I guess? And what else can we surmise?' he demanded sarcastically. 'Seeking asylum? Fiddling the welfare system?'

Quietly ignoring this outburst, Denise looked to Catherine for questions. But Catherine had no questions and no curiosity. The impulse to keep her distance was very strong. It was a matter of self-preservation born out of fear, not of Pavlik directly, but of her own feelings towards him: the fear that she might grow to feel something as exhausting and worthless as hate. Even allowing his name to imprint on her memory was like a small descent.

She would have left Ben to talk to Denise then, but something held her back and she realised she had a question after all.

'Has he done this sort of thing before?' she asked.

'Not as far as we know.'

'He's never attacked anyone?'

'Not that we're aware of.'

'No stalking or anything like that?'

'No.'

Ben interrupted in a tone of aggrievement, 'You never said you'd got a suspect.'

'We thought we just had someone for receiving. Then our investigations led us to realise that we had our man.'

'When did you realise?'

'Two days ago.'

'Two *days*,' he echoed accusingly.

'There was no point in saying anything until we were sure.'

Ben let this go with a sharp frown before asking in a more reasonable tone, 'How long's this Pavlik been over here then?'

'He's lived in London for approximately five years.'

'Age?'

'Twenty-eight.'

'Drifter?'

'No. He had regular work.'

'What sort of work?'

'As a waiter.'

'A *waiter*? Where?'

'Various places,' Denise said, clearly not wanting to be drawn.

'Into drugs?'

'Not that we know of.'

'But theft and robbery and crime, presumably.'

A faint frown sprang over Denise's broad forehead. 'He has no form.'

'But he's not going to be a beginner, is he?'

Denise didn't attempt to answer this.

Again Catherine decided to leave; again something held her back.

Ben asked almost crossly, 'Are you sure you've got the right guy?'

'We feel confident that we have enough evidence to support the charges, yes. We feel confident that the CPS will take the case to court.'

'But what evidence have you got?'

'It's forensic. That's all I can tell you at this stage.'

'You mean fingerprints, DNA, that sort of thing?'

'Well . . .' Denise struggled on that one. 'Loosely . . . yes.'

'And what does this guy say? Does he admit anything?'

'He's denying it, basically.'

'Don't tell me – he was at home with his girlfriend that night.'

'It may well be something along those lines, yes.'

'He's got a lawyer, I suppose.'

'Everyone's allowed a lawyer.'

'But one who knows all the tricks.'

'Most of them know all the tricks, I'm afraid.'

In the small pause that followed, Catherine asked quietly, 'So he was found with my mother's brooch?'

'Yes.'

The thought of avaricious hands on the unassuming amber brooch that her mother had given her at the end of her life was repellent. 'It was worth nothing to him,' she said. 'Not to anyone in fact. Twenty pounds, if that.'

Denise made a sympathetic face. 'You'll get it back after the trial.'

'I won't ever have to see this man, will I?' Catherine said. 'I won't have to go to court?'

'That'll be up to the lawyers to decide, Catherine. Not in our hands.'

Catherine looked away towards the small courtyard garden that she had rebuilt in the early spring, with York stone, raised beds along three walls, and a wall fountain. When she and Ben had left for France the first climbers and perennials had been coming into flower, the garden was showing what Catherine liked to call the first flush of promise. Since then, however, either the watering system hadn't been working properly or Ben had inadvertently turned it off, because many of the plants were missing presumed dead while the remainder were showing all the symptoms of drought and neglect.

'I'm rather cold,' she said. 'I think I'll go and get a cardigan.'

But before she could move, Ben cried, 'I'll go!' as though he'd been itching for just such an opportunity. He was on his feet and out of the door before she had the chance to tell him where to look.

Denise sat forward. 'I know how hard it is to face the business of court and giving evidence, Catherine. But if you do have to attend, I'll be there to see you through. If you like, we can go and look around the court in advance, work out where everyone'll be sitting, what'll happen when you arrive.'

Even before Denise had finished, Catherine had decided she would resist all but the most powerful arguments to give evidence. There was nothing she could say that Ben couldn't say better. He would make a good witness, clear and concise. What was almost as important, it would give him a role. The shrink's words reverberated in her head. *Try to make him feel protective of you.*

Denise added, 'It's hard to face an attacker, but most crime victims find it a lot harder when the offender never gets apprehended, when they have to live with the fact he's still out there, a threat to someone else.'

Catherine thought: Well, if most victims are like that, then I'm the odd one out, aren't I? She said, 'How long before the trial?'

'Hard to say. But months rather than weeks.'

'And until then? He'll be in jail?'

Denise faltered momentarily. 'Could be given bail. Depends on the sort of lawyer he has and the magistrate on the day. The CPS may well oppose bail, but when it's a first offence they don't always win that argument, I'm afraid. I'd be lying if I said they did.' She added hastily, 'If we thought he was likely to be a threat we'd give you protection, Catherine.'

'But you don't think he will be?'

'Nothing to suggest it. DS Wilson and the lads have been through his room. Nothing to show he was a stalker. Nothing to show he'd ever heard of you. So they're pretty confident it was a random attack.'

The dark shadow flickered across Catherine's memory, she saw the advancing figure, the arm swinging rapidly upwards to come down with all its force, and a powerful but unwelcome thought sprang into her mind: He was waiting for me. He meant to come for me. This thought had come to her before a couple of times – if she was honest, maybe a dozen times – but she'd always rejected it, as she rejected it again now, because it was based on nothing more than fear, the irrational rangings of an overcharged imagination.

Denise stood up. 'Well . . .'

Dutifully, Catherine said, 'Thanks for everything. Will you tell the rest of the team that we're very grateful?'

'Sure.' She hesitated in the doorway. 'Nothing else you want to tell me, Catherine?'

'What do you mean?'

'Anything else you remember? Any thoughts?'

'No,' Catherine said warily. 'Why?'

'The phone calls. There's nothing more you can remember about them?'

Catherine maintained her expression. 'There *is* nothing to remember.'

Denise gave a sudden smile. 'Fine. Sorry to have interrupted your birthday, Catherine.'

'Denise?'

She stopped in the doorway.

'The calls weren't from this man. I promise you that.'

Denise greeted this statement with a quick nod. 'Of course.'

Duncan must have shown her out because soon after the front door sounded he put a tentative head into the room and, eyes lighting up, greeted Catherine as he had always greeted her, with a show of joy and unconcealed pride. Like an Italian father, he stood with his arms outstretched, his head at an angle, his face creased into an emotionally charged smile. He bent to kiss her. When he pulled back, his lower lip was trembling slightly. 'Darling girl! The happiest birthday in the whole world to my darling girl! And to be home. At last. *Home.*' He took a rapturous breath, his expression see-sawed between elation and other more lachrymose emotions. Abruptly, he cried, 'Champagne!' and threw a hand into the air, as if to summon a wine waiter. He beamed conspiratorially. 'Nothing less than bubbly will do, eh?'

This rallying cry had reverberated throughout Catherine's childhood, for her father had never needed much of an excuse for a celebration. He loved the ritual of champagne, the weighing of the bottle in his hands, the appraisal of the label – though as Catherine had got older the labels had got brasher and less worthy of reverence – the extracting of the cork, and the pouring of the first glasses. He was never happier than when he was master of ceremonies, setting the whole household into motion, as he did now, calling out to Emma for glasses, to an absent Ben for the ice bucket, to Alice for general unspecified assistance.

Catherine laid a hand on his sleeve. 'I need to find my

cardigan, Pa. I think it's in the front room. Would you take me through?'

'Of course, darling!' He went about the task with all the gallantry of the military man he was frequently taken to be, opening the door with a flourish, skirting back round the wheelchair to push her carefully through into the hall, and executing a neat turn into the terracotta hospital room. Diligently, he asked where the cardigan might be.

'Pa?'

'Darling girl.'

'I was wondering . . . I'm a bit short of money.'

He threw out a hand: a problem easily solved. 'Got plenty! Just been to the cash machine. How much do you need, darling? Thirty? Fifty?'

'No, Pa.' All sort of thoughts went through her mind, of his generosity in small things, of his lifelong difficulties with larger sums, of his old age, not so far away. 'No, it's more – capital. Ben and I find we're rather in debt. It's all been a bit much recently, with all the extra expenses. I was wondering if you could manage a loan. Just for a year or so. Until we can pay you back.'

'Darling girl, you know I'd give you the earth . . .' His eyes travelled the floor. 'The earth.'

'Whatever you could manage, Pa.'

His mouth moved soundlessly, he made a hesitant gesture. 'Would five thousand be any good? I might be able to stretch to six.'

Somewhere, in a foolish and optimistic part of her brain, she'd hoped the restructuring of the wine business might have changed things, that he might have managed to put something substantial in the bank, but history and experience should have taught her otherwise. She mustered a grateful smile. 'That's very kind, Pa.'

He brightened. 'Just wish I could manage more, darling, but you know how it is . . . first the recession, then the pound, then these blasted day-trippers bringing wine in by the van-load.

Company's struggling a bit. But it'll help, will it, the odd five thousand?'

'Yes.'

'You're sure?'

'Thank you, Pa. In fact, we might not even need it at the end of the day. But it's nice to know it's there.'

'Darling girl – *anything*!' He creased up his face into the endearing smile she knew so well.

Seeking reassurance where she could find it, she asked, 'You're all right for money generally, are you, Pa?'

'Me? Oh *yes*, darling. It's never easy, of course, managing to do everything one wants to do in this life. But I'm perfectly content. Got to count one's blessings.'

'No debts hanging over you? No mortgage?'

'No, no,' he cried resoundingly. 'Not a thing.'

He lived in a flat on the southern borders of Belgravia, in what the pedantic might describe as Pimlico. The place was overlooked and dark, the rooms poky, but it was handy for evenings spent at his club in Pall Mall, or as the spare man at dinner parties, for which he was in great demand.

'That business with Terry Devlin, it's all over and done with, is it?'

His face darkened a little. 'Thank *God*. Horrid little man.'

'What happened exactly, Pa?'

He viewed the question with faint disapproval. 'Darling . . . best forgotten, believe me.'

'I'd like to know.'

His expression slowly shifted through one of suspicion to profound alarm. 'You're not thinking of—? You wouldn't—? You don't need money *that* badly, darling girl?'

In attempting to shrug it off, she heard herself laugh falsely. 'No, no. I was just curious, that's all.'

'For a dreadful moment . . .' Grimacing, he relaxed again.

'You always said he'd cheated you. I wanted to know how, that's all.'

'How?' he repeated, looking unsettled again. 'Darling, very

briefly – very simply – he called in the debt when I couldn't pay it, when he *knew* I couldn't pay it. Insisted on taking Morne. What could I do? How could I save it? Had to let it go. Broke my heart, as you know. Poor Mummy – I felt I'd failed her, that I'd betrayed her last wishes, to leave it to you and Alice. To sell if you wished!' He held up a hand as if to deny suggestions to the contrary. 'Oh yes, you could always have sold it – she was quite clear about that. But it was to be *your* decision after I'd gone.' His voice shook. 'But what could I do? He had the deeds of the house as security and when I couldn't pay he made me sign them over to him. It wasn't in the spirit of the agreement. Wasn't cricket. But then, what could you expect? That's how he's got where he is today, isn't it? By never missing a trick. By taking every advantage, and to hell with who gets hammered along the way.'

He turned his old soldier's face to the window, stoic in defeat. 'And after all we did for him,' he mused sadly. 'You would have thought, wouldn't you?'

He patted her arm, he smiled his most uplifting smile. 'Enough of unpleasant things. It's your birthday! We're celebrating! Now where's this cardigan?'

The search for her overnight bag was carried out with a brisk efficiency that took him round the room and out into the hall, where she heard him calling for Ben and Alice.

Alone, Catherine was soon oppressed by the dark musty room and the mockery of the narrow bed, and soon followed her father out into the hall to find that he had vanished. Hearing clattering from the back extension, she looked down the passage and saw Alice silhouetted against the kitchen window, chopping with a vigour that would have done credit to a commis chef. Energy was not something one readily associated with Alice, and again Catherine thought: She's happy. She must have found a man. On the heels of these thoughts came the worry that Alice would set her hopes too high too quickly, that her uncertainties would drive her to smother the poor fellow with unreasonable demands. Alice had long professed a disdain for men, mainly because over the years she had thrown herself at a whole series of unsuitable and unwinnable men who, in rejecting her, had reconfirmed her views both of the male sex and, fatally, of her own unworthiness. Catherine only hoped that the new figure marked a new confidence, that she would break through the ceiling of distrust and discover some self-belief.

From another part of the house came more elusive sounds. Turning her head to catch them, she traced hushed voices to the upstairs landing. Wheeling herself across the hall into the angle of the stairs she craned her head up and saw through the banisters Emma's back and, barely visible beyond, the top of Ben's head. Emma said something in a soft murmur. Ben responded in a voice pitched equally low. Catherine was about to call up when Ben moved forward and touched Emma's shoulder. It seemed to Catherine that what followed was relayed to her at two speeds, that each move was enacted both rapidly and in slow motion. Ben dropped his hand from Emma's shoulder and, looping both arms around her, pulled her close and leant his head against hers. It might have been Catherine's imagination but it seemed to her that his eyes were closed, as if with strong emotion. Emma, meanwhile, had raised her arms to embrace him around the waist. They stood locked together for what seemed a long time but was probably only seconds. As they began to pull apart, Catherine pushed herself swiftly away out of sight.

It was barely twelve when Duncan poured out the champagne and the family raised their glasses to toast her birthday. Catherine drank the first glass quickly and accepted a second in the full knowledge that, this early in the day, it would make her rapidly and irretrievably drunk.

Alice proclaimed, as though from the battlements, 'They will be gone in five minutes!' and described an enormous arc through the air as if to direct a cavalry charge towards the front door. 'Even if I have to *throw* them into the street with my bare hands.'

Catherine announced, 'I need a man.'

Alice grinned delightedly. 'Don't we all!'

'Preferably strong and sober.'

'Oh, *too much*!' she chortled.

'To get me upstairs.'

'Upstairs? Right – *upstairs*! No sooner said.' Alice waved an imaginary wand. 'Who would you like? Ben? Hugh? Charlie?'

'So many men to choose from!' For no particular reason, Catherine found this thought terribly funny and grinned ludicrously.

Alice's smile faded. She crouched at her side. 'You all right, Cath?'

'I'm *fine*.' This was far from the truth, since Catherine was not only several glasses the wrong side of happy but for the past four hours had been neglecting her bodily chores, the hated tasks, large and small, that averted pressure sores and bladder infections and spasms, sins and omissions for which she would doubtless pay dearly. Already she felt the prickle of sickly heat in her face, a trickle of cooler sweat against her shirt. 'Just need to go upstairs.'

Alice hovered uncertainly before murmuring, 'I'll get Ben.'

'No – Hugh.'

Hugh, an accomplished horseman when he wasn't being a lawyer, was fit and strong and picked Catherine up as if she were a bundle of rags. He grinned leerily down at her. 'I think you're wonderful,' he said, breathing wine and smoked salmon over her.

She laughed a little. 'Why, thank you.'

'We all think you're wonderful.'

Catherine turned her head sharply away so that he shouldn't see the scorn in her face, and asked Alice to fold the wheelchair and bring it upstairs.

As soon as she was safely ensconced on the upper landing,

she whispered to Hugh in a tone of complicity, 'If anyone asks, could you tell them I'm sleeping?'

'Certainly!'

Beckoning him closer, she whispered, 'Unless you'd like to join me?'

He laughed too loud and too long, he couldn't quite conceal the look of embarrassment that crossed his face and when he retreated down the stairs his chuckle had the phoney ring of a stage comedian's.

While Alice went down to fetch her bags from the terracotta room, Catherine wheeled herself into the main bedroom and found not the untidiness and scattering of unwashed shirts she had been expecting but order and a neatly made bed. Before she had time to wonder if Ben had found a cleaning lady, the sweat started from her forehead, she shivered with cold or fever and pushed herself hastily towards the bathroom. Some weeks ago, when the stairlift had first come up for discussion, Ben had measured the upstairs doorways and pronounced them adequate, but his measurements must have been out somewhere because the bathroom door proved to be a tight squeeze, and she had to grasp the doorframe and drag herself through, scraping the wheels against the woodwork in the process. Sponging her face with cold water, she didn't feel much cooler. She closed her eyes but reopened them as her head spun and her stomach tightened with the nauseous acidity that comes from too much champagne and too little food. If she wasn't careful she was going to have a vicious hangover. It was too late to make herself sick, the only thing was water and antacid.

The medicine cabinet was out of reach on the wall and she had to wait for Alice to come back to find aspirin and Resolve. As Alice rummaged through the stock of medicines something on the upper shelf caught Catherine's eye. Light-headed with fever or alcohol or both, it was a moment before she understood what it was. Among the antibiotics and home remedies was a bottle of perfume. Pale amber in smooth glass. Gold top. Not her own.

When Catherine emerged from the bathroom five minutes later, Alice was waiting for her, smiling brightly.

'Anything else, Cath?' she asked, following her into the bedroom.

'A new head?'

'Did you have that much?'

'However much, it was too much.' Catherine waved a hand towards the wardrobes. '*Some* time you're going to have to go through my clothes for me, Ally. Sort 'em out. Chuck 'em out. Everything tight or vaguely tight. Ruthless. To hell with how much it cost.' Realising this was presuming rather a lot, she remembered her manners. 'If you wouldn't mind.'

Alice gave a stiff smile, her eyes shone with a fierce indecipherable light. 'You can't wear them?'

'Too hard to get on and off. Not likely to fit either. My world has gone pear-shaped in more than one sense of the word – words, excuse me. Everything has rather *settled*, you see, around my bum.'

The bed was a low one and Catherine eyed it wearily. 'Now, if I get onto this bloody bed, will I ever get off it again? More to the point, do I care?'

Alice's face had taken on an increasingly appalled expression.

Wondering dimly if she had caused offence, too muddled to work out what it might have been, Catherine held out an appeasing hand, her second of the day. Stepping forward to grasp it, Alice seemed to keep coming, to be falling towards the wheelchair, and instinctively Catherine flinched, pulled her head away, before she understood that the arms which reached out to envelop her roughly, the cheek that bumped awkwardly against hers, were proffered with intense emotion.

'Oh Cath,' Alice cried in a ragged voice, 'any time you need me. Any time at all.'

Catherine felt the absolute stillness, the freezing of sensation, that was her defence against pity. The sympathy she'd received today had brought home to her with dismal clarity the

depressingly pessimistic view that the able-bodied held of dis-
ability. This, they were implying with their relentless compas-
sion, is the end of life as you knew it, the end of almost
everything that made it worthwhile, the end of all you had
hoped to enjoy in the future, the end of beauty and physical
attraction and – their first thought, though they would vigor-
ously deny it – the end of a fulfilling sex life. To them she was
now indistinguishable from her condition: paralysed Catherine,
wheelchair Catherine, poor sad tragic Catherine. *She used to
have it all, you know.* Each pitying smile, each hand laid
tenderly on her shoulder, each compassionate hug was like a
slap in the face. *We think you're wonderful* actually translated
as *You are nothing now, except in terms of the heroic role we
have chosen to bestow on you.* They would not be denied their
right to pity her; they insisted on it, because then they could
face themselves in the mirror with a small glow of self-
congratulation.

And now her sister: Alice who knew better than most the
indignity of finding herself an object of pity.

Catherine thought: The drink's making me bitter.

After Alice had helped her onto the bed, Catherine said, 'I'll
be fine now, thanks.' But as Alice left the room Catherine called
her back. 'Last thing. Would you look under the bed for me?'

Alice made a comical frown. 'Under the bed? What am I
looking for?'

'A baseball bat.'

Dropping to her knees, Alice made a thorough search.
'Nothing here, Cath.'

'You're sure?'

Alice crawled round to the end of the bed and looked from
there. 'Nothing.' She got breathlessly to her feet and laughed,
'What's it for – bit of self-defence?' She started and gave a
sharp groan of horror, knuckle pressed histrionically to her
mouth. 'Sorry, Cath, I didn't mean to . . . Oh, God, *God* – of
course! You're worried about being here on your own! Is that
what it is? Do you want me to stay? I'm happy to stay!'

Catherine wasn't quite ready for Alice in this protective role and spoke a little more sharply than she'd intended. 'Don't be ridiculous. It's nothing like that.'

'Sure?'

'Sure. Now, go away,' she growled. 'And leave me to rest. Everyone's so bloody keen on me *resting*. Well, tell them I'm bloody *resting* like a good girl, will you?'

When she'd gone, Catherine turned herself onto her side and, with her arm stretched across Ben's half of the bed, as though in her dreams she might find him there, fell into the leaden sleep of alcohol and extreme tiredness.

She woke groggily to full darkness and the rocking of the mattress as Ben sat down heavily on the edge of the bed at her back.

'Didn't realise you were up here, Moggy.' His voice was thick and unreadable. 'Thought you were resting downstairs. Why on earth did you come up here?'

She turned onto her back. 'It was too noisy downstairs.' Reaching for his hand, she added, 'And I wanted to be here, in our own bed.'

The light from the landing was too faint for her to see his face but she had the impression that his expression had hardened. She heard him exhale, a long slow breath. His hand was loose in hers.

She asked, 'Has everyone gone?'

'Except Emma. She's cooking supper. Pasta, I think. Do you want to come down? I can't say I'm entirely happy about carrying you, Moggy, not down those stairs, not when I've had a drink or two. But if we go slowly, I suppose . . .'

'I promise not to fall.' If Ben thought she was making a poor attempt at humour he didn't say so.

For a fraction of a second their conversation about the debts had seemed to belong to another time and place, but now it came crowding back through the steady beat of her headache, like an emotional hangover.

'How are you doing?' she asked.

'What?'

'Not worrying too much about the money?'

'Of course I'm worrying about the money,' he said testily.

'We never finished talking. The house – I'm not clear,' she said with dull dread. 'Are we going to have to sell it?'

'Sell it? God, no.'

'There's another way then?'

'A second mortgage. It's all arranged.'

'All arranged?'

'I've got the papers downstairs.'

Something inside her smarted a little at the realisation that he had arranged the whole thing and gathered the paperwork without telling her.

He said, 'We can get Emma to witness our signatures.'

'You mean, tonight?'

'Well, she's here. Might as well make the most of it.'

'Can't we leave it till tomorrow, darling?'

'But Moggy, she's *here*,' he repeated doggedly. 'And nothing's going to be different tomorrow.'

'I'd rather leave it, if you don't—'

He shot to his feet. 'You're not listening, Moggy!' His voice was pitched dangerously low. 'Nothing's going to be different tomorrow! And I need to be sure I'm getting this money – otherwise I might as well go and slit my bloody throat!'

'I'd just like to feel we'd talked it through properly, that's all. To be sure it's the best way.'

His voice rose suddenly. 'I *am* sure! And I'm telling you there *isn't* any other way!'

She'd only seen him this angry once before, during their big row in France. Among their friends he was known for being imperturbable, a reputation that perfectly suited his view of himself as a person who conducted his life on his own terms. It hurt her to see him like this because she knew how much he hated it.

When she finally spoke again it was soothingly. 'Darling, I

didn't mean to suggest you hadn't looked into it properly . . . of course I didn't. It's just – I'd like to know how big this mortgage is going to be. And what happens if we can't keep up the payments.' He was very still and she couldn't make out his expression in the darkness. 'Could we lose everything? That's what I want to know. Because I've no other money, nothing at all—'

'Ah, so that's it!'

They had got onto dangerous ground. He didn't like to be reminded that it was Catherine's money that had paid for the deposit on the house.

'Couldn't we buy a tiny flat?' she asked. 'Have some security at least, and use the spare cash from this place—'

'Christ! No time! No time!'

On old ground one is destined to take the same turnings, and she heard herself say, 'I just think of Mummy. It was all the money she ever had. Everything she'd worked so hard to keep—' She had been about to say *to keep safe*.

'So it's *your* money now, is it?'

'Of course not. It's ours, of course it is. I'm just worried about what'll happen if we lose it.'

'We'll rent, we'll save for another place – God, I don't know! All I know is that if I don't get this cash together I'm bloody sunk! And now you're talking as if we had a whole bundle of options. Well, I'm telling you – there are no options!' He paced the room, he came to a halt in the light of the doorway and clasped a hand to his forehead in a final gesture of exasperation.

Catherine felt the future close in on her, dark and cold.

Appearing to calm himself with an effort, Ben came back and sank onto the bed with a long and heartfelt sigh. 'Oh Moggy . . .' He bent over and rested his cheek against hers. 'If there was any other way . . . We'll be all right, once we're through this. Promise you. We'll be fine.'

But she had lost the simple capacity for optimism. Before the accident, she might have looked on the prospect of hard times as a challenge, a fine test of commitment and loyalty, but now it frightened her. Now, she had special needs, not the least of which was security.

'Hey,' Ben murmured into her ear. Pulling back, he placed his palm against her cheek.

Heart heavy, she heard herself say, 'You can count on me.'

'I knew you wouldn't let me down. I knew it.' He kissed her briefly before scrambling to his feet again. 'Supper? Do you want to come down?'

'I'm not sure I can eat anything.'

'I'll call Emma up, then. I'll go and get the papers. We'll get it all over and done with.'

'Ben?'

He paused in the door.

'What happened to the baseball bat?'

A short pause in which the atmosphere seemed to sharpen. 'Good God,' he exclaimed, 'I don't know. Why do you ask?'

'I thought it might have been used in the attack.'

'*What?*' He gave a small incredulous laugh.

'I thought I was imagining things, and then I wasn't so sure, and now – well, it's gone.'

He moved back to the side of the bed. 'Moggy, you've been having bad dreams. I moved it ages ago.'

'Moved it? Where to?'

'Hell, I don't know,' he said airily. 'Somewhere out of the way. The cupboard under the stairs, I think. Or the study. Maybe the study.'

'Why?'

'Why?' he echoed as if the question were absurd. 'Because it was too dangerous to leave under the bed. They always say intruders grab a weapon and use it against you, don't they? Thought it'd be safer.'

'You don't think that this man' – she couldn't bring herself to say his name – 'could have found it, then?'

'No!' he scoffed dismissively. 'I moved it ages ago!'

'And it's still there, wherever you put it?'

He rolled his eyes and shook his head and completed the show of disbelief with a heavy sigh. 'I'll go and get it if you like!'

'Oh, don't bother now . . .'

'No, no!' he said with a weary half laugh. 'Never let it be said.' He was already on his way out of the room. She heard a cupboard door being opened in the study, followed by a clattering, then the sound of his feet thudding down the stairs, followed by faint rattling in the hall. He must have run up the stairs much more quietly than he had gone down because the next thing she realised he was striding back into the room, holding the baseball bat up like a trophy. In a juxtaposition of light and dark, time and memory, she saw the attacker freeze-framed, as if lit by a flashbulb, the weapon high in his hand. The image vanished as quickly as it had come.

'There,' Ben declared, offering the bat up to her.

'God. I was so sure . . .'

'Think you had a few too many, Moggy. You were certainly well away down there! But you're feeling better now, eh? Slept it off?'

'I wasn't feeling well.'

'I'm not surprised,' he said in the same knowing tone.

Swinging the bat lightly in one hand he strode out of the room, leaving the door open. She saw him hesitate and, with the faintest glance back in her direction, take a right turn into the bathroom. A minute later the lavatory flushed, the plumbing hissed as the cold tap was run, and it may have been her imagination, it may have been a trick of an overwrought mind, but she thought she heard the click of the bathroom cabinet.

She saw him cross the landing and head downstairs. Within a couple of minutes, he was back with the documents in his hand. Emma appeared shortly afterwards, wiping her hands on an apron. She would have chattered, but Ben cut her short, and she made a comical face over his shoulder, a schoolgirl rebuked for talking in class.

'Shall I sit you up a little, Moggy?' Ben asked.

He fed the documents to her one by one, then took them to Emma and stood over her while she witnessed them, alert for any misaligned word.

'There!' he said, smiling. 'How about some supper, then?'

Catherine repeated, 'Not for me.'

Ben hurried off with the documents while Emma helped Catherine into the wheelchair for a trip to the bathroom. Once inside, Catherine ran the tap to disguise any noise and levered open the medicine cabinet with the lavatory brush. The bottle of perfume had gone.

Seeing her back to bed, Emma waved conspiratorially and whispered that she'd be back soon.

It seemed a long time before she returned. By then Catherine's brain felt heavy, there was a clamminess on her skin like the beginnings of fever.

Emma drew up a chair and began to chat. As she illuminated some comment with a sweep of one hand Catherine found herself trying to catch her scent, and thought: This way misery lies. Even as she tried to banish the idea from her mind, she interrupted Emma with, 'What's that perfume you're wearing?'

'Perfume?' She had to consider for a moment. 'Help. It's Givenchy, I think. Yes – Givenchy. Why, darling? Do you like it? Shall I buy you some? Let me buy you some. An extra birthday presie.' With a flick of her hair she leant forward excitedly. 'Thought we might go to Harvey Nicks when you're next home, eh?' She rolled her eyes, she lifted both shoulders, she hugged her fists together like a small child. Breaking off only to light a cigarette, she hurried on. 'Starting on the first floor – where *else*. Then on to raid the cashmeres – what do you think? Yeah? Then a boozy lunch on the top floor. Then' – she thrust her head forward, she gave a wild grin – 'a facial? Haircut? God, we could spend the *earth*!' Her smile died slowly, overtaken by a look of concern. 'You okay, Cath? You look so tired. Do you want to me to go away and let you sleep?'

'Tell me something first.'

'Of course!'

'Ben . . . has he been okay?'

Emma hesitated, as if to make sure she'd understood her correctly. 'Ben? You mean – recently? Generally? I think he's been fine. I mean, working hard. *Terribly* hard. No one ever gets to see him. And worried about you, of course. Fretting about getting the house adapted, getting the things you need. It's all he ever talks about, you know – how he wants to get everything right for you. How he wants to care for you.' At this, two thoughts sprang unbidden into Catherine's mind, that a caring role was not one that Ben would have chosen in a dozen lifetimes, and that even in the most dedicated of carers a sense of obligation didn't always sit easily with love and desire. Emma cast around for any last ideas before declaring firmly, 'But otherwise – no, *fine*.' She added tentatively, 'Why?'

'No one gets to see him, you say?'

'Absolutely not. Hasn't made a single party since I can't think when. Not the Hamilton wedding, not even Dunny's birthday, and you know how he adores Dunny. Oh – he *did* get to Jack's do – you know, his annual bash. Had a great time, the life and soul of the party.'

This was what Catherine always failed to allow for – Ben's skill at concealment, his ability to put on a front, especially for his friends, who doted on his irreverent sense of fun. In times of stress, there's a certain comfort to be gained from clichés, and now she heard herself ask, 'If there was something I should know, you would be the first to tell me, wouldn't you, Emms?'

Emma made a gesture of bewilderment, an arc of her cigarette. 'Something you should know? What *do* you mean, darling?'

'You know that old saying about the wife being the last to know.'

Emma's mouth dropped open, she rounded her eyes in a show of astonishment and incredulity. '*Darling* . . .' She was momentarily speechless. She gave a short nervous laugh. 'No

. . . I've heard nothing like that. Really, darling. Nothing at all!' She took a deep breath, as if getting over the shock. 'Where on earth did you get that idea?'

Catherine closed her eyes. 'Nowhere, I expect.'

'No, Cath, *really*,' Emma argued again. 'Haven't heard a thing. And you know how everyone is with the gossip. They can't wait!'

'Tired now,' Catherine murmured. 'Leave the door open, would you? And the light?'

'Of course, darling.' She stood up and paused uncertainly before creeping out of the room.

Long after she'd gone, Catherine heard laughter downstairs and felt the worm of doubt turn once again in her stomach. After another fifteen minutes or so, the front door sounded and the house was quiet.

She dozed and waited, but it was an hour before she heard a stair creak and watched Ben steal into view. Seeing that she was awake, his body sagged into a stance of disapproval, he came into the room with a shake of his head. 'Thought you'd be asleep, Moggy. You must get your sleep, you know! Look, I'm going to work for a while, make a few calls to Singapore. Bound to finish late, so I'll crash downstairs. Don't want to disturb you.' When she didn't reply, he busied himself pulling the curtains more closely together and fetching water she didn't need. 'Now are you all right? Got everything you want?' He cast a critical eye over the room before turning the bedside light off. 'Night, Moggy.'

His kiss was dry and firm.

'Don't sleep downstairs,' she said, hating the note of entreaty in her voice. 'I don't care how late it is.'

A minute hesitation, like death. 'Of course,' he said lightly. 'If that's what you want, Moggy.'

It was three when he crept into the room and slid into the far side of the bed. When she shifted herself close to his back and reached an arm around his waist he squeezed her hand briefly and murmured good night. A few minutes later his breathing had settled into the slow steady rhythm of sleep.

She was woken at seven by a dull pain in her kidneys and the scorch of fever on her skin. She was alone in the bed and when she called out there was no reply. It was eight before she heard him moving around downstairs and managed to make him hear her. When the doctor came he measured her fever at over thirty-nine and, after dosing her with antibiotics, recommended she go straight back to the unit for specialised treatment.

# Chapter Nine

―――・――

SIMON ORDERED the cab to stop a prudent fifty yards from the magistrates' court and walked the rest of the way at a pace that was neither so leisurely nor so hurried that it would attract attention. He observed the people loitering outside the entrance in the skirring wind: a slick youth with a loosened tie, shouting into a mobile phone; a group of slovenly women with rounded shoulders and sour mouths, sucking on cigarettes. From the opposite direction a couple of lawyers appeared, striding along in the rapid ostentatious manner of the professional, briefcases clutched like proof of office.

Beyond the metal detector and security check, in the halls and passageways, were more families and defendants in various postures of anxiety or hostility. Again, Simon's quick glance took them in; again, no face was familiar. The daily list showed that Pavlik was fourth in Court 2. Simon slipped into the public gallery and sat in the back of the two rows.

The building was solid Edwardian but the courtroom had been refurbished in pale wood and day-bright lighting. The public gallery was not as he had imagined, on a higher level and set well back, but down on the floor of the court, separated from it by a tall screen of wood and glass. The bench was just to the left, giving the public a close and unexpurgated view of the law, personified this morning at one minute past ten thirty by a rotund stipendiary magistrate with a dyspeptic frown. To the right was the dock, with, at the rear, steps leading up from the basement cells. Finding his first choice of seat rather exposed, Simon moved back to a seat hidden by the corner of the screen.

The first case was a remand for assault and took a bare five minutes. The second was a drug-dealing offence that had been held over for pre-sentence reports. Reams of paper had been produced by probation officers, social workers and psychiatrists. The magistrate asked questions and the probation officer spoke. Simon counted the professionals involved, calculated their time and costs and thought savagely: No wonder the system's in a state of collapse. All this to administer justice to a hopeless youth who will take the first opportunity to reoffend because it wasn't his fault he was addicted to heroin and cocaine and had to undertake the arduous chore of dealing to pay for his habit. Nothing was anyone's fault any more, not by the time the social workers and pseudo-psychologists had pleaded their liberal rubbish. It made him furious just to listen to it.

The drug dealer was given six months and the third case called, a bag-snatcher seeking bail. Some noisy relatives lumbered into the gallery. A woman with a heavy cold and a filthy handkerchief sneezed her way out. Simon paid no attention when the door sounded again. It was only when an expanse of cream trouser suit appeared at his side and a hand touched his arm that he jerked his head up. Even then, it was a full second before he comprehended that the lipsticked smile, the short hair, the polished make-up belonged to Alice.

He gasped an unintelligible greeting.

Before he could think of anything to say, she squeezed past him into the row and sat down. 'I haven't missed anything, have I?'

He tried unsuccessfully to push the astonishment out of his face. 'I didn't know you were coming.'

'Wanted to see what he looked like,' she whispered. 'Wanted to be able to report to Cath.' She seemed chatty, even friendly, but, deciding not to take any chances, Simon gave the smallest of nods before turning his attention back to the proceedings.

Alice put her mouth to his ear. 'She's been ill, did you know?'

'Yes, I heard.'

'A kidney infection. But they caught it in time. She's better now.'

He made an expression of relief and felt her gaze linger on his face long after he had looked away again.

In his shock at her arrival, he realised that he had forgotten a simple and terrifying fact. It came to him now with a spring of cold sweat that her presence could ruin everything. Usually his mind was a clear one, he could see his way through most problems, but sometimes when he met a situation he had failed to foresee a strange panic would overtake him. He felt it now, a sort of mental gridlock in which his only lucid thought was that he was unable to think.

'What's going to happen today, then?' Her mouth was so close to his ear that he could feel her breath.

'He'll be remanded again, probably for a month.'

'Oh.' She sounded disappointed.

'And he's likely to apply for bail.'

'But he won't get it, will he?'

'It's more than possible.'

'*What?* And let him go and terrorise other women? How can they allow that?'

'They get more rights than their victims, I'm afraid.' The panic had eased a little, his mind was beginning to clear. He needed to explain his presence. Steeling himself to meet her gaze, he whispered, 'This charge was a surprise – they thought he was just handling stolen property, didn't they? So I thought I'd better come and see what was happening. Let Ben know, keep the family in the picture. I didn't realise you were coming, otherwise I'd have left it to you—' In danger of gabbling, he broke off abruptly.

If she thought his argument less than convincing, she made no sign. 'Oh, it's good of you to come,' she declared without hesitation. 'And good of you to be such a support to Catherine. She won't let anyone else visit her, you know. Apart from Emma, of course. It really worries us.'

'Oh, it's a pleasure to see her. An honour.' Immediately, he wished this rephrased. It had sounded too abject.

Again, mystifyingly, Alice seemed entirely pleased with him. Dropping her head a little, she cast him an upward glance and said, with a brief bite of her lower lip, 'I'm sorry I was so defensive before.'

Her soft voice, her smile, flustered him. He couldn't make out if this friendliness was a trick or a game, if she would suddenly turn on him. Her face seemed very close. He could see every detail of the make-up around her eyes, so cleverly applied, of her glossy pink lips, her hair, which had been cut in a short bouncy style. He felt the tension come into his cheek. 'That's all right.'

'I was just overreacting. You know – shock.'

He made an ambiguous gesture, he smiled blandly: nothing that could be taken as a judgement. Seizing the opportunity to forestall difficulties later, he said quickly, 'In case you think I'm rude, I'm going to have to dash immediately after the case.'

'Oh?' Her quick eyes appraised him openly. 'Perhaps we could meet later? After work?'

He couldn't make out why she was suggesting this. Did she want to compare notes? Discuss Pavlik?

The puzzlement must have shown in his face because she whispered, 'Just a drink.'

His cheek gave a jerk that almost caused his left eye to close, like some ghastly wink, and he lowered his head furiously. 'I might be late at the office. I'm not sure when I'll finish.'

'Why don't we make contact later?' She reached into her bag and gave him a card, then, producing pen and paper, waited for him to scribble his mobile phone number down. 'I'm free from about seven,' she smiled.

There was sudden movement in the court and his panic resurfaced, he felt the heat rise into his face. The bag-snatcher, having got bail, was strutting out of the court with a smirk on his face, followed by a lawyer with an armful of papers. The usher called Pavlik's name and the warder disappeared down the steps to the cells. There was a pause in which there was no movement save for the clerk's pen as she wrote up her notes. Simon shrank back a little as the warder reappeared, followed at last by Pavlik.

It seemed to Simon that everything in his mind and body tautened as he watched Pavlik saunter up the last few steps and take his place in the dock. He appeared relaxed to the point of unconcern; he didn't look around the court, didn't look towards the gallery, but kept his eyes on the bench. Simon tried to read his expression, to guess at his state of mind, but his face was devoid of emotion. He might have been up for a parking offence.

'Is that him?' hissed Alice.

Without removing his eyes from Pavlik Simon gave a sharp peremptory nod. Pavlik was short, something like five four or five, but, standing next to a warder who must have been well over six foot, he looked positively stunted. However, his broad, well-shaped shoulders, his thick neck, revealed the body of a man who kept in shape. He was wearing a light blue shirt, well-pressed, no tie, and dark blue chinos. His black hair was newly washed and very shiny. Simon thought: So much for the deprivations of jail.

Alice leant close again. 'He's not what I expected!'

But Simon had transferred his gaze to the lawyers' tables, where a new face had appeared, a short rather moth-eaten man with an unhealthy pallor, collar-length white hair and pebble glasses, wearing an ancient pinstriped suit purchased in slimmer days. When the usher announced, 'Number four on your list, sir, represented by Mr Gresham,' he stood up and nodded to the bench and made an application for bail. The woman from the CPS objected on the grounds that the charge was a serious one, that the police had not had time to make full inquiries as to suitability for bail and, last but not least, the accused was an illegal immigrant who would have every possible reason to abscond. The pinstriped suit lumbered to his feet again and stated that, though Pavlik had entered the country illegally, he had in fact applied for political asylum. Since the members of his family who remained in the Czech Republic were suffering considerable persecution as gypsies, he had every reason to believe his application would be successful. He had been in this country for five years during which time he had never been in trouble with the law in any shape or form, had held down a steady job as a waiter for four years, had been resident in the same area for two years. Given bail, he had every intention of resuming his normal life, residing in his home and, if his job was still open, returning to his work. Furthermore, surety could be provided if necessary.

The magistrate commented crossly, 'It would have to be a substantial surety.'

'Yes, sir, that would be no problem.'

'Who's offering surety?'

'A friend of my client who has every faith in him.'

'And who is this friend?'

'Mr David Frankel, a retired solicitor.'

The magistrate looked over his spectacles. 'Mr Frankel is offering this surety in a personal capacity?'

'He is indeed, sir.'

'Is he here today?'

'No, sir, but I have authorisation.'

'How long has he known your client?'

The pinstriped suit referred to his notes. 'Two years.'

'Is he fully aware of all the circumstances? Not least that your client is an illegal immigrant?'

'He is, sir.'

Behind the magistrate's perpetual scowl, it was clear he was softening. 'Does Mr Frankel live close to your client? Will he keep in regular contact?'

'Mr Frankel lives in Hendon, sir. My client lives in West Kilburn, not so far away. And yes, Mr Frankel will be in regular contact.'

'And where would your client live while on bail?'

The pinstripe read out an address. 'It's the room he's been renting for the past six months.'

The magistrate considered. 'This is a serious charge. The accused is an illegal immigrant. I must ask for surety of fifteen thousand pounds. Is Mr Frankel prepared to stand surety for that amount?'

'He is, sir.'

The magistrate gave a small sigh. 'In that case . . . unless the CPS has other grounds for refusing bail?' The woman from the CPS bobbed up and shook her head. 'Bail is granted on a recognisance of fifteen thousand pounds and on condition that the accused reports to his local police station once a day and lives and sleeps at his address. Does he have a passport to surrender?'

'Sir, his only passport is a Czech passport, which is out of date.'

'And they're letting him out?' hissed Alice. 'I don't believe it!'

Simon cupped a hand to his ear, so as not to miss anything.

'Do you fully understand the conditions, Mr Pavlik?' the magistrate asked.

'I understand.' The words were strongly spoken.

'And you must report back to this court on the date that will be notified to you. Any failure to follow the conditions of the bail or to appear when notified and you will find yourself charged with a separate offence and go straight to prison. Is that clear?'

'It is, sir.'

The pinstriped suit ambled across to the clerk to lodge the surety while a warder directed Pavlik back towards the cells. Pavlik appeared to argue, or at least to question this, and the warder paused to explain something to him before Pavlik acquiesced with a nod and made his way down the stairs.

Retrieving his bag from the floor, Simon got hastily to his feet. 'That's it,' he said.

Alice exclaimed, 'You mean, he's out? He's free?'

Simon was already on his way to the door. 'He will be shortly.'

'That's outrageous!' She hurried after him into the hall.

Halting, Simon held out a hand to make it clear that he had to hurry away

Tilting her head to one side, she said, 'But where are you going? Why don't we share a cab?'

'I've got an appointment out in the sticks.' In a moment of inspiration, he added something approaching the truth. 'But I thought I'd try and find out one or two things about Pavlik first.'

Before she had the chance to say anything else he lifted a hand in farewell and walked briskly over to the gaolers' window to confirm that Pavlik was being returned to Brixton for release. Looking back, he saw the pinstriped suit emerge from court and shamble arthritically across the hall in the direction of the main doors.

Back on plan, Simon thought exultantly. Nothing amiss, nothing to give him away. Only his own stilted movements and the sweat like rain inside his shirt.

He thought of Catherine, as he often did in times of stress or rapture, and this steadied him.

*It'll be fine*, he spoke to her. *Leave it all to me.*

An hour later he sat in the back of a parked minicab in a quiet road in Brixton.

'How long we wait?' The driver was Turkish or Lebanese. His eyes in the mirror were black as treacle.

'As long as we have to.'

'One hour? Two hour?'

'I'm paying, aren't I? I told you, I don't know.'

They were parked in a small residential road with a view back across Brixton Hill to Jebb Avenue and the barriers to the prison.

Simon had already slipped off his suit jacket and tie and,

folding them carefully, had lodged them in his bag with his shoes. Over his shirt he had put on a casual zip-up jacket and on his feet a pair of trainers. Ready on the seat beside him was a baseball cap and in his pocket some dark glasses, a weekly travel card, and cash in varying denominations should he need to take another cab and pay it off hurriedly. Finally, he had attached a strap to his bag so that he'd be able to carry it over his shoulder, just like a tourist, a student, or a waiter on his way to the evening shift. If nothing else, he owed himself the satisfaction of having prepared fully. He ran through the details again in his mind, but could think of nothing he'd forgotten.

While he watched the comings and goings from the prison, he made calls on his mobile, marking each one off on the card that he had prepared the previous night. After an hour he was able to tick off the last call – a deal he was setting up in Argentina – and to place the card in the inner pocket of his jacket, where it lodged with such gratifying exactitude.

As two o'clock came and the time dragged on, he allowed himself to daydream gently of Catherine. In so far as such a thing was possible, he tried to ration his thoughts of her. When he'd discovered she was ill and not seeing visitors, he'd sent her a card and some Belgian chocolates from Fortnum & Mason because he thought she would appreciate something a little frivolous for a change. He imagined her face on receiving them, he saw her smiling a little as she read the card. He was amazingly sure of this smile, just as he was sure that she spoke warmly of him to other people. She was a steadfast person, Catherine, she would never speak unkindly behind his back. When he thought of the way their friendship had grown over the months, the warmth and devotion she had shown him, he felt a piercing sense of pride. If they could continue as they were, he would be more than happy, though when he allowed his daydreams full rein he couldn't help imagining the two of them living in a beautiful flat together, an airy modern place, high up with lots of natural light and a large terrace with a roof garden and a view, so that when he was away Catherine could look out over the city and tend her plants. At other times this vision was transposed to the country, to an eighteenth-century house, possibly a barn conversion, with an abundant garden and wonderful antiques. In both of these homes he could see each room, the decor, the colours, the china they ate off, the food they served, the lunch parties, the quiet dinners à deux. These images were so perfect, so richly formed that the contemplation of them caused him an exquisite suffering. He didn't need to be told that he was feeling the terrible joy of the unattainable.

The sight of the tall white-sided prison transport coming up Brixton Hill and slowing to turn into Jebb Avenue jolted him back to life. He checked the time: barely three. This could be the one: only the magistrates' courts disgorged their prisoners this early.

Adding another hour to the driver's time, he calculated the fare and paid, with the firm instruction that the driver was to wait the full time. In the unlikely event of Pavlik having transport, Simon didn't want to be left standing by the kerb. Pulling on the cap and sunglasses, stringing the bag over his shoulder, he climbed out and, crossing the main road, waited at a point where he could see along Jebb Avenue to the side of the prison but, with just two steps back, could move rapidly out of view.

After ten minutes, a youth clutching a brown-paper bag stepped out of the wicket gate. Five minutes later came an old man, puffing on a cigarette. Then, after another ten minutes, Pavlik. From the way he strode up Jebb Avenue he was not expecting transport.

With a lurch of excitement, Simon began to walk away from the prison in the wrong direction for town. When he glanced back, Pavlik had turned into the main road, heading north. Doubling back, Simon followed at a distance. Obligingly, Pavlik was wearing a bright blue jacket, which, with his dark hair and distinctive build, made him stand out like a beacon. Once, he paused for no apparent reason and looked round. Simon had to force himself to keep walking naturally, but it seemed Pavlik was only checking the route advertised on an approaching bus because, once it got close enough to read, he lost interest and resumed his earlier pace.

On reaching the bottom of Brixton Hill, he made for the underground. Closing up, Simon was four treads behind him on the escalator. A train drew out as they came onto the platform. For a time they were the only people waiting. Simon sauntered up to a chocolate dispensing machine and, hunting for some coins, selected an Aero bar. Other people dribbled onto the platform. Glancing back, he saw Pavlik waiting patiently, staring at the advertising hoarding on the other side of the track, apparently unaware that he was being followed.

When a train drew in, Simon got into the next-door carriage and kept an eye on Pavlik through the glass windows of the communicating doors. At Green Park, Pavlik got off and transferred to the Piccadilly Line. Again Simon took the precaution of getting into the next carriage, but as this train was far more crowded he didn't attempt to keep Pavlik in view but stuck his head out of the open doors at each stop. He didn't have to wait long; the bright blue jacket emerged at Leicester Square.

The walk up through Chinatown was rather pleasant in the weak sunshine. Simon began to relax a little. This whole business was proving far easier than he'd expected, although, as he hastily reminded himself, this was due not to any skill on his part but to Pavlik's total lack of suspicion.

Pavlik crossed Shaftesbury Avenue into Dean Street and, just when Simon was wondering where he might be heading, he disappeared into a pub on the corner of Old Compton Street. A stiff drink after a week in the clink; Simon didn't blame him. Simon rounded the opposite corner and leant a shoulder against the plate-glass window of a pasta restaurant that offered a view of the pub door across a table of gobbling tourists.

Pavlik didn't drink for long – he must have kept it to a quick double – before he was on his way out again, and coming straight for Simon. Simon hastened off ahead of him down Old

Compton Street and walked briskly into a sandwich bar. After Pavlik had passed, he came out again and followed him round the next corner into Frith Street. Pavlik slowed up now, going at a pace that was almost thoughtful, before stopping and smoothing his hair in the reflection of a glass shopfront. Apparently satisfied, he went a few more paces and stepped in through a door. Getting closer, Simon saw an old-fashioned Italian restaurant with pot plants and straw-clad Chianti bottles in the window. La Rondine.

The workplace, presumably. Would the management have kept his job open for him? If Gresham was to be believed, Pavlik had been in the same job for four years, a veritable old-timer in the flighty world of Soho. But Simon suspected that a few months would be more like it, and plenty of moonlighting after hours. Did illegal immigrants pay taxes? Presumably not. Asylum seekers got benefits, though. A beneficiary of the black economy twice over, then.

It was almost five and nearing the start of the evening shift. Simon was beginning to think he had an exceedingly long wait in front of him when Pavlik reappeared, heading back the way he had come. Turning hastily away, Simon found himself standing next to two slack-mouthed men, staring into a dark cavernous doorway lit by garish photographs advertising the bloated breasts and brassy attentions available in the basement beneath.

Following again at a safe distance, he had to hurry to match Pavlik's pace as he turned west along Old Compton Street and down into Shaftesbury Avenue. He was walking so much faster now that Simon almost lost him in the crowds near Piccadilly Circus, only picking him up as he bought an *Evening Standard* at the top of the subway steps. Three minutes later Simon was safely ensconced in the next-door carriage to Pavlik on a Bakerloo Line train, heading north. It was no surprise when Pavlik got off at Queen's Park, on the northern edge of West Kilburn.

As Simon followed him into the maze of residential roads

that must surely mark the end of the trail, his exhilaration was overtaken by doubt. What next? Where was this really leading?

Pavlik stopped at a Pakistani corner shop, emerging a few minutes later with a full carrier bag. Simon judged his distance carefully now, staying far enough back not to be noticeable but not so far that he couldn't identify the house once Pavlik finally got home.

In the event, he needn't have worried. When Pavlik turned in through a black metal gate in a long street of identical two-storey villas he didn't disappear immediately but paused for several moments in the porch, giving Simon plenty of time to mark the precise doorway. Striding briskly past a minute later, Simon noted the brass number on the door, and a single bell. He'd been expecting two or three bells, denoting rooms or flatlets, but unless they had been placed somewhere unusual and he had missed them, the place had all the appearance of a single house. Was Pavlik a lodger then? Or a guest?

The road was called, in improbable imitation of grander places, Fifth Avenue, and when Simon examined the *A–Z* later he saw that it was indeed one of six.

His luck continued when, immediately on reaching the Harrow Road, a free cab appeared, going his way. Safely inside, speeding along against the flow of rush-hour traffic, he allowed himself some small sense of achievement. At least he'd established that Pavlik was intending to live at the address he'd given to the court. Now, at the slightest sign of trouble, Simon would know where to come. What he might do once he got there was, of course, an entirely different matter. He took refuge in the solemn promise he'd made in his heart to Catherine. *I'll make sure no one ever harms you again.*

There was only one aspect of the day that did not slot neatly away in his orderly mind. The house in Fifth Avenue had looked too prosperous to take in lodgers. The fresh paintwork, polished brass house number, new plantation-style shutters in the upstairs windows, fancy window boxes and plant tubs spoke of money to spare. As he realised too late that the cab was heading for Lancaster Gate and the bottleneck across the park, an answer presented itself. Pavlik was athletic and good-looking, one to stand out in a crowd. He might have a lover, a luster after firm flesh who kept him in style in Fifth Avenue.

The tailback across the park started at Lancaster Gate; it would be a long crawl. He retrieved his mobile phone from his document bag and switched it on. Before he had the chance to pick up his messages, however, it rang. He had forgotten about Alice until her voice sang, 'How are you doing? Ready for that drink yet?'

Gripped by a mild euphoria, he agreed immediately and with an enthusiasm that surprised him. An hour later, having been home to shower and change, he found himself back in Soho, walking into the Atlantic Bar. Alice was waiting at the long curved counter, perched on a stool. She smiled when she saw him. Her appearance took him aback. She had changed out of the cream trouser suit into a black dress that was low-cut and flimsy. Since her figure was by any standards full, it was a dress that displayed its contents rather too conspicuously. When she took a breath her breasts bulged over the rim of the dress, and he took care to keep his eyes firmly above her neck.

She was drinking something bright green called a Japanese Slipper, and, though he usually stuck to white wine, he allowed himself a rare impulse and joined her. She asked what he'd managed to find out about Pavlik and didn't seem surprised or concerned when he reported a lack of success. Then, duty apparently done, she chattered about her life, which seemed to consist of a long succession of parties, dinners, and country weekends. She dismissed her work in an estate agent's as boring, while the parties were spoken of with excitement, as though she regarded a packed social life as the only real mark of success. Once again, Simon wondered why she should bother with him, why she had gone to all this trouble to meet him for a drink. He didn't doubt there was a purpose behind it all. At one point, he turned the conversation towards Catherine in case this should provide a cue, but she didn't pick up on it.

'So,' she said with a soft smile, 'what about you? Busy?'

While he talked of Bahrain and Argentina she listened attentively, with bright eyes that never left his face. He had the feeling he was being minutely appraised, and that so far, against all odds, he appeared to be passing muster. Under the searchlight of her gaze he ordered another round of the green drink – a concoction of vodka, lime and something he'd never heard of – and, trying to enter into the spirit of this strange encounter, offered a breezy smile.

Alice said something that was lost in the general din. He bent closer. Whether it was the misguided smile that had encouraged her or she'd been planning to ask him all along, she said in her low musical voice, 'You don't have a significant other, do you?'

'Not significant, no.'

'I didn't think so,' she said mysteriously. 'Why not?' She tilted her head, she leant forward a little, and her bosom came towards him like – he remembered reading such a description in a book somewhere – a blancmange about to slide off its dish.

He said, 'Too busy, too much work, no talent for commitment.'

'Ah . . . commitment.' She smiled with mock wistfulness. 'What about non-significant others?'

'Oh, we all have those, don't we?'

'Do we?' she said, clearly relishing the idea. Then, with a cat-like smile, a narrowing of her eyes: 'So you're not looking for a significant other?'

'Not particularly, no.'

'Don't want to be tied down?'

'Something like that.'

'Quite right!'

She seemed pleased by his response. She flashed her eyes at him over her drink. It occurred to him that in other circumstances, with anyone but Alice, he might have suspected that he was being flirted with. He found this thought sufficiently alarming to change the subject. 'You know that I'm leaving RNP, that Ben and I are going our separate ways?'

Smiling dreamily, eyes still fastened teasingly on his, she came to this subject slowly. 'Mmm?' When he'd repeated the question, she said, 'I'd heard, yes.' Then, seriously: 'I'm not surprised.'

'Oh?'

'Well, Ben's a difficult sod, isn't he?'

Simon made a show of considering this idea as if it were entirely new to him. 'Yes, I suppose he is.'

'You know, I always used to envy Cath,' she said unexpectedly. 'When we were kids. And later. You know. Looks. Could eat all day long without putting on weight. Never had spots. And there I was . . . *well*!' She rolled her eyes self-deprecatingly.

Feeling some response was expected of him, Simon framed a frown of denial.

Misreading this, she declared defensively, 'Oh, don't get me wrong, I didn't actually *mind*. God, no! Quite the opposite.' She attempted a laugh. 'It quite suited me, you see. I could just get on with my life, do my own thing, and no one was any the wiser. Got away with far more than Cath. God, yes! Pa was always eagle-eyed where she was concerned, wanting to know where she'd been, what she'd been up to. But me . . .' Her eyes slid away, as though she'd said more than she'd intended to. 'So – when Cath got Ben, we all thought she'd found herself the best, just like we'd always thought she would. Got the golden man, the pick of the bunch.' She gave a small shrug, she said enigmatically, 'But now . . . well, I rather think she's got her work cut out for her, don't you?'

Simon found himself arguing Ben's case. 'Whatever else, he's doing his best for Catherine.'

'Do you think so?' The disdain in her voice left no doubt as to her opinion. 'It depends what you consider his *best*.'

'What are you trying to say?'

She paused, she eyed him thoughtfully. 'I don't think he's behaving very well. I think he's doing the dirty on her.'

'Oh? And why do you think that?'

She raised an eyebrow. 'I *could* tell you it was just a feeling. I *could* tell you I'm just a clever judge of character.'

'But?'

'*But*,' she said with a heavy sigh, 'I know he's seeing someone else.'

Simon stared at his drink. He felt sick with sudden excitement, as if in one accelerated action Catherine had found out and the way was open for him to step in. 'Ouch,' he murmured, to give himself more time. Then, with a look of suitable concern, he asked, 'Who's the woman?'

'That I don't know.'

He couldn't make out if she was holding out on him.

'But you know there's someone?'

'Oh yes. It was when I went round early one morning to collect something for Cath. I heard someone moving around upstairs. Ben tried to make a clatter, to hide it. But I heard all right – there was definitely someone up there.'

'It couldn't have been – I don't know – someone else? A friend?'

She let her head fall to one side, she rounded her eyes in a knowing expression of doubt.

'No,' he conceded. 'Just ships in the night, then? A one nighter?'

She shook her head. 'She'd left her car keys on the hall table. Think about it.' She raised a forefinger. 'It's only a regular routine that makes a woman do that.'

'You didn't recognise the keys?'

'No.'

His euphoria had quite gone. He'd lost all taste for the gaudy green cocktail. The clamour of the bar seemed to rise around him, unacceptably loud. 'It wouldn't be the first time,' he said casually.

Alice stared at him, as if to be sure of his meaning. 'Since they've been married, you mean?'

He gave a light shrug.

'Who was it?'

'I couldn't say.'

'But there was someone?'

He met her eyes, and it was a confirmation.

'The bastard,' she said.

She was thinking of pressing him further, but he made a show of looking at his watch. 'Sorry, I've got to go.'

He caught the flash of disappointment under the forced smile. 'Oh, I was hoping to lure you off to supper,' she said.

'It's work. Can't escape. But another time.'

'Definitely?' She was still looking at him with something like suspicion, and it struck him that he must tread carefully with her.

'Definitely. In fact, next week? Tuesday?'

'Tuesday.' Brightening a little, she smiled lazily. 'I must let you go, then.' When she leant forward it was for a traditional meeting of cheeks, a token pouting of the lips. But then, as he straightened up, she reached up and, framing his face in her hands, neatly guided his mouth down to hers and kissed him full on the lips. Her mouth was slightly open and it seemed to him that the taste of her stayed with him for hours afterwards.

# Chapter Ten

———•———

'NO PERSONAL mail, no,' said Bridget's voice in Dublin. 'And none at Foxrock either.'

Sitting alone in the hotel suite, the phone tight against his ear, Terry stared unseeing at the gauze curtains stirring in the sluggish air, and thought: Well, what did I expect, for heaven's sake? With half an ear to Bridget as she ran through the arrangements for his return to Dublin, he finally accepted what had been obvious from the start: Catherine would never reply. It had been ridiculous to think she would.

When Bridget had rung off he went to the window and, parting the swathes of fabric, watched the dusk creep up from the Mayfair streets into a crystalline sky. Hoping for a response had been foolish, though perhaps not so foolish as the belief that friendly words and weekly letters could overcome the resentments of the past. It was the arrogance of success, of course, to assume that everything could be fixed, that nothing, not even grievances, could resist the forces of determination and money. And what had he been out to achieve anyway? Forgiveness? Peace of mind? Just salves to his own conscience, he noted severely, surely one of the more shameful forms of vanity.

No, there would be no letter from Catherine, and he would write no more to her either. He should have learnt his lesson the first time and realised that the written word did not serve him well so far as Catherine was concerned. The letter he'd written her during the summer of Lizzie's illness was incised painfully on his memory. He had never understood how he had come to misjudge the situation so badly, but misjudge it he had. There was no undoing it then, and there was no undoing it now. He would have liked his thoughts of that time to be filled entirely with recollections of Lizzie, to remember the many moments of laughter and celebration that had overlaid the recognition of her slow deterioration. But the choice of memories was another thing that willpower alone couldn't provide.

When Lizzie had started treatment, he'd managed to visit her most Saturdays and the occasional mid-week evening. Later, he'd rented a house a mile or so away from Morne and taken short weekends. Finally, at Maeve's instigation – she said he needed a rest – he'd taken a whole month's holiday, an event unheard of before or since, though holiday was a relative term for him, six hours a day on the phone instead of sixteen, and three meetings a week instead of twenty.

At first he saw Catherine only occasionally when she flew in from England, where she was studying under some famous garden designer. He noticed in passing her freshness and exuberance, apparently undulled by four years in London, and her looks, which had settled on her well, which to his mind meant unaffectedly. If he was aware of feeling, it was the great and clear affection he felt for Lizzie. If he'd been asked to describe his heart, he would have said it was full.

In July, a week into his so-called holiday, Catherine came for a two-week stay which extended indefinitely, and they began to walk together. She was a fast walker; he, for reasons his doctor could have spelt out, less so. Eventually, however, they found a pace, and the walks became a regular fixture of the afternoons while Lizzie was sleeping, and some of the early mornings too. Catherine told him about her life in London and the people she'd met and the gardens she was working on, and he felt he was listening to two people, the single girl enjoying the big city, and the working woman who viewed the world with more detachment. On some of their more adventurous expeditions, they began to talk of all the other things that two people discuss on long walks: wars and governments and the nature of progress; ambition and friendship and love. She was an optimist, he a realist; she was what she liked to term a benevolent atheist, he a more-or-less practising Catholic; and so, coming from opposing philosophies, they agreed on many things.

At other times, he teased her as he'd teased her when she was a child, and she rose enthusiastically to the well-remembered challenge, answering as she used to answer, with nonsense and wild exaggeration. Then, towards the end of each walk they would quietly revert to the subject that generally began and ended their outings, the matter of Lizzie's wellbeing and how to improve it. If their relationship felt comfortable he told himself it was because it had both boundaries and purpose; if he felt an affinity for her, it sprang from the ties of familiarity and time, and their mutual determination to support Lizzie through the weeks of her treatment.

Which moment changed everything? Which of them had got it wrong? Apparently it was him, though for the life of him he still couldn't work out how. He'd deconstructed and re-examined the succession of events time and again, but still couldn't see how he'd misread the situation quite so thoroughly.

The first moment that stuck in his mind came on an early morning walk over the black hill to the north of Morne. They'd left Lizzie looking better than for some days, and Catherine was in a buoyant mood. They were talking about holidays and going abroad, and the relative merits of Paris and Rome, which they'd both visited, when Catherine paused abruptly and for no apparent reason turned to him and declared, straight-faced, 'I've been thinking – most women would do far better to go for older men, you know.'

This was a way of hers, to throw a provocative statement into the air and see how it would fall.

'And why is that?' he asked mildly.

'Because then they wouldn't run out of things to talk about on holiday.'

'Is that a danger with younger men?'

She gave a theatrical sigh, all breath and affectation. 'God, yes! The only thing they can talk about is sport. Oh, and bad jokes – why do they love bad jokes?'

'Don't be too hard on them.'

She walked on, pretending exasperation. 'No, they're worse than useless. Older men would suit us all much better. They've been to places, done things. They know what they want, they're much more relaxed with women.'

'Older men would certainly warm to an idea like that with no trouble at all. But how much older are we talking about here?'

She hadn't thought about this of course. Shrugging, she lobbed a figure up at random. 'Ten years? Fifteen?'

'Careful, at that rate you might consign a bright young thing to a decrepit old man like me.'

'Terry!' She touched his arm and grinned at him. 'You're not old! How old are you?'

'I need notice of that question.' He pretended to work it out. 'If Buddy Holly died in fifty-nine, then . . . I'm thirty-six.'

'Just a child.' She walked on for a while before stopping just as abruptly. 'Will you marry again?'

'Oh, for heaven's sake.' He wasn't quite ready for that question. 'Who can say?'

'Of course you will! You'd be a catch.'

He snorted, 'I think that's very much a matter of opinion.'

'Well, *I* think you'd be a catch.'

'Just goes to show your ideas about men are fatally misguided. Who'd want a workaholic heading for a heart attack?'

'Sounds perfect to me.' Then she'd leant across and kissed him lightly on the cheek. 'Seriously, I'm beginning to see you in an entirely new light. Careful!'

She was joking of course, it was a moment of light flirtation, gone in a trice, though not so light that it didn't add a small frisson to their next conversation, a frisson that might nevertheless have remained entirely harmless if a short while later, in an incident emblazoned just as strongly on his memory, she hadn't looped her arm through his and said, 'I love it here, Terry. Ireland will always be my home. I'm not sure I'll ever feel really comfortable in England.'

'Come back, then. Money galore in Ireland now – there must be plenty of people who want their gardens uprooted.'

'Oh, it's not the work – there'd be plenty of work – it's the life here. Or rather, it's the social life.' She chuckled, 'By which I suppose I mean the men! Or rather, the *lack* of them. Too many good Catholic boys, Terry.'

'Religion's never stopped a man yet.'

She pulled a face of doubt. 'It's Madonnas or whores here.'

'You mean there's something in between?'

'Ha, ha.'

'So – if there was the right man, you'd stay.'

The laughter left her face, she considered this seriously. 'Yes,' she declared at last, as though the realisation had surprised her. 'Yes, do you know, I think I would.' Then, in a lightning switch, she cast him a mischievous look and said, 'I'd stay for someone like you.' He thought she was joking again, she was certainly laughing as she said it, but then she muddied the waters all over again by pushing herself up on her toes and kissing him full on the lips, a kiss that was not so brief that it could be judged an assertion of friendship, yet not quite so long that it constituted a firm declaration of interest either. He was tantalised and baffled in equal measure until he reminded himself that it was a strange intense time for them all, that under the strain of worrying and caring for her mother it was natural for Catherine to look for light relief in games of love and desire. He told himself this, but deep down the idea of loving her was just there, waiting to leap heartlessly to the surface.

She phoned with the dinner invitation the next day. Looking back now, he could see that this was the point at which perspective and judgement began to desert him. At the time, though, it was easy to convince himself that the invitation was Catherine's idea, that as the one person who had Duncan's ear she'd persuaded her father that the time had finally come to treat Terry as one of the family. He saw it as a sign of her growing affection for him.

From this distance, the extent of his self-delusion cut him sharply. And when he really wanted to give himself a hard time, he let himself believe that the real reason for the summons had nothing to do with friendship or acceptance, and everything to do with Duncan's need for money, and that this had been as plain as the nose on his face, if only he'd chosen to see.

During the summer Duncan had been away a lot on business, which, as Terry well knew, meant buying mediocre wine expensively in France and wondering why he was then unable to shift it at a profit in Dublin. On the few occasions the two men had bumped into each other at Morne, Duncan had looked at Terry with his customary vague smile, delivered the equivocal greeting at which he was so adept, the muttered, 'Oh . . . Terry, I didn't know you were here', and, wearing a vacant expression, departed for another end of the house. So when, after twenty-odd years in which dinner invitations had been conspicuous by their absence, Terry suddenly found himself on Lizzie's right, very much the honoured guest, he took it as a sea change. The fatted calf was on the table, the silver was out, a half-decent claret filled his glass. Duncan was at his most gracious and urbane, the complete host, the practised raconteur, the all-round bon vivant. Lizzie, with echoes of her old self, sparkled with pleasure at having so many of her loved ones at the same table and stayed up until almost ten, which was late for her. Catherine was quieter than usual, distracted or thoughtful, though Terry in his half-unhinged state managed to translate this into a beguiling serenity. At a quarter past ten Catherine announced she was going upstairs to make sure Lizzie was all right. He had no doubt this was precisely what she had done, yet when he raked over this part of the evening later he couldn't help wondering if it was entirely by chance that he was left alone with Duncan.

Not that he was in the least surprised when Duncan brought

up the subject of money; over the previous six or seven years it had become something of an annual event for Duncan to be in need of 'the odd loan'. Terry braced himself, however, because on the last occasion, just eight months before, Duncan had asked for quite a bit more than before. In the early years it had been two or three thousand, but suddenly it had jumped to twelve, and Terry hadn't yet been rich enough for long enough that every penny wasn't still precious to him. He'd had to remind himself that this was a duty, like giving to his own family, and that normal considerations didn't apply. There were always going to be certain people in your life, related by blood or circumstance, who only had to look at money for it to vanish. His brother was one, his uncle another. Giving to them was a matter of obligation, you didn't quibble, you wrote it off and never dwelt on it again.

'And what can you offer by way of security?' he'd asked Duncan on the occasion of the twelve thousand because they always went through the pretence of putting the loans on a business footing.

'I thought, the sporting rights for a couple of years?'

Since the oak wood had long since been cut down and the wood pigeon departed – there was no question of snipe – Terry had supposed he was talking about the fishing, though by the time the local poachers had finished with the brown trout that didn't add up to more than a couple of minnows. But he'd accepted because honour, however transparent, had to be satisfied.

This time, Duncan began in his customary way, with some bleak observations about the business climate, before announcing that he was experiencing a few 'on-going difficulties', which were forcing him to reconsider his entire position, lock, stock and barrel. Not to beat about the bush, would Terry be interested in a business proposition? This, of course, was beating around every bush in sight, but Terry managed to hold his tongue while Duncan meandered back and forth, skirting the issue with a skill that would have done credit to a Cold War diplomat, before coming in at an oblique angle, with what might or might not have been a firm clue as to what he was after.

'So . . . I was thinking of going for a total restructuring,' he said.

'Your business finances, this is?'

Duncan made the gesture of a negotiator who didn't care to be drawn too soon, a hand twisted one way then the other. 'Well . . . could be a bit of both.'

'How much did you have in mind?'

Duncan gave a deprecating chuckle, as if the idea of stating anything so bald as the precise sum he had in mind would be far too crass at this stage in the proceedings. 'Well . . .' He had the lazy insipid smile of a man who'd learnt at an early stage that an easy manner and ready charm could get you a surprisingly long way in life.

Without warning, Terry reached some limit of his patience. Leaning an elbow on the table, unfolding a hand towards Duncan, he demanded firmly, 'Now, what are we talking here, Duncan? Cash? A lot of cash? Because if we are, I think we might have a difficulty. You see, I'm not interested in the wine business. I've no wish to buy into it, I've no wish to have a stake in it. And I don't believe there's anything else we can usefully discuss in terms of a deal. There's really nothing I want to buy. So you see . . . there's a difficulty, Duncan.'

Duncan made a show of taking this in good part, because according to the dictates of his simple philosophy one kept smiling through thick and thin. He reminded Terry of a dog that keeps trying to please, even when it's down. 'Of course, of course. I wouldn't expect you to be interested in anything you didn't want. Lord, no!'

Terry raised an eyebrow, awaiting enlightenment.

'No, no . . .' insisted Duncan. 'I was thinking you might be interested in Morne.'

There was a pause that for Terry was nothing less than electric.

'Obviously, not immediately . . . with things as they are . . .'
Duncan struck the brave sorrowful note of the loving husband
who can only wait and hope. 'When Lizzie's better.' This was
delivered in hushed tones.

'You mean . . .' And Terry could hardly say it. 'You want
to sell Morne?'

'Sadly, it's the only sensible option. Business conditions are
too difficult here. Far better in England. People actually *appreciate* wine there.'

Terry was groping for understanding. 'But you don't want
to sell quite yet?'

'I was thinking of delayed completion.'

Which meant the money now, and the house handed over
at his convenience.

'But, forgive me – isn't the house going to be Catherine's
and Alice's? For some reason I had the idea that Lizzie was
going to pass it on to the girls.'

Behind the bland eyes there was a shadow of annoyance.
'No, no – never the intention. Lizzie and I were always going
to sell in the fullness of time. Go and live abroad. No, no – it's
been settled for ages.'

'I see,' Terry murmured, though he didn't see at all. In
twenty years of conversations with Lizzie he'd never heard the
slightest suggestion of living abroad; quite the opposite. 'And
you're sure this is the only option?'

Duncan went through the charade of considering this. 'I
think it's the most realistic.'

Which meant, thought Terry, his debts have got completely
out of hand. 'And . . . if I were unable to buy?'

'Oh, then I'd put it on the open market. Lots of Germans
buying around here. Plenty of interest. No, I just thought with
your ties to the area it might just suit you. A place to keep for
your retirement, perhaps.' He spun a hand, plucking possibilities out of the air. 'A holiday home. A long-term investment.'

And still Terry couldn't quite take it in. 'So . . . one way or
another, you're determined to sell?'

A gentle sigh. 'Sadly.'

'But you'd prefer to stay a while—'

'Until Lizzie's better.'

'Until she's better.' Terry felt the need to spell everything out in great detail. 'Which of course you couldn't do if you were to sell to a German?'

Duncan tilted his elegant head while he pondered this for a while, as though the thought hadn't quite occurred to him in this form before. 'That's right,' he agreed with a solemn nod. 'It would be – disruptive.'

Terry thought: So here we have it, this is the deal. He was to buy time for Lizzie, he was to provide for her happiness by letting her stay in the house that she loved for as long as she lived. He was to pay for this privilege, undoubtedly through the nose, and be content to wait for possession until such time as Duncan decided to move out.

It was the solution of Solomon, and Terry could only bow to Duncan's masterly reading of his character. At the same time he was pursued by a deep unease. 'What about Catherine and Alice?' he asked. 'How do they feel? Not to mention Lizzie.'

'Oh, they're not to know. *Mustn't* know,' Duncan cried with a pale laugh. 'It would upset them dreadfully. Not a good time to think of *change*, you know.'

'But . . . the girls do realise they're not to get the house.'

'They've known it for a long time. There's never been any question.'

'Nevertheless, wouldn't it be best to mention this business to them?'

'Best? I think *not*, Terry. Not for them, not for me. Not for any of us.'

'If you say so,' he agreed reluctantly. 'A private arrangement, then.'

Duncan was thrilled that Terry should finally grasp the essence of the scheme. He tapped his arm. 'That's it!'

'But Lizzie will have to sign the contract. She'll have to see it.'

'No, no – she won't need to be bothered with the contents, she won't need to be told what it's about,' said Duncan in the certain tone of a man who knows what's best for his wife, and again Terry's stomach tightened unhappily. Later, he assuaged his unease with the reminder that Duncan would have sold the house anyway, and doing it this way Lizzie would at least remain in ignorance of it.

Thereafter, the details were, in a sense, academic. It was a question of establishing how much Duncan needed immediately, on signature of contract, a sum that probably equated to his current debts and then some, and how much he wanted when the deeds were handed over, an indicator of how much he thought he'd need in the next year. Thereafter Terry offered yearly instalments, or a lump sum on vacant possession, or a combination of both up to the sum agreed. For form's sake he beat Duncan down on the total price, but by the time he shook on the deal he reckoned it was costing him sixty to seventy per cent more than Morne was worth at the fanciest possible market price.

This transaction did nothing for his peace of mind. He didn't want Morne, he felt uncomfortable at the idea of buying it behind Lizzie and Catherine's back, and, so far as the money was concerned, he didn't trust Duncan not to come back for more. And underlying all this anxiety, lapping just beneath the surface of his consciousness, were his tumultuous feelings for Catherine.

A couple of days later, he brought Maeve over to Morne for a picnic in the walled garden. Alice was there, and some neighbours and cousins. With all the comings and goings there was no chance to speak to Catherine alone, but when she glanced his way and smiled it seemed to him that there was a very private and particular message in her gaze. Imagination? Wishful thinking? The longings of a lonely man?

Early the following morning he arrived at Morne for their customary walk, but it was raining too hard and they stayed in the kitchen instead. Catherine was drained after tending to Lizzie in the night. Her eyes looked enormous and empty in the flat white light. After a while, though, she began to emerge from her tiredness, even to tease him a little, which always cheered her up, and when he suggested an expedition to Castledermot later for a spot of supper she agreed immediately.

The evening had stayed with him as a series of conversations interwoven by a long unspoken dialogue. He saw her face animated, sad, thoughtful, but most of all he saw her eyes, which seemed to contain but one simple message. As the evening wore on – could he have been so wrong? – it seemed to him that the two of them were gathered up in a growing and unequivocal understanding.

Two days later, in a state of agonised hope, he sent the letter. An invitation to go to Donegal for the weekend, but also, clearly spelt out between the lines, a man asking a woman if she wouldn't like to take things further, the nearest a man could get in such undemonstrative times to a declaration. He signed it 'with greatest love'.

The letter was written on perfectly ordinary paper, cream if he remembered correctly, but for all its apparent fragility it might have been written in stone.


Promptly at six thirty the desk rang up to announce Fergal. Wherever Fergal's natural habitat might be, it was clearly not the fin-de-siècle opulence of Claridge's Hotel. In his faded baggy-kneed trousers, his crumpled linen jacket with the drooping hem, his recalcitrant hair, he reminded Terry of a rather shambolic priest entering a lady's boudoir. As if to reinforce this impression, Fergal looked around him with curiosity and faint disapproval.

Settling himself as best he could in a cabriole-legged chair with roseate padded upholstery, Fergal swivelled his eyes, as if to encompass the whole building. 'Not thinking of buying this one, then?'

'Not just at the moment, Fergal.' Terry offered him a drink, which he declined with a spread of his hand.

'How's Maeve?'

'She's truly fine. She's off now with Dinah, buying up Bond Street and Knightsbridge and probably the rest of London as well.'

'She's well recovered, then?'

'Almost there, I do believe.' Terry sat down opposite. 'So?' he prompted fretfully.

Reaching into a sagging pocket, Fergal pulled out his note-book and flipped it open. But either he didn't need reminding of what it said or he hadn't written anything down anyway, because he closed it again and spoke from memory. 'Pavlik,' he stated solemnly, his shaggy eyebrows knotted together in what might have been weariness. 'Bail application successful. Fifteen thousand pounds surety. Required to report once a day to the local police station.'

'So. As expected, more or less. The lawyer—' He gestured a lapse of memory.

'Gresham.'

'Gresham. Any good?'

'Wily enough, I'd say.'

'The question is, will Pavlik keep to the bail terms? Or will he try to do a skip?'

'Hard to say. He has no passport, no papers to speak of, except for a forged national insurance card. He doesn't have too many alternatives, really.'

'He might get frightened into it.'

Fergal gave a laconic shrug. 'Thus far he's shown every indication of resuming his life, returning to his haunts. On release from Brixton he made his way to the restaurant where he works, presumably to tell them he is back in circulation, then on to West Kilburn, to the address given to the court. It's a house owned by a Mr Christopher Addleston. It seems Mr Addleston deals in antiques when he's out of work as an actor, which is much of the time.'

'So. That's it for the moment, is it?' Terry brought his hands down decisively on the chair arms in a move that invited agreement.

'Not quite. There are two complications,' said Fergal in a brogue that was suddenly very Irish indeed. 'Firstly, I was not the only person following Pavlik home.'

Terry felt a beat of alarm. 'What do you mean?' he asked, though he had heard him perfectly well the first time.

'There were three of us along the way. A bit of a procession, you might say.'

'Who was this other person?'

'I don't know. Sadly I wasn't able to follow him once he left Pavlik's because he managed to find the only free cab on the whole of the Harrow Road. I'm fairly sure he was an amateur, though. Certainly not police, and not a private eye. Though he took a lot of trouble, I'll say that for him. He was in the public gallery when Pavlik came up at the magistrate's. Wearing a smart suit, designer-style, young professional. Then when I spotted him outside Brixton he was in casual clothes, wearing a cap, dark glasses. But it was the same fella all right, no doubt about that. Early thirties, five ten or eleven, darkish hair, pale complexion.'

Sitting high in his chair, back board-straight, Terry made a wide gesture of incomprehension that was also an appeal. 'I don't understand. Who could it be, for heaven's sake?'

'There's one thing. He was joined in the public gallery of the court by a woman he knew, also young, also smartly dressed. I'm guessing here, but I don't think he was expecting her. I would say he was startled to see her. They talked a lot – well, whispered. Then, after Pavlik's appearance, they left the gallery together and parted in the hall.'

'And she? What did she look like?'

'Darkish hair. Medium height. What you might call – I think the term is – statuesque.'

'A big girl?' He was thinking of Alice.

'Oh, no. Trim, but curvaceous.'

'Black hair, you say?'

'No, somewhere between red and mid-brown. That rich glossy colour that catches every kind of light,' said Fergal, turning poetical. 'The colour, you might say, of mahogany.'

'And the style?'

'The style? Ah . . .' Fergal's vocabulary failed him here. He put a hand to the side of his head and made a corkscrew gesture that might have denoted Medusan locks. 'Short,' he offered feebly. 'In layers, I suppose.'

None of this fitted Alice. 'For God's sake, Fergal!' he cried in annoyance. Jumping up, he strode across the room and stopped by a window. 'What have we here? What's going on?'

'What we have here is someone who wanted to make sure Pavlik got home safe and sound,' said Fergal mildly. 'Or . . .'

Terry strode back and stood over him. '*Or?*'

'Possibly someone who wished to harm him.'

Terry almost laughed. 'And if someone did wish to harm him?'

For a moment they stared at each other in mutual incomprehension.

Terry shrugged. 'I meant, would we terribly care, for God's sake?'

Fergal looked mildly disappointed in him, as though he had betrayed a singular lack of judgement. 'I don't think it would be terribly useful.'

Terry gave a heavy sigh. 'I suppose not,' he agreed glumly and headed for the drinks tray. Having returned from a weekend at Longchamps in which he seemed to have passed precious few moments without a glass in his hand, he had been determined to abstain, at least for a few days, but now he poured himself a large Scotch. 'So what are you suggesting?' he added darkly. 'That we *protect* him?'

Fergal let this remark pass in silence.

Pacing back to his chair, perching on the edge of his seat, Terry declared, 'It may be that these people are going to try to make him talk, Fergal! It may be that they're after information. One way or another, we should *know*.'

'Ah. That brings me to the other thing.' Fergal paused to add weight to his words. 'Apparently he *did* talk to the police. Briefly. When he realised the seriousness of the accusations. Before Gresham got to him and told him to shut up.'

'Jesus!' Terry gasped. As the full implications sank in, he cried more fiercely, '*Jesus!* And what did he say?'

'He said that he'd been put up to the burglary, but denied absolutely the assault. Said he wasn't even there when it took place.'

Terry stared at him furiously. 'Put up to it? But he didn't say who by?'

'No. He just said he'd been hired to go in and burgle the place.'

'Curse it! Why didn't we know this before, for God's sake? Why weren't we told?'

'My contact isn't on the case himself. He can only get so much information at one time.'

'We should have paid him more then, shouldn't we!'

Fergal didn't deign to answer such madness, but continued in his calm voice, 'Pavlik said he broke in during the early hours of that Sunday morning, a good sixteen hours *before* the assault.'

Terry exclaimed, 'Hah!'

'Later he withdrew his comment about being put up to it. Refused to say a word. Just stuck to the story about breaking in well before the Galitzas arrived home.'

'Anything to back his story?'

'Pavlik said he spent Sunday evening with two acquaintances in a pub. But the police haven't been able to find them.'

'Not looking especially hard, I don't imagine,' Terry declared scathingly. 'But he knew these men, he knew their names?'

'Apparently so, yes.'

'Can we get them?'

'At a price.'

'Well, then!' Terry pushed himself restlessly to his feet once more. 'Well!' He paced to the far side of the room and back again. And still he couldn't remain in one spot; he turned, offered first one profile to Fergal, then the other. 'Only one thing for it, isn't there?'

'Find him his alibi?'

Terry jabbed a finger at Fergal. 'Get it in black and white, watertight, no possibility for error! Yes – find him his alibi!'

'It might take some extra men.'

Terry made a sweeping gesture. 'Whatever it takes.' His mind returned to the other disturbing element in the story. 'Just so long as these other people don't get to Pavlik first. We must find out who they are, Fergal.'

'Without more to go on . . .'

'Get whatever you need.'

'It's not a question of more men,' Fergal pointed out patiently. 'It's a question of there being nowhere to start.'

'There has to be!'

Fergal didn't answer but fixed his attention on a spot some three feet in front of his chair, in the depths of the Aubousson-style carpet.

'Well, do what you can,' Terry offered weakly, which was the best he could do by way of apology. He knocked back his drink, and, telling himself it had done him good, immediately went and poured himself another. 'Curse be to hell,' he muttered under his breath. 'Curse be to hell and back!'

Fergal waited until this small storm had passed before murmuring, 'I've made a few more enquiries about Ben Galitza, but failed to turn up anything new.'

'Nor me!' Terry exclaimed hotly, and for an instant it looked as though the storm would blow up again, worse than before. 'And not for want of trying, that's for sure! I have these facts, I have a *mountain* of facts, but much good they've done me. There's no sense in any of it, Fergal. No sense at all. It's like a play going on in the theatre next door – someone understands what's going on, but it certainly isn't me!'

'If I can help . . .'

He levelled his glass at Fergal. 'You can have a drink for a start.'

Fergal was not fond of Scotch, but took the drink and sipped at it dutifully because it was easier to go along with Terry in this mood.

Terry sat down again, and hunched forward with a weary sigh. 'Right . . . this is the story. You will not be surprised to hear that it is a tale of money, greed and what should have been large profits,' he began, in the manner of a fable or a parody. 'It is also a tale of promises, broken and unbroken. The story takes us across many frontiers and many banking systems. We start in Poland, which is famous for its electrical cable and generator industries. We have a valuable consignment of generators that have been built for some hospitals in Germany. However, the order is cancelled – a contractual dispute over specifications. The person put in charge of finding a new buyer for these generators is a fixer called, let us say, Mr X. Mr X puts feelers out. In no time there is a firm bite. It all looks good. The price is fair. There's a middleman or two who wants his introduction fee, but then that's the way business is done over there. Mr X makes checks on these people he is intending to do business with. They are British, though reassuringly they speak Polish. He discovers they are known in Poland and some other countries in the old Eastern Bloc. They have done business in Hungary, the Czech Republic, Slovenia. They have a reputation for driving a hard bargain, but once terms are agreed they meet their contracts, they deliver on time, everything is done by the book. So, here we have it . . . it's all looking good for a deal that is going to be worth roughly fifty million US.'

'Has Mr X ever done such deals before?' Fergal asked quietly.

'Nothing like this. But he has a reputation for being

nobody's fool. Canny. He's been wheeling and dealing locally for years.' Draining his glass, it seemed to Terry that he could see Mr X, that Mr X was large and pasty-faced, with bullet eyes and unfortunate manners. 'Then,' he resumed rapidly, 'for no apparent reason, the deal goes up in smoke. The middlemen don't get their money. Naturally, they are put out, but they offer their services again, they offer to find another buyer. However, Mr X is not interested. He says he is unable to sell the generators after all, that a decision has been taken by a higher authority – he hints at a government department – and the machines are off the market. End of story, we would believe. But some time later one of the middlemen hears on reliable authority that the generators have been shipped out of the country. Sent, he is told, to Gdansk. But where did they go from Gdansk?'

Recognising a narrative pause when he heard one, Fergal waited mutely.

'Cintel's best efforts were required here,' Terry commented. 'It took time . . . but they discovered that the ship carrying the generators was bound for Mexico, Colombia and Venezuela. In the meantime, back in Warsaw, Mr X has bought a BMW, he is renovating his house, he has sent his daughter to America for a couple of years. He says she's gone to be an au pair, but in fact she's attending an expensive college, and is able to accompany her richest classmates to Aspen on skiing trips.'

He pulled in a sharp breath, he shook his head; this was the end of his story. He rotated a hand towards Fergal. 'First thoughts, off the top of your head.'

Taking a long slow breath, Fergal went through the motions of setting his mind to this conundrum, his eyes narrowed as if against a fierce light, his mouth puckered in concentration, while Terry waited impatiently, alert to any change of expression.

'Clearly, Mr X or his masters struck a better deal,' intoned Fergal at last. 'But you have to ask why, having scented the improved deal, Mr X didn't go back to the first buyers to see if they would be prepared to better their price. In effect, to have an auction. Perhaps the second price was so much better there was no point.'

'But why would it be?' Terry demanded. 'Why offer a crazy price?'

Fergal circled a hand loosely to show that he was entering the realms of guesswork. 'It could be that Mr X was providing a service for the buyers, something quite separate from the provision of the generators. Who can say? Perhaps he was close to someone in the government who could put another far more lucrative contract their way, perhaps he could bribe an official to allow something in or out of the country . . .' The circling hand became more agitated. 'There's an endless list of possibilities. But in broad terms – there was more to the deal than meets the eye.'

'Okay,' Terry agreed. 'Another question. Who got rich out of this?'

Fergal regarded him with caution, suspecting, rightly, that this was a trick question. 'Everyone but the first unsuccessful buyers?'

'You would think so, yes.'

'The first buyers *did* get rich, then?'

'No.'

Tiring of this game, Fergal waited.

'No,' murmured Terry. 'They didn't get rich. They got very short of money indeed.'

'Ah.'

Sounds came from the next room, the chatter of Maeve and Dinah returning from their shopping trip.

'But one of them was *expecting* to get rich, Fergal. One of them was expecting to get very rich indeed.'

With a shake of his head, a setting of his mouth, Fergal unwound himself from the chair and got to his feet. He could offer no more opinions without additional information.

'Will you give my warmest regards to Maeve?' he asked as he left. 'And tell her that I've found her that book. She'll know the one I mean.'

Terry promised, but in the hurry to get changed and off to the theatre before curtain up it slipped his mind.

Rebecca made a fine entrance, with her firm stride, her head high, her strong austere beauty set off by the whiteness of her skin and the severity of her black suit.

'Well!' Terry declared as he got up to kiss her. 'Time has treated you well.' It was true. She had slimmed down and she had developed a style that managed to look both simple and sophisticated. Her dark hair was straight and loose around her shoulders and closer to auburn than he remembered. She wore little make-up, but with her bold eyes and clear skin she didn't need to.

She cast him an appraising glance. 'You're looking affluent.'

'You're a cruel woman, Rebecca.'

She laughed. 'I meant just that – affluent.'

'What you meant was that I'd put on weight.'

'It doesn't matter in a man.'

'Ah, but how I wish that were true.'

She ordered a salad but refused wine. He had invited her to the Connaught because it was quiet and the tables were well spaced, and because it was she who had contacted him and he didn't think she would have done so unless she had something to say.

To begin with, however, she made him tell her all about his business, his horses, and his life, though for her life was just another word for love life. He did his best to avoid answering that one. 'Oh, you know,' he said equivocally when she pressed him.

'No, I don't!'

There was curiosity in her persistence, but also, behind her brittle smile, a wistfulness. In the end she wore him down and he admitted, 'Well, there is someone, yes. A companion.'

'Ouch! What a word – *companion*. That says it all, Terry. God! *Companion*. That's *awful*. Is she married or something?'

'No.'

'*Companion*. You're not in love with her then,' she accused.

Finding some sort of consolation in honesty, he said, 'I don't know.'

'Don't know, won't know,' Rebecca remarked cryptically. 'In love with someone else?'

He laughed mildly at this. 'No.'

'Hoping to be in love with someone else?'

'I'm not a dreamer, Rebecca.'

She feigned horror. 'We're all dreamers, Terry.'

But he wasn't having it. 'I've got most things I want, I work hard, I have a good life. And the things I can't have I don't think about.'

'Wish I could say the same,' she said wryly. She told him about the changes in her life, the sale of the marital home in Hampstead, the new flat she had bought off Eaton Square, the progress of her divorce, which was going smoothly, she said, only because they'd refused to fight over money. 'But then neither of us need to,' she said matter-of-factly. 'My father died a couple of years ago.'

'I'm sorry.' He couldn't remember where the family money had come from, but he knew there was plenty of it.

'So here I am, rich and single, God help me.' She cast her eyes heavenward. 'Looking for Mr Right.'

'He'll come along.'

She shook her head at his naivety. 'Nah! I'm a difficult woman to please, Terry. I'll never be happy with a lawyer, doctor, all-round regular guy who wants me to stay at home like a good girl. I like my own life too much. I like my own *way* too much,' she declared regretfully. 'Used to getting what I want.'

'A bit hard on yourself.'

'Just honest.' She pushed her food around her plate. 'That's why Ben and I were so well suited.' She left this thought hanging in the air for a moment before looking up at him and giving the tiniest shrug. 'We were both coming from the same place. We both wanted the same things.'

'I wouldn't have put you and Ben in quite the same category so far as ambition went.'

'Oh, I wouldn't be so sure, Terry. I'm fairly determined when I want to be.' She gave an ironic smile that didn't entirely hide the self-disdain beneath. 'I often think back to that week-end in Ireland, you know,' she said reminiscently. 'The day at the Curragh. We were having such a good time.' She meant: before Catherine came along, before she lost Ben. 'And that other weekend we had with you, when you took us to the west coast. Though I have to say I did feel a bit – I suppose – *guilty*.'

'You, Rebecca? Why?'

'I knew what Ben was up to behind the scenes.'

'Oh, did you now?' said Terry calmly. 'And what was Ben up to?'

'Oh, trying it on,' she said with a chuckle. 'Financing that Mick what's-his-name to buy that hotel for a song, and then selling it straight on to you at a big profit.'

'It was still a good buy, mind.'

'But you pulled out.'

'Yes, I pulled out.'

She tilted her head, inviting explanations.

'I don't like people being untruthful – people who're meant to be on my side, at any rate.'

'Ben was furious.'

'Was he now? And why should that be?' Terry asked facetiously, though not without the small hope, albeit remote, of gaining some insight into Ben's character, which had long been a mystery to him.

'Oh, you'd blocked him, that's what you'd done. And he didn't think he'd done anything to deserve it. He didn't think he'd done anything wrong certainly. By his reckoning you'd encouraged him to set the whole thing up and then left him in the lurch. Ben's always been very good at seeing things from his own – well, *individual* – point of view.' She shook her head indulgently. 'He's never forgiven you.'

'One of his more curious decisions. Like not marrying you.'

Having shuffled her salad to one side of the plate, Rebecca finally gave up on it. 'You're quite wrong,' she said firmly. 'It would have been a disaster to marry me. He couldn't have stomached a wife with money, you see. He needed to be the one earning, the one wearing the financial trousers. Oh, Catherine could play around with her gardens, but it wasn't serious money, was it? No, from that point of view Catherine was perfect. Minor gentry down on their luck. Class without cash. Perfect!'

Terry had never had any pretensions to psychological insight; instinct had served him well enough over the years. He could only listen to this judgement with quiet dismay.

Rebecca said, 'There's another side to that coin, of course. A man who likes to feel in charge of his life, who's dead set on making his own way – he's not too good when things start going wrong.'

This speech made Terry wary in a way he couldn't quite identify.

'Don't get me wrong,' Rebecca added. 'I don't mean he'd get difficult or – *nasty*. No, rather that he's the sort to fall apart. Quite a pussycat really.'

He understood suddenly; she had made it obvious in so many ways. 'You've seen him recently?'

She met his eyes with a spark of acknowledgement.

Terry felt his stomach tighten unpleasantly. 'In what capacity? If I may ask?'

She reached into her handbag and pulled out a packet of cigarettes. 'I'm meant to have given up,' she murmured. 'But it's these or the weight.' Coming to the question in her own time, she said, 'Shoulder to cry on.'

'I see,' he said stiffly. 'And what does Ben have to cry about?'

'Plenty, actually.'

'Tell me, do.'

The scorn must have been strong in his voice because she looked at him sharply and hesitated. 'He's got money troubles,' she said cautiously.

'I can't say I'm entirely surprised.'

'Oh?'

'Always biting off more than he can chew.'

'But he's always been successful in the past, Terry. Always done well.'

'So these troubles are exceptional?'

'Absolutely! It's something totally unforeseen. Something desperately unfair, Terry. I wish I could tell you just how unfair. The thing is' – her dark eyes widened soulfully – 'I was going to ask if you might be able to manage some help . . .'

'For Ben? I rather think you've come to the wrong place, Rebecca.'

She leant closer and said earnestly, 'I know Ben hasn't done you any favours, Terry. I know he's been . . . less than clever in his dealings with you. But at heart he's not bad, he's just thoughtless.' Reading his expression, seeing she wasn't going to make progress on that tack, she withdrew the argument with an uplifted palm, a splay of her fingers. 'Listen . . .' She dropped her voice. 'Can I tell you something in absolute confidence? Will you promise not to tell anyone?'

'I'd rather not be entrusted with secrets that shouldn't be mine to keep, Rebecca.'

She gave a small sigh of frustration, then, after what appeared to be an intense inner debate, decided to trust him anyway. 'He's been blackmailed,' she said abruptly.

Terry did not alter his expression.

'I don't know the details, but it's something – *bad*. He's completely broke. Desperate for money. I thought maybe . . .' Taking a plunge, she said baldly, 'I thought you might want to help him because of . . . the situation. Because of Catherine. I'd lend them money myself, but my father knew me too well, I'm afraid. It's all tied up in trusts.'

Terry sipped his wine and suppressed the urge to knock back the rest of the glass in one. 'Blackmailers don't go away. They keep coming back. He should go to the police.'

'He can't.'

'Can't?' he enquired carefully. 'Or won't?'

'Can't.' She leant across and touched his arm. 'But look – this is the last payment. Definitely. If he can just get through this . . .'

'But, Rebecca, there's never a last payment.'

'Oh, but there is! The blackmailer said right at the outset that he only wanted half a million.'

'Only half a million?' Terry repeated caustically. 'That is a large amount of money by anyone's standards.'

'That was the amount that . . . was in dispute. I can't say any more.' By the sudden doubt in her face, she looked as though she had already said too much.

He folded his napkin and called for the bill. 'Rebecca, I'm not the person to ask. I'm sorry.'

She attempted a thin smile. 'Damn.'

'And, Rebecca?'

'Mmm?' She was hardly listening.

'Don't do anything you will later regret.'

Her eyes flashed defensively. 'Meaning?'

'Catherine needs her husband.'

'Hey,' she said with a lightness that didn't conceal her indignation, 'you don't have to tell me. I know that one thousand per cent. No, you've got me wrong if you think I've got ambitions in that direction, Terry. Believe me, once bitten! I wouldn't want Ben on a platter, not if he were free, single and on my doorstep. Besides which,' she argued more fiercely still, 'he won't ever leave her. He's determined to stay. Through thick and thin.' She shook her head firmly. 'No, Terry, you've got him wrong if you think he'd ever give up on her.'

Terry bowed to her judgement, though nothing could dislodge his impression that the lady had protested too much.

*Dear Terry, Forgive me for not having replied before but I've received so many letters – something like four hundred, many from people I've never met – that I'm only just beginning to get to grips with them all.* Catherine had started other letters the same way, which gave the words a sense of neutrality, but now she must thank him, and that required more careful thought. Eventually she wrote: *Thanks for writing so regularly, and thanks for the flowers from Morne, which were an extraordinary reminder.* He could read into that what he may. She went on: *Concerning the garden, I can't say that Mrs Kent's ideas are right or wrong, I can only say it all depends on what sort of a garden you want. Gardens do change and metamorphose. I think it's a mistake to try to keep them exactly the same. However, from what you describe of Mrs Kent's ideas, it sounds as though she's trying to create an English garden rather than an Irish one. While this might suit some places I suspect it would be wrong for Morne, where the strength of the garden has always been its relative lack of structure and the way it merges so perfectly into the surrounding countryside.*

Catherine paused, feeling cold and a little faint. The infection had left her exhausted. Even now, the pen shook slightly in her hand.

*I will be glad to draw up some ideas for you, if you would still like me to. The best thing would be for me to produce some outline plans from memory, then if you approve them to draw up more detailed plans. If you want to take things further, I could arrange for the preparation of the site, the building of paths and structures as appropriate, the purchase and planting of trees and plants, plus follow-up care for the first season if this is required.*

*My fee for outline plans would be . . .* She wondered how

much she could get away with and put down a figure that was three times her usual charge. She did the same for the other options. If he agreed to all three options she would also get a commission on the plants, which could bring the job in at well over ten thousand. She told herself that he could afford it.

*If this is acceptable I could send you some outline ideas in a couple of months when I'm back at my desk.*

She finished it *Yours, with thanks,* and added at the bottom *Perhaps you could reply to the above address in the first instance.*

Rather formal. Decidedly cool. Entirely reasonable.

She folded it and stuck it in the envelope before she had the urge to redraft it.

They'd given her a side room while she recuperated, and she took the opportunity to sleep through the afternoon. She was woken by Julie.

'Visitor,' she announced.

'Who?'

'Female and young.'

'But who?'

'Foreign-sounding name. Maeve?'

When Catherine eventually got herself to the front hall, she didn't immediately recognise the pale figure in black sitting in the waiting area. It was only as the woman stood up and stepped forward that Catherine realised with a slight shock that it was indeed Maeve.

'I hardly recognised you!' she declared.

'I've done a bad thing,' Maeve confessed, standing with her hands clasped, palms up, her elbows pinched in to her waist, like a supplicant. 'I've come unannounced. And that was wrong of me.'

Catherine reached out to grip her hand. 'There aren't many people I'm glad to see, but you're one of them.'

It was a blustery day with spitting rain but after a week in a stuffy sickroom Catherine was desperate for air, so they went outside and sat in a sheltered corner of the garden, by beds of thriving weeds and wilting roses whose petals were torn aloft by the scurrying wind.

'Are you warm enough?' Catherine asked.

'Me? Oh yes. And you?' Maeve was wearing a loose black jacket over a long black skirt and a woollen scarf wrapped several times around her neck, but no amount of clothing could disguise her obvious frailty. Her face was pinched, her hands thin and bony, there was not an ounce of flesh on her.

'Your father told me you'd been ill,' Catherine said.

'Oh.' She shook her head gently, as if the subject were hardly worthy of discussion. 'I'm on the mend now.'

'What was wrong?'

Maeve addressed this question hesitantly. 'It began with an infection, which turned into septicaemia. I was in intensive care for a week. And then just when I was getting over that I had a bad reaction to one of the drugs and went into a form of shock. So I managed to give everyone a second fright. And since then – well, it's been slow.' She spoke solemnly and unemotionally, her eyes lowered a little, her body so still that she might have been a figure in a painting, with her pale skin, her dark eyes, her hair held back in a band. Only the loose strands at her forehead provided movement as they were pulled to and fro by the wind. 'Anyway, I'm all right now,' she said.

'And what about the nursing? Are you still studying for that?' Asking this, Catherine remembered the shy chubby girl with rounded cheeks and a sweet smile in the garden at Morne, talking about her plans to study at a London teaching hospital.

'I'm switching to nursery nursing. I'm starting at a college in Dublin soon.'

'How lovely.'

'I'll be happier with children. It takes a special sort of dedication to care for the sick.'

'I'm sure you'll make a fine nursery nurse.'

Maeve glanced away, and once again Catherine was struck

by the changes in her, the fragility of her body and the gravity of her expression. 'I'm so glad you came,' she said.

'Oh, I've wanted to for a long time, but it's only now . . . I'm on a trip with Dadda, you see. We've just come from Paris.'

'How nice.'

'Oh, I'd rather stay at home. I'm not a one for the race meetings or the restaurants or the shopping. But it pleases him to take me, so now and again I go along.'

'Your father – he's been writing to me every week.'

'Yes . . . he said.'

'I'm just in the process of replying. Will you tell him?'

'I'll tell him.'

'It's been hard to get round to letters.'

'I'm sure it has,' she replied in the same solemn manner.

'And the garden at Morne, tell him I'll be accepting his offer to redesign it—' Catching Maeve's look of astonishment, she paused. 'You didn't know?'

Maeve stared hastily down at her hands, frowning fiercely. 'I had no idea. I can't imagine why he should expect you to . . . why he should ask such a thing.'

'I gather he has doubts about Mrs Kent.'

Maeve was still breathing rapidly. 'Yes. Mrs Kent.'

There was a long pause in which Maeve continued to stare at her hands. Then, with an obvious effort to pick up the conversation again, she asked, 'And you, Catherine? How are things with you?'

'Things? Oh, they're as well as can be expected.'

'Will you get better?' she asked simply.

'If you mean, will I get back to how I was before, the answer's no.' Maeve watched her with rapt attention as she explained the limitations on her mobility, the walking on smooth surfaces, the crutches and callipers. 'But there we are. There are worse things. I might be quadriplegic, I might be dead. It's all a question of how you look at it. The usual thing – cup half empty, cup half full.'

'And how much longer will you be here?'

'Oh, out quite soon now. Got to get back to work!'

Maeve continued to gaze at her for a long while after she'd finished speaking. Then, seeming to come to a decision, she reached slowly into her handbag and pulled out an envelope. 'Catherine . . . Here are the keys to my flat. I want you to have them in case you should ever need them.'

Catherine was bemused. 'Maeve, I . . .'

'It's just off Regent's Park. The address is in there with the keys. Dadda wants me to keep the place but I won't use it again, I know I won't. I'd like you to feel you can use it any time you want to, any time at all. For as long as you need it. I want you to know there's somewhere safe for you, somewhere that no one will . . . *bother* you.'

'Maeve, I . . . it's very kind of you, but I really don't think I'll ever need it . . .'

'Oh, it's got a lift,' Maeve said hastily, as if this might clinch the argument. 'And nice wide doors. And the toilet's got space beside it – I checked everything very carefully with the spinal injuries people.'

'But . . .'

Before she could think of anything to say Maeve leant forward and, folding Catherine's hands around the envelope, laid her own hands over the top. '*Please* – it would make me so happy to feel that you knew it was there.'

'But I have my home. With Ben.'

'Yes, of course. But it would make me happy.'

'I can't imagine I'd ever . . .'

'No. But still.'

Catherine gave in then, because it was easier to do so. 'Thank you,' she shrugged.

Maeve stood up. 'I have to go now. But I'm so very glad to have seen you, Catherine. You are in my thoughts and prayers always.'

When Maeve bent down to kiss her on the cheek, Catherine was reminded of a bird, her touch was so light.

Ten minutes later Emma came into sight, battling against the wind on the far side of the rose garden. Spotting Catherine, she altered course towards her with a quick wave. 'God, darling, it's wild out here! Aren't you dying? Listen – you'll never guess who *I've* just met.' Her eyes flashed.

'A girl called Maeve?'

'No, her daddy. The famous Terry. We've been chatting!'

Catherine stared at her.

'He was waiting in the hall. We had a long talk. He may be a villain, Cath, but I have to say he's rather good company.' When Catherine didn't speak, Emma added inconsequentially, 'He had a horse at Longchamps that lost by a head.' Then, not so inconsequentially. 'He's charming and he's rich. I tell you, a girl could be tempted!' With a shake of her head, she laughed at herself before pushing Catherine back through the gale.

# Chapter Eleven

———◆———

THE CAB from the airport jolted along as far as South Kensington where it had a small but ill-tempered altercation with a white Transit van and Simon abandoned it to walk the last half mile. To add to his woes there was a vicious wind, an advanced blast of midwinter, which cut through his thin raincoat and chilled his jetlagged bones, still somewhere on Argentinian time. '. . . *the wind's like a whetted knife* . . .'

He lived in a thirties block at the Brompton Road end of Draycott Avenue. Seen through weary eyes in the early darkness, the box-like flat seemed arid and cheerless. He'd rented it as a temporary measure some eighteen months ago but, without the time or single-mindedness to find a place of his own, had stayed put. It was like a hotel room, just a place for marking time. The furnishings were bland and characterless, the style international-chintz, with skirted sofas and easy chairs in a floral design which, with relentless regard for uniformity, matched the curtains and tie-backs. In a fruitless attempt to stamp his mark on the place he'd bought some modern pictures, but they'd looked wrong under the low ceilings and had stayed where he'd left them, propped against a wall in the bedroom. The bathroom was tiny, the shower inadequate, the lighting execrable and the heating uncontrollable. Come what may, he had determined to buy a place of his own in January and move in immediately, onto bare boards if necessary.

The answering machine was showing eight messages, but he didn't attempt to listen to them until he'd taken a bath. He lay in water as hot as he could take for ten minutes, then went straight into a cold shower and felt the jetlag lift a little. He dressed for an evening that would take him to a drinks party, maybe a quick dinner if the company looked promising, and an early night.

He poured himself a glass of white wine before flipping on the answering machine, hoping, but not really daring to hope, that there'd be something from Catherine, who was now back at home. He'd called her from Argentina, but the first time her mobile had been switched off and he'd had to leave a message; the second time, irritatingly, Ben had answered, though Simon had deliberately not used the house line. Then this morning he'd called from the baggage hall at Heathrow to find her phone switched off again.

The tape spewed out its messages. There were two invitations to supper parties at flats shared by chaotic girls in Wandsworth and Battersea, neither of which tempted him, and another from a rather impressive girl he'd met at Cheltenham and never imagined hearing from again, which he would definitely accept. But his spirits, having lifted sharply at this, sank onto a more troubled plain as the next message brought Alice's low lingering voice into the room, wanting to know if he was back and whether he was free the next evening. Alice remained a puzzle to him. He'd taken her out to dinner twice and gone along with her to parties on another two evenings. After the second dinner she'd come for him in the cab with a voracious kiss, mouth open, breasts thrust hard against him, no possible doubt as to what she'd had in mind, and he'd had to plead an incipient cold to be sure of getting home intact and alone. Then at a party the next week Alice had been all over another man in full sight of him and everyone else. She seemed to live in a permanent frenzy, trying to do everything, go everywhere and, it would seem, have every man who happened her way. Sometimes he wondered if she was on drugs; at other times he thought she was trying to make up for time lost to her excess weight, now almost vanished. More recently, it had occurred to him with the abruptness of the obvious that her excesses might have rather more to do with Catherine, that, however terrible Catherine's accident, it had in a strange way allowed Alice to break free from cruel comparisons. What he couldn't work out, and what caused him suspicion, was where he was meant to fit into all this.

If he expected the last two messages to bring more welcome invitations he was soon disappointed. The next voice, which opened with a combative, 'Hello? If you're there, could you answer, please?' froze him gently, like an icy hand on his shoulder. Even before the voice announced itself as his aunt Betty he knew what was coming. 'It's no good, I'm at the end of my tether. I don't know what to do with her. She'll have to be admitted, Simon. I'm sorry, it's more than I can take. Could you please call *immediately*. This time I mean it! I'm at my wits' end. I have no life, I have no peace . . .' The voice broke into a sob. He saw the little house in Chigwell, with the garish purple-pink wallpaper, wriggly stripes above and stippling below a livid purple frieze, frilly curtains at the mock-leaded windows, cheap knick-knacks and dolls on the sills: straw-hatted Spaniards astride donkeys, flamenco dancers tossing their shawls. He saw the bedroom upstairs into which his mother barricaded herself on her days of fury, the multitude of ethnic-Indian cushions spilling off the bed, vying with the clutter of clothes and magazines and suitcases for floor space, for her revolt against tidiness was another gleeful source of conflict with her sister. He saw her in the darkness, lying slumped on the bed, head bent awkwardly against the wall, with the television on full blast and vodka, cigarettes and the cat for company.

He didn't have to imagine her language because it came blasting into the room with the next message. 'Simon? Come and get me – *now!* Do you hear me? Right *now!*' She was half choking, half sobbing with rage. 'You have *no* idea what it's like in this dead-end hell-hole. I'll go mad – *mad* – if I have to stay a moment longer. *Where are you, for God's sake?* You little bastard! You *shit!* Come and get me out of this *fucking* –

*awful – place*! Do you hear me?' What he heard was the ominous hiss of her breath as she filled her lungs for the long agonised wail of fury and thwarted will that he knew so well, a moan that to his ears had come to sound like an animal's. Rasping for breath, she ranted incoherently for a while, the phone seemingly forgotten as she was caught up in a fever of grievances. Then came the sly wheedling tone of entreaty. 'Darling, darling, are you there? Are you? My darling boy, my baby, come and take your mum away. Come . . . If you only knew how vicious and cruel she is to me. *Vicious*. She's always hated me – always, *always*! Oh, she always seems so *sweet*! Butter wouldn't melt. Little miss fucking *perfect*. But darling, you've no idea – she *tortures* me, she makes my life a *misery*. She won't even let me go *out*. She locks me in, the bitch, and I can't get out! She takes my *money*. I've nothing – *nothing*. Darling, darling . . . come and take me away. Please, darling. Please, please, please . . . *please*. Your mumsy needs you . . . Your mumsy loves you more than anything in the whole world . . .'

The earlier she started on the vodka, the fiercer her voice became, though the screaming and tears were always the same whatever time she started. He lowered the volume and watched the tape turning and turning while he dialled the house. It was still turning when Betty answered.

'She's broken the bedroom window,' Betty said without preamble. 'I was almost hoping she'd jump out.'

'What about the doctor?'

'He won't see her. He says if she won't take her antidepressants then there's nothing he can do. There's nothing I can do either, Simon. I've had it. She smashed the mirror yesterday.' He heard the niggardly note in her voice, the sound of someone counting the cost of the disruption. 'She's up there now, music on to wake the dead and the neighbours complaining. I tell you, I've had it this time!'

'I'll come tomorrow.'

'*Tomorrow*! I can't last till tomorrow. *Tonight*, Simon.'

And so he found himself looking in on the drinks party for a brief half hour before driving out through the unlovely regions of Leyton and Wanstead to Chigwell. He heard the music as he parked the car, and he heard her jeering at the world as he climbed the stairs. He called to her as he pushed his way past the makeshift barricade but she pretended not to hear him, nor to see him when he turned on the lamp, throwing her hands up over her head as if to repel him. It took him half an hour to calm her, to still the stream of invective and rage, and then she wept with great heaving sobs and clung to him, her fingers clawing at his arm, her tears and snot leaving trails down his shirt. Her unwashed hair smelt of filth and cigarette smoke and self-loathing. And all the time he tried to keep in his mind the image of her dancing the leading role in *Daphnis and Chloe*, the black and white shot of the impossibly high arabesque that he kept on the chest of drawers in his bedroom, because then he could almost forgive her.

These 'bouts', as they had all come to call them, followed a routine, and there was no departing from the tyranny of the progression, no short cuts to be expected or hoped for. The tears followed the rage; and after the tears came the slurred ramble of complaint and denunciation. To anyone else, the jumble of protest would have been incomprehensible, but he knew the script so well that it was like shorthand to him, he could extrapolate a sentence from a single word. Why was everyone against her? Why had she been abandoned? What had she done to deserve it? First the Company had turned against her, plotted to get her out, and after all she'd done for them, staying on through thick and thin, bad times and good. Who else had gone on stage sick, who else had danced time and again through the pain of injuries? And how had they thanked her? By kicking her in the teeth. Everyone was against her. Everyone. Men – all bloody bastards, Simon's father worst of all. Ditching her for that common tart, sloping away like a rat, making her beg for the money he owed her. Just out for what he could get, an easy time, burning money on booze and prostitutes, the worst sort, coming back with their stink on him. A bloody bastard, just like the rest of them . . .

The whining lament of self-pity followed the familiar path, winding back and forth through endless repetitions, illogical-ities and lost endings, until finally the last stage was reached, the vengeful semi-comatose silence, the ugly glare of distrust that followed him blearily around the room as he tried to impose some sort of order on the dump that was the floor.

Then, at long last, she slept.

By the time he'd bathed her face and hands and put her to bed and gone down to have his ear bashed by Betty for the best part of an hour over a bottle of wine, it was almost midnight. To get away at all he had to promise that he'd book another stint at a clinic, though they both knew it would change nothing because his mother's paranoia would always triumph over any shaky resolve to stop drinking.

The road back to town was clear, but that didn't stop it seeming to go on for ever, and by the time he found a parking space near the flat he was more than ready for his solitary bed.

He viewed the message light on the answering machine with suspicion, fearing it might be Betty again, or worse still, his mother, re-energised by her own resentment, but the voice that floated into the room sent his heart thudding with joy.

'Simon?' Catherine murmured faintly. 'Oh . . .'

His joy stalled as she gasped in a tone of panic or distress, 'Look . . . if you're not back too late, would you . . . could you . . . call . . . please . . . I'm on my own, and . . .' A gasp. 'If you could call.'

Christ, what a time to have left his mobile off! Tonight of all nights! What a bloody idiot! He cried aloud, 'God! God!' But it was also a cry of happiness and exhilaration because she needed him.

In his haste to dial the house he got it wrong and had to tap the number out again. As it began to ring he noticed the time was almost one. When it kept ringing without reply he won-dered if she'd switched the phone off in her bedroom, if she'd simply gone to sleep, or . . . He tried her mobile. This too rang unanswered until the automatic message service picked up.

He grabbed his keys and raced for the car. Stealing across one set of red lights, openly jumping another, he reached Notting Hill in exactly thirteen minutes and, double-parking outside the darkened house, ran to the door and pressed long and hard on the bell before shouting her name through the letter box. He pressed his ear to the flap but heard nothing. There were no lights showing, not so much as a glimmer. He was about to beat on the door when he picked up a faint sound and, putting his ear back to the letter box, heard her call his name.

'Yes, it's me!' he called back, with a leap of elation. 'It's Simon! Are you all right?'

The rattle of a chain, the turn of one deadlock then another, and the door opened a fraction. In his haste to get in he crashed the door against her wheelchair.

'Wait,' she cried.

He retreated momentarily before opening the door more carefully to find she had moved herself well back. He went forward and squatted at her side. The hall was very dark except for a strip of street lighting that slanted across her mouth.

'Catherine, are you all right? What is it?'

Her mouth moved but it was a moment before she managed to whisper, 'I'm all right.'

'What's happened? What is it?'

'Shut the door. Please.'

Pushing the door to, he found the light switch and they both blinked in the sudden glare.

Crouching again, he took her hand. 'What is it?'

She took a steadying breath. 'There was someone there.'

'Outside?'

'Yes.'

'Who was it?'

'I don't know.'

'Did he come to the door? Did he threaten you?'

She shook her head.

'Did he try to get in?'

'No. No . . . he was just *there*.'

'Well, you're all right now,' he assured her. 'You're safe. Nothing can happen now. Nothing!'

She nodded with more certainty, as though she was just beginning to believe it might be true. 'Thank you for coming,' she said forlornly.

'Oh, Catherine!' His throat seized up, he shivered with emotion. Reaching forward, he put his arms round her and pulled her into an embrace that was necessarily a little awkward because of the chair but none the less sublime because, after a short pause, she brought her hands up to his back and returned the embrace. He continued to soothe her. 'It's okay, it's okay.' And all the time he wanted to shout with joy because he was holding her and she needed him.

Eventually he sat back on his heels and suggested a cup of tea, and smiled a little at the banality of it. He wheeled her into the kitchen and put the kettle on. She was still very dazed. Only when some life had come into her face did he finally ask with great gentleness, 'So . . . tell me exactly what happened.'

'It was probably nothing,' she said resolutely, as though she might somehow convince herself of this. 'Probably just a drunk.' Despite the time, she was still fully dressed, and he realised she'd intended to sit up all night alone in the dark.

'You saw him, though?'

'Yes.'

'Where?'

'Over the road.'

'What was he doing?'

She hesitated. 'Standing.'

He made a show of absorbing this thoughtfully. 'Watching the house, you mean?'

'I thought so . . .' Screwing up her face, she seemed to lose all confidence in her own judgement.

Before she could change her mind altogether, he moved her firmly forward. 'How long was he there?'

'I don't know . . . half an hour? Maybe longer.'

'And what time was this?'

But either she hadn't heard or her mind was somewhere else because she shook her head and frowned more deeply. 'What happened was . . . I've had this feeling . . . since Ben's been away . . .' A final hesitation and she got it out. 'I think some-one's been following me.' She glanced at him as though she half expected to be disbelieved.

'Ben's *away*?'

'In Warsaw.'

Simon thought: How could he leave her? How could he do it? He asked, 'This person – this man – when did you first see him?'

'It was three days ago, when I went shopping. Emma was with me. I thought I was imagining things. It was only by chance . . . I just happened to notice this man in the super-market, and then again when we went to lunch.'

'What did he look like?'

'That's the thing,' she admitted unhappily, 'I didn't really get a look at him.'

'But you think it was the same man?'

'He was wearing this . . . hat.' She sketched a circle in the air over her head. 'More of a cap, really. Blue, faded, sort of cotton.'

'And you saw him twice on the same day?'

'Yes.'

'Any other day?'

She clamped her lips together as if to prevent herself from saying anything too hasty. 'I don't know,' she whispered. 'Sometimes I'm absolutely convinced there's someone there and then – well, I think I'm just being hysterical. The truth is, I'm not sure about any of it any more.'

He put a hand on her shoulder and she tilted her head over as though she might rest it against his arm. She said bleakly, 'It's quite difficult . . . being here on my own.'

'I bet it is.' Saying this, he thought with fresh fury: Typical of Ben to leave her alone. Typical of his thoughtlessness.

'It's the practical things,' she said, 'it's not being able to go and check the windows easily. Not being able to get upstairs if I hear something. I thought I'd be all right about that, but I'm not.'

She'd been back from the unit exactly three weeks. 'Of course you're not all right about these things,' he cried, kneeling at her side. 'Nobody would be. There should be someone here with you all the time. You shouldn't be alone.'

'My carer comes in twice a day.'

'But that's the day.'

She clasped a hand over her eyes.

'It's all right,' he said, laying his fingers lightly on her arm. 'You're safe now.'

'It's not just that, it's . . .'

He waited uncertainly. Eventually he asked, 'There's something else?'

She bit her lip.

'Do you want to talk about it?'

'Can't.'

He waited again before saying firmly, 'Well, try to forget about everything now. Just think about getting some sleep. Listen, why I don't I stay downstairs tonight?' Realising that this might be where she herself slept, he added swiftly, 'Or wherever you think I'd make the best guard dog.' He made a feeble joke of it. 'Across the front doormat?'

Her hand came away from her face. 'I couldn't ask you to . . . I couldn't . . .' But her relief was transparent. 'I phoned Daddy, you see, but I forgot he'd gone to France. And Emma – she was out. And . . .' She fixed him with her extraordinary oval eyes. 'You really wouldn't mind?'

'It'd be an honour,' he said solemnly, feeling a sharp thrill of responsibility and pride. His offer was rewarded by a soft murmur of thanks and the vestige of a smile.

'We'll leave everything else till tomorrow. Sort it all out then. The police and so on.'

'The police?'

'We have to tell them about this man, Catherine.'

She looked unhappy again. 'But I'm not sure. I'm not sure it was the same man.'

'We should at least give them a description.'

'But what would I say?'

'Well, the man last night, for example – was he tall, medium, short?'

She was already shaking her head. 'It was so dark . . .'

'What about the man in the blue cap – what sort of height was he?'

She thought about this for some time. 'It's no good . . . I just don't remember. So you see – what could I tell them?'

'Well, one way and another, you can't stay here alone, that's for sure.'

'I suppose not.'

'I really don't think it's safe to stay here. I really don't!'

But she closed her eyes, beyond discussion. She wanted to sleep upstairs so he carried her there. She was light in his arms. When her hair brushed his cheek it was soft and sweet-smelling, and he drew in its scent as though it might purify him of that other hair in Chigwell. He set up the wheelchair for her and turned on a couple of lights, then, taking the bedding she gave him, bade her a rather formal goodnight.

He took keys and went to re-park the car, calling up to tell her when he left and when he returned. He checked the locks twice, rattling them loudly so she should hear the sound and be reassured. He called a last goodnight, softly, and felt a thrill when she responded. The sofa was comfortable enough, but it was an hour before he slept, and then his night was broken by racing thoughts and anguished dreams. He didn't sleep deeply until very late, and then woke sluggishly long after he'd meant to, at eight.

He washed as best he could at the basin in the downstairs cloakroom before going into the hall and listening for Catherine. Hearing a muffled sound, he called up to her.

'In the study,' she replied.

The study was a converted bedroom with a small red sofa, a slatted wooden blind at the window, and two desks set against adjoining walls, Ben's minimal chrome, Catherine's a battered Victorian antique. In the corner was a round table laden with boxes, books and, perched on the top, one of the hats from Ben's collection of exotic headwear, an embroidered cap, Indian or Tibetan. The walls were decorated with Ben's school photographs and holiday snaps, but most of all with the hats, everything from solar topees and helmets to fedoras and deerstalkers, with, in pride of place, a Foreign Legion kepi, complete with neck flap.

He noted the evidence of Ben's struggle with the intruder, the deep gouge down one side of the Victorian desk, the splintered worktop, still unrepaired, while a new chair had appeared in place of the one reduced to matchwood. He knew that many of the pictures had new glass in them because he had collected them up himself and taken them to the framers in the first days after the incident.

Catherine was bent over her desk, sorting through a large pile of papers. 'Oh, I'm glad you're here,' she said in a strange intense voice, hardly glancing at him. 'Could you reach something for me, please?' Indicating a shelf above her head, she directed him to a ring file that was marked 'Clients Corr'. The moment he handed it to her she started leafing through it avidly, snapping the pages across.

He waited uncertainly, casting an eye over Ben's desk, which was also covered in a chaotic pile of papers. 'Would you like tea or coffee?' he asked after a time.

And still she was immersed in her search. 'It's here somewhere . . . I just can't remember which . . .'

'Can I help?'

'I'm looking for a letter.'

'Who from?'

'I don't know. But it would have been somewhere around November, December. Though it might have been an order . . . God, yes,' she sighed, 'it could have been an order.'

'What am I looking for?'

'What? Oh, a phone number pencilled on the top of something.'

It was hard to know where to start but he began a desultory shuffle through the letters and bills on the desk.

'No,' Catherine announced, riffling quickly through the file once again. 'It's not here. Could you reach me the suppliers file, please?'

When she'd started on this file he resumed his search of the desk and couldn't help noticing that there were quite a number of bills in red, as well as a last notice from the electricity company and a threatening letter from the council.

Catherine gave a soft gasp. 'Here it is,' she whispered.

He looked over her shoulder and saw a letter from a garden furniture company. Across the top was a number scribbled in pencil. Now that she'd found it, however, all the energy seemed to drain out of her, and she stared at it gloomily.

Simon pulled up a chair and waited in silence.

'It takes me hours to get up stairs on my own,' she said. 'On my bum. And then of course once I'm here I'm lost without my sticks or the wheelchair. So I haven't really had the chance to look before now. And perhaps . . . I've been putting it off.'

She looked at him directly at last. Her eyes were dull with tiredness and he guessed she hadn't slept much either. 'This,' she said, lifting the sheet of paper up like an exhibit, 'is what the police wanted to know about. This is the number of the nuisance caller.' She dropped the paper onto the desk from the tips of her fingers as though it were faintly unclean and began to recount grimly, 'One night when I was up here doing the accounts there was a call. I knew who it was straight away because the calls were always the same. Silence but with that strong feeling there was someone there. And quite often, breathing . . . I can't really describe it. It was only later that I realised the call had come through on the ordinary phone, not the mobile. They'd always come through on the mobile before. It was just chance that no one else rang up in the meantime. So I dialled 1471, thinking I'd get one of those 'number not available' messages. But no – this was what I got.'

He reached for the letter and saw a central London number with an exchange that he didn't recognise. 'Did you try the number?'

She propped her head on her hand and closed her eyes for a long moment. 'No,' she murmured. 'No . . . I thought about it but then I decided I didn't terribly want to find out who was at the other end.' She said heavily, 'I was pretty sure it was a woman, you see.' She cast him a defiant look that told him it shouldn't be too difficult to work out the rest. Then, slowly: 'But now I do want to know. I want to know who it is.'

In the silence that followed he groped for the appropriate thing to say, and could think of nothing. It would have been equally false to protest disbelief at the idea of Ben's infidelity as to sympathise. He felt his eye twitch and rubbed a hand over his forehead to forestall it. Then a memory came back to him in a rush. 'But wasn't it a *man*? I thought you said it was a man?'

'That's what I *said*, yes. I didn't want them delving into our private life.'

'But that's what you told Emma.'

'Oh, she got it wrong initially – she always gets things wrong – and then I didn't bother to put her right. By that time, I'd realised, you see. And I didn't want anyone to know.'

'You're sure it was a woman?'

'Oh, yes.'

He looked down at the scribbled figures. 'Would you like me to give the number a try?'

'Would you?' In her gaze there was a gleam of fear, but also determination.

He reached across the desk for the phone and, pausing to rehearse some sort of speech, tapped in the number.

It rang, and continued to ring. After a full minute, he raised his eyebrows and she signalled for him to give up.

'Oh, well,' she said.

'Do you want me to find out who the number belongs to?'

'Can you do that?'

'I'll find a way.'

She thought about it, then shot him a grateful look. 'If you would.'

He stood up. 'Now, how about some breakfast?' he suggested busily, starting to plan all the other things he would do for her this morning, revelling in his new role as her carer.

She didn't seem to have heard. She was gazing past him in an unfocused way, fixed on some distant thought. 'I'm leaving,' she murmured softly.

He echoed, 'Leaving?'

'Leaving here. Going to live somewhere else for a while.'

'I have to say I think that's very sensible. You can't stay here alone.'

'What?' She frowned at him as if he had missed the point. 'No, I want to live on my own for a while. Somewhere else. I want to leave Ben.' She looked away to the window.

He sat down again, slowly. 'Because of this woman?'

She said in the same dreamlike murmur, 'I knew he wasn't going to be the easiest man to live with. I knew that I was going to have to be the one to make it work.' She paused and for a time he thought she wasn't going to go on. 'It wasn't that he wasn't keen to try – he was. Still is, in a way. He loves the idea of marriage. That's the trouble, really – he idealises it, he sees it as something separate, which it isn't – it's just a relationship with a label. You still have to get through all the day-to-day things. He didn't want to see the difficulties, he didn't want to think of it as anything but perfect, special, sort of apart.' She took a long breath. For an instant she focused on him before resuming her scrutiny of the window. 'I knew he'd be away a lot. I knew he'd look at other women. I knew that eventually the practicalities of marriage would wear him down and he'd feel disappointed in it and that he'd be unfaithful. What I didn't expect was for it to happen quite so quickly. I thought it would take years and years, a couple of children, boredom, the usual things. And then I imagined I'd probably take a deep breath and decide to live with it, pretend it wasn't happening, do what the smart women do, rise above it. In one way, I knew it was bad to be thinking like that, right at the start of our marriage, but I told myself it was realistic, it was practical, it was the price of loving someone . . . *complicated*. What I hadn't allowed for was . . .' She trailed off. She grew so still that she might have been in a trance. 'What I hadn't allowed for', she said at last with an effort, 'was to find that I was no longer loved. I think almost anything's bearable if you feel you're loved. Oh, he does all the practical things, he's there for me, he declares he'll never leave me, but it's like a mantra, something he keeps repeating to make himself believe it. It's like a grim act of faith for him, a penance. The truth is . . .' She swallowed suddenly, a tremor of emotion filled her eyes. 'The truth is he doesn't love me any more. Not as I am now, anyway. This new person wasn't part of the deal. This new person is too . . . *different*.' She gave a smile that shocked him, it was so bitter. 'Oh, his intentions are good, he tries to love me. But the fact is he can't.' She inhaled sharply. 'And that's all there is to it.'

Simon could hardly breathe for the ache in his heart. Never had he felt such tenderness, such a wish to protect and defend another human being.

Catherine absent-mindedly touched the papers on the desk. 'Just to add to everything else, we're broke. Not just a little broke either – horrendously terrifyingly broke. Normally . . . well, I'd stay and see it through. I'd wait till we'd sorted ourselves out. But' – the fire leapt into her face – 'he's been spending money on this or another *person*. That's what really hurts! That's what I can't take! We've remortgaged the house, we've risked everything – and he's been taking some woman to expensive restaurants.' Grabbing a piece of paper off the desk, she brandished it furiously. 'One of those bloody places in the food guide with Michelin stars, for God's sake! Two hundred and fifty fucking quid!'

Simon concealed an uneasy shiver. His admiration was

threatened by dismay. It offended him to see Catherine in such a state of anger. Her dignity had seemed unshakeable, her courage fierce enough to withstand anything; it unsettled him to see her stripped of the very qualities that had always set her apart.

'So . . . I'm leaving today,' she announced in an uneven voice.

'But where will you go?'

'A friend's place.'

'Emma's?'

'No. Somewhere else. Somewhere secret.'

Immediately he saw a hidden place that only the two of them would know about, a place of clandestine visits and secret phone calls, where he would care for her. His spirits soared again, and he said passionately, 'Somewhere you'll be safe.'

'Yes.'

'Somewhere no one can follow you.'

'Somewhere Ben can't find me and talk me into coming back,' she said. 'I know myself too well, you see. I'd weaken. And I mustn't do that. I must have time on my own. I must have time to think. And to work again. I must have my work. It's hopeless here!' She was getting upset again. 'I can't get to my desk unless Ben's here to carry me up or I spend hours bumming my way up on my own. And I hate it downstairs, I hate it! I can't work down there!'

Again he was disconcerted by her fretfulness, which was somehow unworthy of her.

'So where is this place?' he asked.

'Oh . . . in the middle of town.'

'Is it suitable? Will you be able to manage there?'

'I'll manage,' she said with a touch of bravado.

'When do you want to go? I'll drive you.'

'No, no. You've done enough. No . . . And I've so much to sort out before I leave.' She grimaced at the pile of papers.

'Let me do that,' he said. 'Sort it all out.'

'Thanks, but it's all bills. Though God only knows how I'm going to pay them.'

'That's what I mean. I'll do it.'

She looked slightly shocked at the idea; money was an intimacy too far. 'No. Thanks, but no.'

He didn't argue. 'I'll wait downstairs then. Until you're ready to leave.'

She avoided his eye. 'Emma's going to take me,' she blurted. 'It's best that no one knows where I'm going.'

His heart lurched painfully. The familiar coldness came over him. 'I wouldn't tell anyone,' he said stiffly. 'I wouldn't dream of it.'

'No, of course you wouldn't. But I couldn't have you knowing and not Ben – it wouldn't be right.'

'Well, Emma's not going to keep the secret long, is she?' He tried to suppress the peevishness in his voice. 'Ben'll soon wheedle it out of her.'

This hadn't occurred to her. 'Do you think so?'

'Absolutely. When Ben sets his mind to something he doesn't give up. And Emma's not the most reliable of people. I wouldn't tell anyone, if I were you. You'll be on the mobile, won't you? Everyone'll be able to reach you, everyone'll be able to talk to you. No – if I were you I wouldn't tell a soul. Then you can be absolutely sure of your peace and quiet.'

'Yes, I . . .' She was full of doubt.

'I'll take you,' he said in a tone that didn't allow for argument.

'I'll tell Denise Cox where I'm going,' she decided finally. 'And I'll tell Daddy. I must tell Daddy.'

'Of course.' He stood up. 'I'll wait till you're ready to come down then.'

She looked at him contritely. 'I've upset you.'

'No, not at all.' His denial was too hasty; it rang with desperation.

'You've been so kind to me, Simon. The best possible friend.'

'It's an honour.' He managed a thin smile.

'Perhaps . . .' She indicated the papers. 'If you *would* sort a few things out . . .'

It was a peace offering. 'Of course. Why don't I put things into piles, ready for you to look through?'

'That would be lovely.' She squeezed his hand. 'You really are very good to me.'

It confused him that she should blow hot and cold in this way; it brought echoes of anguished times. But he forgave her because he'd taught himself that forgiveness was the most dignified way.

He brought up some coffee and, while Catherine went to the bedroom to collect some clothes, he began on the paper-work. The bills made by far the largest pile. A quick tally brought the damage to five thousand pounds or so, and that was just what lay on Catherine's desk. Listening for Catherine, he crossed the room and took a quick look at the scatter of papers on Ben's desk. There were documents relating to mort-gages and cashed-in insurance policies, lawyers' and building society letters, but only two bills. One was from Ben's account-ant, who Simon knew from the occasional work he'd done for RNP, the other from a law firm Simon had never heard of, for 'Fees as agreed'. Leaving these alone, he went back to the household bills and, coming to a decision, rolled them up and put them in his breast pocket.

By the time Catherine came back he'd filed some of the redundant stuff, had put the papers without an obvious home into a tray, leaving just a handful of letters on the desk top.

'But where are the bills?' she asked immediately.

'I've got them. I'll pay them. You can repay me when things improve.' He held up a hand to forestall argument. 'It's no big deal. I've got the cash, I wasn't planning to use it for anything.'

She cried, 'No!'

'The money's just sitting there.' He laughed it off. 'That's the advantage of no wife, no children, no mortgage – I've nothing to spend it on.'

She was torn, she began to argue, she fought one way and the other before giving in with a small sigh of resignation. 'I'll pay you back within a month,' she insisted. 'I've got this commission, a large garden. Starting in a couple of days. I'll pay you back as soon as I get the money. Oh, how I hate all this bloody debt! It's so destructive.'

'But fixable,' he said.

He asked her about the garden commission when they were loaded and in the car.

'It's in Ireland,' she told him.

'Great! Just come up, has it?'

'It's only been confirmed recently.'

'Near your old home?'

'Pretty near, yes,' she said.

'You're going there?'

'I'm flying on Thursday.'

'Can I help with transport?'

'No. It's all being arranged, thank you.'

He wondered how she was going to manage. He also wondered why she hadn't mentioned the job before.

Following her directions, he made for the Marylebone Road and turned into a small street tucked in behind one of the Nash terraces on Regent's Park. The flat was in a mansion block with a wheelchair ramp, a porter and a lift. Number twenty was on the top floor with a view over the roofs of the Nash terrace to the treetops beyond. A quick tour revealed a sitting room, two bedrooms, a bathroom, and a kitchen with a table and four chairs. The place had the look of a pied-à-terre, well done up but rarely used. There were no photographs on show, no mementoes or waiting mail.

'Who does it belong to?' Simon asked.

'Oh . . . a childhood friend.'

'It's a nice place.'

Catherine stayed in the hall, looking rather lost, as though the enormity of her decision was only just sinking in.

Simon moved the bags into the larger bedroom and taking

a closer look at the bathroom saw that it had a special shower for disabled people, one with low doors and a swing-out seat. 'Your friend's disabled as well, is she?' he called to Catherine.

She wheeled herself in and stared at the shower with bemusement. 'No.'

They were both silent for a moment.

'Well,' he murmured, 'it seems you were well and truly expected then.'

The note was attached to the fridge with a magnet. *Dear Catherine, Please feel you can stay here as long as you like – the place would only be empty and likely to stay that way for at least a year. The porter can bring in deliveries, and there's a nice man next door in Flat 19 who is the best possible neighbour and can be called on in emergencies. There's a car company (details on the attached card) who will take you wherever you want to go. The car service is my present to you, with love and affection, M.*

Catherine shook her head when he gave it to her to read. 'So incredibly kind.'

On his way to the car to collect more of Catherine's belongings, Simon knocked on the porter's door, which was opened by a wizened man in a uniformed jacket with the top two buttons unfastened.

'I'm just moving Mrs Galitza into number twenty,' Simon said conversationally.

'Ah yes?' The porter smiled, showing stained uneven teeth. 'That'll be your car out at the front then, will it?' he said in the accent of a stage Irishman.

'That's right.'

'Would you be wanting a hand?' He walked lightly ahead on the bowed spindly legs of an ex-jockey, leaving the reek of stale cigarettes and stout in his wake. 'Have to watch the wardens round here. Sharp as they come.'

'I bet.'

'But I'll keep an eye,' he promised as he lifted some books out of the boot.

'Mrs Galitza's not sure how long she's staying.'

'No, that's right.'

'She might need help now and then.'

'Oh, and I'll be glad to give it to her.'

'Your name?'

'Doyle.'

'The owner's being very kind, to offer the flat.'

'Indeed. Indeed.'

'I feel stupid – I've forgotten the owner's name.'

Doyle gave a fleeting smile, as if to commiserate on the state of his memory, before turning away and carrying the books into the building.

In the lift, Simon prompted him again.

'Oh, I couldn't be sure about the names,' Doyle stated breezily. 'Most flats here are company owned. People come and go. Come and go.'

'So which company owns number twenty?'

Doyle affected an air of deep thought. 'Now wait a moment,' he mused, 'maybe it's an agency that deals with it. Yes, indeed, I believe it might be an agency, and I'm not sure I have the name.' His eyes held steady on the floor of the lift cage, and Simon finally understood that such information was not going to be made available to him.

Emerging from the lift, they passed an open door, the entrance to Flat 19, and went on down the corridor to find the door to Flat 20 also open, and a tall man leaning against the doorjamb, talking to Catherine.

The man turned and Simon felt himself appraised by a pair of hooded grey eyes set in a long lugubrious face.

'You are?' Simon asked challengingly.

'From next door,' the man explained softly. 'Just saying hello.' He could have been any age from fifty onwards, with a lanky frame, unkempt greying hair and the baggy uniform of an intellectual, shapeless trousers and brown corduroy jacket.

Since he showed no sign of introducing himself, Simon asked his name.

'Latimer,' he said before rooting around in his breast pocket for a card, which he handed to Catherine. 'Anything you need, just phone me. That's my mobile number. I'm never far away. I'm glad to do any shopping, errands . . . I'm usually back and forth several times a day, so don't hesitate to ask.'

Catherine gave him an open smile, which advertised an immediate liking for her neighbour.

Pricked by doubts he couldn't name and envies he knew too well, Simon voiced caution as soon as they were alone. 'It might be wise to keep to yourself.'

'But he's just a neighbour!'

'I wish I lived next door to you. I wish I could watch over you.'

She gave a long patient sigh. 'Oh, Simon.' But words failed her and with an attempt at a smile she went to unpack her books.

# Chapter Twelve

———·———

TO APPROACH Morne was to leave the world by stages. First, the small turning off the main road at the signpost bearing the single place name, then, half a mile along a worn and uncertain road, the village. Few tourists ventured this way, and, as the jokers used to have it, those that came were only lost for the way out again, yet coming into the familiar straggle of houses Catherine saw that a bright new craft shop promoting linen and replica Celtic jewellery had been set up in what had been Reilly's drapery store, while at the far end of the narrow road that passed for a main street Paddy O'Donnell's pub, which had long sported mouldering wood for its door and window frames, had acquired a fresh coat of vivid green paint. Otherwise little had changed. Catherine was old enough to be glad of this, because she liked the place just as it was, and young enough to be sorry, because people her age still had to go elsewhere for work, albeit in these prosperous times no further than Dublin.

Beyond the village a gap in the high bank marked an unsigned turning onto a single-track road that wound up through hedgerows towards the brow of the hill and the gates of Morne: the stretch known simply as 'the lane'.

From the moment she'd left the flat, Catherine had experienced the sensation of being effortlessly conveyed. In London, she'd used the car service that Maeve had arranged, in Dublin Bridget had met her at the arrivals gate, accompanied by Pat, the driver, and escorted her to the Mercedes that stood at the kerb, guarded by another man, never identified, who immediately disappeared. On leaving the airport, Bridget had used her mobile phone to report to a nameless presence, who could only be Terry, that they were safely on their way. Bridget had then gone through the day's itinerary: the expected time of arrival, the lunch arrangements, the departure time, the check-in for the return flight. Nothing had been left to chance, and on this, Catherine's first solo expedition, she wasn't quite so brave or so proud that she wasn't glad of the assistance.

As the journey progressed Catherine found herself thinking: So this is money, this is how it feels. It was not after all a matter of ostentation, though there was an element of that in the Mercedes, but of seamless arrangements, of having people to check and double-check each detail to ensure that everything ran smoothly; people, moreover, who took their cue from those they served, who answered questions when asked, who chatted a little when prompted, but otherwise kept a measured silence.

The lane looked completely different, and this almost succeeded in unnerving her. The hedgerows had been trimmed so savagely that the branches, once tall and overhanging, had been reduced to woody stumps, which let a cold white light flood the road. For a crazy moment Catherine wondered if Terry's gardener hadn't been let loose here too, perhaps had blighted the entire neighbourhood. At the last bend, she prepared herself to see the house over a wasteland of uprooted shrubs, even – it was too terrible to imagine – completely denuded of its cover, whole trees or thickets gone. But when the gates came into view all the trees were standing, and when they turned up the drive it was between wide plantings of lusty new rhododendrons, most over two metres high, leaves shiny with nursery-nourished health and heavy with buds, and hardly a glimpse of the house until the very last turn.

The house looked both strange and utterly familiar, a place she might have left three years ago or yesterday. It was a moment before she understood that nothing had changed since the final months of her father's occupation, when times had been difficult and gardeners unreliable.

Fragments from Terry's letters came back to her, snippets that talked of wild tanglewoods and rampaging roses and unpruned trees and creepers with trumpet-like flowers unknown to the reference books. Never for a moment had she taken him seriously: she had thought it pure exaggeration, designed to amuse. Though the rhododendrons might have been slain, she had pictured the rest of the place in ruthless order, new gravel on the drive, fresh paint on the windows and all plant life firmly under control. Yet here was the past held still and magnified, the gravel thin and dusted with weeds, the strange mossy stain still clinging obdurately to the foot of the front wall like verdigris, climbers taking light from windows, lichen patterning the roof, and the tulip-shaped yew still sporting a ruff of nettles.

As Pat brought the wheelchair round from the back, a black dog ran up to the car, barking benevolently. It was a mongrel with one crooked leg and a rolling gait that reminded Catherine irresistibly of her own rather singular walk. 'Hello, Conn.'

Whether by chance or design, Terry didn't appear until she was in her chair, footrests set up, and ready to move. He came striding round the side of the house, dressed for the garden in ancient grass-stained trousers, a baggy sweater and a battered tweed hat. To complete the picture, he carried a pair of secateurs in one hand, and she couldn't help thinking that he had chosen both wardrobe and props very deliberately, to strike a casual note no doubt, but also to put her in mind of the days when he had carried out general maintenance for the Langley family at two pounds an hour.

She had rehearsed a pleasant but neutral tone. 'Pruning?'

'A desperate and futile attempt to bestow order on the roses.'

The hand he offered was large and warm, which reinforced her impression of a big man grown even bigger and more bear-like.

'There's coffee freshly made,' he said.

'And then if we could get straight to work? There's a lot to get through.'

'Of course.' He inclined his head, as if bowing to her professionalism, before flicking the briefest of glances over her head, a signal, it appeared, for Pat to begin pushing her towards the door while Terry went ahead.

On the few occasions when Catherine had bothered to imagine what Terry might have done to the interior of Morne, she had pictured rooms furnished in the country style peddled by department stores, largely floral, largely insipid, and largely bogus. Then, on reflection, she'd decided that Terry would have brought in one of the more esoteric designers, someone widely acknowledged to have seriously good taste, which she knew from her own experience of working for the newly rich was the quality they coveted most keenly, and that the resultant style would be somewhat austere, the rooms painted from head to toe in soft white or palest cream to offset a collection of spectacularly beautiful and expensive antiques. Nothing in her imaginings had prepared her for the sight that met her astonished gaze. Bare floorboards, a scattering of unattractive rugs, skimpy ill-fitting curtains, peeling paint in familiar if faded colours, walls with the ghostly outlines of the long-departed pictures she had known so well. In the dining room, camp chairs around a trestle table, and, visible through the drawing-room door, a strange modern sofa and what might have been a matching chair, looking shipwrecked amid plain walls and bare boards.

'I haven't done too much to the place,' Terry said vaguely.

Catherine could only think he was attempting irony.

'Would you care to freshen up?' he asked rather formally.

In another orchestrated move, the two men disappeared and Bridget stepped forward to offer help, which Catherine accepted as far as the cloakroom door. This room at least was furnished in recognisably country style, with a clutter of fishing rods, waterproofs, battered tweed hats and boots in every state of decrepitude.

When she emerged, Terry was waiting in the hall alone. He had taken off his hat, and she saw that his hair was receding and had begun to grey, and that it wasn't only his face that had grown rounder, but his waistline too. Again, she was reminded of a bear, though his eyes, which were grey-blue and steady, belonged to an altogether more watchful animal.

He smiled. 'Where would you like to start?'

She said crisply, 'If we could look at the plans somewhere?'

He directed her to the dining room where coffee was laid out on the trestle table: cafetière, cups, milk, cream, two kinds of sugar. 'Unless you'd prefer tea?'

She would have preferred tea, but she said coffee would be fine because she didn't want to delay things. While Terry poured, she caught fresh glimpses of the past: a faint damp-stain high on the wall in the shape of a seahorse, an area of chipped paint on the doorframe, the smudge of fingermarks around the lightswitch, dilapidations that had gone unnoticed in the last years of her parents' occupation, but which, like the absent pictures and dispersed furniture, were a source of sharp nostalgia.

As Terry put the coffee tray to one side and sat down, she took the graphics from her folder and began to spread them out over the table. 'These are computer simulations of the garden from various vantage points,' she began in a rush, 'and at different intervals, after a year, two years, five years, and showing the different layouts and options, which I've kept to three, though of course they can be mixed and matched a bit if that's what you want.' She glanced up to find Terry watching her steadily and thoughtfully, with little sign of having absorbed what she was saying. 'Obviously these are very approximate,' she pressed on. 'They can only give you a rough idea, and the effect very much depends on the maturity of the trees and shrubs that you decide to plant.' As she went through the visuals in detail and explained the various options at some length, she became increasingly aware of his inattention. 'Are you clear so far?' she demanded briskly.

'I believe so.'

She decided to test him. 'So how do you feel about the woodland? Which option do you think you'd prefer?'

A gleam of understanding lit his face, as though he had read and appreciated her motives. 'I think I'd prefer to have the largest possible area of woodland,' he said, with a show of great seriousness. 'Either side of the glen and all the way down to the meadow and right along to the bridge. Complete with glades, as you suggest, and some coppicing to the north, to attract the birds. That was your second option, I believe, wasn't it?' He didn't pause to relish his moment of triumph. 'And I'd prefer wholly indigenous trees, or – how did you put it? – trees that have been growing here for at least a thousand years. *Almost* indigenous. Like most of the Irish, you might say. And four species sounds plenty to me. Oak, elm, hazel and . . . yew, was it? Yes, I think that will look very fine. And if it's fifty years to maturity – well, I grudgingly accept the risk of not being around to see them in their full glory.'

She should have realised that, even with minimal concentration, he would have an effortless grasp of content and detail.

'Only one thing . . .' He lifted a hand and rotated it in a gesture of unexpected grace. 'I don't think I can resist one item from your list of exotic species. A handkerchief tree. The name appeals to me. The idea appeals to me. I believe I've seen a picture of one. Would that be allowed?'

If he was being facetious, he hid it well.

'It's not a question of anything not being allowed,' she said. 'You can have whatever tree you like, wherever you like, so long as the soil's right. A handkerchief tree would probably be best on the edge of the lawn, in the rough grass, as a focal point.'

'In solitary splendour?'

'I would think so, yes.'

'When does it produce all those handkerchiefs?'

'May or thereabouts.'

'So . . . I should hold back on all my tears till springtime, then.' He said it lightly, but not so lightly that there wasn't a reflectiveness in his tone, and it struck her that for all his money and success life hadn't gone entirely his way.

She said, 'This woodland . . . You do realise the size of the undertaking?'

He bowed his head again and smiled. 'You've explained it very clearly.'

'It'll take some time to cost it accurately, but if you want semi-mature trees we're talking tens of thousands.'

He gave a considered shrug.

'You want to go ahead, then?'

'I believe so.'

'But why?' The instant the question was out, she wished it unsaid. She felt the heat come into her face.

He paused to make sure he had understood her. 'You mean, why bother?'

'I meant . . . I didn't realise you had such a feeling for trees.'

This explanation didn't fool him for a moment, but he answered it all the same, albeit wryly. 'Ireland has so little woodland, does it not? It's a small investment for the future. A gesture if you like. We'll all be moving on soon enough, won't we, but the trees, they'll still be here. My small piece of immortality.' He smiled broadly to show he didn't really take thoughts of immortality too seriously. 'Not much else one can leave behind. Besides, I was always sad that the old woods went.'

He was talking about the oak wood that had been felled before she was born in what must have been one of her father's first acts on marrying into the family and taking over the house. While she was growing up, this event had never been mentioned at Morne, except by unwitting neighbours, who'd soon found it a poor subject for conversation. She supposed it had been done for the money.

'You might say the woods here gave me some of my

happiest memories,' Terry said. She'd forgotten his smile, the way it lifted one side of his mouth before spreading up into his eyes.

'The poaching, you mean?'

He drew in a soft breath of mock offence. 'Vermin control.'

'Ah.' She began to fold up the plans. 'Done from the goodness of your heart, then?'

'The pigeon were terrible. The rabbits worse.'

'And that was it, was it?'

Pretending seriousness, he made a show of searching his memory. 'I believe so.'

'Mummy said you used to take the brown trout.'

'I might have glimpsed them in passing, but they were too quick for me,' he said ruefully. 'Never could master the tickle.'

'She said you used nets.'

'No, no, that was Paddy O'Brien!' he said firmly. 'He was a devil for the nets and the explosives. Your mamma always had that wrong,' he said fondly. 'For all the years I knew her, she had that wrong.'

Rather briskly, Catherine put the visuals back in their folder.

Taking his cue, Terry straightened up and placed both hands flat on the table. 'The garden,' he said, 'would you want to have a look around straight away or after lunch?'

She chose to go straight away. This contingency, like everything else, had been planned for. A golf buggy had appeared at the front of the house, as if by magic.

'Is this yours?' she asked disapprovingly, hating the thought that he had bought it specially.

'I borrowed it from a golf club over by Carlow,' he said immediately. 'The alternative was the quad, but I wasn't sure if it was your sort of thing.'

He was right, she couldn't have ridden pillion, not without her arms locked precariously around the driver's waist. At the same time, she viewed the buggy with resentment because it was everything that was safe and dull. 'A quad is just my sort of thing actually,' she declared childishly. 'But not very practical when I'm working and taking notes.'

Pat lifted her out of her chair into the buggy and wrapped a rug around her legs against a gathering wind. She thought again: The detail, the detail. And wondered yet again why Terry should go to all this trouble, what he could possibly want from her. In the next instant she persuaded herself that it really didn't matter. When the fee was large and you needed the money, explanations were something of a luxury.

'We've had a go at the worst of it,' Terry said cryptically as they set off around the side of the house onto the grass. 'Tidied things up a bit.'

'From what you described, it sounded like Sleeping Beauty's castle.'

'Ah, but we fought the worst of the brambles off the house. We hacked them back.'

As they emerged onto the lawn she saw beds with only a mild sprinkling of weeds and hedges with the barest stubble of new growth. 'Looks fine,' she commented.

'Wait till you see the shrubbery,' Terry said, rolling his eyes in mock despair.

'The machete?'

'Believe me, that would have been merciful.'

'And you've managed to restrain him since, your gardener?'

'We've had him chained hand and foot, worse than a felon.'

Led by the dog, zigzagging rapidly ahead, the buggy trundled across the lawn to the long walk, where she saw real work to be done on the avenue of yews, deadwood to be cut out, and tops to be tapered to let the light down. At the far end of the walk, framed by the long promenade of yews, was the ancient arbour encased in a tangle of rose stems, also in need of pruning, and when they reached the opening half way along the avenue, she saw that the wrought-iron gate was badly overgrown. Making the calculations that came automatically to her, she reckoned it would take a good gardener seven or eight weeks to get the remedial work done, and that was before any preparation for spring planting.

At the arbour, Terry turned the buggy onto the narrow grass path that led into the area of scrub known as the wilderness, and stopped. Before them, the ground sloped away through coarse grass and bracken, rowan and young hazel to the lip of the small gorge, which sheltered, deep in its cleft, the concealed stream. Further down the glen was the bridge, also hidden from this point, and visible on the far side, the wild-flower meadow with its autumn cover, a sea of tall silvery grasses that rippled and shivered in the wind.

'It will be a derry,' Terry announced as he surveyed the wilderness. 'I think I'm right in saying that means oak grove in old Irish, aren't I? When you think of all the smaller places, the crofts and the like, which are called something-or-another-derry you realise what the country must have looked like in the olden times.'

She was aware of him gazing at her again. 'So . . .' he murmured softly, as though passing from one thought to another.

She glanced at him expectantly, and was surprised to see him drop his eyes in what in any other man could have been a momentary shyness.

He indicated the wilderness. 'Will it be possible to grow wild flowers under the trees?' he asked, like a diligent pupil.

'While the trees are young, you'll be able to grow them almost everywhere. Later, well . . . there're one or two species that tolerate shade. But in the glades – that'll be the wonderful thing about the glades, walking out of the trees into a sea of wild flowers.'

When she looked back at him he seemed distracted.

'Thank you again for sending the wild flowers,' she said, wanting to get this out of the way. 'They were . . .' She hesitated and settled on, 'different'.

'They probably didn't keep too long.'

'No, but that didn't matter.'

'You didn't mind then, that I sent them?'

'Mind? No. No, I . . . they were lovely.'

He seemed relieved. 'I'd wondered maybe . . .' But with a sudden smile he left this thought aside and said brightly, 'Now, tell me something, Catherine – if it were up to you, how would you choose to do this garden? Here in the wilderness, for example, would you make a woodland of it?'

'I couldn't say. It's not my garden. That's the whole point – it's an individual thing.'

'But it used to be your garden.'

'Never *mine*,' she protested. 'My family's. My mother's.'

'All right,' he conceded easily. 'So if it were yours now, at this moment, what would you do with it?'

'You're asking the impossible . . . It all depends on how one feels about a place, how one sees it. I don't live here any more, I couldn't have a view on that.'

He made a face of disappointment. 'So I can't have the benefit of your opinion?'

'You told me what you were looking for in a garden. I must go by that.'

He searched his memory. 'What did I say exactly?'

'You said . . . natural, tranquil, wooded.'

'Ah. I might have been concocting a thing or two there,' he said in the manner of the confessional. 'I don't think I really knew what I wanted. In truth, I'm still not too sure. Most of the time, I don't feel like a proprietor at all, you see. More like a caretaker who happened along.'

Her anger caught her unawares. 'We're all caretakers, aren't we?' Shuddering inwardly at the banality, she added, 'But you got the place. You acquired it.'

'Well . . . I ended up with it at any rate.'

'*Ended up with it?* You sound as though you didn't want it!' she retorted. Before he could answer she said with a pretence of indifference, 'But that's none of my business. And nothing to do with the garden. Which is what we're here to discuss, isn't it?'

There was a taut pause.

Terry said in a low voice, 'I think lunch will be ready and waiting. If you need to see anything else, perhaps we might do it later.'

He reversed the buggy back onto the main walk, and they returned to the house in a silence that she might have broken if she could have thought of anything pleasant to say.

The house was warm, the trestle table had been laid for two. Catherine could hear Bridget and another woman in the kitchen, chattering softly. Terry brought in soup and warm bread, and some wine. It was good wine, and Catherine decided she'd have at least two glasses, which was one more than the doctor had deemed healthy for her kidneys, or it might have been her liver, it suited her to forget which.

The skirmish still turning in her mind, Catherine maintained a deliberate coolness as they began to eat, but if Terry noticed or minded he gave no sign. He talked companionably about the latest neighbourhood gossip, the scandals and mishaps, 'though I've only half an ear to what's *really* going on.'

She'd forgotten quite how easy and unassuming his manner was, how his blend of banter and attentiveness made you feel you were the one person in the world he wanted to talk to. She'd forgotten how effectively he used this approach to draw you into a sense of friendship and intimacy, and how easy it was to believe in it. There had been a time in the long summer of her mother's illness when she'd been beguiled by this, when she'd come to look forward to their walks and their rambling absurd intense conversations, had even – it made her shudder now – begun to think of him with great fondness. But – thank God – she had found him out in time.

She accepted a third glass of wine even before he brought the main course.

'It was good to see Maeve at the unit that day,' she said. 'But you were there too. You should have come in and said hello.'

'I thought best not,' he said pleasantly. 'I thought one of us was probably enough.'

'How's she enjoying the nursery nursing? The new college?'

'A success, it seems.'

'And her health?'

'Oh, stronger, you know. Better by the day.'

'She was very ill, she said.'

'She nearly died.'

'Septicaemia.'

Lowering his fork, he said sharply, 'It was the incompetence of the doctors.'

'They didn't spot it in time?'

'Too busy banking their fees. I'd like to sue them to kingdom come, I'd like to see every last one of them struck off.' The quietness of his voice did not disguise the enmity beneath, and it seemed to Catherine that this gave the lie to the quiet charm that had gone before, that here at last was the vengeful man who did not take kindly to being thwarted. Then, as if to turn this impression on its head, he gave a long and heartfelt sigh. 'I'd do it if I believed for a moment that it could make up for the suffering Maeve has been through. But sometimes at the end of the day it's wiser to think about your future, your health, and whether you want something like that hanging over you, poisoning your life, for years and years to come. If you can't forgive, you can at least try to forget and put it behind you. This is Maeve's view. And it is mine.' He looked at her in a strange way, as though he wanted to say more, before changing the subject abruptly. 'But now, what about you, Catherine? How are you getting on?'

'Me?' She was immediately on her guard. 'Oh, well enough. I can't run like I used to, of course.'

Far from being embarrassed, he seemed to understand her need for bad jokes. 'But you're managing all right?'

'Oh yes.'

'It must be a matter of the practicalities, of a hundred small annoyances.'

'I've never tried counting them, but yes, the annoyances. And other people.'

He grasped her meaning immediately. 'Ah, they try too hard, do they? Kind to a fault?'

'They gush. They talk as though I were a child. That, or they look above me, past me, through me. I become invisible.'

'It could have advantages, being invisible . . . But perhaps not that many.'

'Not that many.'

'But you have your family, your friends.'

She said evasively, 'I have all I need.'

'And the house, it's been adapted? You're managing there?'

This answered the question that had been on her mind for some days: whether Terry knew she was living in the flat, whether Maeve had kept her promise of secrecy. 'The house . . . is not ideal,' she admitted. She hadn't intended to tell him about the difficulties of living in a two-storey house without a stairlift but he was a patient and attentive listener, and perhaps she'd got to the stage where she needed to tell somebody, but she found herself going through it at some length, finishing on a note of exasperation. In case this had given away too much, she added, 'Of course, we'd have put in a stairlift if we were sure about keeping the house. But we're still thinking about moving. We haven't made up our minds yet.'

'But what happens when Ben's away – you're not on your own there, are you?'

She stiffened. 'Occasionally.'

A long pause in which he fiddled with a spoon and seemed noticeably ill at ease. Several times he seemed on the point of speaking before he finally asked, 'And the trial of this man?'

'It starts next week.'

'Are you going to have to appear yourself?'

'No.'

'But still a strain, I imagine.'

'Only if I let it be.'

'You have plenty of support?'

He had asked it with such open concern that she answered this too. 'Yes. The police are very good.'

'Support's very important,' he muttered vaguely.

Another silence during which Terry laced and unlaced his fingers several times. 'Ben's still in partnership with Mr Jardine, is he?' he asked eventually.

She queried the subject with a frown.

'I was just curious,' he said.

'Actually, no,' she answered cautiously. 'Simon decided to go his own way.'

'I see. Since when?'

'Oh, quite recently.'

'Ah. But it was a mutual thing, was it?'

'Completely.'

And with that, the strange stilted questions came to an end.

There was a pudding, but she couldn't eat it. There was more wine, which she could manage very well. Over coffee, he asked about her work, but aware that the wine was in danger of making her garrulous she got him to talk about his work instead.

'Oh, it reached the stage last year where I had no life of my own, working insane hours, so I decided to pull back a little, to give myself a bit more time to stand and stare, to travel a bit.'

'With Maeve?'

'Ah, when I can. No, usually with Dinah, my lady friend.'

This took Catherine completely by surprise, it was an effort to keep the astonishment out of her face, though the moment she stopped to think about it she realised that Terry would never have stayed unattached for long. In Dublin circles – in any circles – he was probably seen as a great catch. No, what had caught her out was the passage of time. In her mind he was still the rather solitary man from five years ago, the widower of under two years with the touching devotion to her mother. Also, and unforgivably, he was the arrogant self-made man who'd managed to equate love with power, and had the nerve to suggest a relationship with her at the very moment when he was in the process of defrauding her father.

'So,' she said carefully, 'this spare time – will you be spending it at Morne?'

'I'm always trying to come more often.'

'How often do you get here at the moment?'

'Ah. Not as often as I'd like,' he said a touch sheepishly.

'Weekends?' she persisted.

'Once a month, if I'm lucky. Bit of a waste, really.'

It could have been the wine, it could have been the reminders of the past, but the resentment welled up in her again. 'Yet you were so anxious to get hold of this place.'

He paused. 'I wouldn't say anxious exactly.'

'Well, you didn't miss the opportunity.'

'I never saw it as an opportunity, Catherine.'

'It was a favour, then?' She hated the sarcasm in her voice.

'No,' he said with dignity, 'not that, either.'

And still she wouldn't let go. 'So Morne just fell into your lap.'

His eyes darkened, he gazed at her with something like disappointment. 'I didn't seek to come here, Catherine.'

She shook her head at him in mute anger.

Slowly, with the air of someone undergoing an ordeal he would rather avoid, Terry slid his elbows onto the table and made a cage of his fingers, before saying in a considered tone, 'I never wanted this house, Catherine. In fact, I've never known what to do with it. I'd sell it tomorrow if I felt it was the right thing to do.'

'But you took over the mortgage, you . . . foreclosed on it – or whatever it is. You were bound to end up with the place.'

Again, he chose his words carefully. 'I only did what I was asked to do.'

'You're suggesting Daddy *wanted* to give up the house?'

'It wasn't quite as simple as that, Catherine.'

'So how complicated was it? Either my father wanted to stay or he didn't.'

'Perhaps you should ask him.'

'I already have.'

He dropped his eyes, he sat back in his seat with a small

gesture of submission, and said quietly, 'Then you must take that as your answer, mustn't you?'

The dependency clinic stood in the grounds of a private hospital serving the commuter belts of Kent and East Sussex. It was the cheapest Simon had been able to find, which wasn't saying a great deal because all the private clinics were daylight robbery. But National Health places were impossible to find unless the addict was prepared to wait months. So far as his mother was concerned no amount of waiting would ever make the time right, of course, but the six weeks would at least offer a respite for Betty. And for me, he thought. Most of all for me.

Following accepted practice, his mother was to share a room; following normal routine, she informed the nurse that this would be out of the question. The inevitable scene ensued. First the imperious *froideur*, the grand inspection of the premises and the announcement that it wouldn't do, as though she'd booked the Ritz and been shown a seedy B & B; then the reasoned argument, delivered in a sweet voice of injured innocence.

Some token tears followed, then, when these proved futile, came the venom, delivered with skill and precision because she knew exactly what she was doing when she was sober.

'I only have to look at him to feel sick,' she told the staff. 'Because he's just like his father – a two-faced shit.'

The lexicon varied but the substance always remained the same. When he finally got her into the room and unpacked, she sat on the bed like a martyr, face set, mouth pulled down, eyes drooping, talking of suicide. He remonstrated, as he always did, but she wouldn't be denied her outpouring of bitterness, her chance to visit her anger on him in the name of his father.

The next stage brought a familiar turmoil, a surge of heat and tension, like the spiking of an old wound. She told him things about his father that no mother should ever tell a son, things that as a child he'd barely understood except to know that they were hurtful and loathsome and must surely be his fault, things that as he'd grown older he'd heard with growing confusion and despair, and something else dark and shameful which he dare not name.

He listened as he always listened, silently, obediently, feeling the heat and disgust which had long ago become indistinguishable to him, until they reached the last stage, the long process of pacifying her, of repeating the reassurances and promises of devotion that she'd heard a hundred times before, but still demanded of him feverishly, like a liturgy from an abandoned religion.

He returned to London with a sense of deep fatigue and nagging dread, knowing it was only a matter of time before she threatened to walk out, wondering as always how many phone calls and blandishments it would take to dissuade her.

His mood didn't improve when he realised he was going to be late for his meeting with Wilson. Nearing town, it began spotting with rain. By the time he parked in Notting Hill it was bucketing down. He jogged into the police station exactly forty-five minutes late. Fortunately Wilson hadn't gone out. While he waited for him to come down to the lobby, Simon ran a comb quickly through his dripping hair and dried his spectacles with a handkerchief.

'Mr Jardine! Brought the weather with you, I see.' In keeping with his little quip, Wilson seemed lively, almost cheerful: the clear-up rate improved perhaps, or no murders this week. 'How's Catherine?' he asked.

'Fine, thank you.'

Wilson took him through the pass door. 'She did better than expected, I gather. Earned herself early release.'

'She said she couldn't take more of the physio's sadism. That and the quiz nights.'

Wilson gave the obligatory laugh, then, finding a vacant interview room, waved Simon to a seat. 'So, what can I do for you?' he demanded crisply.

'I just wanted to catch up really. I've been away—'

'Argentina, you said?' Sitting on the other side of the table, he made a show of racking his brains. 'Pampas? Or have I got that completely wrong?'

There seemed no limit to his bonhomie today. Simon replied pleasantly, 'I only got as far as Buenos Aires.'

'Ah. No pampas then.'

'Not a lot.' Hoping this had exhausted the travel talk, Simon ventured, 'There were a couple of things I wanted to ask, if that's all right.'

Wilson gestured him on with a flip of his hand, as if he'd be the last person to hold things up.

'This is a bit difficult,' Simon began with a suitably awkward laugh. 'I don't want Catherine to think I'm going behind her back. It's just that . . . well, she happened to mention that she'd come across the number of that nuisance caller. She made a note of it late one night, thought she'd lost it, then found it again a couple of days ago.'

Wilson made a face of great puzzlement. 'But the calls came through on her mobile telephone. There was no easy way to trace them.'

'That's right. But this time the call came through on the house line, and she used 1471 to get the number.'

Wilson tightened his lips. 'But this call – it was silent, like the rest?'

'As I understand it.'

'So it could have been someone else altogether?'

'Possibly,' Simon conceded rapidly. 'But Catherine thought not. She thought it was the same person.'

'Though the person didn't speak?'

'That's right.'

They exchanged a complicit smile, as if to say: this is the way women are, intuitive, beyond simple logic.

'And we're not talking wrong numbers any more?'

Simon chose to answer this with a diplomatic shrug.

'I never thought we were,' Wilson remarked heavily. 'Not for a second.'

Under Wilson's unwavering gaze, Simon reached into his wallet for the slip of paper he'd prepared and handed it over. Wilson laid the number on the table without looking at it. 'I'll get it checked this afternoon.'

'You'll let me know, obviously? Rather than Catherine? So she's not bothered.'

When Wilson's eyes narrowed Simon thought for a moment he'd gone too far. But apparently it was just Wilson's way, to consider all requests with circumspection, because the next moment he nodded unconcernedly and lifted his eyebrows, ready for the other item on the agenda.

'Yes . . . Again, I'm going a bit behind Catherine's back.' Simon frowned to show that even the mildest subterfuge was distasteful to him. 'She didn't want to tell you in case it was nothing, in case it caused unnecessary fuss, but I thought you should know. The thing is, Catherine had the idea that someone might be following her earlier this week.'

Wilson's look of polite interest sharpened into something more terrier-like. 'Did she get a look at this person?'

'No. Not enough to give a description anyway. It happened twice. She *thinks* it happened twice. The first time, she was out shopping and saw this man in a blue cap twice within the space of an hour. Sort of loitering nearby. Then on Tuesday night there was someone standing opposite the house for quite a while. But she couldn't say if it was the same man.'

'A blue cap? Loitering?' Wilson asked in a flat tone of disappointment. 'That was it?' Then, without waiting for an answer: 'And the man outside the house – she only saw him the once?'

'Apparently.'

'Did he appear to be watching the house? Or just hanging about?'

'It was very dark.' Simon made a regretful face.

'Height? Age? Weight? Ethnic group?' Wilson rattled the questions off without expectation of anything useful by way of reply.

'Nothing.'

'And no similar incidents since?'

'No, but then she's moved into this flat for the time being, and it's quite a long way from the house.'

'Ah yes, WPC Cox did inform me.'

'I encouraged her to go. While her husband's away.'

'Good idea,' Wilson muttered vaguely.

'It was just to be on the safe side.'

Coming to a decision, Wilson said, 'Yes, best thing all round, because I regret to say we won't be able to follow up on these incidents. Without a description to go on, without any certainty that she was being followed . . .' He gestured sympathy. 'Perhaps she's just a bit nervous, what with the trial coming up. A bit jumpy with her husband being away.'

'You don't think it could have been Pavlik?'

'Pavlik? Not likely.'

'Why?'

'Never been a stalker. No reason to start now. No motive to try to intimidate Catherine. She can't identify him as her assailant.'

'He's been keeping to his bail conditions?'

'He must be reporting daily to his local nick, otherwise we'd have heard soon enough.'

'And the other conditions?'

'We assume everything's all right unless we hear to the contrary.'

Simon wanted to say: Well, he wasn't bloody working at La Rondine last night for a start, and the house in Fifth Avenue was deserted till at least three in the morning, so I don't know how you can sit there and assume anything at all.

'We did check things out at the beginning,' Wilson volunteered smoothly. 'Visited his landlord.' He added with what might have been a sneer, 'Though landlord is not the word some might choose.'

Simon was silent.

'Protector,' Wilson threw into the air. 'Admirer. An older

man with – what shall we say? – charming manners and a voice to match.' He made a knowing face.

'Gay, you mean?'

'It would seem so, yes.'

'But . . .' In a theatrical gesture of incomprehension, Simon touched his fingertips to his temples. 'I thought . . . You mentioned sexual overtones . . . in the attack. You talked about a possible stalker.'

'That's right.'

'But if Pavlik's gay, then surely . . .?'

With the manner of someone only too glad to enlighten others, Wilson said, 'I'm no psychologist, Mr Jardine, but from what the experts tell me Pavlik wouldn't be the first homosexual to have violently mixed feelings about women. Apparently some of them adore and worship women from afar, but once they get close, then something called – I think I'm right – *heterophobia* kicks in. All mixed up with Oedipus-type feelings. Revulsion, revenge. Getting back at mother and women in general for all the imaginary wrongs they've suffered. Confused sexual feelings. I've explained it badly, but it's something like that.'

'What about these *objects* that were found? The ones that made you think he was psychotic?'

'Yes . . .' Wilson grunted. 'But in the end they may not feature much in the trial.'

'Why not?'

Wilson hesitated. 'There's a question mark over whether the CPS will be able to make much use of them. There's no way of linking the items to Pavlik, you see. Nothing forensic.'

'And what were these items?'

'Some lace panties. A lady's scarf.'

Simon frowned. 'Catherine's?'

Wilson shook his head.

'They were found near her?'

'The panties under her head, soaked with her own blood. The scarf . . . tucked up her skirt. With blood on it, but not hers.'

Simon's heart gave a cold thump. He felt a blend of revulsion and curiosity. He looked away and took a long breath, to give himself time. 'And you think these items were put there by Pavlik?'

'We think he carried them around with him, ready for a moment like this. A collector, you might say. An enthusiast for deviant little items. Probably graduated from thieving off washing lines.'

And still Simon couldn't make any sense of this information.

Wilson peered at him. 'You all right?'

'Yes, I'm just . . . shocked.'

'Catherine didn't tell you then?'

Simon's throat swelled, his voice choked slightly as he said, 'No, she never mentioned it.'

'Well, I'm sure she just wanted to put it out of her mind.'

Sensing that Wilson was about to call a halt, Simon asked hastily, 'But tell me, why can't this be used against him?'

'Oh, it'll be used, but the CPS won't go strong on it. If Pavlik had been a known stalker, a known collector of women's underwear, if there'd been forensic evidence . . . When Pavlik agreed to a body sample we thought we'd get him on some DNA traces, something on the scarf at least, but' – he pursed his mouth – 'no such luck.'

Simon said with a light laugh, 'So what evidence *do* you have against Pavlik?'

'Oh, we can prove he was in the house. We can prove he was upstairs in the second bedroom. We've got four different strands of fibre plus some specks of very unusual paint. Then, what else . . .?' He checked his memory. 'We've got a witness who'll say Pavlik boasted about breaking and entering. And of course he was caught trying to flog the jewellery.'

'That's going to be enough, is it?'

Wilson gave the mirthless chuckle of someone who'd seen too many prosecutions turn to dust. 'Mr Jardine, you're a lawyer. You know how it is. There're no certainties in this game. It only takes a smart barrister. It only takes a jury who're easily swayed. I wish I could promise you that Pavlik's going to be put away. But I can't. According to the defence disclosures, two men are going to swear they spent the whole of that Sunday evening with Pavlik.'

Simon made a show of absorbing this. 'And will it stand up, this alibi?'

'Who knows?' Wilson exclaimed contemptuously. 'Pavlik's got a very sharp legal team. Presumably they wouldn't be fielding these two witnesses unless they thought it might be of benefit to them. As I say, I can't give you any guarantees.'

A sliver of fear slid into Simon's stomach. 'A sharp legal team? What do you mean?'

'The CPS people know them. Top firm of solicitors. Top QC.'

'Top firm?' he said incredulously. 'What, this man Gresham?'

Wilson offered this up to his memory. 'No, no – he's changed them all. No, the solicitor's something else like . . . Blake? Black? And the QC, one of those that comes at ten thousand a day.'

Feeling slightly sick, Simon continued to hold very still. 'A totally new team?'

'No expense spared.'

'But how can Pavlik afford people like that?'

'Mr Jardine, I don't think we have to look very far to work out who's paying, do we?' Wilson said in the tone of a schoolmaster explaining the basics to a dim pupil. 'Pavlik lives with an older man. An older man with a bit of money.' He shrugged to suggest that this settled the argument, and, pushing back his chair, got briskly to his feet.

Simon moved slowly, with a sense of being weighed down. 'So he might get off? You're saying there's a good chance he'll get off?'

'I'm saying that I can't give you any assurances, Mr Jardine. That's all. But it wouldn't be fair to anyone to promise he's going to be put away.'

# Chapter Thirteen

THE PLANE was late leaving and late arriving. By the time the car reached Regent's Park Catherine was in that state of exhaustion and muddle-headedness that comes from a long day punctuated by wine and ranging emotions, otherwise she wouldn't have turned down the driver's offer to escort her up to the door of the flat, wouldn't have assured him when they reached the lift that she'd be able to manage the rest of the way on her own.

The lift rose smoothly, the doors opened all right, but when she wheeled herself out it was to see strange numbers on the doors of the flats because she was one floor too low. Then, as if her patience needed further testing, on recalling the lift and reaching the door of number twenty, it was to wrench the keys from her bag with clumsy fingers and see them fly from her hand and fall to the floor, where they hit the polished wooden strip beside the runner and slid into a deep corner, the one place she couldn't reach from the chair.

Early on in this long game of adjustment and transformation, she'd learnt either to laugh at such mishaps, as she'd laughed at her birthday skirmish with the escaping wheelchair and the gutter, or more often to rage, for which she'd acquired a voluptuous repertoire of short sharp swear words; but never, if she could help it, to get upset, not because she was in the least stoic, far from it, but because tears infuriated her far more than whatever had caused them. Nothing was worth the sense of defeat, certainly not anything so measly as a set of keys, because one thing was certain, there were going to be plenty more lost keys and annoyances to come. Tonight, however, she had little energy for exasperation, and certainly none for laughter, and resorted to a muttered commentary that took her back along the passage to a radiator casing, where she removed the armrest from the wheelchair and, hanging onto the top of the casing, swung herself out and down to the floor. Doing a bummer, as it was known in the trade, was like sex, best practised in private. Sliding herself along the floor on her backside, she reached the keys and dropped them in her lap, turned herself round and shuffled back to the flat door. Resting against the jamb for a few moments, she addressed an indifferent world like some bag lady in a shop doorway. 'Well, you've got this far at least. Well done! Well done! Got *something* half right . . .'

The answering voice seemed to spring out of the darkness. 'Are you all right, Catherine?'

With a gasp, she looked up to see her neighbour from Flat 19. 'God!' she cried with a nervous laugh. 'You gave me a shock!'

He made a penitent face. 'I apologise. I didn't mean to startle you. How can I help?' he enquired solicitously. 'Shall I bring your wheelchair over?'

'Thank you . . .' She couldn't think how he'd crept up on her. She hadn't heard his door open, hadn't heard him approach. As he padded off to fetch the wheelchair she looked at his feet, wondering if he'd be barefoot, and saw battered suede shoes with crêpe soles.

Parking the wheelchair at her side, he waited with a grave expression on his long face.

'Thank you, Mr Latimer.'

'Please – call me Fergal.'

'Fergal. You really did give me a bit of a fright there.'

'My apologies.'

'I didn't hear you come out.'

'I was looking for the cat. One has to go stealthily to have a chance of catching him.'

'A cat? I haven't seen a cat.'

'A tortoiseshell called Bertie. He's Maeve's cat really. And a bit of an escape artist. Likes to roam the corridors unsupervised at night.'

She said, 'Rather like me, you mean?' and held up her arms to be lifted. 'If you wouldn't mind?'

He picked her up and sat her in the chair and, unprompted, slotted the armrest back in place as though he were a master of wheelchair assembly. He unlocked the door for her and reached inside to switch on the lights before returning to the corridor to collect her briefcase. 'Now, can I get you anything? Tea? Coffee? A kettle for a hot-water bottle? Something a little stronger?'

There was an accent she hadn't caught before. Matching it to his name she said in a tone of mild accusation, 'You're Irish.'

He dipped his head in acknowledgement.

'But I've just been to Ireland today,' she said. 'I've just come back.'

'Ah. Is that so?' The comment was polite but incurious. 'It must have been a very long day for you.'

'Yes.' Voicing it, she felt a fresh wave of weariness.

'Can I make you a drink?'

There was a steadfastness about Fergal, a calm unhurried quality that made her surrender herself to his care without question. 'Tea would be lovely.'

While Fergal padded around in the kitchen, filling a kettle, she retrieved her mobile from the hall table where she'd left it that morning and dialled in for her messages, which, according to the robotic voice, totalled six. As expected, there was the daily call from her father, dutiful questions first, asking how she was managing, did she need anything, his tone fervent and anxious, then – his voice warming instantly – a list of treats she might like to consider: a glass of champagne at the American Bar, a trip to the theatre, a dozen oysters at Bentley's. She had no interest in such outings, she had told him so more than once, but there was no deterring him because for Duncan life without treats was a life unlived.

There were messages from Emma and Alice, both sounding hurt, both wanting to know where the hell was she and what she meant by hiding herself away like this. The similarity of the phrasing made her suspect they had been agreeing tactics.

Then Ben.

Her heart tightened at the sound of his voice, which seemed very close for Poland.

'Catherine? Where are you?' he began coldly. 'What the hell's going on? What does this note mean – gone away? Gone away *where*, for God's sake?'

She realised then: he was home. Her stomach lurched, she felt she could hardly breathe.

'Are you feeling all right? Has something happened? I mean, this note – it sounds like you've bloody *left home*. No address, no nothing. What the hell does it mean? It sounds like . . .' There was a sharp hiss. 'Christ! I do wish someone would bloody tell me what the hell's going on. I couldn't get any sense out of your father. Nothing that didn't scare the shit out of me anyway. Talked about you being somewhere and he couldn't say *where*. What the hell did he mean? Pissed, I suppose. Your father, I mean.' A rapid sigh. 'Well, I'm *here* anyway. I'm *back*. I got an early plane. *Specially*.' Another sigh. 'And *if* it's not too much to ask I'd like to know where you are and when you'll be back!' The message ended abruptly.

The next message also brought Ben's voice, but calmer.

'Moggy, sorry if I was . . . angry. It was just a hell of a shock. You know – getting back to find this strange note and an empty house. Darling, where are you? Please call me. I'm so worried. This note sounds so . . .' His voice broke. 'Moggy, I love you. I'll be worried sick until you call. Christ, this note frightens me. You will call? *Please*.'

Fergal appeared with the tea. Wordlessly, he put it beside her and, in the absence of chairs in the tiny hall, wedged his lanky frame into the corner and looked away into a distance of his own making.

The final call was – inevitably – from Simon. Her keeper, her guardian, who yesterday had taken it on himself to phone four times and drop by in the evening with some food she hadn't asked for and didn't need. Hearing his voice she prepared herself for the diligent questions, the request to phone him, his hope of seeing her the next day. Tonight, however, his voice took her by surprise, it was so taut, so urgent. 'It's really very important that you call me, Catherine. However late you get in. You must call me straight away. Please, it's extremely important! And, Catherine, I know this sounds strange – I can't explain – but trust me, please – don't speak to *anyone* until you've spoken to me. No one at all.' He made a sound of frustration. 'Really, Catherine – *no one*. And – it's nothing to be worried about – but don't open your door to anyone, will you? *No one*. Not even . . . Just no one!'

'I guessed at milk no sugar,' Fergal said as she switched off the phone.

'Thank you.'

'Is there anything else I can get you?' His voice was very soft.

She shook her head. 'Where do you come from, Fergal?'

'Dublin.'

'You go back sometimes?'

'Now and again.'

'You have family there?'

But a part of her had ceased to listen, and sensing this he soon fell quiet again. She was thinking: Who should I call? Ben? Simon? Neither of them? Arguments with Ben demanded energy and agility, and she was short of both tonight. Even when she was feeling reasonably sharp-witted he could usually outmanoeuvre her. He had a way of leaving an argument just as she was getting to grips with it, and launching off into another, with no backtracking permitted. And she knew how it would be this time. He would take the high moral ground: the injured party, hurt and bewildered, innocent of all charges, declaring devotion. The expensive dinner would be business or an old friend. The double room at the country house hotel would be booked for a Pole and his girlfriend who hadn't turned up. If that didn't work he would cajole, charm, bully, plead with her, and then start from the beginning all over again. He wouldn't stop – wouldn't allow her to ring off – until he'd extracted a promise to return to him. The prospect of such determination might have touched her if she hadn't suspected it was driven as much by anxiety as love, for though Ben was desperate to do his duty, by far the sharpest and least ambiguous emotion in his soul was the fear of losing control.

Fergal, at ease with silence, waited quietly in his corner perch, his gaze fixed on some inner world.

Catherine said, 'How peaceful it is here.'

'For the centre of London.' He produced the closest thing she had seen to a smile. 'Now, you're sure there's nothing more I can get for you?'

You could get me a hard heart, thought Catherine. You could get me a heart that could shut Ben's message out of my mind and let me go to sleep without guilt. 'No, thanks.'

'In that case . . .' He straightened up slowly. Standing, he resembled a tall stork-like bird, with his long loose limbs and his shoulders raised high around his ears, an impression reinforced by the enquiring tilt at which he held his head. 'I'll wish you a good night. Oh!' He thrust a hand into his pocket and pulled out a card. 'I gave you my mobile number before. But for the night perhaps you should have the number next door. Just in case.' He placed it on the table beside her before making for the door. 'You're going to be all right now?'

'Fine, thanks. Good night.'

'Take care, Catherine.'

This time she heard the door of his flat sound as he closed it behind him. She heard a fainter click, which might have been an internal door opening, and then the soft rush of a communal pipe somewhere between the walls. The tea cooled in her hand. At some point she must have put it down, but she had no recollection of it. Her memory was caught elsewhere, in a place she couldn't name.

*Take care, Catherine.*

It's the tiredness, she decided. It must be the tiredness because it makes no sense.

*You're going to be all right now.*

She tried to capture the precise sound, word, intonation that had jogged the dark corner of her memory.

*Catherine . . . You're all right, Catherine. You're going to be all right.*

It was the softness of his voice, it was his choice of words. It meant nothing, couldn't mean anything unless . . . Thoughts seized in her mind, caught on improbabilities, rushed off again, stopped and stalled.

At some point her eyes fell to the card on the table beside her. There seemed no order to events after that; they might have happened all at once or minutes apart. She looked at the number and it meant nothing and everything. Like his voice it belonged to another time, another place. She closed her mind to it; she opened her reason to it: she knew, but refused to know that she had seen it before.

The entry-phone buzzer sounded, and that also seemed to come from another world. She held still as if this might deny the sound, but it buzzed again, and she thought dimly: Simon.

But it was her father's voice that spoke her name. Then: 'Let me in, darling.'

She pressed the door-release and waited for him calmly, with a sense of disconnection. Whatever had happened here, whatever she had begun to grasp in these few minutes were like secrets, to be hidden away until another time.

Before opening the flat door, she folded the card and slipped it deep into her pocket.

At the sight of her, Duncan gave a show of immense relief, a clutching of both hands together, a heavenward roll of his eyes. 'Thank the Lord you're safe, darling! I can't tell you how worried we've been!'

As he opened his arms and stooped to embrace her she saw over his shoulder the dark figure of Simon, caught in the shadows between the passage and the doorway. Her father straightened up and stood aside with a glance towards Simon, who came slowly forward into the light.

'Thank God,' Simon said forcefully, his mouth working with suppressed emotion. 'Thank God.'

'For heaven's sake,' Catherine sighed with sharp impatience. 'What is it?'

Her father gestured towards Simon.

'Well?' she demanded.

'The nuisance caller,' Simon announced gravely. 'I'm sorry to have to tell you, Catherine' – he lowered his voice to a confidential murmur – 'but the phone number belongs to the flat next door.'

There was a pause in which she held his gaze. 'Yes,' she said very deliberately, 'I know.'

Simon blinked at her. 'The flat next door to *here*, I mean.'

'Yes.'

He frowned at her, before saying, in the manner of a further announcement, 'We've told the police.'

'*What?*'

'They would have come anyway,' he argued defensively.

'Oh, why did you have to do that? I wish you hadn't done that!'

'But they traced the number for us. And Denise Cox knows you're living here – they'd have worked it out for themselves.'

'You shouldn't have gone behind my back, Simon. You should have asked me first!'

Simon appeared to shudder, his cheek danced furiously, for an instant his eyes were very dark.

Duncan touched Simon's arm to gesture him to one side, and said to Catherine, 'But darling heart, these calls, this place—'

'It isn't something for the police, Pa.'

'My dear girl, listen . . . I'm sorry to have to tell you . . . it may come as a bit of a shock . . .' He half crouched to bring himself down to her level. 'Darling, darling . . .' His expression suggested he would do anything to spare her such news. 'The thing is, both this flat and the one next door are owned by this company,' he began unhappily. 'And the thing is, darling girl, the company is controlled by – I wish I didn't have to tell you this' – he made a gesture as if to berate the gods – 'well, dear heart, they're both owned by Terry Devlin.' He paused mournfully, waiting for some sign that she had understood. 'This one *and* the one next door,' he repeated for clarity. Glancing to Simon as if for help, he resumed unhappily, 'You see . . . this Latimer and his nasty calls – the thing is, darling girl, I'm afraid to say it was all a vile way of trying to get at Ben through you.' He took her hand, his face creased with mortification. 'I'm so terribly sorry, darling.'

'Get at Ben?' she echoed.

'I'm afraid so.'

'But why?'

'I know it's hard to take it all in,' Duncan said, ignoring her question. 'I know you thought that nice daughter of Devlin's was just being kind. I know, I *know* how *painful* and *beastly* it must be to realise just how badly you've been taken in—'

'For God's sake, Pa,' she protested. 'This is crazy! This is madness! Why would Terry want to get at Ben?' She looked from her father to Simon and back again.

Duncan's eyes slid away helplessly. 'Darling girl . . .' He patted her hand abruptly and straightened up. 'Best if Ben explains it all, I think. Definitely best. He can tell you.'

'I can tell you,' Simon cut in, his face animated by a strange excitement. 'It's all about money.'

Duncan shot him a reproving glance. 'I don't think it's for *you* to talk about this, Jardine. This is something for Ben!'

Simon said directly to Catherine, 'It's very simple. Ben owes Devlin money, and Devlin wants it back.'

Duncan said rather pompously, 'Can we *please* leave this to Ben. He'll be here any minute.'

Catherine stared at her father. 'You've told Ben I'm here?'

'I know I promised, darling, but I thought it best . . . in all the circumstances . . . The thing is, darling girl, he's absolutely frantic. Frantic! I can't tell you! And he can explain everything, you see. Much better than me, better than either of us!' His gaze flittered everywhere but to her face; he was ill at ease with explanations of betrayal. 'And we thought, since it's not safe for you here, that you'd want to go home, you see. We thought he should come and take you home . . .' Hoping the worst was over, he ventured to look her in the eye, armed with his most defenceless smile.

She said, 'I understand, Pa,' because there was nothing else to say.

He beamed, his entire face dissolved into an expression of relief. 'For the best, darling!'

But she wasn't ready to forgive the summoning of the police, and Simon must have read this in her face because he said in a voice that quivered with self-justification, 'It was out of my hands. Ben's making an official complaint. He wants Latimer arrested. There was nothing I could do.'

She shook her head obdurately.

Simon's face was very white. 'I would have done anything, *anything* . . .' But the words blocked in his throat, he seemed almost dazed, and with a strange gasp he turned on his heel and left.

Every night, work-day or weekend, Soho was the same nowadays, crowds of secretaries and traders up from their East End strongholds, armed with bulging pay packets and raucous laughter, spilling out of the pubs to block the pavements, even in late November. Stepping past them, forced out into the street itself, Simon thought: To the coarse and loud-mouthed, the modern world. Only La Rondine retained the flavour of a gentler era. The post-theatre diners were few and soberly dressed and, keen to catch the last trains back to the garden suburbs, were all gone by midnight. From the other side of the street Simon watched the illuminated sign of the swallow fall dark and a waiter hastily relay the last table with white cloth and crimson napkins.

On arriving, he'd made a close pass of the frontage and spotted Pavlik in full waiterly stride, swerving rapidly between tables with a cluster of stemmed glasses high in one hand. The sight of him had produced a shiver of relief or terror, he didn't care to identify which, while the knife in his pocket might have been molten steel, it seemed to sear his hand so badly.

When Pavlik emerged, Simon prepared himself to match a fast pace. But Pavlik seemed tired tonight, he stepped out slowly. He shrugged his leather jacket higher onto his shoulders before ambling off through the crowds, hands thrust into his pockets, head low. He turned into Old Compton Street, apparently making for Piccadilly and the tube, only to take the next right into Dean Street, which was not the direction for home at all. When Simon rounded the corner it was to see him on the opposite pavement, slowing up to turn into an entrance with a smoked glass door and no sign to say what sort of a place it was.

Simon gave it five minutes and pushed open the glass door to a reception area, a long passage dimly lit by downlighters and the throb of bass music rising from the basement. Guarding the entrance were two men at a desk, clones with shaved heads, heavy moustaches, earrings, black leather jackets copiously adorned with studs; a clear and unambiguous indication, if any were needed, of the style and tone of the establishment beneath.

It was a membership club, no ID, no questions asked, a year's subscription in advance. Simon retreated to the street in a state of jittery frustration. This was all he needed, Pavlik on the pull. Two minutes, two hours: he might be all bloody night. Even then he might appear with a ghastly pick-up, or someone eager to take him home, though from the look of the place it wasn't for tender hearts. Simon decided to give it an hour, and took up his cold vigil in an office doorway, which smelt of disinfectant and rotting vegetables.

Watching the comings and goings at the smoked glass door, he tried to make out if the club's clients stayed for long, but it was impossible to tell because they all began to look the same to him, like soldiers in an outlandish inter-galactic army, with their uniform black jackets and convict hair and strutting steps.

One fifteen; and the hopelessness crept up on him in a tide of loss and yearning. He'd blown it. This would achieve nothing; Pavlik would walk free from court and have his revenge; Catherine would hate him for ever. He slumped a little in the doorway, counting off the regrets and lost opportunities, pondering the unfairness of a life half lived.

Pavlik emerged just after one thirty. He was alone. He came out fast, heading south at a stride just short of a run, quickly vanishing into Old Compton Street. In his haste to follow, Simon ran across the street, dodged between some dawdlers on the corner and promptly cannoned into two men on the far side, one of whom declared comically to his vanishing back, 'Excuse *me*!' Simon sped on and saw Pavlik disappearing round a bend ahead, at the same frantic pace.

Simon caught him again in Brewer Street, going west. Following a few yards behind, he almost had heart failure when Pavlik glanced back over his shoulder. But either he didn't see him, or he was looking for something else entirely, because he hurried on in the same way as before, without looking back again.

Within sight of Regent Street, with no warning at all, Pavlik suddenly broke into a sprint, flat out, arms pumping, head back, and jumping a barrier wove through a line of oncoming traffic to disappear behind a stationary bus on the far side of the street.

Simon ground to an unsteady halt, panting hard, and watched Pavlik take his seat on the N36 bus as it drew away, going north.

The first cabbie he tried had left his adventurous spirit with his sense of humour, in another life, and drove off with a sour grimace. The second driver laughed, game for anything that broke the routine, even if it was a predictable succession of stops and starts along Oxford Street and up the Edgware Road, towards Paddington and the north-west.

When the bus reached the Harrow Road, Simon told the cabbie to overtake and drop him just short of Fifth Avenue.

He walked fast and chose a spot opposite the house in the shadows of an overhanging shrub. Pavlik's lover didn't seem to be at home: there were no lights on, not even a porch light, and the ground-floor curtains were undrawn. He waited impatiently, the sweat cold on his back, the blood hammering in his ears, the knife sharp and unwieldy and terrifying as he fingered it in his pocket. How hard did you have to push it in? And where? Just under the ribs? The neck? God, God, he wanted to be sick. He had the shakes. His guts churned hotly, threatening action.

How much longer? *Where are you, you shit?*

Just when he thought he might have made a ludicrous misjudgement, that Pavlik might have turned around and gone in a different direction, he saw in the steady beam of a street lamp the squat athletic figure walking unhurriedly up the road, head low, eyes on the pavement, no scent of danger.

Simon slipped his spectacles into his pocket and waited for Pavlik to turn in through the gate, then, blood running high, nerves thrumming, he began to run lightly across the road. At the point where he adjusted his stride to leap onto the opposite pavement he still believed he might reach him undetected. In the moment when he landed awkwardly and one foot brushed roughly against the paving stone, he knew that he wouldn't, and then the blood sang in his ears, he felt the blind lust of pursuit. As he covered the last two yards, he watched Pavlik twist around defensively.

The sight of Pavlik's half-raised hands sent a shot of doubt into Simon's heart and in an action he hadn't planned and certainly didn't have time to think through he cranked his left forearm back to take a swipe across Pavlik's head or neck, while keeping the knife low in his right hand, ready to thrust upwards.

He had caught Pavlik by surprise, but not so much by surprise that his reflexes weren't working perfectly. He ducked to one side and twisted away so that Simon's left fist glanced ineffectually off the top of his head, and when Simon thrust the knife up he found air and then something hard: brick or stone, the blade bounced off it all the same. Pavlik must have seen the blade, or heard it, because he caught Simon's wrist and chopped down hard on it with such force that the knife might have been blown from Simon's hand, it left his grasp so quickly.

For some reason Pavlik let go of Simon's wrist, perhaps to swing at him, but Simon was too fast for him. Driven by panic or fury, he grabbed the front of Pavlik's jacket in both hands and, bunching it up under his jaw, jammed his head hard against the door. The sound of Pavlik's howl seemed to fill the whole street.

Simon yelled into his face, 'You shit!'

Pavlik fell silent, or maybe he couldn't breathe. His eyes bulged, the whites gleaming in the dull light, his lips were drawn back over his teeth. He gave a sharp hiss, a sound of contempt or fear.

'You're a dead man, you bastard,' Simon roared, voice juddering, 'unless you tell me – who the hell's bought you? Who's paying you?'

Pavlik gasped something that Simon didn't hear.

'Come on, *come on*! Who's bought you, you fucker? *Who's bought you?*'

Pavlik stared down his nose at him, and Simon caught the stench of alcohol on his breath. 'Talk crazy,' he hissed.

'Who the hell is it? Galitza? Devlin? *Give me the name, you shit!*'

Even before Pavlik's face contorted and swelled, even before Simon heard the long intake of breath and felt the sturdy arms coming up against his chest, he felt the panic of the weaker man. As Pavlik shoved him forcefully away, Simon saw the hurried jab coming and managed to duck it by a hair's breadth. He got in one feeble upward blow to Pavlik's side – it was like hitting stone – before he realised that Pavlik was cranking his fist back for something far more serious. In an effort to forestall him, Simon lunged for a neck-lock that didn't come off though it succeeded in throwing Pavlik off-balance and disabling the blow. Reaching out blindly, Simon grabbed desperately for clothing, flesh, anything and finally got some sort of a grip on an arm. They wrestled fiercely, toppling a dustbin, and almost fell before regaining their feet. Simon tried for the neck-lock again, but Pavlik had his balance this time, rooted and square to the ground, and pushed Simon's arm aside as if it were matchwood. An instant later Simon felt an explosion against his ribs, a hammer-blow that doubled him over in a jackknife and drove the air from his lungs in an agonised rush. The second fist caught the side of his head, a cracking blow that sent him sprawling to the ground, grating his face over concrete or stone. He rolled over – he was somewhere in the doorway – and came up in a crouch, gasping. From the corner of his eye he saw Pavlik turning to run for it, and felt a fresh surge of anger. Scrambling after him, his empty lungs fighting for air that wouldn't come, Simon made a dive for him. He managed to grab one leg at knee level and for a ludicrous moment they were caught in a grotesque pavement ballet, one man hopping and kicking, the other hanging on grimly. Then Pavlik twisted round and swung a fist onto the side of Simon's head, precisely where he'd struck it before, and Simon yelped as the pain shot through his brain like fire. He had the impression of passing out, though he remembered rolling onto his back and shouting after Pavlik, 'I'll kill you!'

He heard savage sobs and realised they were his own. He curled up on his side and, cradling his head with his arm, vomited until the nausea faded.

Eventually, he staggered to his feet and, groaning aloud,

made his uncertain way to the Harrow Road. The first two cabs sailed past, the drivers' eyes carefully averted, and it was only by stepping out in front of the next that he got it to stop at all. Even then, he had to persuade the cabbie that he'd been mugged, and no, he wouldn't bleed all over his precious interior, and yes, he still had enough money for the sodding fare.

At Draycott Avenue he thrust a note at the cabbie and waited doggedly for every penny of his change, no bloody tip, before stumbling towards the entrance. As he fumbled for his key he heard a woman call his name and, disorientated, looked around open-mouthed.

'Simon!'

He stared stupidly at Alice.

'*God!*' she cried, getting a proper look at him. She helped him into the lobby. 'What the hell happened to you?'

He looked down and saw that his suit and shirt were covered in blood.

Up in the flat she bathed and disinfected his face where it had scraped along the stonework, and put ice to the lump on his head, and prodded his ribs gently to see if they were broken.

'The party was so boring. I was hoping you'd liven things up a bit,' she said, laughing at the absurdity of it all.

He told her he'd been mugged, but didn't want to bother with the police.

They had a large brandy each, his washed down with two painkillers, before she put him to bed. He was glad when she slid in next to him. He wanted sympathy, he wanted the proximity of a warm body, most of all he wanted to obliterate his fear in the transitory joy of sex.


'Let's get some sleep now, Moggy. It's very late.' Ben reached for the bedside lamp.

'I still don't understand.'

Abandoning the lamp switch, Ben took a long breath of ill-concealed dismay and, rolling back, dropping his arm heavily onto his stomach, turned his head on the pillow to look at her. 'What is it you don't understand, Moggy? God knows, I've tried to explain. I've told you twice – *three* times – there *is* no other woman. The bloody hotel room was for that stupid oaf Casimir and his ghastly blonde totty. I took Rebecca out to lunch – *once*. The last of the big spenders. Guilty as charged. That's it!'

'It's not that. I've got all that,' Catherine said quietly, though there were things she had chosen not to mention, like the perfume in the bathroom cabinet, and what had or hadn't passed between him and Emma. 'It's this business with Terry Devlin,' she said slowly. 'I don't understand why . . . I thought you'd fallen out years ago. I thought you hated him. I thought you were never going to do business with him again.'

'God alone knows, so did I!' he agreed lavishly. 'Last thing I wanted! But a deal's a deal. If it looks like a good one, you have to go with it, even if it means supping with the devil. Or you *think* you have to go with it,' he added with a grunt of regret.

'So you ended up owing him all this money?'

'Darling love,' he said heavily. 'It wasn't quite as simple as that. It was a business thing.'

Softening her voice, she persevered, 'I need to understand. Please tell me.'

He became so still, his eyes so vacant, that he might have been lost to the conversation altogether. 'Okay,' he said at last, coming to a decision. 'Basically . . . Terry advanced some money against the prospect of this deal in Poland. That's all there was to it really. The deal was going to take a year or so to complete. Maybe longer. He knew that, there was never any question of a fixed time.'

'This deal . . . what was it for?'

Another pause, a slight shrug. 'A hotel.'

'I didn't think RNP went in for that sort of thing.'

He gave her a narrow look. 'It doesn't. This was a one-off. Nothing to do with RNP.'

She absorbed this with surprise before struggling on. 'And something went wrong?'

'It appears so. *I* thought we had an agreement. The terms were perfectly reasonable. He agreed to them quickly enough anyway! But then . . . then he went and decided he wanted to – *foreclose.*'

'And he threatened you?'

'Let's just say he wasn't going to be put off.'

'He was going to use this . . . bad thing against you?'

'Yeah,' he mused distractedly. 'Yeah.'

'You're saying that Terry was the blackmailer?'

'I'm saying that Terry knows how to get his way when he wants it badly enough.'

There was a part of Ben that had always taken refuge in abstruseness, and she was too tired to press him further. 'It's all over now, though, is it?' she asked. 'He's got his money back?'

'Mmm?' Again, a vagueness came over him. Again, it was a moment before he answered. 'Oh yeah. I've kept my part of the bargain all right.'

'And . . . the nuisance calls?'

'Oh, bully-boy stuff. Latimer's his errand boy.'

'But why *me*? Coming through on *my* phone?'

He said, shame-faced, 'I got them, too, Moggy. Calls.'

She stared at him and pushed herself up on one elbow to see his face more clearly. 'You never told me that.'

'Didn't want to worry you.' His brusqueness had given way to a sort of misery.

'But . . .' She bowed her head for a moment while she caught her breath. 'Is there anything else you haven't told me?'

He shook his head and putting a hand on her shoulder caressed it softly. 'It's been a dreadful time, Moggy. Not being able to tell you the half of it.'

'But it would have been far, far better if you'd told me. Far better.'

'Not too late now?'

And still she hung her head.

'Moggy – I'm sorry. I'm really sorry.'

She looked up to find him smiling contritely, the child asking for forgiveness. When this didn't produce an effect he breathed, 'Oh, Moggy . . .' He touched her hair and his eyes took on the liquid glint that in the dim days of uncomplicated happiness had so often formed a prelude to love-making.

He guided her head back to the pillow and they lay side by side, faces inches apart, caught in the stillness of the night and in the awareness of each other. It was astonishing to have forgotten the force of this stillness, the slow deepening of sensation, the closeness that was all the more potent because their bodies were not quite touching. But forgotten it she had, partly from a need to protect herself from the ache of rejection, partly because no amount of remembering could ever do justice to it. She had wanted this moment for so long, had fixed her hopes on it so unquestioningly, that now . . . As he murmured the endearments that were the first waymarks along the familiar path, she felt something stall inside her, she was caught up by a huge emptiness. Her body responded with a host of old and new sensations, some mechanical, some lost for ever, some that would need to be reinterpreted or re-learned. But her mind was somewhere else, floating in a sea of loss that had no name.

# Chapter Fourteen

———

CATHERINE WAS ready and waiting by the front door in her long coat and scarf when she heard the car halt in the road outside and the sound of brisk footsteps on the pavement. Reaching up to slip the latch, she saw in the early gloom the face of Mike, the driver who'd taken her to the airport for the flight to Dublin. He held the door open for her as she levered herself upright and made her way out, then, following her directions, locked up and slid the keys into her pocket.

It was four o'clock and already pitch dark. There was a cold snapping wind, a hint of snow. Her breath vaporised and was sucked away into the murky swirl of the streetlights.

Mike helped her off the pavement; she wasn't yet so confident with crutches that she could swing them forward from one level to another and be absolutely sure her legs would follow. He saw her into the car, understanding immediately how this must be done. She thought how they all followed a type, these people who worked for Terry Devlin, willing, efficient and taciturn.

Before setting off, Mike passed her an evening newspaper, and she thought at first that he meant her to read something about the trial, but when she searched the news pages it was to find nothing but blizzards in the east, snowstorms in the north and the doom merchants blaming the early winter on global warming. She flicked through the paper once again, but if there was anything about the case it must have been very small. At the start of the trial the papers had carried reports of the prosecution's opening case under extravagant headlines, the most restrained of which was 'Burglar accused of throwing TV girl from landing'. Reading these accounts – all with a sensational slant, all containing errors of fact – she'd had the impression of reading about a fictional character loosely connected to herself by name and – when they got it right – by age, a person who'd been constructed from a series of stereotypical images to form a more digestible version of herself. Redrawn in this way, she had become 'beautiful', her career as a 'popular presenter' had been 'blossoming', she was newly married to a 'dynamic entrepreneur', and of course she was 'paralysed'. It was like viewing herself through the wrong end of a telescope: she saw a person who was diminished and indistinct.

At the mansion block, Doyle must have been looking out for them because the moment they drew up he came scuttling out like a crab, head tucked down, shoulders hunched against the wind, to open her door. She replied to his greeting absent-mindedly, because her attention had been caught by the sight of Fergal emerging from the entrance.

'How are you, Catherine?' he said, coming forward to help her up the steps.

'They haven't locked you away then, Fergal?'

He cast her a small admonitory frown, as though it were inappropriate to make light of such things. In the lobby he said rather formally, 'I'm glad you telephoned. Had you been trying for long?'

'For two or three days, off and on. In the rush I lost your mobile number.'

'I was away in Dublin, seeing my mother.'

'The police – they've finished with you then, have they?'

'I believe so.'

'What did you tell them?'

'I told them that it was a mistake.'

'And what sort of a mistake, may I ask?'

He didn't reply until the lift had arrived. 'I told them,' he said in a considered voice, 'that it was a private matter.'

She held her tongue with difficulty. Once in the lift, however, she asked firmly, 'And the man following me?'

'I know nothing of anyone following you, Catherine.'

'No?' She would have argued with him, because in recent
weeks she had learnt to question all facts offered to her by way
of explanation, but something held her back. She realised, with
mild surprise, that it was a belief in his honesty. 'Oh, well,' she
sighed, 'I was never sure there was anyone anyway.'

The lift stopped, the door opened, Fergal held a hand over
the sensor to stop it from closing again. His lugubrious face
took on an expression of great solemnity and some discomfort.
'I have to tell you though, Catherine, that there was someone
watching over you in the night. The man outside your house –
I can only offer my sincere apologies that the fool should have
alarmed you and caused you distress.' With this speech, Fergal
himself became almost agitated. 'He was meant to stay in the
car, to keep his distance. He disobeyed his instructions. He was
dismissed immediately.'

There was a long moment in which Catherine couldn't
speak, except to breathe in a tone of incredulity, 'My God.'

The silence was broken by a sharp buzz as someone tried to
summon the lift. Fergal stepped out and, restraining the door
once more, helped Catherine onto the landing. The door closed
with an impatient whir.

'Terry asked you to set it up, did he?' Catherine asked with
iron calmness. 'This – *watch*?'

'Yes.'

'How long has it been going on?'

'It was simply for those few days. While you were on your
own in the house.'

'You *knew* I was on my own? But how did you—' She
broke off as the answer came to her. Ben had gone to Poland;
he must have gone with Terry's knowledge, perhaps even his
blessing, to sort out this business of theirs, or to raise money,
or . . . But she had tired of trying to understand the crazy world
of Ben's dealings. 'But why put a man outside?' she asked.

Then, as her anger began to goad her more fiercely, she repeated with indignation, '*Why?*'

'To watch over you. Nothing more, Catherine.'

'But the reason, Fergal. Why should you want to do that? What am I saying? I mean, of course, why should *Terry* want to do that? To spy on me?'

'Never to spy, Catherine. Never that.' Fergal spoke with the sadness of misunderstanding. 'It was merely to make sure you came to no harm.'

'But who would want to harm me? Tell me! Do you know of someone who wants to harm me? *Do* you, Fergal?' All pretence of calm left her then, and she exclaimed bitterly, 'Why, oh why do I feel that I'm the last to be told anything! Why do I feel that I'm being treated like a child! Or worse – like a *nothing*, a *nobody*!'

Fergal said placatingly, 'I myself am not aware of any particular person who wishes to harm you, Catherine.'

'But Terry knows of someone perhaps? Is that it? *Is* it?' She snorted, 'But I suppose you would have to get his permission to answer that!' With this retort, she turned perilously fast, maintaining her balance only by a panicky jolting move of one crutch, and started her unwieldy progress towards the flat.

Reaching the bend in the passage, she saw Maeve standing in the open doorway of number twenty, so still that Catherine felt sure she must have been there for some time and heard her spat with Fergal. Maeve came forward tentatively, hands out as if to embrace Catherine, before losing her nerve and coming to a sudden halt with her hands clasped tightly together. 'Come in,' she whispered at the floor, before leading the way.

Catherine glanced back, but there was no sign of Fergal. Watching, presumably, and waiting.

An elderly tortoiseshell trotted determinedly into the flat just ahead of Catherine. Maeve shooed him into the kitchen with a brief awkward smile before gesturing Catherine towards the sitting room.

'Oh, Catherine, how I've been dreading this moment,' she

said, taking Catherine's coat. 'And how I've wished to talk to you for so long.'

Once Catherine was settled in an armchair, Maeve seemed to lose what small amount of confidence she might have had. Wringing her hands, she cast around in desperation. 'Oh, there's tea,' she said breathlessly. 'I made some tea. Will you?' As she pointed jerkily towards a nearby table Catherine saw that her hand was trembling.

'Thank you,' Catherine said formally.

Maeve went to the side table and moved to pick up the teapot, then the milk, then the teapot again, before appearing to forget why she was there. As her hand paused indecisively in midair, the rest of her also seemed to be in imminent danger of stalling. She swayed slightly and gasped.

'Why don't you sit down?' Catherine suggested. 'We could have tea later.'

Blinking rapidly, Maeve half turned and, taking this in at last, gave a dazed nod. It was another few seconds before she managed to unlock her limbs and manoeuvre herself to a chair.

'Are you all right?'

She whispered, 'Yes, I . . . Forgive me. I . . . stupid . . .'

Appearing to remember some instruction she had been given for just such an occasion, she closed her eyes and took a long slow breath, holding on to it for several seconds before exhaling at the same measured rate. She did this twice before opening her eyes again. 'I forget to breathe,' she gasped. 'Then I breathe too much. Hyperventilation. It makes me feel faint.'

With her transparent skin she looked even paler than in the rose garden, and, if anything, thinner, though this may have been the effect of her clothes, a black ribbed sweater that clung to her body and a long straight skirt through which her hip bones protruded in sharp crescents. Without make-up, her wide-set eyes appeared to float in her face, adding to her air of distraction.

Pressing a hand to her chest, appearing to recover a little, she managed to say, 'The trial – Fergal said the verdict's due any minute.'

'They thought today. But now it'll be tomorrow. Probably.'

Maeve absorbed this slowly. 'Aha. And you yourself, Catherine,' she asked in her soft whispering voice, 'did you have to go to the court and appear?'

Suppressing her impatience, Catherine answered mildly, 'They didn't need me there. Or rather, I told them I wasn't going, so they had no choice but to manage without me. They had Ben, of course. He gave evidence.'

Again Maeve pondered this for some time, and again Catherine had to curb her restlessness.

'And what's going to happen at the trial?' Maeve asked in the same halting voice. 'Will he be sent to prison?'

'Will he be sent to prison?' Catherine repeated vaguely, as though she hadn't given this much thought. 'I think, all in all, from what people tell me, reading between the lines – probably not.'

'Oh . . . *Oh*! I'm so very sorry.'

'It doesn't bother me.'

Maeve searched Catherine's face in open bewilderment. 'You don't mind?'

'I mind, yes. But I'm not going to let it rule my life.'

'But, Catherine, I don't understand – why won't he go to prison?'

'He has an alibi. Apparently it's rather a good one.'

'Oh. But is that enough? How can that be enough?'

Catherine shrugged.

'What a pity no one saw him!' she declared with sudden passion.

Catherine said drily, 'Quite.'

With a surge of colour, Maeve stared hastily at the floor and became stranded once more in a world where she could neither breathe nor speak.

Catherine prompted firmly, 'So . . . this flat, Maeve – it isn't yours?'

Maeve looked startled by the question, but also relieved.

'No,' she agreed meekly, 'This flat is Dadda's. Mine's next door. I mean – it used to be mine, when I was here.'

'And you phoned from there?'

She whispered, 'Sometimes, yes.'

'Why me, Maeve? Why not Ben? It was Ben you wanted, wasn't it?'

'I never meant you any harm, Catherine,' she moaned wretchedly. 'Never. Please believe me. *Please*.'

'But you've been' – she chose one of the more delicate expressions – '*seeing* Ben?'

'I wish— I didn't mean to— I . . .' Maeve's face contorted, her eyes gleamed with tears.

'When did it start?'

Her gaze fixed pleadingly on Catherine. 'Oh, it was all over before your marriage. I swear. I *swear*!'

Catherine kept very still.

'That was one thing I could not have done. Not that! Never! No – once you were married! I promise! For the rest . . .' She bowed her head. 'I cannot justify anything to you. Not a single thing. What I did was wicked, utterly wicked. When I think back now, I can't believe that I could have behaved in that way, telling myself I was doing no harm, knowing full well that I was doing dreadful harm to everybody, to the Lord, to myself, to . . . *you*. I can only say that I seemed to lose all power over myself, that I couldn't seem to stop myself, or to fight my way free. It's not enough to say that though, is it? You can always stop yourself if you try hard enough! I just couldn't – *couldn't* – stop.' She sank forward, caging her eyes with rigid fingers, until her forehead was virtually resting on her knees.

'And when did it finish?' Catherine asked in a voice that conceded nothing.

A gasp. 'That September.'

Maeve would have been nineteen then, which pushed Catherine towards the question: 'How long had it been going on?'

Maeve's reply was almost inaudible, and Catherine had to repeat it for confirmation. 'A year?' She thought: That would be about right. By then she and Ben had been together two years, long enough for him to welcome a little diversion before settling down to the serious business of marriage. And of course – the really irresistible attraction of such a diversion – with Terry Devlin's daughter

'A year . . .' she murmured again. It was only with the greatest effort that she asked, 'And . . . how did it happen, Maeve? How did it start?'

Maeve lifted her head a little. 'It was me. I . . . called him.'

'Just like that?'

'He'd . . . said to call him. I knew no one in London. He said to call him for lunch and . . .'

'You'd seen him, though. Somewhere. Not long before.'

'At the races.'

Of course, Catherine thought. The races. Where it appeared that everyone in her life was doomed to meet and part. 'And how often did you see him?' she asked.

'Perhaps . . . once every two weeks.' Her head was going down again, her voice fading.

Catherine pondered the questions that sprang into a hurt and saddened mind. What did you do? Where did you go? When in the day did you meet? How many hours did you spend together? Did he say he cared for you? Did he promise to look after you?

Strangely – but perhaps not so strangely after all – she hoped Ben had been kind to her.

'What did you want when you phoned the house, Maeve? Why call?'

Maeve was crying, the tears dripping from her nose and cheeks unchecked. 'I just wanted him to *speak* to me,' she sobbed. 'To accept that I still existed, that he couldn't just pretend I wasn't *there* any more. I wanted to make him speak to me – that's all! Oh, it was a dreadful *madness*, Catherine – a dreadful *madness*. I couldn't think of anything else at all.

Nothing, nothing! My studies, my friends – I did nothing, saw nobody for weeks and weeks. All I could think about was making him talk to me! Just talk to me.' She raised a hand as if to deflect an accusation. 'Oh, don't think for a moment I had any other ideas! No, no, I knew he'd never want to see me again, not like that. No, I just wanted to . . . *talk*, to make him *realise* . . .' She struggled to express some other idea, but gave up with a gesture of hopelessness.

'And your illness?'

'Oh, I wanted to die,' she announced matter-of-factly. 'I rejoiced at the thought of dying. Lord forgive me, but I hoped and prayed for it. It was like a terrible darkness all around me, the wish to die. I couldn't see my way clear. I couldn't imagine the darkness going away. That's what happens when you're very ill – you can't see a way clear, you can't imagine it's ever going to end. I'd learnt about such things in college, I knew it was a terrible illness, depression, but you don't understand it when it's happening to you. The only thing you know is that the pain is unbearable. I realise now that I was in great need of treatment, that I was very, very ill – ill in my body and ill in my mind, that I needed the right drugs. I know that *now* . . .'

Catherine softened a little. It was impossible to feel angry in the face of such unhappiness. 'But you almost died, you said. You were seriously ill.'

'Yes,' she answered in a flat voice directed at her knees. 'I hadn't been eating, I'd lost weight, too much weight. And when I got ill, I didn't go to the doctor. I never thought . . . It didn't seem important, you know? It was only when I got a fever. Even then I didn't think to tell anyone. And the next thing I knew I was in the hospital.' She finished this speech as she had begun it, in the same measured delivery.

Catherine let the silence draw out before asking, 'And me, Maeve? Why did you make the calls to me?'

'I thought – I thought—' She started again. 'I was beyond reason, Catherine, beyond reason . . . I thought that we might meet, you and I, that we might talk . . . Oh, not that I was going to say anything to you. No, no – not a word. No, I simply thought that if we talked, then . . .' Her voice faded again in shame or disbelief. '. . . *I might just see him.*'

This brought a parallel memory to Catherine, of a time when she'd been young and impressionable and had formed a mercifully brief obsession for an older man she'd met at a polo match. He was beautiful and rich and amusing; in the short time before she realised he was also self-indulgent, lazy and unkind she'd waited in for his calls, caught up in a frenzy of hope.

She murmured, 'On the phone once, I heard you crying.'

'Oh, I didn't mean for that to happen,' Maeve protested. 'I always meant to speak to you, even if it was just to say hello, but I never could.' She directed a groan of scorn at herself. 'Of course I couldn't! It was part of the madness, to think I could talk to you as if nothing had happened. Lord help me!'

'But you spoke to Ben sometimes?'

'Yes.'

'And?' she asked with an attempt at lightness. 'What did he say?' She had to interrupt Maeve's whispered reply to ask her to speak up. 'My hearing,' she explained patiently, 'is not so good as it used to be.'

'He said he couldn't see me,' Maeve said in a voice that was barely more audible. 'He said it wouldn't be possible.'

'So you never saw him?'

'No.'

Catherine waited for the rest of it. It was a while coming, a minute or more, and arrived obliquely in a flurry of unconnected fragments and repetitions, told in the same rushed whisper, which she had to strain to hear. 'Oh, I understood,' Maeve began, apparently referring to Ben's refusal to see her. 'I knew it wasn't possible . . . I knew, but at the same time . . . I went to Mauritius, I went to Italy. But it was no good, I couldn't bear it. I only wanted to . . . It wasn't that I expected anything – no, no. But I had this terrible *need* to . . . This, this—' She made a gesture of frustration. 'It was as though I had no room for anything else in my head. I used to imagine so often, used to think about it all the time, day and night . . . I didn't *expect* anything, I just . . .' She lost her way altogether then. She pressed a palm to her forehead. When she picked up the threads again, it was with new resolve. 'I wanted my say,' she declared, with a sense of discovery. 'I wanted a proper end to it, a moment I could look back on and think: That was the end of it and I had my say. I wanted peace. That's all. Peace.' She added bleakly, 'Of course, there was nothing to be said. And no peace to be had. But that was how I felt at the time.'

She searched in her sleeve for a handkerchief and blew her nose. She was calmer now, and when she continued her story it was in a steadier voice, her eyes fixed on a point somewhere near the foot of Catherine's chair. 'I managed to speak to Ben just before you went to France. Of course he didn't want to speak to me, to see me, but I begged, I used every argument, I said it would just be for five minutes. He finally agreed. Just to keep me quiet, of course. But he agreed. He said he'd be back early from France, on the Sunday. He said you were staying on longer. He said he'd call me when he got in. I knew he wouldn't, of course. I knew he'd . . . well, I just knew he wouldn't. So I decided to wait for him.'

She wrapped her arms tightly around her waist, as though to ward off the cold, before pushing herself onwards. 'I arrived at the house in the morning and there was no one in. I went to a coffee place in Portobello, and came back again, then one of your neighbours kept looking at me, so I went and had some lunch and came back again. I don't know how many times I came back – four, five times? Then . . .' She stiffened, her voice rose. 'When it was getting dark I thought I saw a light in the house. I rang the bell and waited. And then—' She glanced uncertainly at Catherine. 'I looked up and I thought I saw the blind move. Oh, I tell you, I've gone through it in my mind time and again! *Time and again!* And I'm never sure if it really moved or it was a trick of the light or . . . You know how it is when you look up suddenly and it's almost dark and you're not sure what you've seen. But of course I was ready to convince myself that it was Ben. I thought he'd spotted me and was hiding from me, pretending he wasn't there. I pressed on the bell and kept pressing and pressing . . .' Unwrapping her arms from her waist, she immediately crossed them again over her thin chest and gripped her upper arms, as though for protection. 'I went and waited across the street. I was upset. I thought – Oh, I was in a dire state, Catherine. What can I tell you? Angry. Wretched. Crying my eyes out.'

Her voice had risen dangerously, her breath was coming in short gasps, and it was only by a visible effort that she slowed herself down. 'Then I realised I had to calm myself. It was no good being in a state like that. If it was him in there, I didn't want him to see me like that. Hysterical, pathetic. So I went to the pub round the corner and cleaned myself up and dried my face and had a glass of wine for some courage. It must have been about fifteen, twenty minutes before I got back. Then . . . well . . .' She made a small agonised gesture, a plea to be spared the last of the story.

But for Catherine the story was everything. She said implacably, 'You found the front door open?'

'Yes.'

Still Maeve hoped for a reprieve, and still Catherine wouldn't give it to her. 'Was it dark inside?'

'More . . . dim,' she replied with a droop of resignation. 'There was a light at the back somewhere. That's why I didn't see you to begin with. I stood in the doorway and called out. Not loudly, just a sort of hello. I called several times, then I plucked up courage to go in. And then . . .'

'You saw me.'

The tears had returned silently. 'It was like the most terrible nightmare in the world – to see you there. The blood – oh, the blood! It was like a black lake. I thought you were dead. I felt sure you were dead!' A shudder snatched at her body.

'But I wasn't.'

She closed her eyes at the memory of her relief.

'And then?'

'Then . . . oh, I wish I could tell you I did everything possible for you, everything I was trained to do! I wish I could say I went through all the right procedures! But my mind was in a state. I couldn't think. It was like a dream – I didn't feel I was there at all. I can't remember very much . . . Everything was all mixed up. I was crying and carrying on. I felt it was all my fault, Catherine. I felt somehow I was to blame! And the blood – all I could see was the blood. There was so much of it! I was desperate to stop it. *Desperate.* I tried hankies . . . I tried anything I could find. Eventually – I don't know how long it was – I began to come out of it, to wake up, to think about what I should do. Finally I went and turned on a light and felt your pulse. I knew I mustn't move you – at least I knew that! I knew I mustn't even straighten your head. But Catherine – I completely forgot to check your pupils and your breathing and your airways and to make sure you weren't choking. I completely forgot!' She cried in disgust, 'Why did I ever think I could make a nurse! It was madness to think I could ever be a nurse!'

Refolding the handkerchief in trembling fingers, she used it to rub the tears ferociously from her cheeks. 'Then Fergal arrived. He was everything that I was not. Practical and calm. He phoned for the ambulance. He did all the things I should have done – checked your airways, your breathing. He went upstairs and found Ben and checked on him as well. Fergal is one of those people – there is nothing he can't do.'

A growing listlessness crept over her. Her grip on her arms loosened, her hands dropped, she settled back in her chair and closed her eyes momentarily as her head sank against the cushion. 'Fergal told me to go and wait in the car. He said he'd deal with everything else. I wanted to stay, I was desperate to stay, but he made me go. He said it wouldn't do any good if I was still there when the ambulance arrived. He said it would only make things difficult for everyone. That's what I mean,' she said wonderingly, 'he thinks of everything.'

'But, Maeve, why was Fergal there in the first place? What brought him?'

'Why?' Maeve echoed as if this should have been obvious. 'Oh,' she breathed with a show of understanding, 'because of Dadda! Dadda had told him to keep an eye on me. To follow me, really. Fergal was there to watch over me.'

Another person to be watched over. But the deeper realisations came to Catherine in slow stages, first as small nudges of suspicion, then as lurches of shock and comprehension. 'Fergal was there all day?'

'Oh no, he didn't come until that minute. No, I fooled him into thinking I'd gone to the doctor and then out with a friend. No, it was only when I didn't come back . . .'

'But he knew where to come? He knew where to find you?'

She gave a single nod.

'He knew about Ben?'

Catherine missed her murmured reply, but then the answer was written in her expression.

'And your father – did he know too?'

She nodded again, miserably.

Catherine's heart squeezed coldly. 'When did he find out about you and Ben?'

Maeve's expression was full of pain. She didn't answer.

'When did he find out?' Catherine repeated with quiet insistence.

'When I was ill,' Maeve breathed.

'He knows the full story?'

Her frown said yes.

At this, a whole succession of possibilities cascaded into Catherine's mind, one building on another, each more disturbing than the one before. At each realisation she pricked with fresh anger and mortification. He had known! He had known all along! She pictured the scene at Morne, the tour of the garden, the lunch, and all she could think was: He looked at me and he knew! And when he wrote all those letters – he had known then too. The letters that had given her such secret pleasure, which she had looked forward to each week – this knowledge had infected every word. And in the midst of this long rocky storm of feeling, one thought wedged firmly in her mind. A father does not forgive the man who takes his daughter's innocence.

Catherine picked up her shoulder bag to leave. 'One thing, Maeve. The ambulance men found some panties under my head. They were yours, were they? You put them there to stop the bleeding?'

Maeve stared aghast. 'Panties . . . Did I . . .? Oh . . . Oh.' She flushed and dropped her head. 'Oh, I didn't realise. Oh . . .'

'There were yours?' Catherine persisted.

'Yes, I . . . always have some . . . in case . . . in my bag . . . in case of . . . you know . . . emergencies.'

Catherine assumed she meant emergencies of the feminine kind, and wondered at her fastidiousness. 'And the scarf, Maeve – whose blood was on it?'

'Scarf?' she repeated dully.

'It *was* yours, wasn't it?'

Again the confusion, the flush of what looked like shame.

'Whose blood was on it?' Catherine repeated.

'It was mine.'

'You'd hurt yourself?'

Her eyes slid away, her voice faded to a whisper. 'No . . . it was from before.'

Catherine waited silently.

'From . . . when I was bleeding and . . . he cared for me.'

Catherine couldn't disguise the incredulity in her voice. 'That was why you kept it?'

Maeve nodded silently, with a heartbreaking tenderness, which Catherine could only gaze at with a kind of awe.

'I'll be going now,' she said to break the spell.

Maeve jumped to the front of her seat in renewed agitation. 'Oh, Catherine – I'm so very sorry for everything! I feel it's all my fault. I feel I'm to blame for everything!'

'Why? Don't be silly.'

'But if I'd got there sooner. If I'd stayed outside the house and waited. I can't stop thinking, *If only, if only*.'

'There was nothing you could have done.'

'But I might have seen him! I might have stopped him! I can't help going over it again and again. I can't help thinking that I must have caused it to happen . . . I can't explain. There was even a time when I thought—' She started guiltily.

Catherine asked quietly, 'What was it you thought?'

Maeve gave a strange laugh. 'Oh, nothing!'

But her fresh open face was incapable of concealment, and Catherine read something there that made her insist, 'Tell me.'

'Oh, it was just . . . When I was in a state – a real state! – I thought – really, it's nonsensical' – she made a face of disbelief – 'I thought it was Dadda!'

Catherine held her expression. 'In what way?'

'Oh . . .' Again, Maeve tried to brush it aside. 'That he wanted to see Ben hurt. That he'd sent someone.'

'Does he do that? Send people?'

'Oh *no*! *No!*' In her horror, Maeve kept repeating this. 'No, no. It was just *me*. I was imagining it! No, Dadda would never do a thing like that! No, never. It was just the madness in my head.'

The moment Catherine began to manoeuvre herself upright, Maeve leapt to her feet.

'Oh, Catherine, I'm so terribly sorry for everything.'

'Don't feel sorry about the accident,' Catherine insisted. 'You probably saved my life, you and Fergal. Someone else might have tried to move me and succeeded in finishing me off.'

'I didn't even check your airways,' Maeve sighed inconsolably. 'I didn't check your breathing. Oh, I'm no use, Catherine. No use to anyone!'

When Catherine kissed her cheek, she had the sense of kissing a forsaken child.

*

In the car Mike said, 'There was an item on the news, Mrs Galitza. I don't know if you've heard—'

'About the trial?'

'Yes, the man, he—'

'Not now, Mike, thank you.'

A surprised pause, before he said humbly, 'Right ho.'

She wasn't ready for more; not yet. There was only so much that could be absorbed at one time. She needed to catch her breath, to make sense of her emotions. Her heart was raging; her heart was icy. She felt calm; she felt wild with bitterness. She kept thinking: How could he? How could he betray me so deeply? And then, almost as passionately: How could he destroy Maeve? She had no idea what she felt for him any more. She loved him, she despised him; she yearned for him, she felt sick at the thought of him; he was achingly familiar to her, he was a stranger, unnerving and suspect. One minute she strived to forgive him, to make allowances for his troubled nature; the next she wanted to be rid of him for ever. She hated to give up, but she knew it was essential to give up sometimes if one was to hold on to some shred of self-respect.

And all the time the facts kept racketing around her head, stinging and tormenting her: the whole year that it had lasted, the very year that she and Ben had been planning their future together, gone house-hunting, found and bought; the subterfuge that Ben had exercised so flawlessly, the late meetings, some of which couldn't have been business meetings at all, the evenings when he'd reported on his day and must have reported lies; the declarations of love and devotion that had meant whatever had suited him at the time, nothing, something, everything.

But if the facts were hard to bear, the unknown was worse, because there was no stopping your thoughts then, the only limits were the limits of imagination, and just then it felt as though her imagination had no limits at all. She saw the two of them together, she saw Ben's foxy grin, she saw Maeve's childlike gaze, and for a while she let the images run on painfully, in the hope they might burn themselves out.

The car swept down from the overpass towards Padding-ton: ten minutes to home. Ten minutes to prepare. One morn-ing recently, Catherine had woken to a vivid nightmare in which she'd been struggling in deep water, her legs useless because they were dragged down with weights. Lying there in half sleep, she'd thought dramatically, with a surge of self-pity: That's how it is for me – I'm drowning by degrees. I can't survive any more! But in the full light of day she'd seen her situation rather more prosaically. You could always survive, so long as you took things slowly, with time to catch your breath in between.

Well, she was getting her breath back now, and as the car skirted the north side of Paddington Station, she had the strength to say, 'Sorry, Mike – what was it you heard on the radio?'

He met her eye in the mirror to check that he hadn't misheard. 'There was an item about the trial of the burglar, ma'am.'

'And what did they say?'

Again, the anxious glance in the mirror. 'Not guilty of the GBH, ma'am. Guilty of something lesser.'

'Thank you, Mike.'

In the remaining minutes before reaching home she had imposed some semblance of calm. She thought: I'm getting as bad as Ben, all cover and pretence.

At the house, someone must have been looking out for her because the front door swung open as Mike helped her up onto the pavement.

It was Emma who ran out, crying, 'We've been worried sick about you, Cath! Where've you been?'

'Is Ben here?'

'And your father. And Denise Cox. Where've you been? I got here sharp at four and you weren't here! You gave me heart failure, Cath!'

'I left a note for Ben saying I was going out.'

'Well, no one told *me*!' In the frosty air Emma's breath

plumed sharply, like steam. 'But come on in, darling – it's so *cold*.'

Denise and her father stood just inside the door, solicitously, like mourners at a funeral.

'I heard the news,' Catherine declared before she crossed the threshold.

'I'm sorry,' Denise said, stepping back to let her pass. 'Sometimes these things happen, and you never know what you could have done differently.'

'Darling heart,' her father cried, wrapping her in a tortured embrace, 'there's no damned justice! None at all!'

Catherine sat down to take off her coat, and remarked in the same brisk tone as before, 'I forgot to ask – is he out and walking free?'

'One year suspended,' Denise said. 'For the burglary. We lost the GBH on the alibi.'

'The damned alibi!' Duncan muttered furiously. 'The jury swallowed it hook, line and sinker. Believe anything, these people!'

'Emma?' Catherine called. 'I'd love some tea.'

Emma pulled the cigarette she was about to light hastily out of her mouth. 'Of course, darling,' she agreed effusively and hurried away.

Catherine laid a hand on her father's arm. 'Pa, would you get my wheelchair for me? I'm too tired to walk any more today.'

'Darling girl, of course!' Clutching her shoulder, he compressed his mouth in a grimace of unbearable pride. 'Walking! All this walking! I tell you!' He flung a look at Denise, inviting her to share a moment of celebration.

'Just explain it to me,' Catherine asked Denise once Duncan was out of earshot.

'He admitted burglary, but sixteen hours earlier. He said he'd broken in, taken the valuables. But that was it. He said he'd left the door open and unlatched, and anyone could have walked in off the street, and presumably did. When you arrived home at ten on the Sunday night, he had these two witnesses to swear that he was drinking with them in a pub in Soho. They were independent witnesses, that's what really swung it in Pavlik's favour. Neither knew him particularly well. No axe to grind. And definite about the date.' She made a face as if to say, what can one do? 'And the legal team – this top QC – they made it watertight.'

'I'm sure they did.'

A door slammed above and Ben came running down the stairs, wearing his harassed face. 'Christ, the phone – it hasn't stopped.' Twisting to a halt in front of Catherine, he adjusted his expression to one of grave concern. 'Denise has told you?' He looked to Denise for confirmation before crouching lightly at Catherine's feet. 'What a bummer, eh, darling? What an absolute bastard.' He took her hands in his and held them delicately, with a sort of reverence. 'Have to look on it as the closing of a chapter, I'm afraid. Have to look ahead to new and better things.'

Catherine always forgot how perfectly he could match his mood to the occasion. 'New and better things?' She laughed darkly and unnaturally.

A flicker of doubt crossed Ben's face before he too laughed, falsely. Duncan, appearing with the wheelchair, lifted his head enthusiastically to the sound. 'That's right, damnation to them all!'

Denise was pulling her coat on.

Catherine said jauntily, 'This is goodbye then!'

'The case will stay open, you know. For as long as it takes,' she said. 'We won't give up on it.' And promptly spoilt the effect by dropping her eyes.

After she'd gone, they sat in the sitting room to drink the tea that Emma had made and few wanted. Duncan opted for a stiff whisky.

'Sun safely over the yardarm, I think. Not drinking alone, am I? What about you, Ben?'

Ben flicked a thoughtful glance at Catherine. 'No, Duncan, not for the moment.'

'Emma?' Duncan asked with mock despair.

'No, I'm going to stick with tea,' Emma said, directing a complicit smile at Catherine, as if to show that she was prepared to stand by her even in the smallest things.

Securely ensconced in an armchair with his glass cradled to his chest, Duncan launched forth on the subject of juries and their deplorable gullibility, and – a favourite lament – the lack of education among the populace as a whole. Emma, on the other hand, was more inclined to put the jury's failure down to the modern practice of passing the buck, of ducking every type of responsibility that society asked of them, responsibility for themselves, their families, their health and welfare. Citizenly responsibilities came *way* down their list of priorities, in fact so close to rock bottom as made no difference. Now it was a who-cares-and-stuff-everybody-else society. Most people's aim was to get by with the minimum bother. The jury had found it easier to let Pavlik off than go through the mental effort of weighing up the evidence.

Duncan waved his glass airily and proclaimed that this proved his point precisely, it was the fault of appalling educational standards.

And all the while, Catherine gazed out into the black, dead garden and felt Ben watching her.

Finally, when Duncan and Emma had heartily agreed on the underhand tactics of the defence lawyers and the CPS's lamentable cross-examination of the alibi witnesses, who'd obviously been put up to it – you could tell by the shiftiness in their eyes – a silence fell. By chance, everyone looked at Catherine at the same moment.

'I want to thank you for your support,' she said, 'for everything you've done for me. But now I want you to go.'

Emma must have caught something in her tone because as she bent to kiss her goodbye she said, 'You all right, darling?'

'*Me?*' Catherine declared in a voice that was pitched too high. 'I'm fine!'

Duncan, shielded by good intentions, oblivious to the finer

nuances of atmosphere, beamed happily at her. 'There's my girl! Leave you to a cosy evening, my darling. Just know that we all love you. In my case, to absolute bits!'

He planted a loud kiss on her cheek. As he drew back, Catherine saw a face on which life and love and loss had left no mark, and could only envy him.

'Well!' Ben said a little too brightly once he had seen them out. 'Would you like that drink now, Moggy?'

'You have one.'

Unable to gauge her mood, he eyed her warily. 'Don't want to drink alone.'

'I've gone on the wagon, so I'm no good to you.'

'Is there something wrong?' he asked solicitously. 'I mean, is it the trial or something else?' He sat down in the chair next to her and, sitting forward with his arms resting on his knees, offered a cautious smile.

The games that she might play. The traps that she might lay for him before delivering up the series of ugly little truths that would mark the point of no return. The temptation was there, part of her wanted the satisfaction of humiliating him, yet the victories would be cheap, the process antagonising, and at the end of the day she yearned for peace.

'It's over,' she said a little unsteadily. 'Between you and me. It's all finished. I know about Maeve. I know about the phone calls – everything. And I don't think there can be any going back, do you? So I'd like you to leave. I'd like you to move out.'

For a full five seconds he didn't move. His eyes stayed fixed on hers. She felt he was weighing up the various approaches he might take and finding them all wanting.

'Oh, Moggy, I'm so terribly sorry,' he cried at last, in a racked and hoarse voice, and she realised that he had decided on the full and frank approach, the placing of his head on the block. 'What can I say? It was unforgivable. I could tell you it was a last fling, I could say that I called a halt long before the wedding but she threatened to kill herself – I was terrified that she *would* kill herself – I could make a dozen different excuses, but—' He paused with a deep contrite sigh. 'In the end there are no excuses, are there? It was totally wrong.' He dropped his head onto his hands, he gasped miserably. Raising his head again, he looked at her imploringly. 'Moggy, if I could undo it all I would. Believe me. I've never stopped loving you. Never! In fact, I know this sounds crazy' – in the tiny pause that followed she had the feeling that he was assessing just how crazy it might sound – 'but it was a way of proving to myself how *right* you were for me, how much I *truly* loved you. It was a sort of confirmation of everything we were aiming for, if that doesn't sound too insane. I loved you so much – *so much!* – but I still had this ridiculous fear of the commitment we were making. I mean, marriage is such a huge and daunting thing, isn't it? And I thought that a last fling, a last sort of *test*.' Again the glance, again the measurement of progress. She was careful to show nothing in her face, and this encouraged him to continue in the same vein. 'The crazy thing is that I knew straight away that it meant nothing – *nothing* – that it was just as I'd thought – you were everything to me, Moggy. *Everything*. But by then – well, she was being difficult, threatening to phone, come round, you name it. Basically to try and ruin our lives.' He slumped a little, he gave a long laboured breath. 'I was weak, Moggy. Utterly weak. I can only say I haven't stopped regretting it for a single moment ever since.'

'*You* were weak?'

He didn't like that. His eyes narrowed, his voice took on a note of self-justification. 'Look, I wanted to be kind to her, I tried my best to be kind to her, but it was the worst possible thing with someone like that. You've no idea – she kept phoning and saying she was going to take mouthfuls of tablets. She was wildly unstable, absolutely hysterical. Someone like that – you can't reason with them. You can't begin to deal with them.' But the conviction was fading from his voice. Standing up, he paced across the room and came back to stand over her, restless and fretful. Sitting down again, he declared in a tone of near despair, 'I don't want us to be finished, Moggy! I don't want it at all. I'd be lost without you. Completely lost. We make a great team, you and me! Admit it, Moggy – we're good together!'

He was waiting doggedly for an answer. She murmured, 'I used to think so, yes.'

Grasping at this, he tried his old winning smile, the roguish half-closed eyes: the handsome devilish son of a gun. 'Could be again, Moggy.' He ducked his head to catch her gaze. 'No reason why not! You and me. Hey,' he sang in the soft fluid tone he used to bring her round to his point of view.

Looking at him, she felt an immense distance. She thought: It's all a technique, it's all a game, it means nothing. And yet like an autonomic reflex part of her responded, an unbidden sway of the flesh and the heart.

He covered her hand with his. She looked down at it, she felt the warmth of it, and thought: But there can't be any going back.

She murmured, 'I'd like to know – on the night of the burglary, were you expecting to see Maeve?'

He pursed his mouth at having to go back to Maeve. '*See* her? Christ, no.'

'But you told her you would.'

'What? No, no, I just told her something – anything – to get her off the phone.'

'So you weren't expecting her?'

He pulled up his mouth in mystification. 'Christ, no! *Hardly*. Why would I be expecting her?'

'No, I . . . It was just something she said.'

He caressed her hand, as if to soften the mood again, and cast her a hopeful gaze. 'So, Moggy . . .' Lifting her hand, he bent and kissed it. His voice was low and tender again. 'Could be a team again, you and me. Hey? What do you say?'

Taking her silence as a sign of encouragement, he moved forward as if to embrace her, but she pulled her hand away very deliberately and said with a tremor of anger, 'There's been

someone else though, hasn't there, Ben? Since Maeve. In fact –
recently.'

He sank back onto the edge of his seat. 'What?' He glared
at her defensively. 'For God's sake, where did you get that idea
from?' Then, with a show of indignation: 'No, Moggy –
absolutely not. That's a crazy idea.'

But she had startled him, she knew she had. As if to
underline this, he repeated in a blustery tone, 'No, I'd like to
know where you got that idea from. Was it that lunch with
Rebecca? That stupid hotel room? I told you what that bloody
hotel room was about – precisely *nothing*. Bloody Casimir and
his blonde! There *was* no story. What more can I say?' His eyes
flashed angrily.

'And the perfume in the bathroom?'

He held her gaze just a little too long, she saw the flicker of
realisation. 'Perfume?' he responded, too late. 'I don't know
anything about perfume. What perfume?' When she didn't say
anything, he repeated angrily, '*What perfume?*'

'It doesn't matter.'

'Doesn't matter! You've accused me of something and now
you won't even talk about it.'

'It's hard to talk when . . .' She took a steadying breath.
'When there've been so many lies. All that time you were seeing
Maeve. The phone calls. Saying you were being blackmailed.
Was there any blackmail?' she asked wearily. 'No,' she added
immediately, 'don't bother to answer that. It's not important.'

'Christ! You think I'd make up something like that?' he
retorted, taking the offensive. 'You think I'd *pretend* I was
being taken to the financial cleaners! God, I may have done a
few things – but not *that*!' Shooting angrily to his feet, he went
across to the drinks tray to pour himself a whisky. Glass in
hand, he leant back against the table and said sulkily, 'So that's
it, is it? Just write the whole thing off. No thinking about it,
talking it through, giving it time?'

'I don't think there's much point.'

He lifted one shoulder, he pushed out his lip in a Gallic

gesture of indifference. When he drank, the gaze that met hers over the rim of his glass was blank and cold.

She said, 'I might have felt differently if . . .' Here were the most painful words of all. 'If I thought you still loved me.'

'But I've said so! I do!'

'I think you've tried very hard, but I think that it's all a terrible effort for you. The burglary, the attack . . we've both changed. I know you find it hard to love me as I am now.'

'So you don't even believe me when I say I love you!'

'I suppose that's it, yes,' she agreed.

'Great!' he scoffed sarcastically. 'So everything's been a lie, has it? All the good times. All the fun we've had together.'

'The fun's over, Ben.'

'Well, that sums it up, doesn't it. You don't want to know. You're not interested in even trying! You're giving up!'

'Yes.'

'And just when the going gets tough!'

She said reasonably, 'The going got difficult when you began seeing Maeve.' She suppressed the urge to say, *and this other woman.*

'The money – I mean the money. This is when I need your support.'

'You've had my support. You'll still have my support so far as the money goes.'

'Fat lot of good,' he mumbled.

They didn't look at each other. The silence stretched out and settled around them like darkness.

Abruptly, he tossed the rest of his drink back and slapped the glass down. 'I'm to leave then. Is that what you want?'

'I think it's best.'

'*Best? Best?* Who for, for God's sake? You don't know what you're doing, you really don't!' He had got himself into a strange fury that was almost like a panic. 'This is going to be the *end* for me. *And* for this house. The house'll have to go, you do realise that, don't you? Don't think we can keep it because we can't! It'll have to go!'

She shrugged.

'You don't seem to understand what I'm saying.'

'I do, it's got nothing to do with *us*.'

'It's got everything—' He broke off with a shudder of exasperation. 'You just don't understand!'

She looked away. 'Apparently not.'

He stalked to the door. 'Well, don't blame me, that's all,' he flung back reproachfully. 'Don't bloody say I haven't tried!'

She made herself a proper supper, no half measures. It was quite a performance, levering herself up to hook things out of the higher cupboards, hunting for pans that had been put away in strange places, but it was occupation, it was therapy, it was all the things that the unit encouraged. Occupational therapy, and get the hell on with life and, if that didn't do the trick, there was always the help line and the quiet voice of the sister–brother, trained in advice and anodyne sympathy.

Well, she wanted to get the hell on with life, which at this precise moment was pasta with tomato and basil sauce, salad with dressing, freshly made and no modifying the recipe. She opened a bottle of vintage burgundy, one Ben had been keeping for a special occasion, and, pouring a glass, holding it up as if in a toast, made herself a promise, that if she couldn't stick to the one glass she'd give up booze altogether, for at least a year, absolutely no cheating, even if everyone said she was miserable as sin.

She sat at the small table in the kitchen. Knife, fork, cheapskate napkin of kitchen paper. Meal in front of her, glass of wine: a small cause for celebration. She turned on the counter-top television and flicked through the channels. There was a programme she actually wanted to see. She thought: There! Not so very hard after all. Only her jittery stomach threatened trouble. The first mouthful went down, however, and stayed down, smoothed by the wine. Smoothed *enormously* by the wine, she thought as the doorbell rang, long and loud.

Her heart lurched and plummeted. He'd come back. He couldn't bear to stay away. Then she remembered with both relief and disappointment that he had his key, of course he still had his key: he had no reason to ring.

Her father, then. Or Emma.

She sat immobile, wishing the world away. The bell sounded again, and still she didn't move.

'Cathcrine?' The voice that came drifting down the passage was muffled, but unmistakably Simon's.

She wheeled herself to the door and, unfastening it, opened it just a short distance, to show that she was not at home to anyone, not even friends.

He loomed into the doorway, shoulders hunched high, face pale, looking frozen or worn out.

She said, 'Simon, it's not a very convenient time, I'm afraid.'

'Is Ben here?' he asked.

His eyes gleamed in the half light. She thought: He's come to sympathise about the verdict, he wants to wallow in it, chew over every detail.

'He's out, but . . .'

'I can come in then,' he said, gasping a little.

'Another day, Simon. I've just made supper and then I'm going straight to bed. I'm sorry.'

'But I must see you,' he said with a hint of desperation. He put a hand on the edge of the door as if to push his way in and she heard the rasping of his breath, as though he'd been running. 'Please, Catherine. *Please.*'

'Can't it wait?'

'No,' he cried urgently. 'There's something I have to tell you. Something very important!'

He seemed to stagger as he came in, like someone near exhaustion. When he turned to face her, she saw that his hair was awry and hanging damply over his forehead and his spectacles were spotted with moisture. As he struggled to speak she became aware of the breathlessness again.

'What *is* the matter, Simon?'

'I – I've got bad news.'

'What is it?' For a wild moment she thought: It's Ben. He's hurt.

'Pavlik,' he gasped. 'He left court and walked straight into the arms of Terry Devlin's people!' He seemed to think she should understand the implications of this because he waited in agitation for a reaction. When none came, he cried, 'Don't you see?'

Her stomach tightened. 'No.'

He began to gabble, 'His defence was bought and paid for by Devlin. *Devlin!* I knew there was somebody, I knew there had to be. Devlin went and found his alibi for him. The two men in the pub – well, the police couldn't find them, could they? Couldn't find them *anywhere*. But *Devlin* did. Just like that. Must have put them up to it, mustn't he? You see? Bought and paid for. And the legal team – the solicitor, the QC – all paid for by Devlin! All part of the deal! I tell you, he just walked straight into the arms of that man Latimer! They just – walked off together!'

'Slow down,' she begged, throwing up both hands.

Fresh damp had sprung onto his forehead, his cheek was jerking so violently that it brought up the corner of his mouth like a leer.

Beckoning him to follow, she led the way down the passage to the kitchen and pointed to a chair. 'Sit down.'

She fetched a glass and poured him some wine. 'Drink it,' she commanded, 'and start again, please. Slowly.'

He knocked back half the glass, and it seemed to steady him a little. His eyes hunted around the room before they finally settled somewhere on the table in front of her. Between the staccato statements, his gaze flicked up to hers. 'Devlin paid for Pavlik's defence. He found the witnesses, the ones that got him off the charge. Pavlik's there with them now, with Devlin's people. Bought and paid for.'

'Are you trying to say . . .' She paused to get it right. 'Are you saying that Terry Devlin hired Pavlik to come and break in?'

Simon gazed at her with a bitter expression, and nodded slowly and deliberately three or four times. 'He was after the papers. The papers in the strongbox. He wanted them. And he got them.'

'Papers,' she repeated dully.

Leaning forward, Simon spoke avidly, his eyes glinting behind the misted glasses. 'The papers that proved Ben was cheating him. That Ben had done a secret deal. That he was stealing all the profit. *And* . . .' His voice rose to a fierce note. 'The generators? From Warsaw? Ben took an extra ten million and shuffled it on to Bermuda and the Caymans for his clients in Colombia. It was dirty money, Catherine. *Dirty money.*' He shivered with disgust. 'The bank codes and transfer details were in the strongbox, and that's what he wanted, Devlin wanted the proof. And he got it! He got the proof!'

She felt oddly calm, as though all this were happening in another life. She looked away to the pinboard with the display of postcards and party snaps. She saw a clipping from the society pages of a *Tatler*-style freebie magazine, showing Ben and herself at a wedding. Mr and Mrs Ben Galitza, smiling confidently into the future.

'*Catherine?* Do you understand what I'm saying? It was Devlin. *Devlin.*'

'Yes,' she said, 'I understand.'

Her lack of reaction confounded him, he clutched at her hand, but she was in the past somewhere, thinking about Ben and Maeve.

When she finally focused on Simon again, it was to say, 'You look terrible. You mustn't take all this to heart, you know. It's not the end of the world.'

But he wouldn't have it, there was no consoling him.

'Go home,' she said. 'Get some sleep.'

'I don't want to leave you.'

'I'll be fine.'

'What time's Ben coming back?'

'He isn't coming back.'

He gasped slightly. 'Then . . . can I guard you again tonight, Catherine? Can I watch over you? It would make me so . . . *happy*.' He said the word gently, as though in the midst of all his distress he were trying it out for size and finding it perfect.

# Chapter Fifteen

SHE WOKE to the sound of knocking, so faint it might have belonged to her dream. After a while it came again, a tentative brush of fingertips against wood. In the second or two before she answered, Catherine placed herself in time, and the previous day came back to her in a series of interlocking layers, each lit by a stark image: Maeve bent forward, weeping into her hands; Ben's eyes staring coldly at her over his drink; and Terry pondering his next move at the massive desk that her imagination had drawn for him silhouetted against a tall window. Truth and lies, but blurring now, and gaining distance. In one of those insights that seem so revelational in the waking hours but always fail to survive the light of day, she decided: The truth is not so important as the leaving of it behind.

She didn't give Simon any thought until she remembered the knock.

'I've brought up some breakfast,' he announced when she called out to him.

The bedside clock said eight; she was surprised at how long and how well she had slept. She ran a hand through her hair and, pulling herself up against the pillows, told him to come in.

His head came slowly round the door. 'How are you feeling, Catherine? Are you all right?'

'I'm fine.'

Encouraged by this, his shoulders appeared. 'Shall I bring the breakfast in now?'

'Why not?'

He put the tray on the bed and when he straightened up his

face was empty of all expression. He said, 'All safe and sound.' It was a watchman's report.

'Thank you.'

'I found some cranberry juice – is that okay? And a croissant, and some toast.' He was like a zealous waiter running through a difficult order. 'I've made both tea and coffee. I'll drink whichever you don't want.'

There was butter and marmalade. The tray had a proper cloth, and a napkin lay folded on one side. She murmured, 'Spoilt.'

'Of course. What else?' His smile flickered uncertainly. He glanced around for a seat, only to change his mind and lean against the door frame, hands in pockets, in a casual pose that succeeded in making him look rather stiff. His clothes were slightly crumpled and his chin was dark with stubble, but his hair was damped down and neatly combed, his spectacles were polished. She had the feeling he'd been up for some hours.

'I'm sorry about last night,' he said in a thick voice. 'Coming out with everything in such a rush like that. I must have frightened you. I'm sorry. I wasn't thinking straight. The last thing I wanted was to frighten you.'

It occurred to her that if anyone had been frightened, it had been Simon, though incensed might have been a better word.

'It was just the shock – the complete disbelief,' he said, as if to confirm this.

'Of course.'

Straightening up, he moved restlessly towards her. 'And the powerlessness of seeing it happen under your very nose.'

'Forget it. Really. *I* have.'

But with Simon, forgetting was never an easy matter.

An evangelical light had come into his eyes, and when he began to talk it was in a rapid insistent voice that echoed the strange fury of the previous night. 'You see, I thought I'd hang around after the verdict. I just thought, *I wonder, I wonder*. It was just a hunch, that was all. Just a feeling that there might be something to see. Some *evidence*. But never, *never*, did I think that it'd be so absolutely *blatant*. Latimer was waiting for him right there at the door of the court – right there, Catherine! Went up and greeted him, then shook the barrister's hand. Congratulating him for a job well done, presumably. And Pavlik over the moon, of course. The bastard actually laughed. *Laughed*. Then they went off together, him and Latimer. Obviously all planned, all set up, because there was a car waiting. Driver, engine running, the lot. Just swept them away. Gone!'

She picked up the coffee and held it out to him. He came forward jerkily, and when he grasped the saucer, the cup rattled. Stilling it swiftly with one hand, he met her gaze and finally seemed to read the message there, that enough was enough, that for her it was too early in the day for all this, or perhaps too late for any day at all.

'Sorry,' he said solemnly. 'Here I am worrying you again. I didn't mean to. Absolutely not . . . *Sorry*.'

His concern touched her because it was so confused and earnest, but also because it was nice not to wake to an empty house. She hadn't been brought breakfast in bed since the early days with Ben.

'Take the coffee,' she said.

Settling self-consciously on the edge of the bed, he gave that odd disjointed laugh of his, the small gasp that came out of nowhere. 'No,' he smiled, trying to make himself come alive, 'what I really wanted to say – what I came up especially to say – was how about going away for the day? I wasn't planning to do very much work today anyway. Why don't we go somewhere? Give ourselves time away from the madding crowd! Go somewhere marvellous for lunch. The *Manoir*, perhaps. And a drive in the country. Perhaps to the coast. Or' – he took a stab at spontaneity – 'Paris! How about Paris?'

'It's a lovely thought, Simon, but I've so much to do. Money to earn for a start. Rather urgently, in fact.'

'But it's just one day, Catherine. The weather's cleared up a bit. It's much warmer than it looks. Please.' There was a feverishness in his pleading.

'It's tempting, it really is, but another time.'

'But tomorrow might never come,' he said with intense seriousness. 'We could go on postponing the important things for ever, Catherine – for *ever* – and wake up one day to find we'd done none of the things we really wanted to do!'

'Don't remind me,' she agreed lightly.

'*Please*, Catherine. It would be so perfect. The whole day together. *Please*.' Then, with a drop of his head and a quick upward glance: 'I do have a slight ulterior motive.' He said it with the air of laying himself at her mercy, but also with a gleam of excitement.

'Oh yes?'

'There's a house. Just the other side of Oxford. I want you to come and look at it with me.'

She was slow on the uptake. 'What house? Why?'

'A place I want to buy.' His eyes were glittering now, he put his coffee cup hurriedly on the tray. 'A stunning Queen Anne house. Would you come and see it with me? Would you, Catherine? It looks perfect from the photographs. I haven't fixed a viewing, but if the agent can't arrange anything in time I thought we could see it from the outside, get an idea, ask if we can at least see the gardens. The gardens, Catherine – they look amazing. Though you mightn't think so, of course! You might think they're all wrong, that they need a lot of work. But there's a knot garden and a walled garden and a rose garden, and a lake and—'

'A lake! God, it sounds *enormous*.'

'No, no,' he retreated immediately. 'The lake's really quite small, I think. And the house – well, it's got eight bedrooms, so not too large. Then there're the outhouses and two cottages. And the grounds – fifteen acres in all.'

'And just the other side of Oxford? But, Simon, you're talking really serious money for a house like that. Two million at least.'

'Quite a bit, yes.'

She made a face of incredulity.

'Oh, I can manage it all right,' he said with a touchy modesty. 'I've been doing rather well on my own. More than well. Never seem to get round to spending it.' Then, hastily, as though fearing some loss of momentum: 'You'll tell me what you'd like changed, won't you, Catherine? In the house and the garden?'

Still absorbing the surprise of his new-found prosperity, she missed the reference to the house. 'Is this a commission then?' she teased mildly. 'Are you signing me on?'

'In a way,' he said enigmatically, and, looking away hastily, wouldn't be drawn further.

In the terrace off Eaton Square the morning light arrived early, reflected by the immaculate white stucco and sparkling windows. For the rich, even the winter dawn looms brighter.

In the car, Terry sat hunched in the back and thought longingly of home. In his mind even the overdressed house at Foxrock had taken on an emotional appeal out of all proportion to its real place in his affections. He found himself thinking with overt fondness of the heavy damasks and drapes and curlicues, of the Hollywood bathrooms and gilt taps, because it was there, in his memory at least, that he had lived simply with Maeve, and, God willing, hoped to live as simply again. He felt the overblown yearning of the exile stuck in an alien land by an interminable and futile war. With luck he should be back in Dublin by evening, yet each moment he had to stay in London was a moment too long, because his heart had gone out of the fight, and his soul too, and the duties that faced him this morning seemed irksome and repugnant. The campaign had gone on too long, the victory had been short and unsatisfactory. He was tired, but most of all he was tired of the struggle, which for him was tantamount to declaring a tiredness for life.

In the front of the car, Fergal murmured something to Mike then fell silent again, bowing his head contemplatively.

As eight came and went, Terry kept his eyes doggedly on

the portico of number fifty-three, waiting for the swing of the black door. A succession of people emerged or gained admittance from the adjoining houses, City men and domestics and decorators, and the occasional well-dressed young woman, bolting off to work. And still Terry watched the one door, with patience, because he knew it was about to be repaid, but also with exasperation, because it was typical of Ben Galitza to make him wait.

It was ten past when Ben finally ambled out and paused on the top step. In the short unguarded moment before Fergal got out of the car and proclaimed their whereabouts, Ben's mouth was compressed sourly, he wore a troubled frown, and Terry found himself thinking: Good! I hope you're hurting!

At the sight of Fergal, a mask of indifference slipped over Ben's face. He sauntered over and got into the back of the car without meeting Terry's gaze, which was probably just as well because Terry wasn't attempting to hide anything in his expression just then.

'Charming,' Ben declared sarcastically, without preamble. 'But then you have absolutely no shame, have you, Terry? Your instincts automatically reduce you to the lowest of the low because it's all you know.'

Terry watched Mike close the car door behind him and walk round the bonnet to join Fergal on the pavement.

'So, you've had me followed and now you think you've proved a point,' Ben continued caustically, addressing the windscreen. 'You're going to call in the guarantee and you're going to destroy my life, and I hope it brings you nothing but misery because you'll be wrong, you see. Not that you'll be interested in hearing anything to do with the *truth*, of course. *Oh no*, because you'll have your mind made up. Because you had your mind made up right from the beginning.' He gave a long sigh of disgust. '*Christ.*'

Terry was silent. His mind was on the call he'd made at seven thirty this morning to the third-floor flat high above them, and the sound of Rebecca's angry hiss as she exclaimed,

'Who the hell is this? Do you realise what time it is?' and then the startled pause as he'd asked for Ben, and – it might have been his imagination – the intake of breath as she'd recognised Terry's voice.

'You're such an arrogant sod, Terry!' Ben snapped, with a sudden display of fury that came from nowhere. 'You and your pathetic *terms*! I told you at the outset they were completely unworkable and bloody patronising and deeply offensive '

'They were cheap at the price,' Terry interjected quietly.

'*Only* someone who thought he was God bloody Almighty would try to interfere in other people's lives the way *you* do,' Ben scoffed viciously. 'You think you can control everyone's lives the way you control your workers and your minions and your bloody empire and all the people who think you're God. Well, I've got news for you – there're a whole world of people who think you're a bloody dangerous officious sanctimonious tyrant and won't put up with it.' In his fury, he spluttered incoherently before delivering his final salvo. 'You should take your half-baked Catholic morals back to the bogs where they belong, and mind your own bloody business.'

And still Terry didn't speak. He was recalling their conversation at The Shelbourne all those months ago. He was remembering Ben's protestations of devotion to Catherine, of the absolute irrelevance of money in his conduct towards her, of how nothing that Terry could say or do would in any way influence him in what love and duty would have compelled him to do anyway, which was to stay firmly by her side. The very idea that he could be induced to stay was deeply insulting. Only someone who believed that people could be bought and sold would have suggested such a despicable thing. And all the time Terry had reminded himself that you might misjudge a man once, but only a fool did it a second time. This was the man who had set out to cheat him over a deal from which they both stood to make a fair profit, had exploited Maeve pitilessly while he was betraying Catherine, and for all he knew in those confused and tumultuous days was also the man who had brought about the whole catastrophe of Catherine's accident. This was the man who, despite his protestations, was going to accept Terry's terms because his outrage was grounded less on scruples than an aversion to having restrictions placed on his god-given freedom to do exactly as he pleased.

'So you haven't broken the terms then?' Terry enquired mildly. 'Is that what you're saying?'

'I'm saying you're going to believe what you choose to bloody believe, so what's the point.'

'Try me.'

With a harsh sigh of forbearance, Ben announced in the heavy contemptuous tones of someone who's wasting his breath, 'The situation *is* that the situation's out of my hands. Catherine's decided she needs some space for a while. She's asked me to move out, maybe for the short term, maybe for ever. So I *can't* take care of her because she doesn't *want* me to. So you see? The terms can't bloody apply, because she's made the decision to leave me, and that's all there is to it. And before you start thinking precisely what I can *see* you're thinking, it was nothing that I did, and nothing that I failed to do. She just wants to be on her own, it's *her* decision, and there's nothing I can do about it. Okay? Absolutely *nothing*. I've stood by her a thousand per cent, I've done everything I could possibly do to make her happy – everything I would have done *anyway*, I may add, without your bloody interference – but she wants out. All right? And I came here to Rebecca's because I had nowhere else to bloody go.' He rolled his eyes. 'Christ, the very fact that I'm having to *explain* this to you . . .'

Terry said nothing. He was wondering if this was what Catherine really wanted. If so, he secretly rejoiced for her.

'And if you don't bloody believe me – which you won't, of course – go and ask her yourself,' Ben muttered petulantly. 'Or ask the entire world – everyone'll know soon enough, I'm sure. Though of course they'll go and blame *me*. *Inevitably*. So much more convenient to cast me as the villain. I'm not crippled, I just tried to kill the bastard who attacked her. *No* allowing for the fact that it's Catherine who wants out, no allowing for the fact that it's Catherine who's broken—' He bit hard on his lip, as if to stifle his despair, before muttering scathingly, 'Oh, for God's sake, what do I care what you believe? Withdraw the bloody guarantee. I'm not going to beg. Do your bloody worst.'

Terry said with the same appearance of great calm, 'I didn't come about that, in fact.'

There was a pause while Ben turned to look at him for the first time. 'What do you mean? You had me bloody followed, for Christ's sake! You've caught me at Rebecca's. What else is this about if it's not that?'

'I've only had you followed since last night,' Terry remarked wearily. 'And only because I needed to know where to find you.'

And still Ben stared, though now his curiosity was tinged with resentment at the realisation that he had poured out his excuses and aired his humiliation for nothing. 'So what the hell *is* it about then? Why the hell go to all this trouble?'

Terry said unhurriedly, 'Rightly or wrongly, I took it on myself to find out who burgled your house and why, and I thought you might be interested to know what I've discovered. Oh, and I wanted to ask you a few questions. Yes,' he said carefully, as if correcting a lapse, 'to ask you to fill in the gaps.'

Ben's eyes were very sharp and very still. 'You *know*?'

'I took the precaution of buying Pavlik the best defence in town.'

'You *what*?'

Terry thrust up a quieting hand. 'And I found him his alibi – or rather, I located the witnesses who could attest to his alibi, the ones the police in all their diligence had failed to find – or failed to look for. It was true, you see. Pavlik was not there at the time of the attack. He was innocent of that charge. So . . . in exchange for this service, Pavlik told me who had paid him to break in. And why. Well, more or less why. I think that's where you might be able to fill in some of the details.' Without waiting for an answer, Terry continued in a musing tone, 'Pavlik's *employer* – if that's the word – had already bought him a defence of sorts, but Pavlik didn't trust his employer one inch. He had the feeling that the defence lawyer he'd been given might be renowned more for his obscurity and incompetence than for his talent, and that he, Pavlik, might have been cast in the role of sacrificial lamb. He feared to tell the police the truth because he feared for his life, and he had no name for his employer anyway, no proper name, so he doubted very much that they would believe him. With good reason, I would suspect.'

Ben seemed overwhelmed or frozen, or both, so Terry continued, 'I will say straight away that I began these investigations with the idea that you yourself might have a very great deal to answer for. More, I mean, than you have to answer for already. I had the idea that you had meant to harm Catherine—'

'For God's sake!' Ben exclaimed, emerging from his daze with a jolt.

'Allow me to finish,' said Terry on a warning note. 'I thought you might have harmed her because you believed she was someone else – because you believed she was Maeve.'

The short but startled pause that followed was broken by Terry whose voice maintained an iron calm. 'You were expecting Maeve – or rather, you should have been expecting her if you had bothered to remember the arrangement you'd made. And, as I saw it, there she was, turning up at an inconvenient moment, a nuisance to you, an encumbrance' – his voice broke a little, it was all he could do to steady it – 'she'd become ill and bothersome, you wanted well rid of her, her sudden arrival was the last straw.'

'But I didn't—'

'That was how I *believed* it to be,' Terry interrupted, with his first show of impatience. 'That was how I saw it at the *beginning*. For a long time it was hard to make out what had happened because when Maeve returned she was wild with grief. Inconsolable. Because – you must have realised – it was she who discovered Catherine on the floor.'

Ben looked defensive. 'Oh.'

'At first I knew only what Maeve was able to tell me, and for a long time she could say very little. She was in a terrible state. Finding Catherine like that, thinking she was dead. And coming on top of her other griefs, which, as you will know better than anyone, were considerable and had been going on for some time.'

Ben dropped his head, though whether it was from anything as decent as shame it was impossible to tell.

There was another pause in which Ben turned to stare out of the window and Terry fought old battles with his own grief and anguish. The temptation to rage at Ben was very strong, he longed to beat his arrogant head against a wall and demand to know what had been going through his mind when he took Maeve's innocence and generosity and trampled on it so mercilessly, he wanted to ask what kind of man could take satisfaction from such destruction. But he made the supreme effort to restrain himself, partly because he strongly suspected that Ben's satisfaction had come precisely from the fact that Maeve was his daughter, and partly because at the end of the day there was no arguing with a man with only the slenderest grasp on decency and morality, there was no winning a quarrel in which painful revelations might come to light, only to haunt him cruelly for ever afterwards. It was almost more than he could bear, to stay quiet, but he told himself there was more to be gained by keeping a dignified silence.

'Then I heard that Pavlik had a story to tell,' Terry resumed after a moment. 'For a price. So I struck the deal, not because I especially wanted to nail *you* – though the Lord only knows, that would have given me the most enormous satisfaction – but because I wanted the truth for Catherine. I wanted her to know that it was your dealings that had brought it all about.'

Ben opened his mouth as if to protest, only to think better of it and draw in his lips tightly.

'Pavlik told us he'd been hired to break into the house so that his employer could remove or copy some papers. What were the papers, Galitza?'

Again Ben seemed on the point of arguing, again he decided against it. 'Details of financial transactions,' he replied in a flat sulky voice.

'What transactions?'

'Normal business transactions,' he said as if explaining the obvious to an ignoramus. 'Money coming in and going out again. Bank details and statements. Access codes. The *normal* things.'

Without warning, something overturned in Terry, his stomach lurched, his anger flowed over him like a red-hot sea, his throat seized and it was all he could do not to shout. '*Details!*' he echoed in a voice that shook audibly. 'Come on, *come on*. What details? Of money laundering? Of the profits from the secret deal for the generators that you pulled off behind everyone's backs? *Come on*, let's have a little truth for a change! I know it comes hard to you, the truth, but humour me, let me have a little flavour of it! What was it about – money that you had forgotten to pass on? Money that you had forgotten to share? Money that was illegally obtained? Come now – let's have something like the unvarnished truth here!'

'All right, all right!' Ben replied savagely. 'It was money I was passing on for some customers. I didn't ask where it came from, I didn't ask where it was going, I only knew where it had to go when it left my hands, and that's where I sent it.' He added in a more reasonable tone, 'But I guess I upset some people along the way. There's a dealer in Warsaw, a middleman I've dealt with for years, someone who's got fingers in every pie – or so he likes to think. He got miffed when he realised I'd cut him out.'

'So it was him, is that what you're saying? It was him who sent the employer to come and reclaim the money?'

'Yup. He as good as told me he was coming after it.'

'What did he get for his burglary?' Terry demanded, not letting up for a moment. '*Precisely*.'

Ben didn't want to answer that one, he would have shrugged it off, but something in Terry's expression made him give in with bad grace. 'He managed to empty my bank account—'

'So he got all the pass-codes and access details!'

Ben didn't like being reminded of his stupidity. 'Yes!' he hissed sardonically.

'Foreign banks?'

'Bermuda, the Caymans.'

'But he wanted more?'

'He demanded the same again in lieu of his cut.'

'*Or else?* There has to be an *or else*.'

'Or a photocopy of the transaction details to the authorities.'

'So – stymied. Your profit gone, and then blackmailed to boot. That must have hurt. My Lord, that must have hurt!'

Not sure whether this was offered in a spirit of gloating or irony. Ben clenched his jaw furiously.

Terry continued in the same tone of jaunty sarcasm, 'This middleman must have felt as sore as a scalded cat to go to all that trouble. Polish Mafia, was he? Dabbling in drugs and all sorts, didn't like you muscling in – was that it? Still . . . to go to all that trouble. But then, I suppose the money alone was worth it. Your cut was – what? – a million dollars or so? And then the million in recompense. So, two million dollars. Well, yes, that would have gone a long way to making him feel better. It would make anyone feel better, would it not?'

'None of it excuses what was done to Catherine!' Ben cried bitterly, finding his voice again. 'Nothing I've done could ever justify *that* sort of thuggery!'

'No,' Terry agreed abruptly, calming down at last. 'No, nothing at all.'

He watched a pretty woman coming out of a house opposite, carrying a small child on one hip, its short legs straddling her waist. She had a large bag over her other shoulder, and a folded pushchair in her hand. Despite all the paraphernalia, she made her way down the steps with assurance and grace, and in some unfocused way Terry was reminded of

Catherine. Except that Catherine would never know the simple pleasure of carrying her child on her hip and depositing it – crying now – into a pushchair.

'Did it never occur to you', Terry murmured, his eyes still on the woman, 'to try to get even with this man after what he'd done?'

'What – declare war against the Polish business community? This guy's still doing a whole bundle of legitimate deals. He's got influence. He'd make my name mud. I'd never be able to do a deal there again.'

'So you decided to take your medicine instead.' He added, with the slightest touch of irony, 'Like a man.'

Ben closed his eyes expressively.

The moment of revelation had almost come. Yet again Terry felt no sense of triumph, only emptiness. 'It never occurred to you to look closer to home?'

He got Ben's full attention then, the eyes swung round, alert, wary.

'You didn't think there was anyone here who might have felt entitled to that money?'

'Like?'

'Someone you'd cut out of a deal he was expecting to share in?'

'No.'

Ben might have cunning, he might be quick, but Terry always forgot to allow for the fact that he wasn't outstandingly bright. 'What about your company? Wasn't it expecting the benefit of your profits?'

'You mean . . .' Ben hesitated, he thought it through, he dismissed it with a laugh. 'Simon?'

Terry lifted his eyebrows.

'*Simon?*'

'Pavlik met him in a gay club, knew him as someone called Christian. It was a cash deal, the burglary. Half up front, half after the break in.'

Ben was already shaking his head with a superior knowing smile. 'Simon couldn't – wouldn't – he's incapable . . . No, no, for God's sake . . . We were – *are* – friends.' With each denial he was slowly but surely talking himself into the possibility. 'And a gay club? He's never been that way – I mean, not to *my* knowledge! And why would he want to – I've never cut him out of anything–' He stalled suddenly, his eyes flickered crossly, he became indignant. 'Christ, he did okay, we made money, he had nothing to complain about. I mean, he was my number two, for God's sake. I mean, we were partners, I gave him half of everything, of *course* I did, but I did all the *deals*, I had all the contacts, nothing would have happened without me. And then he goes and–' He made a dismissive exclamation, then in the next breath demanded coldly: 'You're *sure*?'

'Pavlik described him, we showed him a photograph.'

'But he only met him – the once, was it? – in a club! How could he be sure?'

Terry paused, embarrassed. 'According to Pavlik, they had a, er – transient relationship.'

Ben pulled back, startled. 'Jesus. *Jesus*.' His face slowly contorted as his fury grew. 'And Pavlik identified him from a photograph?'

'For sure.'

'That bastard! He cleaned me bloody out! Took everything! And had the brass nerve to— And after all we did together! God – what a two-faced— *God!*' He had flushed with anger, his handsome mouth was pinched and rigid. Then his expression clouded as fresh realisations and doubts came to him. Twisting round in his seat, he stared at Terry. 'He was the one who attacked me?' It took him a moment to absorb this. 'God, if I could . . .' He clenched his fists like a schoolboy itching to get his own back. Again he turned to Terry and stared. 'And Catherine?' He couldn't bring himself to spell it out. 'He did *that* to Catherine? He . . .' Then, with confusion, 'But he *adores* her, he's always hanging around her, he's like her bloody shadow! He's like a lapdog!' And finally, in a murmur: 'The burglar alarm, he knew the code of course. It was the same as the office. Yes, yes . . . he knew the code.'

He was finally there. He understood it all.

Now that the unpleasant task was over, Terry was suddenly desperate to be away. The sense of revulsion rose in him like a panic, he felt he would suffocate if he stayed in the same space as Galitza for a second longer.

'I propose to tell the police this morning,' he announced, opening the window to a blast of cold air.

Ben raised his head to this. 'Hey, what about *me*? I don't want them bloody nosing about in my affairs. No, I think that would be an appalling idea!'

'I'll leave it twelve hours, then. That will give you time to settle on your story.'

'You *shit*.'

Ignoring this, beginning to feel more cheerful all of a sudden, Terry asked, 'Where's Jardine now, do you know?'

'No idea.' Then he hissed bleakly, 'Spending my money, presumably.'


Heavy clouds swept low over the valley, driving veils of thin sleet up the ramp of fields into the exposed garden, agitating the animals in the topiary and swirling plumes of leaves up into the branches of the black-limbed beeches.

'Not much point in seeing more,' Catherine said.

'But it gives you an idea?'

'Oh yes.'

Simon turned the wheelchair round and pushed her back along the path through a brick arch into the relative sanctuary of the rose garden.

'It's beautifully maintained,' she called back over her shoulder.

'You like it?'

'I think it's a splendid garden.'

'You wouldn't want to change it?'

'Not in any major way. It'd be a waste of your money.'

He turned the chair round and tipped it backwards a little to pull it up some shallow steps. 'But it could be improved?' he asked.

'Oh, the planting could be improved, I'm sure, but you'd have to see it through an entire season before you'd know what you wanted to do.'

'So if I bought it now . . .?'

'You'd begin to have a good idea by May.'

They came round the side of the house onto the gravel sweep where the car was parked. 'Six months then,' he said.

'More or less.'

He opened the car door for her and held the chair steady while she transferred herself. He waited until she was settled then brought a rug round from the back to lay over her knees.

'Really, I'm fine,' she insisted, but he was already crouching down to wrap the rug around her legs.

'Just until the car warms up,' he said protectively, and cast her a diffident smile.

When he'd stowed the wheelchair he sat in the driver's seat with the door open and his feet on the gravel and changed his shoes, placing the dirty ones in a plastic bag, which he carried round to the boot. He then took off his waterproof jacket and, shaking the rain from it, folded it neatly and laid it with care on the back seat. Watching this, Catherine wondered how he was going to manage country life, in which mud, dirt and wet clothes had a way of sneaking into the best-defended homes. But then the whole day had been overlaid with an odd sense of unreality. Leaving shortly before ten, they had taken the slow road along the Thames through Henley and Cliveden, arriving at Bray at exactly twelve thirty – Simon had speeded up a little so they shouldn't be late – where they'd eaten a rich ornate lunch. Simon had talked a lot about lifestyle, the importance of getting it right, of the futility of working hard unless you had something worthwhile to come home to, how the bedrock of a good life was non-negotiable: strong values and a united family and unstinting loyalty and solid friends. The house, still unseen, appeared to be central to this vision, a pivot or a symbol, and the garden too, though by his own admission he'd never felt the need for one in the past. He'd rambled a bit, repeated himself a great deal, but there was no doubting his passion and sincerity, nor the sharp edge of desperation beneath, as though by focusing so closely on his dream, having earned the money to realise it, he knew it would slip from his grasp. He was suffused with a nervous jumpy energy that had the moods chasing over his face faster than she could follow them. Hope, despair, anxiety – she had never seen him in such turmoil. His cheek trembled almost continuously, he had developed a new habit of sucking in his lips, and now and again when he looked away it seemed to her that his eyes contained desolation.

Climbing into the car at last, Simon sat with his hands on the wheel and looked up at the façade. 'Well,' he said, 'what do you think?'

He had asked this several times during their tour of the house. She could only repeat, 'I think it's stunning.' She added on a cautionary note, 'Though I hate to think what they're asking for it.'

'It's a fair price.'

'You'll need to add a lot for the furnishings,' she warned him. 'And then there'll be the maintenance, of course. A full-time gardener, I'd have thought. And probably a housekeeper too.'

He said softly, 'Could you live here, Catherine?'

She was about to make some mundane reply when, glancing across at him, she found him watching her with a strange intensity, and paused. She was struck by the uncomfortable thought that he was serious. 'Me? I'd love to live in a beautiful place, of course I would. *But,*' she added hastily, 'I think something smaller would suit me far better.'

And still his brilliant eyes remained fixed on her face. 'But . . . if you found yourself here . . . you could like it?'

Oh God, she thought, he's about to make a declaration. 'You can like all sorts of places, can't you?' she said in a tone that was deliberately offhand. 'It all depends on—' She was about to say, *on who you're with and whether you're happy*, but pulled herself up just in time, and said lightly, 'On where you happen to find yourself.' She ducked forward to look up at the sky. 'Could we get going now?' she asked breezily. 'It'll be dark soon. And I'd like to get home.'

'But Ben and you,' he said relentlessly, 'it's over, isn't it? He's gone? You're going to need someone to look after you.'

'I really can't discuss Ben.'

'But Catherine – wouldn't you be happy here?' His voice had risen, his breath was coming fast. 'We both like the same things. We could make it the most beautiful house in the world. Antiques and pictures, and people in for lunch. Not *all* the time of course! We could go abroad for some of the winter, we could travel. But this would be our home, we could make the garden the best garden for miles. Oh, God,' he groaned furiously, 'I'm making it sound as though it's all about *that*! It's not – what I mean is, what I've been saying very badly, is that I want to look after you, Catherine, take care of you. I want that more than anything in the world.'

'Simon, *please*.' She waved a hand inarticulately. 'Not now. This isn't the time. I'm sorry.' She exhaled slowly. 'If we could just go home.' She looked firmly ahead through the windscreen.

'Oh, I do realise it's rather soon,' he gasped in a voice of sudden reason. 'Of course I do. I realise you're still upset about Rebecca. That's natural . . .'

The name resounded darkly in her head. *Rebecca*.

'. . . You're bound to be. And I appreciate that you can't actually decide at the moment. That you can't make promises. I wouldn't expect you to.'

Rebecca. In the instant that she felt the first stab of anguish, she also understood that Rebecca was the obvious choice for Ben in a time of trouble. He would have wanted sympathy, familiarity and lack of complications, more or less in that order;

he would have wanted someone who understood this instinctively, someone who knew him well, an old lover without expectations; or, with expectations and the shrewdness to hide them.

Ben and Rebecca. A story that she had interrupted.

She had missed much of what Simon had been saying. Now he was asking insistently, '*Catherine?* Will you? *Will you?*'

She looked at him helplessly, she made as if to touch his arm by way of apology. 'Have you known about Rebecca for long?' she asked.

He didn't want to talk about Rebecca, he frowned. 'I saw them together once. I was trying to catch Ben one morning and . . . I saw them.'

'At the house. She was at the house?'

He looked mildly abashed, as if he'd said too much, but not so abashed that he didn't nod in confirmation, before resuming with quiet insistence, 'Just say you'll think about it, Catherine.'

'Sorry?'

'Say you won't rule it out. That's all.' He gave a laugh that seemed to catch in his throat, there was a sheen of nervousness on his temple. 'We'd be so happy here, I know we would. Think – this garden with two garden makers!'

The attempt at light-heartedness only succeeded in striking a note of pathos, and again it seemed to her that his longing hid a deep pessimism, that he knew his chances were hopeless.

She began to recite the ritualistic words of rejection. 'Simon, I'm terribly flattered, and I'm terribly honoured, but I can't possibly begin to think about the future at the moment, not in any shape or form. I have no idea where my marriage is. I have no idea what I want myself.' Seeing his pain, she ploughed on, forcing an overt note of kindness into her voice, hating the string of platitudes. 'I like you, of course I do, I value your friendship, but I have to say that I've never thought of you as anything but a friend. And I can't say that's ever going to change. I just can't. I'm sorry.'

He turned his head sharply to look away through the

windscreen. After a while he started the engine. 'I understand,' he said in a voice that was very controlled, but also very close to breaking. 'Thank you at least for being such a good friend.'

'No, no,' she said, far too quickly, 'I'm the one who's grateful to *you*.'

She thought: I got that wrong. No, she corrected herself, we both got it wrong. His timing couldn't have been worse, and he had sprung it on her: he hadn't thought it through at all. He hadn't taken account of the upheavals that had shaken her life over the last two days; or perhaps he had, and rushed at the opportunity. At this thought, her indignation grew, and she began to see his declaration as an intrusion, wildly insensitive and very unfair.

They drove for a long time in silence. Wearied by the tension, she took out her phone and announced in a light voice, 'Just going to pick up my messages.' In the dusk, his profile was severe. He didn't look towards her and he didn't speak.

She hadn't really expected a message from Ben, but she was miffed not to get one all the same. Instead, there was her father's standard message, complete with diversionary ideas – it was a trip to the races now, a lunch with friends. Then Emma's voice, diffident, loyal, a little troubled, possibly hurt, asking if she could do anything for her. In her mind, Catherine apologised: *I thought it was you, Emma, and I was wrong*. It seemed extraordinary now to believe Emma capable of such sustained and accomplished deceit, but a tortured imagination is a wild imagination, in which it's a short step from an embrace to a well-established affair.

After Emma came three or four business calls that she would play back later. Then Alice, in a panicky tone that made Catherine instantly alert.

'Cath, wherever you are, please call me straight away. I went round to the house, but you weren't there. I've got to speak to you. I'm at work. Usual number. But I'll leave my mobile on as well, just in case.' A pause, then, distractedly: 'Hope you're okay.' And urgently: 'Cath – straight away.'

Catherine ruled out a broken love affair; Alice had always been too proud to come to her with those. A family problem then? Pa running up debts and not telling anyone? Or Ben, going to Alice with some sob story about being thrown out? But even as she brought up Alice's name on the display and pressed the dial key, she discounted that one. Ben was frightened of Alice; he would rather choke than confide in her.

'Where are you?' Alice cried hastily.

'On a motorway, coming back from the country.'

'When will you be back?'

'An hour or so.'

'An *hour*?' A sigh of frustration.

'Why? What's happened?' She was thinking of Pa.

As if reading her mind, Alice declared brusquely, 'Oh, it's not Pa. Nothing like that. No, it's . . . to do with your burglary, Cath. Something you should know. Something that the *police* should know.' She was sounding slightly hysterical.

'Give me a clue.'

A hesitation, as if she couldn't make up her mind how much to say. 'It's about Simon,' she said eventually. 'Something really bad, Cath.'

Without thinking, Catherine glanced across at him. His eyes swivelled round and met hers briefly. In the instant before she looked away again, she saw a strange brilliance in his eyes.

'Tell me,' she said, selecting her most casual tone.

'But can you talk? Are you driving?'

'Hardly driving.'

'Oh no, of *course* not. *God*, no – stupid of me. No . . . But it might take a moment. Is it all right? Who're you with? Who's driving you?'

'A colleague.'

She made a nervous exclamation. 'God, I thought for a moment it might have been Simon.'

'So,' Catherine said lightly, 'what's the problem exactly?'

A pause while Alice chose her words, which she delivered with a kind of agonised excitement. 'You remember I went to the court that day when Pavlik first came up? The magistrates' court? And Simon was there too?'

'Aha.'

'Well, when the bail was arranged, they mentioned the name of this man who was going to guarantee the bail – or whatever the word is – and well, I hardly registered the name. I mean, it was no one I knew. I never thought to remember it. And I was so appalled at the fact Pavlik was getting bail that I just didn't pay much attention.'

'No.'

'Anyway, I just realised a couple of hours ago – well, in fact it was last week that I actually heard the name again, but it just didn't click until today, I just couldn't remember where I'd heard it before. You know how it is – you hear names, and you just don't connect them. It was only today that I finally realised it was the *same* guy. And even then I got Denise Cox to check the court records for the name of the man who put the money up. It took her all day to get the information. I couldn't say how urgent it was, of course, and I went almost *mad* waiting, but at last she came through with it, and it was the *same* guy, Cath.'

'The same as who?'

Alice slowed down a little as she said rather stiffly, 'The same as the man who left a message on Simon's machine. While I was there. Last week. In Simon's flat. His name's David Frankel. He's a solicitor. He's the same man. But, Cath, he talked like a *friend* in the message. First name stuff. Sort of, how are you, Simon, and can you phone me some time. But, Cath – why would Simon know him unless . . .? You see what I mean?' she cried on a rising note of fear. 'It's all wrong, isn't it?'

Catherine said calmly, 'I see what you mean, yes.'

'What should we do?'

Catherine said, 'I can't think just at the moment.' And it was true. Her mind had stalled, her thoughts were all over the place.

'But, Cath, if Simon was involved with this man, if they put up the bail, then—'

'I understand what you're saying. Let's talk about this later. I'll call you.'

As she rang off, Simon asked, with echoes of his old anxiety and attentiveness, 'Everything all right, Catherine?'


Reaching the house, he stopped the car with a slight jolt and gripped the top of the wheel, his shoulders hunched, his head bent forward, like some awful parody of a boy racer. 'I'm sorry if I frightened you,' he cried in a rush of anguish. 'It was the last thing I intended. The last thing in the world! I knew it wasn't the best moment, I knew it was a bit too soon. But I could just *see* us there, Catherine! I could see us in that house with all those beautiful rooms, and the garden, and the lake, and the country life. It's what I've always dreamt of, you see. Always. From when I was small, when we lived in a rat-hole flat with filthy windows and dirty carpets. That's what I dreamt of – a place like that!' His voice had risen emotionally, and dipped again. 'I knew it was hoping for a lot, of course, to think you'd want to share it with me. I knew the chances were a bit slim. I knew—' The words seized in his throat, he inhaled unevenly. 'But you've got to dream a bit, haven't you?' His nervous laugh emerged as a ragged gasp. 'You've got to go for things, otherwise what's the use? Got to believe it's going to happen.' He turned to her. 'Forgiven?' When she didn't reply he begged furiously, '*Please*, Catherine.'

'Sure,' she murmured. 'Forget it. It's not important. But I'd like to get into the house now, if you don't mind. I'm tired.'

Something in her voice must have alerted him because he stiffened and gave her a long searching look before climbing out of the car.

When he wheeled her up to the house, he seemed preoccupied, and it wasn't until they were inside that he spoke again.

His words came as a statement delivered in a flat voice. 'You're not forgiving me then.'

'I told you – it's not important.'

He twisted his head, as if to catch her tone. 'There's something else,' he said tightly.

She began to pull off her coat and waved him firmly away when he tried to help. In the car, she'd decided to leave the business of Simon and Frankel to the police, she no longer trusted her judgement on matters involving explanations, excuses and lies. But now as she struggled ineffectually with the sleeves of her coat, her frustration got tangled up with a wider anger, and she said accusingly, 'I'm told that you know some-one called David Frankel.'

Freeing herself from the last sleeve, she threw the coat in the general direction of a chair and looked up to find him staring at her, white-faced, as if someone had struck him.

'Well?'

He seemed frozen. He might not have been breathing.

'David Frankel,' she repeated slowly as if addressing an idiot. 'You know him?'

A barely discernible nod.

'He was the man who put up the bail money.'

He closed his eyes tightly. He seemed to shrivel visibly, to retreat into his body in a dozen minute ways, his head to settle lower into his neck, his hands to shrink against his body, his shoulders to slump by infinitesimal degrees.

'Well?' she demanded in cold exasperation.

'Oh, Catherine . . .' he whispered faintly. He lowered his head.

'You're making me think bad things, Simon.' And now it was her own voice that was shaking. 'You're making me think you arranged Pavlik's defence. You're making me think he was working for you!'

He tried to speak, but only choked.

'For God's sake!' she cried contemptuously.

'Oh, Catherine!' It was an agonised wail, a great cry of despair. Suddenly he clamped his hands over his face, and she realised with astonishment that he'd begun to cry. He tried to say something, which she couldn't at first make out through the increasingly violent sobs. 'I never meant ... Never, never, *never*!'

'For God's sake!' she snapped, in terror at what he might say.

He dropped his hands from his face and flung them down by his sides, palms spread wide. With his bowed head and splayed hands, he was like a supplicant offering himself for retribution. And still he sobbed. The tears dripped off his nose, tracking down a long skein of mucus that dangled from the tip. Spikes of hair had fallen forward, masking his eyes. 'It was a *mistake*! A terrible, ghastly *mistake*!' The 'mistake' was drawn out in a long moan of misery. 'If you knew how I've tortured myself – how I've begged for it not to have happened! God, there hasn't been a *moment*, not a single moment that I haven't *begged* to be struck down, that I haven't longed for it to be me. If *I* could have been the one – I'd have given anything for it to have been me! Oh Catherine, if I could have brought you back, made you whole again – I'd have done anything – I'd have died a thousand deaths – a thousand million deaths. Believe me, Catherine, there hasn't been a moment – not a *second* that I haven't wished it undone – that I haven't *longed* for it not to have happened. I've dreamt so often of catching you as you fell, I've rushed to catch you –'

'It was Pavlik. You hired him. It was Pavlik who attacked me. Is that what you're saying? *Is that it, Simon?*'

He raised his head. His face was distorted and ugly with despair.

She read her answer, and one part of her was in immediate and fierce revolt against it, refused absolutely to accept it, did not want to admit to the message in his eyes, not now, not *ever*, while another part of her was sickened with revulsion and betrayal, was recoiling from the depth of his treachery, though even as the rage shook her, it began to ebb rapidly away.

Simon was gesticulating violently. 'Don't you see, don't you see, Catherine – I didn't realise it was *you*. I had no idea it was *you*. Don't you see . . .' His legs buckled slowly, for a moment he stood like someone who'd been shot and refuses to fall, until he finally sank forward onto his knees, which met the stone with a sharp crack. Like my head, she thought. My head would have sounded like that. *Crack!*

'I thought it was *her*, Catherine!' He held his arms up wide, like a priest. 'I thought it was the girl! I heard her ring, I saw her knocking! I saw the awful sick look on her face that they always get when they're around Ben. The disgusting foul look before they throw themselves at him, just like cheap common tarts! I've seen them time and again, getting that same sick disgusting look in their eyes.' With a whimper, he brought his hands down in a savage cutting motion, as if to haul himself back from some brink. 'I saw her there,' he began again in a shuddering voice. 'Knocking on the door, thinking he was there, desperate to get at him. And, Catherine, I realised he was betraying *you* just like he was betraying *me*! I thought: He's doing to Catherine what he's doing to me! And I felt sick, I felt disgusted, I wanted to kill him with my bare hands!'

He had begun to cry again, his cheek was dancing so violently that his face seemed permanently askew. 'He sold me out, Catherine. Betrayed me!' he sobbed in a voice of fresh despair. 'After all my *work*. After *everything* I'd put into that deal – heart, soul, energy, bloody *devotion* – and what did he do? He went and cut me out. Cheated me! Without a second thought, without a moment's hesitation! Because I was nothing to him, you see. I was just a load of *shit*! Someone he could treat like *dirt*! Just like he was treating you, Catherine. He was going to have that girl, just like he'd had a thousand girls, and not care a shit! The fact that he was married to *you*, to someone as fantastic and wonderful as *you* – well, what would *he* care?

He takes people and uses them. Always has. Greedy, greedy – always wanting more, more, more. Never enough money in the world for him. Never enough women. And loyalty? Christ, what a *joke*! Loyalty means fuck all to him. It's just a *word*! He doesn't begin to know the meaning—' He made the strange choking sound again and, clasping his head in both hands, sucked in long gulps of air as if he were suffocating.

'The girl,' Catherine said in a low voice, 'did you mean to hurt her?'

His head came up slowly, he looked at her, aghast. 'God, no! *No!* She – *you* – took me totally by surprise! I thought when Ben arrived that he was alone – I thought he'd come back from France a day early without you. He was meant to be coming back the next day *on his own*, Catherine! You were meant to be staying on in France. That was what he told me! That was how we left it and when I heard him come in, and I looked down and saw him alone, it never *occurred* to me that you were somewhere behind him. When he caught me upstairs and we fought, I never thought for a second there'd be anyone else!'

He dragged a hand across his eyes, rubbing them viciously. 'It was a complete shock when I heard someone calling. I thought it had to be *her*, I thought it was the *girl* come back, that they'd planned to meet. I only meant to push her out of the way, to make sure she didn't see me. But then . . . then I got angry, I wanted to *punish* her for being in your house, I wanted to *punish* her for behaving like a cheap . . .'

He trailed off, the energy went out of him, he sank back on his haunches and lowered his hands onto his knees. He whispered, 'But it was you.'

There was a long pause in which the only sound was the rasp of his breathing.

Finally she asked, 'And you blackmailed Ben?'

'I wanted my money,' he said dully. 'I wanted him to know what it was like to pay up. I'd got the proof of what he'd been up to. I used it to make sure I got my money.'

'You took what he owed you?'

'Double. Exactly double. He never worked that out! It never occurred to him that I could have done such a thing, you see.' He was still close enough to tears that he laughed easily. 'He thought—'

The doorbell made them both start a little. They exchanged glances, Catherine's bewildered, his afraid.

She moved towards the door. 'Who is it?' she called.

'Catherine, it's Fergal.'

She looked back towards Simon. He was still kneeling, his eyes fixed on the floor.

She opened the door a short way.

Fergal seemed immensely tall against the darkness. His expression was very stern. He said in a voice designed to carry, 'Just calling by to see you're all right, Catherine.'

She took a deep breath. 'I'm all right,' she said.

Flicking his eyes towards the road, Fergal added in a whisper, 'I've got Mike right here. We could have the police round in a jiff.'

From behind her, Simon said flatly, 'He knows, Catherine. He knows everything.'

As she moved back to let Fergal pass, Catherine pretended faint irritation. 'Watching over me again, were you, Fergal?'

'Oh no. Never,' he remonstrated gently. 'No, if you're to thank anyone, Catherine, it should be Mr Devlin.'

# Chapter Sixteen

———————

*Foxrock, 21st February.*

*Dear Catherine, Forgive me for not having been able to meet up with you for so long. Christmas seemed to arrive in a terrible rush, and then as you know I was off to the US for the best part of two weeks, and then back to a situation here that has conspired to keep me chained to my desk ever since. But Fergal tells me that you've had a good offer on the house. I'm glad things have moved so fast. I hope that you'll find what you're looking for in the way of a new place very soon. A fresh start is a great thing.*

*Regarding the financial matters, the final account is now complete. Fergal will give you the details. He is in London from this Saturday evening and will phone you to arrange a time to call.*

*I hope Bridget has been able to provide you with all the necessary liaison over the garden – I'm afraid I haven't had the time or the mind to give it proper attention. But I have every hope of getting down to Morne to see the work begin. And if, as Bridget tells me, you will be coming over before then (to plan the excavations?), then we will definitely meet, though it may have to be in Dublin.*

*Maeve sends her fondest love. She is good and busy.*

*Your friend, as ever,*

*Terry*

\*

Built in sturdy post-modern style on the site of a demolished church in Bayswater, the block was four years old but looked older. The agent had extolled the virtues of the stainless steel kitchens and bathrooms, but Catherine had taken the flat not for the gleam of its plumbing but for its position high on the fifth floor, its south-west-facing terrace, and the reserved parking in the basement garage below.

Arriving on this Sunday morning, letting some air in, she also discovered that you could hear church bells drifting from the direction of Hyde Park, and the faint screech of shunting trains beyond Paddington Station.

While waiting for Fergal, she took measurements and inspected the decorators' progress. The whole place was to be white: a space intentionally blank. She would impose some sort of mark with her antiques, her pictures, and the few bits of modern furniture she had yet to choose. But possessions would be kept to a minimum. She had the instincts of an itinerant now; no sooner camped than ready to move on. It was no coincidence that the feeder road to the Westway was barely fifty yards away.

It was just before eleven when Fergal rang the bell.

'I thought we were doomed to the phone for ever.' Her smile didn't entirely hide the reproach beneath.

He pecked her cheek. 'Not for want of seeing you, Catherine.'

She gave him a conducted tour, which took all of two minutes. 'A tidy little place,' he commented, with the forced interest of a man who expects little of his surroundings.

They sat on two cheap plastic chairs belonging to the decorators. A slow rain speckled the windows.

'So, what's going on, Fergal? Why are you two rushing around like mad? You're bad enough, but *Terry* . . . We've talked twice, I think, since Christmas.'

'Oh, you know how he is, always saying he's going to ease up, and then he's away again, after another hotel, another enterprise.'

'It's not that he's gone off the idea of the garden then?'

'Oh no, it won't be that!' he declared without hesitation. 'No, it'll be the hours he's working, all God made and more. Which isn't to say he won't be keeping an eye. He always keeps an eye. You can be sure he's fully aware of the progress of the garden.'

'So what's this project, Fergal?'

Fergal took on the abstruse expression of someone whose lips are sealed. 'Empire building, you might say.'

Taking her shrug as a display of bewilderment, Fergal hastened to add, 'Oh, it's not for the money that he does it. Never the money. The house at Foxrock, it's not grand, you know, not by the standards of some in Dublin. No, he's a restless spirit, that's the truth of it. It's in his nature to look for the next challenge. Apart from the horses and the racing, there's little to occupy him, you see.'

'But Maeve, he's got Maeve.'

'Aha. But then he hasn't seen so very much of her since Christmas. She's found herself some new friends. Students like herself. They're always away somewhere – walking the hills, or off to the films, or gone to the dancing. It's a great thing for her, the dancing.'

'So she's happy, Fergal?'

He made a speculative gesture. 'She will be, I believe. Yes, one day.'

Catherine had an image of Maeve in a group, dancing, and of Terry going back to an empty house.

'I was hoping to meet Terry at Morne this week,' she said. 'But of course it doesn't look as though he'll be free. When I ask Bridget what to do she just tells me to go ahead.'

'I would do that very thing then,' Fergal suggested calmly. 'Go ahead. Take it as a declaration of faith in your judgement.'

'Supposing he doesn't like the result?'

'You can tell him he should have paid more attention,' Fergal retorted uncompromisingly.

Despite Fergal's reassurances, Catherine couldn't quite rid

herself of the idea that, having done his duty by everyone, Terry had moved on, that, subconsciously or otherwise, he was distancing himself from the past and everything associated with the period of Maeve's obsession. And, as Catherine hardly needed reminding, associations didn't come much stronger than herself.

Fergal cleared his throat in the manner of someone getting down to business. 'So . . . I have brought what Mr Devlin likes to call the final account.' He pulled a paper from his breast pocket and handed it to her. 'He wants to know if it meets with your approval.'

It was a list of six charities, with, against each one, the sum it had received by way of anonymous donation. Since drugs had seemed the most likely source of the money, it had been Catherine's idea that a large proportion of it went to addiction and rehabilitation projects. For the rest, she had left the decisions to Terry. The total came to over three-quarters of a million pounds.

'It looks fine,' she said.

'Mr Devlin also wanted to be sure that you had received everything that was owing to you. That nothing was outstanding.'

This was Fergal's way of asking if Ben had made over the house proceeds and signed the other papers relating to the separation settlement. 'My solicitor tells me it's all gone through,' she said.

'And the house sale?'

'Completion next week.'

'So, you're all set then?'

She had no real reason to disagree. Her work was picking up, she had financial security again, she had this place, and a modified car in the garage below. Everything she needed, and yet, and yet . . . she felt unsettled. She was alone and lonely, of course: that was part of it. But also, somewhere in the long process of drawing a line under the past, she'd developed a sense of unfinished business, of matters unresolved. Gradually, amid the legal discussions, the house clearance, the impending divorce, the shadow of an idea had begun to form on the edge of her mind.

She grasped at it now. 'There's something I've been wanting to ask you.'

He waited attentively.

Catherine began slowly, almost casually. 'It's just a small thing. I don't even know if you'll be able to tell me. About the accident . . . the attack.'

A slight wariness crept into his eyes.

'When you arrived that night, when you saw me there . . . you checked my pulse, my breathing. Presumably you checked on the bleeding too, to see where it was coming from.' She turned this into a question with a lift of her head.

Fergal's shaggy eyebrows drew into a frown. 'I did,' he said.

'And where was it coming from, the blood?'

'Your ear. Your left ear.'

'Aha,' she murmured, attempting to sound indifferent. 'And that was it? Nowhere else?'

'So far as I could tell.'

'And Maeve . . . she'd tried to mop up the blood?'

Fergal's eyes were very still, and she had the feeling he was way ahead of her. 'Apparently so.'

'A pair of panties, wasn't it?'

'I was not aware of what they were at the time. I thought – if I thought at all – that it was a handkerchief.'

Catherine made a show of absorbing this. 'And the scarf? Did you see the scarf?'

There was a taut silence. 'No,' he said.

Catherine shrugged lightly. 'But you knew she'd left a scarf?'

He hesitated. 'Not then. I was told later.'

'And you know where it was found?'

She wasn't sure if it was embarrassment that made him grow uncomfortable, or the confirmation of where this had been leading. 'I believe I heard a while later.'

She looked away to the window and the misty rooftops. 'When Maeve was ill,' she said in a low voice, 'was it just chance that she got septicaemia, Fergal? That she nearly died?'

She left it several seconds before looking back at him.

He was staring at her obdurately.

'Or was there a procedure that went wrong?'

'I couldn't answer that,' he growled, dropping his eyes.

She asked so quietly that it was almost a whisper, 'Was there an abortion, Fergal?'

He tightened his lips. 'I could not say.'

'Could not or must not?'

He didn't reply.

'I understand,' she murmured, turning her head to scrutinise the window once more. 'Suppose, though, that I simply asked you to indicate if I was wrong – nothing more. Just . . . if I was wrong.' She left this thought in the air for a moment while she transferred her gaze to her hands. 'The reason I ask, Fergal, is that I want to leave the whole thing behind. I hardly need tell you how important it is to me. But I'm still finding it difficult. Partly, I'm finding it difficult to understand why Maeve should have been so . . . persistent. But if you were to indicate to me that I wasn't wrong, then it would begin to make sense, you see. I would understand why she did what she did, why she came to the house that day. I would feel very much clearer.' In her mind, she added, *about Ben as well. And about Terry.* 'It would make it that much easier to put it all behind me.'

Unable to explain it any better, she finally brought her eyes up to his.

His frown had returned, deeper than ever, his eyes hunted across the floor as he wrestled with some inner debate. Finally, he seemed to come to a decision. His mournful eyes lifted to hers and he affirmed with a soft sigh, 'No, Catherine, you would not be wrong.'

She embraced him solemnly at the door. 'Tell Bridget I'll

be coming to Morne on Thursday. If she could make the arrangements.'


The sky was still stormy from recent rain, but as the car left the village and turned up the lane the clouds seemed to break up a little, the air to brighten. Passing through the gates, climbing towards the house, the rhododendrons drooped and glistened, tattoos of rain dropped from overhanging branches, and the surface of the drive ran with a web of rivulets.

Catherine had expected a gardener's car, or the golf buggy, or both, but there were three jalopies and two vans outside the house, one with ladders, another with faded signwriting that said *Decorators*.

Though it had stopped raining, the driver insisted on holding an umbrella over her. He promised to return in three hours.

Inside the house there were dustsheets and ladders. The hall had been painted a soft cream, the drawing room was turning a slightly warmer shade of white. The floors had been sanded and sealed. The dining-room walls had been filled and rubbed down, and a sample of eggshell blue daubed across the furthest wall in a broad cross. A selection of curtain samples had been pinned to the shutters. Through the doorway to the kitchen, she glimpsed new units in pale wood and a gleaming hardwood floor.

The men were taking a smoking break in a corner of the drawing room. 'Ah, if you're after Mick, he'll be back directly,' one of them told her.

She waited in the dining room, sitting at the trestle table, most of which had been taken over by paint pots and rolls of lining paper. She tried to clear her mind for the meeting with the landscaping contractors and tree specialists, but all she could think was, *So he's going to use the place after all*. She examined her emotions with curiosity, and decided she was glad.

A vehicle approached the house with a soft hum and drew

up noisily on the gravel. A car door slammed, footsteps sounded, the front door cannoned open and crashed against the stop, and through the open doorway she saw Terry stride across the hall to peer into the drawing room. Half way back across the hall he saw her and hastened forward again.

She laughed as she called out his name.

He took both her hands in his and smiled. When he kissed her, his cheek was smooth and she caught a scent of aftershave.

He stood back and regarded her appraisingly, and she noticed his eyes, which were clear and bright, and very steady.

'You look well, Catherine.'

He seemed taller and to have lost a little weight, though that may have been the effect of his suit, which was dark and beautifully cut and undoubtedly expensive.

'I didn't think you were able to come!' she said.

'It's amazing what Bridget can do with the diary when she really tries.'

He continued to survey her openly and fondly for quite a while before turning to pull a chair up to the table. As he sat down, he slipped the button of his jacket and smoothed his tie, and it occurred to her that he spent most of his life in such well-made clothes, and that the image she'd held of him all these months, the rather self-conscious figure in the misguided gardening outfit, had been quite wrong.

She said, 'Your empire won't crumble while you're away then?'

He grinned. 'It's the vanity of self-made men to think that the ship will hit the rocks the moment their backs are turned.' He rotated a hand, and she remembered the unexpected grace of his gestures. 'I should have two hours at least before danger looms.'

'*That* long.' She turned down her mouth in mock rebuke.

'But I'll take as long as I need today, because it's not often I get the chance to see you, Catherine.'

'Entirely your fault, Terry.'

Beneath his smile, he was rueful as he said, 'Yes, my life is madness at the moment.'

She indicated the room. 'You didn't tell me you were doing the house.'

'Ah? Didn't I?' He affected a bafflement that was entirely unconvincing. 'It's just a quick coat of paint really, to make it presentable.'

'But the kitchen . . . the curtains and colours. You've got someone helping you? A designer?'

He gave her an odd look as though he wasn't entirely sure how to interpret this question. 'A designer? Yes, but no one I know,' he said with a quiet emphasis whose significance she could only guess at. 'Bridget organised someone.'

'And you're going to use the place? You're going to come regularly?'

'Ah, well . . . we'll see.' Abruptly, he changed the subject. 'Now, Catherine, I want to know – the final account? You were happy with it?'

'Oh, yes.'

'Good, because I can tell you, it's been the devil's own job giving away money that you do not own and cannot possibly account for, money that will get you into jail quicker than a raid on the Central Bank. My financial man's been red-eyed and drowned in sweat. Like someone handed a hot coal – trying desperately to pass the damn thing on without dropping it on his foot.' A gleam of mischief came into Terry's eyes, and she had the feeling he had secretly enjoyed the challenge.

'However it was done, it was worth it.'

'Indeed it was, Catherine. Indeed.' Risking the decorators' dust, he slid his elbows onto the table and rested his chin on his hands. 'I also thought it prudent to make some enquiries about our mutual acquaintance.' He added anxiously, 'If you should like to know, that is?'

'Sure.'

'It seems he's in Argentina. Buenos Aires. He's set up an import–export business there.'

She felt nothing at this news except, perhaps, a lack of surprise.

'I still say, Catherine – and this'll be the last time, I swear – I'll not say it again – that you were too generous to him.' He held up a hand as if to forestall her objections. 'I know, I know – he was more of a case for the doctors than the courts, but—'

'Terry, I think he would have killed himself. In fact, I know he would.'

He frowned, he came round to the idea reluctantly. 'Very well. I must accept your judgement on that.'

'And if anyone should have ended up in court, shouldn't it have been Ben?'

His expression clouded, he said with feeling, 'Indeed. And where is he, still . . .?'

'In Eaton Square, so far as I know. Oh, I don't mind, Terry. Why should I mind? Better Rebecca than some poor girl who'd take him seriously and get hurt.'

They fell into a thoughtful silence, broken when they both began to speak at the same instant, broke off, only to speak over each other once again.

'There are two things I—'

'There was something—'

He said immediately, 'No, after you,' and smiled his slow smile that started at one corner of his mouth and spread up into his eyes. She had forgotten how striking his eyes were, more blue than grey, and how unflinching.

She had to look down at her hands before she could find the courage to start. 'Before we discuss the garden, there are a couple of—'

'Oh, I've no need to discuss the garden,' he said quickly.

'What?'

'I'm here to see you. I'm not worried about the garden.'

'Oh,' she repeated uncertainly. 'But all these people are coming—'

'I'll wait. I'll wait for as long as necessary.'

She took a deep breath. 'There are two things I want to say to you before we go any further,' she began with strange formality. 'Firstly, that I owe you an apology. About this house, how you came to own it. My father's never been terribly truthful about money. I've always known it, really. I just found it hard to accept at the time. Somehow, the loss of the house got bound up in Mummy's death. It was too much for me to accept that Pa had sold it under our feet just when Mummy was dying. I'm afraid I believed what he said – all the bad things he told us about you – because it suited me to. The alternative was too painful.' She looked up at him. 'I got some sort of admission out of Pa the other day. Not a lot – you can imagine – but enough to make me suspect that the truth was very different. I don't know what the arrangements were, but I'm sure they were very generous. As always. Whatever else, Terry, you are the most absurdly generous man I know. So . . . I want to apologise. I hope that you'll be able to forgive me.'

Matching the note of formality, he bowed his head in acceptance. When he looked up again he seemed pleased.

In her relief at having got this out of the way, she almost forgot the second matter. 'Oh yes!' she exclaimed. 'I loved your letters.'

She had caught him by surprise. 'I'm sorry?'

'I loved the letters you sent me. I read them all many times. I wanted you to know that they gave me enormous pleasure.'

'But they were a poor effort,' he argued. 'I'm no good at that sort of thing.'

'You're wrong. And in fact . . . I owe you another apology. For sending such an awful reply to that letter you sent me that summer—'

He interrupted sharply, 'No, no – too long ago, Catherine. Best forgotten. Water under the bridge. No, no – an age away!'

But she could see he hadn't forgotten, she could see that the wound still smarted, and she felt an ache of regret and something else that was very like longing.

'I'm sorry, I . . .' But seeing the warning flash in his eyes, she said rapidly, 'What was it you wanted to say? I interrupted you.'

'I think – later,' he said.

It was an hour before the contractors left, an hour that Terry spent alone in the study. She found him hunched over his desk on the phone. At some point he had changed into casual clothes, more country than gardening, which suited him far better.

He mimed a greeting. While she waited for him to finish, she watched him and thought of the letter he had written her that summer. She couldn't recall the exact words he had used, but she remembered that they'd been good honest words, straight from the heart. It occurred to her – perhaps hadn't been far from her mind for a long time – that she had been foolish to turn him down.

'Now then!' he cried as he rang off. 'Time to wrap up!'

The quad stood in the stable yard. He lifted her on and got on behind her. They went slowly because she had to brace herself on the handlebars, and he had to keep one arm tight around her waist.

A short way up the hill, he turned the machine around so they could look back at the house. 'What I wanted to say was – it's yours,' he said. 'I always intended to give it to you.'

She leant to one side so she could look back at his face. 'The house?'

'The house.'

'But I don't want it, Terry!'

'I'm giving it to you anyway.'

'And I can't possibly accept it.'

He gave a sharp sigh. 'Now, why did I think you were going to say that? Unlimited loan then?'

'No.'

He looked down at her. 'Why not?'

'I wouldn't want to live here on my own. It wouldn't be practical for a start.'

He conceded this grudgingly. 'Will you come often then?'
'As often as I'm invited.'
This idea floated tantalisingly between them.
'You drive a hard bargain, Catherine. But I agree.'